'Forgers, thieves, heretics, horse thieves,' he muttered as if he was reciting some kind of litany. 'What kind of army are you trying to build?'

'Once these men are in uniform, I don't care about their pasts. Besides, France cannot afford to be choosy about who wears her colours. We need men. I was sent to Paris to get men. It doesn't matter what *kind* of men. General Jourdan would accept a regiment of cripples at the moment. You saw Barras's signature on my order. I'm here because the Directory wants me to be. Surely *you* are not going to interfere with Directory Business?'

BONAPARTE'S SONS

RICHARD HOWARD

WARNER BOOKS

A *Warner* Book

First published in Great Britain in 1997 by
Little, Brown and Company

This edition published by Warner Books 1998

Copyright © 1997, Richard Howard

The moral right of the author has been asserted.

A CIP catalogue record for this book is
available from the British Library.

ISBN 0 7515 1811 5

Typeset in Sabon by M Rules
Printed and bound in Great Britain by
Clays Ltd, St. Ives plc

Warner Books
A Division of
Little, Brown and Company (UK)
Brettenham House
Lancaster Place
London WC2E 7EN

BONAPARTE'S SONS

PROLOGUE

Alain Lausard peered up at the dull grey light of dawn creeping through the bars of the cell and sighed wearily. The arrival of a new day promised nothing for him. It would be a day like any other. A day of monotony spent alone in his eight-feet-square cell. A day indistinguishable from all those he had already endured and he knew it would continue until those who chose to keep him captive decided otherwise. The soul-destroying predictability would only be interrupted by the arrival of a few slops pushed through the slot at the bottom of the wooden cell door; and these would only come if someone on the other side could be bothered to ladle gruel into the wooden bowls that passed for eating receptacles. Sometimes the meagre meals never even arrived.

Lausard got to his feet and took two paces across the cell to the window. Two strides was all it took to cover the cramped confines of the enclosure. He was a powerfully built man and even the lack of good nourishment for so long had done little to diminish the impressiveness of his physique. His hair was long and badly in need of a wash; lank strands hung down as far as his shoulders, framing a square and somewhat cold face. His appearance was made all the more daunting by piercing blue eyes which fixed on things with unwavering concentration. That gaze now settled on the droplets of moisture running down one wall of the cell, chasing each other like dirty tears over the pock-marked stonework. The floor of the cell was covered with straw rotting in the damp, the stench of which he'd found intolerable at first but now the rancid odour seemed to belong. In fact, looking around the cell, Lausard felt as unfeeling and unforgiving as the rock which hemmed him in. But if there was nothing *inside*, then the world beyond the bars and the walls offered just as little. The world outside was, in its own way, as unforgiving as the place he now called home. The streets and gutters of Paris could be as harsh as any prison, as he had found during the past two years.

Sometimes he forgot how long he'd been scrounging a living on those streets. Time seemed to have lost its meaning even *before* he had been arrested, before his world had been condensed into four damp walls and a floor of rotting straw.

Standing beneath the barred window set about six feet up in the wall, he watched the dawn light creep unwillingly across the floor as if it too were reluctant to enter this place.

Further down the corridor, in one of the dozens of cells identical to his own, he could hear snoring. Someone, at least, was managing to ignore the discomfort and find escape in the oblivion of sleep. Lausard both envied them and resented them for that ability. He himself was rarely that lucky. When the cell was transformed into a black hole by the onset of night, he managed to get only a little sleep, during which time he was momentarily free of the hungry fleas which infested his clothes and hair. He could feel one on the nape of his neck now. He picked it away and crushed it between his thumb and forefinger.

Another day of waiting and wondering. Of languishing in this stone box which imprisoned him with nothing to look forward to but the opening of that one door which led to the outside. Deep in his heart though, Lausard knew that should that door be opened, and the guards finally come for him, then his journey would be one way and it would be final. He waited like the others in the prison with him for release in only one form.

He sat down against one of the damp walls and gazed at the wooden door, almost willing it to open but knowing that if it did, he faced a meeting with the guillotine. His crime carried the death penalty, as did most transgressions in the city. He knew the time would come. All he could do was wait.

He continued to stare at the door.

CHAPTER 1

Captain Nicholas Deschamps reined in the magnificent bay he was riding and patted the animal's neck reassuringly, glancing around at his companion.

Sergeant Legier brought his own mount to a halt and glanced around the prison courtyard, waiting until his superior swung himself from the saddle before he too stepped down. He winced slightly as his booted foot connected with the cobbles beneath. Having injured his hip a couple of days earlier it was still painful.

The Conciergerie was one of the largest of twenty-eight prisons currently in use in Paris. It held over six hundred prisoners and had been home to Marie Antoinette before her execution. Only Bicetre was larger. Some of the jails held as few as thirty captives; Maison de Coignard and Prison Luxembourg boasted thirty-five and thirty-three respectively. Nearly five and a half thousand unfortunates were currently held within the walls of these prisons, charged with crimes ranging from forgery to rape, stealing to heresy. Three years earlier, on Jean Paul Marat's orders, more than one thousand four hundred prisoners throughout the city had been butchered in the space of five days. A year later, Marat himself was dead, stabbed to death in his bath by Charlotte Corday.

The political climate in the city, and in France itself, seemed to change on a daily basis. Those who were enemies on Monday were allies by the Tuesday and sometimes dead by the Wednesday. Any man or woman branded a member of the wrong political party could expect swift and summary treatment. 'The Patriotic Shorte-ner', as the guillotine became affectionately named by the masses, began to work overtime.

When Robespierre came to power, the blade of the killing machine was rarely still. The Jacobin leader had overseen the mass blood-letting known as 'The Terror' before he too had finally come to rest his neck beneath the sharpened steel.

The early morning breeze which whipped across the courtyard was icy but neither Deschamps nor Legier felt its sting. They were both dressed in the green uniforms of dragoons, with thick woollen tunics faced with white lapels, cross-belts and bleached breeches tucked into knee-length boots. As Deschamps walked, his sabre bumped against the polished leather and the breeze whipped the horsehair mane of his brass helmet around his face. He was a big man, close to six feet tall. His colleagues had always joked that his size made him a bigger target and his collection of wounds would seem to bear that out. There were several scars on his face, the worst of which had been acquired during the battle for the Heights of Abraham during the Seven

Years War. A sabre cut had left him with a split upper lip and another wound gave him the appearance of wearing a perpetual smirk, with one corner of his mouth drawn up towards an ear. Thirty-eight years of soldiering. From Canada to Corsica, Valmy to Fleurus. The army was his life and always had been. He had risen through the ranks, attaining his captaincy by his bravery and willingness to risk his life for his country, for the Republic.

Legier had served under him for twenty years. He was a stockier man, powerfully built with a bull-like neck as though his head had been rammed down between his shoulders. His right ear was missing, courtesy of a piece of shrapnel, but he could hear perfectly well through the hole which remained and he made no attempt to disguise the deformity.

The main door which led into the prison itself was unguarded and the two cavalrymen exchanged disdainful glances as they approached it. Deschamps banged twice on the wood. To his surprise it swung open.

He stepped inside and saw a man slumped on the cold stone floor, musket propped against his shoulder, head flopping forward.

He grunted and looked up, trying to scramble to his feet while attempting to blink the sleep from his eyes. Gripping the musket, he lowered it so that the barrel was pointing at Deschamps.

Legier stepped forward, hand falling to the hilt of his sword but the officer waved him back, his gaze locked on to the solitary guard. 'Who are you?' the guard asked, regaining his wits.

'I want to see the Governor of the prison,'

Deschamps said flatly, unconcerned by the Charleville musket pointing at his chest.

'I need identification,' the guard said defiantly. 'The Governor is a busy man. He will not see just anyone.'

Deschamps ran appraising eyes over him. The guard was in his early twenties, dressed in the white jacket of an infantryman with a bicorn hat perched precariously on his head and short trousers holed and threadbare. He wore a pair of gaiters but no boots beneath.

'How old are you?' Deschamps asked.

The youth looked puzzled, as if the question was somehow beyond his powers of reasoning.

'Answer me, boy,' snapped Deschamps. 'You look like a child. How many more children are pretending to be soldiers in this place?'

'Answer,' Legier added menacingly.

'Sixteen,' he said falteringly. 'I am sixteen.'

'Well then, boy soldier,' Deschamps said quietly. 'Do your job. Fetch the Governor now. I have business here.'

The young man looked at each of the dragoons in turn, at the stern expressions, the scars, the uniforms. Then he turned and sprinted up the corridor.

Felix Marcognet was a tall, thin man with sad eyes and a pinched expression. His eyes darted nervously back and forth between the two dragoons, both of whom had declined his offer to sit. Marcognet himself wiped a hand over his balding pate and looked once more at the piece of paper which Deschamps had given him.

The name on the bottom of the paper, signed in bold

strokes, was that of 'Paul Barras'. Barras was one of the Directory of Seven, one of the most powerful men, not just in Paris but the whole of France.

'We need men,' said Deschamps. 'France needs men.'

'I can't help you,' Marcognet told him.

Deschamps fixed him in a withering stare.

'I'm not a well man, I have trouble breathing,' the Prison Governor pleaded. 'And I can't spare any of my guards, I—'

'It's not you *or* your guards that I want,' Deschamps said with irritation. 'You have over six hundred men in this prison. Most of them are fit enough to fight.'

'But they're criminals, scum,' Marcognet protested.

'So are most of the army.'

'I can't let you take them all.'

'I don't want them *all*.'

'I have a job to do here. I have responsibilities!'

'To whom?' Deschamps enquired. 'Your responsibilities are to France. You're a turnkey. Nothing more. You have something I need and I mean to have it.'

Marcognet swallowed hard, his gaze again flickering back and forth between the two uniformed men. Legier was tapping gently with his index finger on the hilt of his sabre.

'You won't find much here,' the Governor said.

'I'll be the judge of that,' Deschamps said. 'In case it has escaped your notice, we are at war. We need all the men we can get. Let their quality as men be of concern to me.'

'There is no quality in them,' Marcognet said scathingly. 'I have already told you what they are.'

'And I'm sure your opinion is unquestionable,' Deschamps sneered. 'Nevertheless, I want to see a full list of names of every man in this prison and I want it now.'

Deschamps paused at each door and peered indifferently through the grille at the occupant of the cell; he squinted to make out the human shape in the gloom within. With the arrival of the dawn the task was made a little easier – the cold grey light of a new morning illuminated slightly the interior of the cells and the wretches who occupied them.

Deschamps looked in at each prisoner while Marcognet read the name from a sheaf of papers and Legier put either a cross or a tick next to the name using a quill pen and ink.

'Do you treat them all as badly?' Deschamps demanded, peering in at one man who was doubled up in the middle of the cell coughing badly and clutching at his chest. He hawked loudly and spat some blood-tinged mucus from his mouth.

'They're criminals,' said Marcognet.

'They're *men*.'

'Look, Captain, I don't think you realise what running a prison entails,' Marcognet said officiously. 'It takes organisation. It takes certain skills which you are not aware of.'

'Such as?' Deschamps slid the wooden slat on the grille shut and passed along to the next cell.

'There are the prisoners to be attended to, the guards who watch them have to be kept in line,' Marcognet said. 'It is a very responsible job.'

'And how did *you* come by such a responsible job?' Deschamps chided.

The Governor coughed theatrically but didn't speak.

'Well?' the dragoon persisted.

'I have a nephew in the Directory,' Marcognet said finally, lowering his voice.

Deschamps looked at Legier who eyed the Governor with disdain and scratched at the hole where his ear had once been.

'Your brother was wounded during the storming of the Bastille, wasn't he, Legier?' Deschamps said.

'Yes, sir, he was,' Legier replied. 'Blinded in one eye when a powder keg blew up.'

'Do you know what was done to the Governor of the Bastille?' Deschamps asked, glancing at Marcognet who shook his head. 'De Launay was his name. The crowd asked him to hand over his gunpowder. He refused. He ordered his men to fire on the crowd. They killed nearly a hundred before the prison was stormed. They cut off De Launay's head with a butcher's knife.'

'What has that got to do with me?' Marcognet questioned.

'Nothing,' Deschamps said, sliding back a wooden partition to peer in at the next prisoner. 'As you say, it is a responsible job. Men in authority are not always the most popular of men and the public are fickle.'

Marcognet swallowed hard.

'Who is this?' Deschamps said, looking at the prisoner.

The Governor consulted the list. 'Roussard,' he said. 'A forger.'

'Open it up,' Deschamps said, nodding towards the door.

Marcognet put a large key from the ring he held into the lock and pushed open the door.

'On your feet,' he snapped and the occupant of the cell did as he was ordered, nodding almost politely at the newcomers.

'Leave us,' said Deschamps, looking at the Governor dismissively.

Legier stepped in front of the closed door as the tall, thin man retreated from the room muttering under his breath.

'Do you want to die in prison, forger?'

'I don't want to die at all,' Roussard said, a thin smile on his lips.

'Everyone dies, it's just a matter of when or how.'

'Perhaps. Why does it bother *you* where I die?'

'I can make sure it isn't in *here*,' Deschamps told him.

'How?'

'France needs fighting men. Better a death with honour, wouldn't you agree?'

'So you're offering me a choice between having my head cut off by the guillotine or being shot by some Englishmen, Prussians, Austrians or Italians? It isn't much of a choice.'

'You're not in a position to bargain.'

Roussard nodded, still smiling.

The two dragoons turned to leave.

'Captain,' Roussard called. 'If you need money to buy horses, I can help you. My francs are a work of art.'

The cell door slammed shut.

'I am a lover, not a fighter,' said Giresse, smiling.

'You're a horse thief,' Marcognet interrupted. 'That's why you're in *here*.'

'A horse thief, in the middle of Paris?' Deschamps said, looking surprised.

'I took some horses from the Tuileries stables,' Giresse replied.

'How many?' Deschamps asked.

'Just two,' said Giresse. 'I was going to sell the meat. Perhaps even give some to my ladies.' He smiled again.

'There will be plenty of women for you when you join the army.'

'I don't need a uniform to attract them,' said Giresse. 'It's knowing how to treat them that matters. Women are like flowers, delicate and fragrant. They need to be nurtured, cared for. I have a gift for tending those delicate blooms. The young ones need a little work to bring out their radiance, the older ones require more perseverance to make them blossom. But all the effort is worth it.'

'You should have been a poet,' Deschamps said.

'When *I'm* with a woman, it *is* poetry.'

Marcognet locked the cell door and hurried along the corridor to keep up with the two soldiers who were moving along to the next cells, studying the men within and whispering amongst themselves as they studied the occupants. Marcognet didn't like the newcomers. They were too brash, too sure of themselves. They undermined his authority. They didn't treat him with the respect he deserved. Particularly the officer. Marcognet wondered if he should speak to his nephew in the Directory about this surly military man.

'This cell.' Deschamps motioned towards the door. 'Open it up.'

Marcognet hesitated, exhaling wearily.

'Forgers, thieves, heretics, horse thieves,' he muttered as if he was reciting some kind of litany. 'What kind of army are you trying to build?'

'Once these men are in uniform, I don't care about their pasts. Besides, France cannot afford to be choosy about who wears her colours. We need men. I was sent to Paris to get men. It doesn't matter what *kind* of men. General Jourdan would accept a regiment of cripples at the moment. You saw Barras's signature on my order. I'm here because the Directory wants me to be. Surely *you* are not going to interfere with Directory business?'

Deschamps held him in an unblinking gaze, then watched as he unlocked the cell.

'Moreau,' he announced. 'A religious maniac.'

The man in the cell was kneeling, facing the barred window. Deschamps realised that he was praying.

Legier took a step towards the man but the officer held up a hand to halt him.

Moreau was a large man with immense hands. Pressed together in prayer, they looked like two hamhocks joined.

'Praying for a way out?' said Marcognet with scorn.

Moreau ignored him, his head still bowed. Finally he crossed himself then rose to his full height, which Deschamps guessed to be around six foot. He regarded the intruders warily.

'What were you praying for?' Deschamps asked.

'Forgiveness,' Moreau said. 'Not for myself. For the rest of mankind.'

'Are you the only one without sin then?' Deschamps queried.

'No one is without sin. But some carry a heavier burden than others. Some need God's forgiveness more than others.'

'Such as who?'

'Men like you for one,' Moreau said reproachfully. 'Soldiers. You kill every day. You take lives which you have no right to take. Only God has the right to decide when a man's time is up.'

'Do you think God cares about France and her people?'

'God cares about everyone.'

'Then why does he let them die in wars?'

'Men make wars, not God.'

'Men do God's will.'

'Do *you* believe in Him?'

'I've been a soldier too long to think that any God would allow some of the things that I've seen,' Deschamps declared. 'And yet I've heard so many men call on Him during those years. Some of them He's ignored. Do you think He's ignored *you*?'

Moreau looked puzzled.

'Leaving you to rot in a stinking hole like this? If he heard your prayers wouldn't he get you out?'

'I don't care about myself. I follow God's will. If it is His will that I be in here then I accept that, but God didn't put the property of the Church at the disposal of the nation. The Assembly did, five years ago.'

'And you didn't agree with that?'

'Church property is God's property,' Moreau rasped. 'No man has a right to take it.'

'You should have been a cleric,' said Deschamps.

Moreau eyed the officer silently.

'Would you fight for France?' Deschamps asked.

'Would you kill her enemies? The same enemies who would destroy your countrymen?'

'"Whosoever destroyeth my flock, I shall so destroy",' Moreau declared.

Deschamps smiled.

'He's insane,' said Marcognet, slamming the cell door on Moreau.

Deschamps peered back through the grille at the big man who had once again dropped to his knees, his huge hands clasped together beneath his chin.

'Why?' the officer asked. 'Because he believes in God?' He glanced at the Governor indifferently. 'What is the official Directory instruction concerning God? Does He exist or doesn't He? Has your nephew told you?'

Marcognet didn't like the note of sarcasm in the officer's voice and glared menacingly at Deschamps, but the gesture went unnoticed by the soldier.

Deschamps and Legier were peering into another cell.

'Rostov,' said Marcognet, seeing the man. 'A Russian. He was arrested as a political undesirable. Foreigners aren't popular here, Captain. You should know that, you spend most of your days killing them.' Marcognet managed a smug smile.

'I kill the enemy,' Deschamps told him. 'The enemies of France.'

'Not all enemies wear a uniform,' Marcognet added.

They passed to the next cell and the Governor slid back the grille.

'Delacor,' he said. 'The rapist. One of the most vicious, dangerous pieces of scum in this prison.'

'Sounds like perfect material for a corporal,' said Deschamps and both he and Legier laughed.

From inside his cell, Delacor heard the sound and looked up. He saw three sets of eyes gazing in at him. He didn't move. He merely sat in the centre of the cell, twirling a piece of straw between his thumb and index finger.

Deschamps looked into those eyes. Deep-set and black as night, they glared back at him from beneath a heavy brow with bushy eyebrows, which made it difficult to see exactly where he was looking. He could almost feel the resentment burning behind them.

'If you take him, Captain,' said Marcognet, 'he'll put a sword in your back the first chance he gets.'

'We'll see,' Deschamps murmured and passed on to the next cell.

And the next.

'Bonet, the schoolmaster,' Marcognet said. 'He refused to teach his pupils what he was told to teach them. He insisted on telling them that history was important *before* those stinking Bourbons were overthrown.'

'History didn't die with Louis the Sixteenth,' Deschamps reminded him. He pointed to one of the scars on his face. '*That's* history,' he snapped. 'Did I imagine *that*?'

'The Directory—'

Deschamps cut him short. 'Is five men. Men,' he hissed. 'They make rules. They can't change history, or its teaching.'

'To hear you speak, Captain,' Marcognet said ominously, 'one would reckon you didn't think too highly of our government.'

'You talk to me of criminals, turnkey,' the dragoon said with scorn. 'These men you keep in here are saints compared to most politicians. Show me a thief or a politician and I'll take the thief every time. At least his motives are honest. He steals because he has no food or money. He steals to feed himself or his family.'

'You want thieves?' said Marcognet defiantly. 'Here's one for you.' He slid back the grille on the next cell.

The man inside looked around at the prying eyes.

'Alain Lausard,' said Marcognet. 'Thief.'

CHAPTER 2

Lausard had heard the footsteps approaching his cell, heard the hushed, almost conspiratorial voices in the corridor beyond and now he heard the hinges of the door squeal as Marcognet opened up the cell.

Lausard looked on in mild bewilderment as the two dragoons entered the small space. Their swords bumped against their highly polished boots and the few early-morning rays of sun that penetrated the barred window bounced off the brass of their helmets.

He studied the features of the officer. The scars and the wrinkles. The hole where the sergeant's right ear used to be. They were both in their fifties, Lausard guessed, but it was difficult to be specific and at that moment it didn't matter to him. What intrigued him was why they were here in his cell at the crack of dawn.

'What did you steal?' Deschamps asked. 'What was so precious that it brought you to this place?'

Lausard met the man's gaze but didn't answer.

'The Captain asked you what you stole,' Marcognet snapped, taking a step towards the prisoner. 'Answer him, you filth.'

Lausard stood his ground, his blue eyes fixed on the Governor who finally took a step back.

'I stole bread,' Lausard said, his words directed at Deschamps but his piercing gaze still pinning Marcognet like an insect to a board. 'If it is so important to you, it was from a shop close to Notre-Dame. How much more do you want to know?'

'And you'd have died for that?' Deschamps said. 'For a few crumbs you risked your life?'

'I'd have died *without* it,' Lausard told him. 'Hunger kills as surely as the guillotine. It just takes longer.' He finally turned his attention to the officer. 'What might be crumbs to you are life or death to many people on the streets of Paris.'

'How long have you been a thief?' Deschamps asked.

'Does that matter to you?' Lausard said.

'Not to me, no,' Deschamps confessed. 'I was just thinking that you can't have been a very good thief to have been caught. How did you survive out there?' The officer gestured towards the window.

'A man learns to adapt to his surroundings. I'd been stealing for two years. My luck ran out. Just like it has for many people in this city, or this country.'

'That sounds like sedition,' Marcognet snapped.

'So what if it does?' Lausard challenged. 'I'm to be executed anyway. Thief or traitor. What difference does it make? Why should I worry about speaking my mind now, of all times? There's nothing more you can do to me anyway.'

'You insolent bastard,' hissed Marcognet, taking another step towards Lausard.

This time the younger man moved forward a pace, fists clenched. 'Thief, traitor or murderer,' he growled.

'The choice is yours. The outcome is the same.'

Marcognet stepped backwards.

'Leave us,' said Deschamps, glancing at Marcognet.

'He's a madman,' Marcognet said dismissively.

'I don't think you need to worry about us,' Deschamps assured him, tapping the hilt of his sabre.

'I'm going to be there watching the day they take your head,' Marcognet said as he stepped out of the cell.

'Perhaps I should have let you kill him,' Deschamps said. 'You wanted to, didn't you?'

'Him and all his kind. Overfed, pampered, *pekinese*. He doesn't have to worry about starving. He sits on his worthless arse because of some relative in the Directory.'

'How do you know that?'

'Word gets around in places like this but I wouldn't expect you to know that.'

'I've been in worse places than this. Have you ever been on a battlefield?'

Lausard shook his head. 'At least there you're free to die as you wish,' he said. 'There's honour in dying while fighting. There's no honour in dying on the guillotine.'

'Is dying with honour important to you?' Deschamps asked.

'It used to be. When I had something worth living for. When I knew the meaning of honour. I'm not so sure I do any more.'

'I can give you that chance again. The chance to die with honour.'

'Why are you here?'

'France needs men. France is bleeding to death.'

'France cut her own wrists. Fighting on three fronts

against nations more powerful. And what do you have for an army?'

'The truth? A collection of maniacs, fanatics and conscripts commanded by incompetents for the most part. And if that sounds like treason then perhaps it is but it's also true.' Deschamps scratched at one scarred cheek. 'France has less than sixty thousand cavalry. In some places there are ten horses to every two hundred men. Why do you think we have so many dragoons? Men have to be able to fight on foot as well as horseback because there aren't usually enough horses for them to fight on.'

'Why are you telling me this?'

'Because I know men and I know something about you already,' Deschamps offered. 'You're no thief.'

'Then why am I in here? I was caught stealing. That makes me a thief, doesn't it?'

'Some men pray,' said Deschamps. 'It doesn't make them priests.' He sucked in a weary breath. 'Prisons all over the country are being emptied. Men like myself and Sergeant Legier, men who should be on a battlefield somewhere, have been reduced to errand boys. We run the errands of the Directory and the latest errand is to collect men. Then we have to turn them into soldiers, or at least something that passes for soldiers. We have to teach men who've never held a musket in their lives how to load and fire a Charleville, how to charge with a bayonet or swing a sabre. We have to teach men who've never saddled a horse how to ride, men who've never marched how to drill.'

'Why you?' Lausard questioned.

'Because I care about France. I want to see her great again. I have no interest in politics. This government uses its commanders like toys. Twenty-four generals have already been executed by this government. I don't fight for them, I fight for France.'

'What kind of troops do you need?'

'Infantry, cavalry, artillery. What difference does it make? I need horsemen. Can you ride?'

'As well as any of your dragoons,' said Lausard.

Deschamps smiled. 'You recognise the uniform?'

'And your rank.'

'You don't belong here.'

'Why not? I'm a thief.'

'There is more to you than that,' Deschamps said. 'Tell me the truth. Who *are* you?'

'I am nothing more than what you see. No different from any other man inside this prison. A common criminal. No more. No less. Do not bestow upon me qualities I do not have.'

'Are you so lacking in qualities?'

'Lacking perhaps in virtues. Unless hatred is a virtue.'

'You're young to have so much hatred inside you,' Deschamps said. He removed his helmet, cradling the brass head-dress beneath one arm. The long horsehair mane stirred gently as he walked slowly back and forth across the cell. 'How old are you?'

'Twenty-six,' Lausard answered, 'or three, if you follow our revolutionary calendar.'

Deschamps chuckled and glanced at Legier who managed a lean grin. The sergeant's gaze had not shifted from Lausard during their time inside his cell. It was as if he was trying to remember every detail of the younger man's features and mannerisms.

'Are you a Republican?' Deschamps enquired.

'I have no allegiance to anyone,' Lausard said without much interest.

'What about your family?'

'I have no family,' said Lausard, 'not any more. They were executed. All of them. My father, my mother, my brother and sister. Enemies of the state they called them.'

'Aristocrats? Was that their crime?'

'Girondins. I have Robespierre to thank for their deaths.'

'And how did you escape?' Deschamps asked.

Lausard exhaled wearily.

'I ran,' he said, a note of disgust in his voice. 'I returned to our home that day and they had been taken, so I ran. I was a coward. Not really the type of man you want for your army, Captain. I did nothing to save them. I hid in the gutters of Paris like some snivelling rat. I stole, I lied, I cheated. Anything to stay alive.'

'Most men would have done the same. The instinct for self-preservation is one of the strongest known to mankind. You did nothing wrong.'

'I did nothing at *all*,' Lausard hissed. 'I watched my family die. You say self-preservation is the strongest instinct, I say it is guilt. It's guilt that eats away at me. It gnaws at me like a disease. It consumes me and it will until I die, until I can be with my family again.'

'In heaven?' Deschamps said, raising an eyebrow.

'I gave up believing in God years ago, Captain.'

'Something else we have in common. Some of your companions inside this prison might think differently. There are some good Catholics in here.'

'The men in here aren't my companions,' Lausard corrected. 'I have nothing in common with them. If they knew my background most of them would probably carry me to the guillotine themselves. And yet I am lower than they are; at least some of them still have pride in themselves.'

'Thieves, rapists, murderers. What do they know of pride?' Deschamps asked.

'How many of them stood by while their family was butchered?' Lausard challenged.

'Self-pity doesn't become you. What happened is in the past – you must learn to live with it. It wasn't your fault. Do you think that I spend time thinking about the men I've killed over the years.'

'They were enemies. Soldiers who would have killed you if they'd had the chance. There's no shame in what you did.'

'Because a man wears a different uniform it doesn't stop him being a man. Those I killed had wives and families.'

'They were soldiers, they knew that death always walked close to them.'

'How close does death stand to you?'

'Not close enough,' Lausard muttered.

'Is death the only way to cleanse this guilt?'

Lausard didn't answer.

Legier took a step towards the younger man but Deschamps raised a hand to wave him back.

'I can promise you nothing but hardship in the army,' he said. 'And perhaps a chance to regain some self-respect.'

'Am I supposed to be grateful for that?'

'You have no choice anyway. I came to take every able-bodied man from this prison, whether they want to go or not.' He slipped the brass helmet back on his head and turned towards the door. 'By the way,' he said, 'where did you learn to ride?'

'The Carabinier School at Chinon,' Lausard said. 'I was there for seven years.'

'You missed your vocation, my friend,' Deschamps told him as the door was opened. 'Perhaps this is your chance to try again.'

Lausard watched as the door slammed shut behind the two dragoons. He heard their footsteps echoing away up the corridor.

CHAPTER 3

The crowd had been gathering for more than thirty minutes. A steady trickle at first which grew into a torrent and now, finally, into a tidal wave.

Those who could read had scanned the proclamation nailed to the walls and word had spread rapidly. Indignation had spread through the masses, growing steadily into anger and then into an inferno of rage.

The Constitution of the Year III, posted all over Paris on that chilly October morning, declared that the Directory had given itself total power.

'They're hypocrites!' someone screamed from the crowd. 'How dare they try to rule us!'

'They sit in the Tuileries now just like the Bourbons before them,' another voice added. 'We removed one set of leeches and now we have more to take their place.'

Ripples of anger spread through this sea of people at great speed.

'We don't have to take this,' another voice intoned. '*We* are the power of Paris, we are the heart of France, not these bastards who would rule us!'

The man stepped forward, ripped the proclamation from the wall and tore it in half, tossing the pieces into the air.

The action was met by a huge cheer and the man was lifted on to the shoulders of two men standing close by. 'They cannot rule us!' he shouted as heads turned to face him. 'No one can rule us!'

An enormous cheer greeted this exclamation.

The man smiled triumphantly.

His name was Auger. A small man with a bull neck and a barrel chest, barefoot like so many of his companions.

'Will you help us?' he bellowed, pointing a finger at a red-coated National Guardsman.

A number of troops had gathered to see the proclamation, their tall bearskins nodding in the light breeze, muskets clutched to their chests.

The first man hesitated then, as the roar of the crowd heightened, he seemed to become intoxicated by the tide of emotion and he nodded, pulled off his bearskin and hoisted it aloft on the point of his bayonet.

'And you?' roared Auger to one of the other soldiers.

He mimicked his companion and, within moments, the soldiers were all waving their headgear in the air like bizarre trophies.

The baying of the crowd grew louder, becoming deafening.

'Who do these bastards in the Directory think they are?' Auger shouted. 'Have they helped to overthrow the Bourbons? Do they suffer as we suffer?'

'NO!' the crowd roared back as one.

'They have made themselves kings by their own hand,' Auger shouted again. 'Can't they remember what happened to the last king?'

More cheers of agreement and appreciation.

Auger was carried through the crowd by the two men, shouting his comments, seeing many faces follow his progress, hearing so many voices echo his anger.

'We must do something,' someone else added. 'We must teach them a lesson as we taught the fat Bourbons. Let *them* feel our anger too.'

Five or six of the National Guardsmen were stalking along behind Auger now, hands slapping appreciatively at their backs, some touching their muskets briefly, feeling the wood and steel.

'*We* have the power, not the Directory!' Auger bellowed. 'Let us show them that power!'

'There are only five thousand regular troops in Paris,' one of the guardsmen shouted. 'We outnumber them four to one if we unite.'

'Unite against this new tyranny,' added another voice, now almost drowned out by the fervent rantings of the crowd. 'Fight.'

'Yes!' another bellowed. 'Fight!'

'Fight,' Auger echoed and a huge explosion of sound erupted from the crowd. 'We will throw these bastards out of power. Kick them into the Seine!'

Every comment was met by a deafening chorus of approval.

'We march on the Tuileries,' Auger roared.

The crowd screamed back its agreement.

'Nothing will stop us. Paris is ours.'

Fists were clenched and raised in salute.

'To the Tuileries!' Auger shouted once more. 'Arm yourselves!'

Napoleon Bonaparte stopped beside one of the eight-pounder cannon and slapped his hand on the bronze barrel. The twenty-six-year-old brigadier-general ran his fingers over the metal lovingly, watched by one of the twelve-man crew who stood in readiness beside the piece.

There were forty cannon arranged across the Rue St Honoré and the thoroughfares immediately adjacent. Bonaparte had demanded them brought from the artillery park at Sablons and that task had been completed by Captain Murat, who now sat astride his magnificent grey horse watching the small man wandering slowly up and down, eyes flicking back and forth. More than once he looked at his watch but, as Murat watched, there seemed to be no urgency about his movements and even as Bonaparte straightened his hat, it seemed to be with slow, deliberate movements.

Up and down the street orders were still being shouted and one of the eight-pounders was being manoeuvred using its hand-spike, the gunners sweating profusely despite the chill in the early-morning air.

Behind the guns were lines of blue-uniformed infantry, muskets sloped, bayonets bristling, sunlight winking wickedly on the points.

Bonaparte moved behind one of the guns and ducked low, checking the barrel trajectory. Like all cannon, this was controlled by a screw mechanism called a cascabel and on top of the smooth-bore barrel was a vent. It was here that one of the gunners would apply the portfire and ignite the powder inside the barrel to send the projectile hurtling towards the target.

In this case it was canister shot.

Canister shot consisted of a tin case which ruptured upon leaving the barrel, transforming the cannon into a massive shotgun as it released up to eighty one-ounce balls which had been packed tightly within. Heavy case was also used, a more lethal version which could send up to forty three-ounce metal balls to its target at a speed in excess of 450 feet per second.

Bonaparte left the gun and wandered across towards Murat who swung himself out of the saddle as his commander-in-chief approached.

'They think we won't fire on them,' Bonaparte said, his accent harsh, still carrying the strong inflection of his Corsican homeland.

'We could try reasoning with them, sir,' Murat offered.

'Barras didn't send me here to reason with them. He sent me to stop them and that's what I intend to do. This isn't a demonstration, Murat, this is a *coup d'état*. I have heard reports that there are more than twenty thousand rising against the Directory. They must be stopped.'

'I understand that, sir,' said the cavalryman. 'But—'

Bonaparte cut him short. 'You will obey my orders when I give them?'

'Of course, sir.'

Bonaparte nodded and turned away from the other man, who watched as the Corsican once more took up position behind one of the eight-pounders.

The guns were aimed at the Church of St Roch and, already, Bonaparte could see people spilling from the building on to its steps. Most of them seemed to be civilians but, amongst them, he saw the red uniforms of the National Guard, even some white-uniformed men. For a moment the Corsican wondered if they were regular army but closer inspection revealed that they were more than likely civilians dressed in stolen tunics. Muskets were brandished in the air. He saw knives, swords, pitchforks, axes and even what looked like a long spear. The noise grew more intense as more figures tumbled out of the church into the street, most of them forming an unruly mass on and around its steps.

A stone was thrown by one of the mob. It struck the cobbles some way in front of them, skidding off the road.

'Reason with them?' Bonaparte called to Murat who looked on impassively.

The sight of the guns seemed to provoke even greater anger amongst the crowd, and they began to form up in ragged lines, as yet more of them spilled from the church. The shouts of anger escalated, and weapons were brandished more openly.

Bonaparte guessed that the closest of the crowd was little more than a hundred yards away. If they decided to rush the guns it would take them less than twenty seconds but then again, he reasoned, to rush the guns would be suicidal.

Another stone came hurtling towards the waiting artillery.

Then another.

A third struck a spongeman on the temple and he fell heavily on the cobbles, blood pouring from a nasty cut just below his hairline. Two colleagues ran to his aid, one pressing a balled-up piece of cloth to the wound.

A command was bellowed and the infantry ordered arms. 'Stand ready!' an officer roared.

Murat estimated that the crowd had already swollen to nearly a thousand. Men and women of all ages were milling around now less than one hundred yards from the mouths of the cannon, shouting angrily, gesturing defiantly at the uniformed troops who barred the way to their objective.

Bonaparte had drawn up his troops to isolate the Tuileries, where he knew the crowd to be heading. All roads leading to the Palace had been closed off, guarded by cannon, troops or both.

The mob seemed unperturbed by the presence of these regular soldiers, presumably because it outnumbered them four to one, and it seemed to the Corsican as though the mob was multiplying before his eyes, ebbing back and forth like some human sea, closing the distance between themselves and the gaping mouths of the eight-pounders by the second. They were about ninety yards away now.

'Portfires, ready,' Bonaparte said quietly to an officer beside him and the order echoed around the Rue St Honoré.

Ventsmen working at the guns hurriedly inserted a 'quick match' into the vent. This piece of cotton soaked in saltpetre and spirits of wine would then be ignited, when ordered, with the portfire, a slow-burning match which comprised a tightly wound cylinder of blue paper soaked in sugar of lead and water, which would burn slowly for up to three hours.

At every gun the portfires burned, the glow like angry fireflies.

'Ready,' officers bellowed, forced to raise their voices

to maximum volume to make themselves heard above the frenzied shouts of the still growing mob.

It seemed as if the vast mass was reproducing within itself, churning out more and more people until the entire thoroughfare was choked with them.

Another hail of stones came flying over but most of the artillerymen stood still, awaiting their moment.

Bonaparte, sheltering behind the four-wheeled caisson of one gun, could almost make out the features of the leading members of the crowd now.

One was a woman, her face contorted with rage, brandishing a meat cleaver in one pudgy hand, holding her skirt up with the other as she advanced towards the guns.

'Traitors!' a voice from the crowd roared and the cry quickly spread.

The mob was advancing steadily towards the guns. It seemed to show no fear. Many of the uniformed men within had joined the front line, and one spat disdainfully in the direction of the eight-pounders.

Another stone was hurled by a youth in his teens. Barefoot and wearing just a worn shirt and threadbare trousers, he looked briefly at the faces of those around him as if for reassurance as he saw how close he was to the waiting cannon.

Next to the youth was a man in his mid-twenties who was holding a pitchfork, the gleaming points aimed at the waiting troops. He wore a bicorn hat but the cockade was missing. In its place he had stuck a feather. He too was barefoot.

Murat looked at the mob then across at Bonaparte, who was still watching calmly.

Suddenly, with less than fifty yards to advance, the

mob rushed forward. As if an order had been given, the deliberate, measured approach became a frenzied dash, the screams and howls of anger rising in volume as they hurtled towards the guns.

'Fire!' shouted Bonaparte and the order was echoed all around the street.

The cannon opened up.

A deafening roar reverberated as the eight-pounders fired, the barrels flaming, thick black clouds of smoke belching out. As they were fired, the guns shot backwards, carried by the savage recoil of so much power. They trundled back a full seven feet.

The cannon which had so far held their fire now let forth with another thunderous barrage.

Everything was momentarily drowned out by the explosions and, for precious seconds, not even the screams of those in the line of fire were audible beneath the massive detonations.

Case shot cut into the crowd, scything it down. Some were lifted off their feet by the impact of the heavy iron balls. In places, those closest to the muzzles were simply blown to pieces by the ferocity of the discharge.

And now, as the roar began to die away, Bonaparte and the others heard the moans of agony from the wounded. Still the smoke hung over the street but as it began to drift slightly, the extent of the carnage was unveiled.

Bodies carpeted the street, in places piled two and three deep, dead lying on top of wounded.

'Reload,' Bonaparte said and the command echoed around the road that had become a slaughterhouse.

Barrels were swabbed out to extinguish any smouldering powder from the previous shot, preventing premature firing. The ventsmen, their thumbs protected by a leather stall, pressed fingers to the vents to stop the current of air from causing blow-back at the spongemen. Then the loaders pushed fresh canisters into the hot barrels, stepping back as they were rammed into place with the opposite ends of the double-headed sponges. Another quick match was inserted. The gunners waited.

The youth who had thrown the stone was lying close to one of the eight-pounders, most of his face blasted away by a lump of metal. A wounded man was crawling across him, trying to drag himself away on what was left of his arms.

A National Guardsman was trying to scream but, with most of his bottom jaw missing, he could only manage a faint gurgle as he swallowed his own blood.

Many of the crowd had fled at the first fusillade, shocked and terrified by its ferocity. Those who remained were pulling back towards the church, some dragging wounded companions with them, others running as quickly as they could in the opposite direction.

Bonaparte watched as one man stopped long enough to pull a pair of shoes from the feet of a corpse before he too disappeared from sight down one of the side streets.

'You wanted me to reason with them, Murat,' said Bonaparte, running a hand through his hair. 'These cannon spoke to them in the only language they understand.' Again he patted one of the barrels.

In front of him, the wounded continued to scream for help.

CHAPTER 4

Lausard glanced around at the ragged lines of men formed up in the main courtyard of the Conciergerie. He guessed there were about one hundred and fifty, perhaps more.

'What the hell is going on?' Rocheteau whispered, shivering slightly in the breeze.

'We're going to be soldiers, boy,' said an older man with a huge moustache, his hair almost white.

'Shut up,' bellowed Sergeant Legier. 'No talking.'

The sergeant paced up and down before the prisoners. Captain Deschamps stood with Marcognet and, on either side of them, uniformed guards held their muskets at the ready, aimed at the prisoners.

Lausard heard the sound of horses' hooves on the cobbles and turned to see a dozen dragoons entering the courtyard from outside the prison. They were tall, powerfully built men with brass head-dresses nodding as they rode, horsehair manes flowing out behind them and carbines bumping against their saddles. Their mounts were brought to a halt behind their captain who swung himself into the saddle, lifting himself into view of the watching prisoners.

'Very pretty,' murmured Delacor, regarding the green uniforms indifferently.

The man standing next to him, a huge man with an enormous belly and thinning hair, shuffled nervously from one foot to the other. 'I can't ride a horse,' he said nervously.

'I wouldn't worry about it,' Delacor told him. 'You'll probably be dead before you get the chance.'

Joubert clasped his hands together, shuffling his fingers like fleshy playing cards.

'You look like you could *eat* a horse, never mind ride it,' Delacor observed.

'At the moment,' the big man said, his stomach rumbling loudly, 'I *could*.' He rubbed his huge gut. 'I can't remember the last time I had a decent meal.'

'You think you're the only one, fat man?' Delacor snapped. 'You've got enough blubber there to exist on for another six months.'

'Shut up!' roared Legier and his voice echoed around the courtyard.

The prisoners' attention was drawn towards the line of dragoons facing them, as the officer on the bay addressed them. 'You are men of France,' he called. 'You are her sons. You are no longer prisoners of the State. From now on you belong to the army. You will do as you are ordered. What you did before is not important. *Who* you were before is not important. You have been given another chance. A chance to regain some honour. A chance to give your lives for France.'

'That's very kind of him,' whispered Rocheteau under his breath.

Lausard never took his eyes from the dragoon captain.

'I can promise you nothing but hunger, hardship and pain,' Deschamps continued. 'But you will be free men again. Look upon that as a gift and look upon your chance to fight for France as a duty. One which you should cherish.'

Lausard lowered his gaze and swallowed hard.

Deschamps nodded to Legier, who spurred his mount forward, the animal trotting towards the main gate of the prison. The other dragoons formed up in lines of six on each side of the prisoners.

'Forward!' shouted Legier and the whole group moved forward, some of the men attempting to march, others walking as briskly as they could, some merely shuffling along.

Deschamps watched the entire ill-disciplined unit moving towards the gate and patted his horse's neck.

'Good luck, Captain,' said Marcognet, smiling.

'Be thankful I didn't take you too,' the officer snapped and rode towards the head of the group to join Legier.

Beyond the gates the prisoners saw not only more dragoons but infantry too, all crammed into the street with such density it looked impossible for them to move. There were civilians too, standing on the road-side watching the activity. A woman lifted her small child up towards one of the waiting dragoons, watching as the trooper gently stroked the child's face with a gloved hand.

'Where do you think they're taking us?' Rocheteau asked, glancing at the emotionless faces of the infantry flanking them. He almost stumbled trying to avoid stepping in a crater.

Roussard wasn't quite so lucky and he cursed as he slipped.

A hand shot out to steady him.

'Thank you,' Roussard said to the man walking next to him, who nodded and smiled, patting him on the back.

Roussard looked at his companion and noticed that the man was totally bald, but his shiny pate wasn't a legacy of old age; his face, red-cheeked and round, was that of a young man, perhaps in his early thirties. He had the bluest eyes Roussard had ever seen but they were virtually hidden by heavy eyelids and an almost protuberant forehead. The man's head had been shaved so closely that not even a hint of stubble remained. It looked as smooth as a cannon ball.

'What is your name?' Roussard asked him.

'Carbonne,' the man told him, wiping one large hand over his bald dome.

Roussard was about to say something when he felt a hand grab at the back of his neck.

'Shut up, scum,' the infantry corporal bellowed in his ear, almost throwing him to the ground. He glared at Carbonne. 'You too.'

The men marched on in silence.

The popping of musket fire seemed to drift on the breeze.

It was hard to tell from how far away it came. A mile, perhaps more.

The thunder of cannon sounded much closer.

Lausard and Rocheteau glanced at each other but neither spoke.

'Keep moving,' one of the NCOs roared and the sound of hundreds of marching feet mingled with that of horses' hooves, the jingling of harnesses and the occasional snorts of the dragoons' mounts.

Once more they heard the distant crackle of sporadic musket fire.

A moment or two of silence then the roar of cannon again.

'Perhaps the Austrians are in Paris already,' Rocheteau said quietly.

Lausard glanced over his shoulder, back at the rows of colourless faces.

Somewhere in the distance he saw smoke rising. A single black plume of it pushing its way up amongst the clouds. Very soon it was joined by another.

No one knew how far they had walked. No one knew exactly how far outside Paris they were. All they knew was that they were cold, hungry and exhausted.

The journey from the prison, which had begun in bright morning sunlight, was ending in the blood-red wash of sunset. The sun itself was a massive burnished orb slipping slowly below the horizon, its dying light turning the sky the colour of bloodstained bronze. Birds returning to their nests were black arrowheads against the crimson backdrop.

The prisoners had been ordered to halt at the foot of a low ridge which was densely wooded. A stream wound through it and the dragoons were watering their horses at the point where it left the confines of the trees. A farmhouse, about a mile to the north, was just visible in the fading light. A thin column of smoke rose from its chimney, like the plumes Lausard had seen earlier in the day as they had left Paris.

The outskirts of the capital were behind them. For

the last two miles they'd trekked along a road barely wide enough to accommodate themselves and the accompanying troops.

The infantry stood or sat cleaning their muskets, using rags taken from their packs. Several dragoons polished their saddles and harnesses.

Lausard noticed Deschamps walking across the uneven ground, clutching a pipe in one hand, puffing slowly on it, with two other officers accompanying him.

A farrier was busy removing a stone from the shoe of a horse, working away expertly while its rider stood by watching and chatting to a companion. One of them had his green cloak slung around his shoulders to ward off the cold wind which the night was bringing. From the nearby woods, birdsong signalled the end of the day and branches rustled gently in the growing breeze.

A group of infantrymen returned from the wood carrying branches. Lausard watched as they used gunpowder from a cartridge to start a fire, feeding pieces of twig in as the blaze became brighter, flames licking hungrily towards the darkening sky.

'It's all right for those bastards,' snapped Delacor. 'What about us? We'll freeze to death.'

'And starve,' Joubert added, rubbing his huge belly.

'Not you, fat man,' Delacor said irritably. 'Perhaps the rest of us should be careful you don't eat *us*.'

A chorus of guffaws greeted the remark from those closest.

'Leave him alone,' said Giresse. 'He's not the only one who's hungry.'

Delacor shot him an angry glance.

'I'd love to be in my father's baker's shop now,'

another man chipped in. 'I can almost smell the freshly baked bread.'

'Stop this torture,' Giresse said, chuckling. 'Who are you anyway?'

'My name is Charvet.' He extended a hand, which Giresse shook firmly.

'What did they lock *you* up for?' Joubert asked.

'Illegal gambling,' Charvet said. 'I was a boxer. A friend of mine used to organise the fights in an abandoned church.'

'Were you any good?' Giresse enquired.

'I never lost a fight,' Charvet told him, raising his fists as if to throw a punch.

'God will punish you,' Moreau said, with an air of finality. 'Fighting in a church. Defiling God's house with violence. You're a disgrace.'

'A friend of the Almighty, that's all we need,' said Rocheteau. 'If you're on intimate terms, couldn't you ask him for a fire and some food?'

'Blasphemy won't help you,' Moreau said.

Some of the other men chuckled.

'I'll tell you what's blasphemy,' Joubert interjected. 'Us not being given any food, that's what.'

'There is such a thing as sustenance for the soul,' Moreau said.

'To hell with that,' Joubert snapped. 'I need sustenance for my stomach.'

There was more laughter.

Rocheteau grunted, his laughter cut short as he felt a boot driven into his back.

He spun round to see a dragoon standing over him, a large moustache bristling beneath his hooked nose. He smoothed a hand over his sergeant's stripes and looked disdainfully at the group of prisoners.

'You, you and you,' he said, jabbing fingers towards Rocheteau, Lausard and Carbonne. 'Get some wood from there.' He hooked a thumb in the direction of the trees. 'Build a fire. I don't want you bastards dying on me in the night. Go.'

The three men got to their feet and trudged towards the woods, the sergeant close behind them.

'My name is Delpierre,' he said. 'Remember that.'

'How could we forget?' hissed Rocheteau under his breath.

He heard the hiss of the sabre being drawn from its scabbard, then he felt the point pressed against the back of his neck, hard enough to draw blood.

'You keep your mouth shut, convict,' Delpierre snapped. 'You don't speak unless I tell you to. If I hear you open your mouth again without permission, I'll gut you like a chicken. Understand?'

'Yes,' said Rocheteau through clenched teeth.

'Yes, *Sergeant*,' the dragoon corrected him.

'Yes, *Sergeant*,' Rocheteau echoed, waiting for the sword to be lowered. Still he felt the cold steel against the nape of his neck and Lausard turned his gaze towards Delpierre. The sergeant's face was deeply pitted, a legacy of smallpox. His eyes were deep-set, almost pig-like.

'What are you looking at?' he snapped at Lausard, finally withdrawing the sabre, running it back into its sheath. 'Pick up some wood and get a move on.'

Lausard and the others started to pick up some fallen branches from the floor of the wood. Carbonne heaved several large lumps of timber up on to his broad shoulders, his muscles bulging beneath the weight.

Rocheteau picked up some more of the drier lumber and held it before him.

'Come on,' snapped Delpierre. 'Hurry, we haven't got all night. You've got a long march ahead of you tomorrow.' He smiled crookedly. 'By the time I've finished with you, you bastards will wish you were still in that prison.'

The men headed back towards their waiting companions, picking their way through the undergrowth with care now. Darkness had descended but for a tiny remnant of blood-red sky, a crimson slash across the black curtain of the night.

Lausard moved sure-footedly through the wood, clutching his bundle of kindling.

Not so Rocheteau. He stumbled over a fallen branch and went headlong, scattering the collected timber before him.

'Pick it up, you scum,' hissed Delpierre taking a stride towards him.

He drove one boot into Rocheteau's side and the thief rolled over, ready to spring up at his tormentor, but Lausard shot out a hand and gripped his shirt.

'Leave it,' he whispered under his breath.

Delpierre looked at Lausard, then at Rocheteau. The thief was still crouched down as if ready to spring.

'Whenever you like, scum,' said Delpierre, grinning.

Lausard kept a firm grip on his companion's shirt.

'What's your name?' Delpierre asked, kicking a piece of wood towards Rocheteau.

'My name is Rocheteau.'

'And you?' He nodded in Lausard's direction.

'Lausard.'

'I'll remember that,' the dragoon said. 'We're going to get to know each other very well during the next few weeks. Now move it.'

He walked away, leaving Rocheteau to gather up the dropped wood.

'I'm going to kill him,' the thief hissed. 'I swear to God I'm going to kill that bastard.'

'Not yet,' Lausard said quietly. 'The time will come.'

'Where do you think they're taking us?'

Lausard gazed into the flames of the fire, watching the yellow tongues leaping and dancing, encouraged by the breeze.

He heard the words and lifted his gaze to see Charvet looking expectantly at the other men huddled by the meagre source of heat. It had been he who had asked the question.

All over the slope men were gathered in groups around camp fires. Prisoners and troops alike. Some were sleeping, others talking in hushed tones. Some of the troops chewed on biscuits, others drank from bottles of wine which they'd taken from their packs.

Two dragoons passed by at a walk, the harnesses of their mounts jingling in the still night air. Several infantrymen stood sentinel near to the woods, muskets sloped, their faces turned towards the prisoners. One or two tents had been set up towards the foot of the slope – for officers, Lausard presumed.

'I said, where do you think—' Charvet began.

'We heard what you said,' Delacor snapped. 'How the hell do we know where they're taking us? It's outside that stinking prison, that's all I care about.'

'How many do you think they took?' Carbonne

wondered, looking around at the smattering of camp fires and huddles of men.

'A hundred and fifty or more,' Rocheteau mused. 'Who knows?'

'Why us?' Charvet persisted.

'They're desperate for men,' Lausard said. 'Conscription didn't work. They're frightened of being overrun.'

'They're not the only ones,' Roussard added.

'The army's in a mess, the country's in a mess,' Lausard offered. 'It must be if they want men like us to help them.'

'I'm proud to fight for my country,' said a huge man seated opposite Lausard. He was well over six feet tall, powerfully built, but when he spoke his words were faltering, as if he had trouble pronouncing them.

'It was your country that locked you up, you half-wit,' Delacor snapped.

'Why were you in prison?' Lausard asked.

'They said I stole food,' the big man replied. 'But I was hungry.'

'You and half of Paris,' Giresse added.

'What's your name?'

'Tabor,' the big man replied.

'He's an idiot,' Delacor said dismissively.

'Perhaps he thinks the same about you,' Lausard chided.

The other men laughed but Delacor sat forward, leaning towards Lausard.

'You'd best be careful how you talk to me,' the rapist hissed.

'If you're trying to frighten me, don't waste your breath,' Lausard dismissed him.

'I won't frighten you, I'll kill you,' Delacor threatened.

'You're welcome to try,' Lausard said softly.

The two men locked stares for a moment longer, the firelight flickering in their glaring eyes, then Delacor sat back.

A long silence followed, finally broken by Charvet. 'So where do you think they're taking us?' he tried again.

'There's a training depot at St Germain,' Lausard said. 'It's my guess they're taking us there.'

'What makes *you* such an expert?' Delacor demanded.

'Trust me,' Lausard said.

'I don't trust anybody.'

'We're better off out of Paris after what happened this morning,' Carbonne suggested. 'I overheard a couple of the dragoons talking earlier. They said the mob had tried to attack the Tuileries. The army fired on them. They said over two hundred had been killed, twice that wounded.'

'Murdering bastards,' Delacor sneered.

'What choice did they have?' Lausard offered. 'If they were being attacked they had to retaliate.'

'The army will end up ruling this country,' Giresse opined.

'Then it's just as well we're going to be a part of it, isn't it?' Rocheteau said, chuckling, and the other men joined him.

Delacor merely glared at the thief.

'There'll be a price to pay,' Moreau interjected. 'God will punish us all for this.'

'I don't think God has got anything to do with what's going on at the moment,' said Lausard.

'He has abandoned us,' Moreau said wearily. 'And who can blame Him?'

'I never asked for His help in the first place,' Delacor rasped.

'You'll call on Him at some time, every man does,' Moreau persisted.

'Does He listen?' Lausard asked. 'Does He *ever* listen.'

'He hears everything.'

'Do you think He'd hear me if I asked Him for some food?' Joubert enquired.

The other men laughed, moving closer to the fire as the leaping flames gradually became flickering whisps. Rocheteau fed more wood to the pyre, waiting for the heat to spring up once again.

'You'd be surprised how long the human body can go without food,' Bonet said. 'I know, I was a schoolmaster before they arrested me.'

'Why would they want to arrest a schoolmaster?' Rocheteau asked.

'The Directory didn't want any history taught that involved the Bourbons,' Bonet said. 'I thought my pupils had a right to know what went on before Louis the Sixteenth died. History is important. It teaches us about ourselves.'

'Very interesting,' Delacor yawned, then he looked over at Carbonne. 'What's your story?'

The bald man swallowed hard. 'I was an executioner. I worked with Sanson for two years. Then, one morning, they brought a man to the guillotine. I was going to pull the lever until I realised it was my brother. I couldn't do it. I was arrested on the spot. My brother still died though.' He lowered his voice.

'You should have died with him, you bloody butcher,' said Delacor.

Carbonne shrugged.

'None of us knows *your* crime,' Lausard said, turning to face Delacor. 'Why so shy? Share it with us.'

'Go to hell!'

'In time,' Lausard countered. 'What was your crime?'

'I committed no crime,' Delacor said, feeling the eyes of the other men upon him. 'The woman was as much to blame, she encouraged me, the bitch. She—'

Lausard cut him short. 'A rapist.'

Delacor's eyes narrowed as he looked at the younger man with an expression of fury.

Rocheteau hawked and spat in Delacor's direction.

Moreau crossed himself.

Roussard shook his head slowly.

Giresse held a hand before his face as if he had just smelled something rank.

'What gives any of *you* the right to judge *me*?' Delacor challenged angrily. 'We're all criminals. You're no better than me.'

All eyes were upon him but no one spoke.

The hillside was becoming darker as the fires burned out. More wood was fed into them but they remained little more than small patches of glowing embers. More and more men settled down on the cold ground to try to sleep as best they could. The whinnying of tethered horses could be heard every now and then through the stillness, along with the occasional barked commands of an NCO.

Lausard lay back, hands clasped behind his head, his gaze directed towards the stars dotting the firmament. It looked as if someone had fired crystal grapeshot at a black velvet blanket. Around him he could hear some of the men snoring but sleep continued to elude him.

When he inhaled, a peculiar cocktail of smells filled his nostrils. The acrid smell of burning wood, sweat from so many unwashed bodies, horse droppings, gun oil, smoke and the scent of grass.

When he sat up he could smell fresh air. It was the smell of freedom. Preferable to the rancid stench of his prison cell. And again Lausard felt a kind of crushing weight on his shoulders. It was as if he had been spared a second time. First he had escaped the clutches of the Jacobins and cheated the guillotine and now the army had saved him from that killing machine. Unlike his family. For fleeting seconds the images of their faces flashed into his mind and he blinked hard to drive the vision away.

He looked across at Moreau, who was sleeping with his face turned towards the fire. No doubt he would have said that God had saved Lausard, but the younger man did not believe in the existence of such a divine entity, let alone in His intervention.

Slowly he regarded the other men around him, men who had been strangers to him hours earlier. Now he knew their names and how they had come to be incarcerated. These men with whom he would share the remainder of his days. Thieves, gamblers, rapists, forgers. All kinds of criminal. And among them were a schoolmaster, an executioner, a near idiot and a Russian. If God did exist, Lausard mused, then He certainly had a sense of humour. These were the men who were going to help defend France. Men as worthless as Lausard himself.

He lay down again and tried to sleep, but again images of his family filled his mind. This time, however, he didn't chase them away; he allowed them to fill his head, allowed himself to feel the pain they brought.

It was a long time before he slept.

CHAPTER 5

As Lausard sat on the frozen hillside he was aware of two things: the cold which dug its invisible nails into him, raising the hairs on his arms, and a growing discord of shouts and curses.

The sun was struggling into a watery sky, spreading a dull dawn across the land. A single plume of smoke rose mournfully from the embers of the fire that the men had huddled around so gratefully the night before.

Rocheteau rolled over and pushed his hands close to the pile of blackened wood, hoping to draw some last vestiges of warmth from it.

Joubert rubbed his huge stomach which rumbled protestingly.

Giresse stretched and yawned.

Moreau crossed himself.

Lausard heard the sounds of a bugle close by. The dragoon trumpeter was blowing the insistent notes designed to wake the sleeping men.

The infantry had already formed up into line; three dragoons rode past, one of their horses shaking its head wildly, its rider forced to tug hard on the reins to keep the animal under control.

The tents at the bottom of the slope were still in place and, from his vantage point, Lausard could just make out the figure of Deschamps puffing on a pipe, still dressed in a shirt and breeches, a forage cap perched jauntily on his head. He was talking to three other men, gesturing up the slope towards the troops and prisoners.

Lausard was still watching the officer when he felt the shove in the back that almost caused him to over-balance.

'Come on, you bastards,' shouted Delpierre, holding Lausard's gaze as the younger man glared at him momentarily. 'On your feet, there's something I want you to see.'

He swung a boot at Delacor who was still struggling to his feet.

The other men scrambled upright, some rubbing their hands together in a futile attempt to generate some warmth in bodies chilled by a heavy frost.

Other NCOs, cavalry and infantry were moving amongst the prisoners, rousing them with similarly brutal methods. Sergeant Legier prodded men with the point of his sabre while an infantry corporal kicked others to force them to their feet.

The troops looked on impassively. Dragoons, already mounted, sat astride their mounts forming a green-coated barrier across the entrance to the woods. The early-morning sunlight twinkled on the brass casques of their helmets.

As Lausard watched, several of them moved their horses to one side and, from the resultant gap,

Delpierre appeared, pushing three men before him.

When one stumbled and fell, the sergeant drove a boot into his side then dragged him to his feet.

'What's going on?' murmured Charvet, watching the tableau before them.

No one answered. Lausard in particular was more concerned by the sight of twelve infantrymen moving into the centre of a clearing, muskets sloped. They formed into two lines, one kneeling ahead of the other, and he watched as they loaded their weapons. The manoeuvre was carried out with drill-book precision. First, each man took a cartridge from his tin-lined cartouche and bit the end off the greased paper tube. Holding the ball in his mouth he drew the hammer back one notch, opened the priming pan and poured a small amount of powder into it. The remaining powder he then poured down the barrel. The infantrymen spat the balls down the barrels, ramming the cartridge paper after it to form a wad, to hold the lead ball in place. The ramrods were replaced in their channels beneath the barrels and the Charlevilles were lifted, with mechanical precision, to blue-coated shoulders.

Delpierre strode in front of the twelve men, dragging one of the prisoners with him. The other two were pushed into position alongside him by a dragoon officer who barely looked old enough to shave.

'These men tried to escape last night,' Delpierre shouted, glancing around at the other watching prisoners. 'They are cowards. They were given the chance to fight for their country and they chose to run instead.'

Rocheteau looked anxiously at Lausard but he was staring intently at the stricken figures before him, at the twelve muskets pointing in their direction.

One of the three fugitives had dropped to his knees.

Delpierre grabbed him by the collar and hauled him to his feet.

'This is *not* the kind of man that France wants,' Delpierre continued. 'When you were in prison you belonged to the State, now you belong to *us*. If you break *our* rules you pay *our* price. These men are deserters. The price *they* must pay is death.'

The man Delpierre was holding suddenly pulled away, pushing the restraining arm aside, and stood defiantly before the levelled muskets.

Delpierre met his gaze for a moment then walked away, nodding in the direction of the infantry sergeant who was standing beside the firing squad.

'Ready,' the man shouted and twelve hammers were drawn back.

Lausard gritted his teeth, the knot of muscles at the side of his jaw pulsing angrily.

Delpierre looked across and the two men locked stares. Lausard was sure he could see a faint smile flickering on the sergeant's lips.

'Fire!' roared the infantry sergeant.

The stillness of the morning was filled with the deafening retort of twelve muskets; a cloud of black smoke belched from the barrels, drifting across the slope. When the sulphurous fog cleared, two of the three men lay on the frosty ground.

Lausard could see several crimson smudges on the shirt of one. The second man was still twitching slightly. Two musket balls had hit him in the stomach, a third had shattered his left arm at the elbow.

The third man remained on his feet, untouched by the fusillade. He stood motionless, his eyes bulging wide, his body quivering slightly, gaze fixed on the firing squad which was in the process of reloading.

'Wait!' ordered Delpierre, striding towards the man.

The sergeant first inspected the bodies of the other two prisoners, prodding each with the toe of one boot. The second man groaned softly, his eyes flickering. He looked up imploringly at the dragoon, blood spilling over his lips, his one good hand now clutching at the ragged wounds in his belly, as if to hold the blood in.

Delpierre drew his sabre, pressed it against the man's throat then drove it forward, puncturing the ground beneath as he skewered the dying man's neck. He quickly pulled the sabre free and wiped the stained blade on the shirt of the prisoner, then turned to face the last of the trio.

Even from such close range, the Charleville musket was notoriously inaccurate and Delpierre wasn't entirely surprised to see that one of the men was unscathed.

'You have either God or the Devil on your side,' he said, grabbing the man by the collar. 'You might be useful.' He shoved the terrified prisoner towards Lausard and his watching companions. The man fell at Lausard's feet, gratefully accepting the helping hand he was offered. His skin was milk-white, his body quivering madly and Lausard could smell the stench of urine as he stood close to him. There was a dark stain on the front of his trousers.

'That is how any attempt to escape will be dealt with,' Delpierre said, motioning towards the two bodies.

Moreau crossed himself.

'You belong to the army now,' Delpierre continued.

'These men were given another chance and they threw it away. The rest of you look closely at them. If any of you were thinking of trying to escape, then forget about it.'

'Why did you run?' Lausard whispered to the surviving prisoner.

'Why do you think?' the man hissed. 'We're all going to die in battle anyway, if we get that far.'

'What's your name?' Lausard asked him.

'Sonnier,' he said, wiping perspiration from his face.

Delpierre was still stalking back and forth in front of the two dead bodies, his narrowed eyes scanning the rows of blank faces before him.

'If any man disobeys he will be flogged,' he shouted. 'If any man tries to run he will be executed. Keep this in your minds.' He turned and looked down at the two corpses. 'They'll be left to rot where they are. Food for scavengers. It's all they're fit for.' He wandered back up the slope to where his horse was waiting. Lausard watched as he swung himself into the saddle.

'It serves them right,' muttered Delacor. 'They shouldn't have run.'

'Do you blame them?' snapped Roussard.

'I blame them for getting caught,' Delacor said disdainfully.

'How the hell can they be deserters when they're not in uniform yet?' Rocheteau argued.

'You heard what he said,' Lausard murmured, nodding towards Delpierre who rode past close to them. 'We belong to the army now.'

'They own us,' Joubert added.

'Nobody owns *me*,' Rocheteau hissed. 'I carry no one's brand.'

'You might be carrying the mark of the lash if you don't do as they tell you,' Joubert offered.

Rocheteau spat indignantly.

'They want us to be soldiers,' said Lausard. 'Let's play their game.'

'This is no game,' Sonnier groaned. 'We'll all be killed.'

'It'll be God's will,' Moreau said.

'God has nothing to do with this,' Lausard snapped. 'And if He's got any sense, He'll keep his nose out of it. If there ever *was* a God He gave up caring a long time ago. We're on our own now. We can live or we can die.' He glanced behind him at the two corpses lying motionless on the slope.

In the sky above, several crows were already circling.

CHAPTER 6

Paul Barras ran his finger around the rim of the glass with a slight smile creasing his face. In his fortieth year, Barras, like his two companions in the room, enjoyed an almost unrivalled power in the turmoil that was revolutionary France. A member of the newly self-appointed Directory, he had amassed considerable personal wealth and used it on the one real vice he had. Women. The power was wonderful, the wealth glorious, but the unbridled affections of so many women seemed like a drug to Barras; the latest in a growing retinue had made him the talk and the envy both of his colleagues in the Directory and of those who moved in high circles. It was her face which Barras pictured in his mind now as he sat at the large table in one of the smaller state rooms of the Tuileries. Joséphine de Beauharnais. The name seemed musical to him as he thought of it, thought of her. The stunning Creole had spent her earliest years in the French West Indies before marrying Vicomte Alexandre de Beauharnais fourteen years ago. He had gone to the guillotine the previous year.

Barras and she had become lovers within a month of the execution. He sipped at his wine, wiping his mouth with the back of his hand, wiping the wistful smile away too. He got to his feet and crossed to one of the huge windows looking out over the rear gardens of the palace. There were several soldiers in sight, dressed in their familiar blue jackets and white *culottes*.

'Don't you find this all a little ironic?' said Barras, still gazing out over the gardens.

The other two men in the room looked at him in bewilderment.

'We run the country from the home of the man we helped to destroy,' Barras continued. 'Once this building belonged to the Bourbons, now it belongs to us.'

'The *country* used to belong to the Bourbons,' said Tallien. 'Now *that* belongs to us too.'

'Such power,' Barras mused, returning to the table.

'*We* didn't destroy the monarchy,' Gohier offered. 'The people did.'

'We *are* the people,' Barras reminded him. 'I for one would be proud to think that I'd been responsible in some way for removing that tyrant.' He swallowed what was left in his glass then refilled it from the container on the table.

'If we are the people, then why did the people try to destroy us?' Tallien asked. 'If they'd reached us they would have killed us. If that *coup* had been successful we'd all have been sneezing into the basket just like the King and his family did.'

'It wasn't a popular rising,' Barras said dismissively.

'It was twenty thousand people, Barras,' Tallien protested. 'How popular does it have to be for you to recognise that we are not liked?'

'Men in power never are, but decisions have to be made and we are the men who make those decisions for the betterment of France *and* her people.'

'The same people who tried to destroy us?' Tallien murmured sardonically.

'The Paris mob is no longer a force,' Barras said. 'What happened the other day has broken them.'

'You sound very sure of that,' Gohier said.

'Over two hundred of them were killed, more than twice that number wounded,' Barras said, a note of pride in his voice. 'They realise now that we are not afraid to use the army against them if necessary.'

'Did you instruct Bonaparte to fire on them?' Gohier asked.

'I ordered him to do his duty,' Barras said. 'I ordered him to protect us.' He jabbed a finger at his companions. 'He's a soldier. He acted as he saw fit.'

'Why did you choose Bonaparte?' Tallien enquired.

'He's a very able man,' Barras replied. 'He proved that at Toulon two years ago. I doubt that siege would ever have been broken without him. You should be grateful to him, Tallien.'

'I *am* grateful but I'm not sure I trust him. After all, he isn't French, is he?'

'He's Corsican,' Barras said and laughed. 'Has his loyalty ever been in doubt?'

'He was a friend of Robespierre, he was arrested,' Gohier offered.

'He was held for two weeks and he wasn't a *friend* of Robespierre's, he was under the patronage of that dictator's brother.' Barras began walking around the table. 'He's a very gifted man, a very intelligent soldier.'

'Does such a thing exist?' snorted Tallien.

'Whoever controls the army, controls the city,' Gohier said. 'If Bonaparte is as intelligent as you say, don't you think that might have occurred to him?'

'His loyalty is not in question,' Barras insisted. 'How many times do I have to say it? It is only because of him that we are here now. I cannot understand your concern. If anything does happen then we simply remove him.'

'It might not be that easy,' Gohier protested. 'If he has the army in his control—'

Barras interjected. 'So if *we* control Bonaparte then we also control the army. There isn't a more able man available.'

'Dugommier. Massena,' Gohier suggested. 'They're both very able men.'

'Bonaparte may be too young,' Tallien said.

'Is his youth cause to doubt his abilities?' Barras queried. 'Massena is the same age and yet you would not hesitate to suggest him. Serurier is a very competent soldier but I feel he is too old.'

'What of Cafferelli?' Tallien said.

'He is an engineer,' Barras countered. 'Commanding troops in the field is not his forte. Why are you all so resistant to Bonaparte? Perhaps we should be discussing how best to thank him for saving our lives and our positions instead of questioning his skills as a soldier.'

There was a long silence, finally broken by Tallien.

'You're right, Barras,' he said, sighing. 'Bonaparte should be rewarded in some way. What had you in mind?'

Barras smiled.

CHAPTER 7

Lausard couldn't be sure how many men were drawn up in the three ragged lines that stretched across the compound. He guessed around a hundred and fifty, perhaps more. He glanced furtively back and forth, his steely gaze moving from man to man.

The compound itself was surrounded by a low stone wall and tall trees. Behind the men was a number of buildings. Stables, an armoury, a commissary, an infirmary and what he could only assume were barracks. There were several water-troughs on the main parade ground and also three eight-pounder cannon, barrels pointed towards the men but unmanned. A tricolour flew proudly from the pole near the barracks, fluttering in the breeze.

The floor of the compound was partly cobbled, partly dark earth, the latter marked by the passage of many hooves and also liberal amounts of droppings. The odour mingled with the pungent smell of perspiration and unwashed bodies, one of which belonged to Lausard himself. He saw one of the men in the line ahead of him scratching a flea bite at the back of his neck. Lausard began scratching his own armpit.

As they'd entered the training camp he'd seen Captain Deschamps and two other officers ride off and now the highest-ranking men left on the parade ground were NCOs, Delpierre and Legier among them. Both of the dragoons were still mounted, Delpierre walking his horse slowly up and down the waiting lines of men.

The infantry had dispersed too. The green-jacketed dragoons were the only sentinels who kept a watch on the prisoners now. They sat, statue-like on immobile horses, watching the unwashed horde and waiting for orders. One was gently patting the neck of his mount. Two held their carbines across their chests. The weapons were identical to the Charleville muskets carried by the infantry, apart from the fact that they were thirty-seven inches long instead of the usual fifty. Like the .70 calibre infantry weapon they could also be fitted with a fifteen-inch bayonet for hand-to-hand fighting.

There were three water pumps within sight and Lausard could see several men in stable dress filling buckets with water, lining them up as neatly as chess-pieces. The men were talking quietly amongst themselves, the odd laugh punctuating the conversation.

'Take a good look around you,' Delpierre shouted, his voice reverberating around the compound. 'This will be your home for the next few weeks. You may grow to love it, you may grow to hate it. That isn't important. What you *will* do is learn. You will obey when you are given an order, you will carry out that order to the letter.' The sergeant guided his horse back and forth, only now he was joined by Legier too, the men riding up and down in opposite directions, passing each other every so often.

'You will train here,' Legier shouted. 'You will become soldiers here. It is our duty to turn you into soldiers. What you were before is not important. Your life before is not important. When you pull on the uniforms you are given you will become men again. Until then you are nothing. You are clay to be moulded.'

'Moulded by *us*,' Delpierre added. 'You smell, you must be cleaned up.' He glanced across at the men working the water pumps. They were still lining up buckets of water. Delpierre rose in his stirrups and looked at the lines of prisoners. 'Strip off,' he bellowed. 'Take off those filthy tatters.'

The men hesitated.

'Now!' Delpierre roared.

Lausard pulled his shirt open, began tugging it off.

Rocheteau did likewise.

Men all along the lines began disrobing, shivering in the chill breeze.

Charvet tugged off his filthy shirt and tossed it aside, almost hitting Carbonne with it. The bald man frowned, pulling off his own dirty trousers, standing naked like so many of the other men in front and behind him. Within a matter of minutes, every prisoner stood naked, shivering in the breeze. A number in the front line clasped their hands across their groins.

'Forget your modesty,' Delpierre said mockingly.

Almost involuntarily, Moreau glanced down at Giresse who was standing beside him with his arms folded, proudly displaying his manhood.

'There are women who would kill for what you now see,' Giresse bragged.

Moreau looked away in disgust.

'I want all those uniforms gathered up now,' Delpierre shouted. 'You, you and you.' He pointed towards three men in the front rank. 'Pile them up.'

The men scuttled around, gathering the filthy rags, hurling them into one large untidy pile.

'You two, help them,' the sergeant said to some more of those waiting patiently in the cold.

The mound of discarded clothes began to grow until it was as tall as a man.

Lausard looked first at the clothes, then at the sergeant who was smiling to himself.

'In groups of five,' he roared. 'Over to the water pumps. Get cleaned up. Move it.'

The first group of men did as they were ordered and were met by a stinging deluge of freezing water, hurled by the five dragoons in fatigues.

Five more followed them. And so it went on.

Joubert spat out some water, shaking uncontrollably from the chill.

Rocheteau ran a hand through his hair, brushing the sodden strands from his face.

Lausard wiped his hands across his cheeks and chest, glad to be cleansed of the filth which clung to him like a second skin but not so happy about the way it was being removed. The cold was almost unbearable.

'What the hell are they doing with our clothes?' Delacor said, grabbing Lausard by the arm.

The prisoners looked on as two dragoons poured pitch over the cloth, ladling it from a large barrel close by. At a signal from Delpierre, the entire bundle was ignited using a small tinderbox. The flame danced and flickered in the breeze then seemed to gain strength.

There was a loud *whump* as the pitch went up, the fire spreading quickly, devouring the soaked clothes. Flames began to spring further up the mound and soon a pall of thick smoke was rising into the air.

Delacor stood watching incredulously until a bucket full of cold water struck him, shocking him back to reality. He glared at the man who'd thrown it but the dragoon merely smiled back.

On the other side of the compound several tables were set up and Lausard could see men standing behind them, stacks of clothing laid out before them. As they were directed towards these tables he saw that the clothes were predominantly blue and white. The familiar blue jackets of the infantry, but many of the tunics were white. Each man was given one bundle of clothes containing a jacket, a pair of trousers, wooden shoes and a belt.

'Put those on,' shouted Delpierre. 'You'll be given the uniforms of cavalry when you're fit to wear them.'

Lausard pulled on the blue jacket, noticing that there was a large hole in one shoulder, the edges singed.

'You'd better hope you're luckier than the man who wore it before you,' said Delpierre, looking down at him.

'I can't get this on,' grumbled Joubert, trying vainly to make the two sides of a white tunic meet across his massive belly.

Roussard was having the opposite problem. The sleeves of his jacket were about six inches too long. His trousers too were like concertinas around his ankles.

'This is a Prussian jacket,' said Bonet, slipping his navy-blue tunic on.

'Who cares where it came from?' Lausard said, fastening his brass buttons.

Tabor fastened the belt around his waist, hoisting his trousers further up, his huge hands fumbling with the material.

'Cavalry,' said Rostov dismissively. 'I've never ridden a horse in my life. How are they supposed to turn us into cavalry?'

Lausard didn't answer, he was gazing around at the other men, all now dressed or dressing in the cast-off infantry uniforms.

'Keep them clean,' Delpierre ordered. 'Others who follow you will have to make use of them.'

Rocheteau sniffed at the armpit of his jacket.

'Whoever had this one didn't bother,' he grunted. 'Why should I?'

'Where did they get them?' Joubert asked.

'The dead,' Lausard said flatly. 'Ours and the allies.'

'Wearing dead men's clothes is bad luck,' Sonnier argued.

'You're lucky someone's not wearing *yours*,' Rocheteau sniggered. 'You complain about bad luck after surviving a firing squad. You must be the luckiest man on earth.'

A number of the men chuckled.

'God decided it wasn't your time,' Moreau said.

'He's got the inaccuracy of the firing squad to thank,' Rocheteau countered. 'Not God.'

More laughter.

'Shut up,' bellowed Delpierre.

'I *said* I was going to kill that bastard,' Rocheteau muttered under his breath. 'And I will.' He shot the sergeant a malevolent glance.

'I wonder when they'll give us weapons,' Roussard mused.

'When they're sure we won't use them to escape, probably,' Lausard said. 'They *daren't* trust us yet.'

'*I'm* not running away again,' Sonnier asserted.

Bonet succeeded in fastening the buttons of the Prussian tunic he'd been given. He smoothed one sleeve, removing a piece of dried mud from the cuff.

'This looks like better quality material,' he said, touching the shoulder of Carbonne's tunic. 'Ours are thinner.'

'Too thin to stop a musket ball,' Lausard interjected, pushing a finger into the hole in his jacket's shoulder.

'Or a sabre cut,' Charvet observed, indicating a slash in the breast of his own jacket which had been hastily stitched. There was still dried blood on the white tunic.

'So many ways to die,' muttered Roussard.

Lausard didn't answer, his gaze was firmly fixed on the pile of burning clothes on the other side of the compound. The plume of thick black smoke was still rising higher, up towards the darkening sky.

A huge metal cauldron containing boiled meat and vegetables had been set up at one end of the barrack room and the smell of food was both welcome and much appreciated. The cook, a huge man with a massive moustache, ladled the broth into the metal plates each man held up, while an assistant broke off pieces of bread and passed it to them. Most ate the bread as soon as it was given to them, others dropped it into the broth.

'I wonder what it is?' Rostov asked, peering ahead of him, past the line of waiting, hungry men.

'Who cares?' Joubert grunted. 'It's food, that's all that matters. I was beginning to think I was going to die of hunger.' He inhaled deeply, savouring the rich aroma of the broth.

'Some kind of blessing should be said before we eat,' Moreau said. 'We should give thanks to God for this food.'

'We should give thanks to whoever cooked it,' Rocheteau chuckled and the other men joined in the chorus of laughter.

'I'm not thanking anyone until I've tasted it,' Lausard said, grinning.

Rocheteau patted him on the shoulder and smiled.

The barrack room itself was about fifty feet long, half that in width. Blankets were laid out on the stone floor at regular intervals. No beds. But at least the men would be spending this and many more nights under cover. They comforted themselves with that thought. Food and shelter was all they asked.

'It's still like being in prison,' Delacor said irritably. 'But at least in there they left us alone, they didn't bother us.'

'No,' Lausard mused. 'They wouldn't have bothered you until the morning they came to take you to the guillotine.'

'I'd have escaped.'

'So escape from here,' Lausard challenged. 'You hate it so much. Get out. Or are you afraid of what they'll do when they catch you?'

'I'm not afraid of anyone,' Delacor snarled, pushing closer to Lausard. 'What makes you so happy here anyway?'

'I'd rather die like a soldier than a rat in a cage.

Deschamps was right, at least there's some honour in that.'

'To hell with honour,' snapped Delacor. 'And to hell with the army.'

'If you run, they'll catch you,' Sonnier interjected. 'I *know*.'

'You got caught because you're stupid,' Delacor scathingly told him.

'Just shut up,' snapped Carbonne. 'Both of you. Haven't we got enough to concern us without bickering all the time?'

Delacor opened his mouth to say something but Lausard raised a hand to silence him. 'He's right,' he said. 'We have to stick together. We're all in this now, one way or the other. They've given us a way out. We should use it.'

'They've given us a way straight into a coffin,' Roussard offered and smiled thinly.

Lausard held out his metal plate, watching as the cook ladled meat and vegetables into it. The broth was thin and watery, the meat and the other ingredients cooked so long that the colour had been boiled from them. But that wasn't important now. All that mattered to Lausard and to everyone else was to quell the raging hunger gnawing away inside their bellies.

When each of them had received his share, they gathered together in a group. Strangers thrust together, linked only by the fact that they had been criminals and that they were now to be soldiers. Men from different backgrounds, and in some cases, different countries. Rostov wasn't the only foreigner in the unit. He'd heard that there was an Austrian, even an Irishman, somewhere amongst the other men. The others were from every region of France but predominantly from Paris and its outlying regions. Men who had enjoyed completely different upbringings, who had been forced to scratch a living as thieves or forgers or horse thieves. Every kind of criminal, every manner of man was present in the barracks.

'What will they do with us?' Charvet wondered. 'Turn us into infantry, cavalry or artillerymen?'

'This was a cavalry training depot,' said Lausard, munching on bread. 'My guess is they'll use us as horsemen.'

'I can't ride a horse,' Tabor said, looking around him anxiously.

Bonet patted his arm reassuringly.

'That's why we're here, you half-wit,' snapped Delacor. 'So they can teach us.' Then he turned to face Lausard. 'Anyway, what makes you such an expert? How do you know this used to be a cavalry training depot?'

'I spoke to Deschamps back at the prison,' Lausard said, dipping his bread into the thin broth. 'He said that the army was short of cavalry. That's why they need us as horsemen.'

'They'll have trouble finding a horse big enough for you, fat man,' said Giresse, smiling, prodding Joubert in the side.

The big man didn't answer, he just continued eating, a satisfied grin on his face.

'They'll have trouble finding horses for any of us,' Bonet interjected. 'I heard that the cavalry are using animals captured from the Austrians.'

'A horse is a horse, who cares where it comes from?' said Rocheteau.

'That's not strictly true,' Bonet said, dropping bread into his broth. 'German horses are larger than most French mounts. Spanish ponies are smaller and quicker and—'

Rocheteau interrupted, holding up his hand. 'All right, schoolmaster, I get the idea.'

Joubert drained what was left on his metal plate by lifting it to his mouth, then licking it to ensure he didn't waste any of the precious fluid. He looked longingly at Rostov who was still sipping at his broth, but the Russian merely met his gaze and shook his head gently.

'That wasn't enough,' said the fat man. 'How can they expect a man to survive on such meagre rations?'

'We all survived on *less* than this when we lived in Paris,' said Rocheteau, mopping his plate with a piece of bread.

Some of the other men nodded approvingly.

'Do you think those bastards in the Directory ever went hungry?' Carbonne asked.

'That's no way to talk about our government,' Bonet said, smiling.

'What are you going to do?' Carbonne challenged good naturedly. 'Report me?'

'I shall report you to Paul Barras personally,' Bonet replied.

The other men laughed.

'Now there's a man who *should* have sneezed into the basket,' Carbonne said and chuckled. 'I'd have done a good job on him.'

'We'd all have queued up to pull the lever,' Rocheteau added.

'That would have been *my* privilege,' Carbonne reminded him.

'He'll get his come-uppance,' Bonet murmured. 'All of them will.'

'From who?' Giresse asked.

'The army,' Lausard interjected. 'You mark my words. In two years, this army will be the power in France.'

'And we'll be a part of it,' Rocheteau said, a thin smile creeping across his face. 'We soldiers.' He got to his feet and saluted, and the gesture was met by a great cheer.

Other men in the barrack room turned to see what the noise was about, then returned to their food or settled down for the night to try to sleep. The candles which lit the room were burning down and night was throwing a dark blanket across the land.

Lausard looked at his companions in their makeshift uniforms then he gently stroked the sleeve of his own threadbare tunic.

'Soldiers,' he said quietly, then smiled.

CHAPTER 8

The men had been divided into groups of between fifteen and twenty and they now stood beneath the weak sun of a chill morning, each group assigned to a different NCO. The dragoons were dressed in short, green single-breasted jackets with no facing colours and wore breeches reinforced with leather over their boots. Sergeant Legier, who was instructing Lausard's group, wore his forage cap too.

Somewhere behind him, Lausard could hear Delpierre's voice bellowing instructions at his own gathering of men. He had also seen Captain Deschamps strolling unhurriedly across the parade ground, puffing on his pipe, apparently unconcerned at the activity all around him. A small detachment of dragoons in full dress had ridden out of the training depot less than ten minutes earlier but Lausard, like his companions, had no idea where they were going. Fewer still cared.

The young man's thoughts were interrupted by a loud metallic hiss as Legier drew his sabre from its scabbard.

'Take a good look at it, boys,' he said, his voice low.

He turned the three-foot-long blade slowly in his hand, the sun winking off the cutting edge. The polished steel blade curved all the way to a tapered point.

'This will be your friend,' Legier continued, holding the weapon at shoulder height, tilting the point towards Delacor who took an involuntary step backwards. 'You'll learn to use a carbine and pistols too, but the sword is the most important weapon you'll carry. Treat it well, learn how to use it.' He stepped towards Roussard, the blade still levelled.

'Do you want to kill me already, Sergeant?' Roussard said.

Legier managed a slight smile but it vanished like fog in a high wind. He looked at the men as he spoke, twisting the weapon in the air, allowing them to see every angle and edge of the instrument.

'There are two methods of striking an enemy,' Legier began. 'The thrust.' He drove the weapon forward, to within inches of Lausard who never took his eyes off the sergeant. 'And the cut.' He lifted the weapon high and brought it down, the blade slicing the air. 'The sword is always held in the right hand. The cut is made from right to left. The backhand cut from left to right. Everyone has their own opinion about which is the more effective. The thrust allows greater reach and the wounds caused by a thrust are more likely to be mortal. A man can survive slash wounds. Believe me.' He touched the empty hole where his ear used to be. 'It is the *point* that kills,' Legier continued. 'Thrust as often as you can. You will defeat all those you touch.' He took a couple of steps back. 'The thrust is delivered by keeping the thumb against the hilt, facing *down*. When cutting, aim for the neck or shoulder. Most men will duck if they see the blow coming, so a cut to the neck may strike the face. Aim higher and you will miss your enemy completely. Strike downward if you can.' He demonstrated once more. 'The sword will penetrate more deeply.'

The men looked on, mesmerised. Only Lausard watched with something approaching real enthusiasm.

'There are tricks too,' Legier continued. He turned the sword so that he still held the blade at shoulder height but the flat of it was horizontal. 'When thrusting into the ribs, hold the sword like this. The blade will enter cleanly *between* the ribs. Its entry will be clean and it can be withdrawn more quickly so that another blow can be struck. I've seen men break their wrists accidentally striking bone. Keep the blade flat. Don't twist it or it'll stick inside your opponent. If he falls from his horse he may even take your weapon with him. Strike quickly and pull free quickly, you will create a sawing effect. If you *do* strike bone, the steel will break it.' He patted the side of the weapon. 'As long as it is held like this.'

Roussard swallowed hard.

'What about infantry?' Tabor asked. 'How do we fight them?'

Legier took a step forward, pressing the point of the sword against the big man's chest.

'Don't speak,' the sergeant said quietly. 'Your job is to listen, *not* ask questions. Do you understand?'

Tabor nodded, glancing down at the sword tip. It didn't seem to bother him. In fact, as Lausard watched, the big man reached out and gently touched the tip.

'It's sharp,' he said, smiling at Legier then at the other men.

Bonet shot out a hand and pulled him back.

'Half-wit,' Delacor murmured under his breath.

'You fight infantry with care,' Legier said, a slight grin hovering momentarily on his lips. 'If attacked by cavalry they will form squares. The trick is to catch them in open order, preferably on open ground where they can't use cover. If you do catch them that way then ride them down. Your horses will try to avoid stepping on men if they can. The Russians, in particular, know this and use it. If their infantry cannot form squares in time they will allow you to ride over them. It is their only protection. Otherwise, strike down at them using the slash I spoke of earlier. Backhand is more effective.' He twisted the sword in his grip. 'You may come up against armoured cavalry too. The Austrian cuirassiers wear a breastplate which deflects most sword swings. Ride past them and strike at their backs. They have no back plate, no protection.'

'What is your group like, Sergeant?'

The men turned as they heard a new voice.

Lausard saw Delpierre striding towards them.

'They will learn,' Legier told him. 'And yours?'

'Cannon fodder,' he said and smirked, picking at one of the scabs on his chin.

He stood next to Legier, his eyes scanning the watching men. 'You have no cavalry uniforms because you do not deserve them yet,' he said. 'Nor do you have any horses. Or weapons.'

'How do you expect us to fight then?' Sonnier asked defiantly.

'The coward has a question,' Delpierre said and chuckled. 'Why do *you* want to know about fighting? You tried to run away.' He took a step towards Sonnier.

'If you want to fight, then fight me. Now.' He drew his sword and hurled it towards Sonnier who took a step back, looking at the blade as it struck the ground at his feet. 'Pick it up,' Delpierre told him.

Sonnier looked at the sword then at the sergeant.

'Pick it up,' Delpierre roared. 'Come on, what are you waiting for? Come on, coward. Pick it up, you spineless, snivelling scum.'

'Pick it up,' hissed Delacor.

'Go on,' Rocheteau urged under his breath. 'Run him through.'

'Cut the bastard,' Carbonne added.

Still Sonnier stood motionless, his gaze flicking back and forth from Delpierre to the sword which lay at his feet.

'Pick it up,' the sergeant shouted again. 'You gutless bastard.'

Lausard stepped in front of Sonnier, lifted the sword by its hilt then turned it in his hand and offered it to Delpierre.

'So, *you* want to fight, do you? You want to protect that coward.'

'I am returning your sword, Sergeant,' Lausard said evenly, his gaze never faltering.

'*You* fight me,' Delpierre hissed. 'Show me what you've learned.'

Delpierre suddenly grabbed the sword by its hilt, pulling it from Lausard's grip, slicing the cutting edge across the palm of his hand. The sharpened metal laid the flesh open and Lausard gasped in pain and anger as he saw blood spurt from the cut.

'Come on,' Delpierre said, grinning. 'I've spilled *your* blood. Now spill mine.'

The knot of muscles at the side of Lausard's jaw pulsed angrily, his steely gaze locked on Delpierre as if magnetised. He could feel his left hand burning and there was blood dripping from the cut.

'I promise not to hurt you,' Delpierre said mockingly.

Lausard heard the hiss as another sabre was drawn and he looked up to see Legier pulling his own blade free of the scabbard. He tossed it towards Lausard who caught it with his right hand.

Legier nodded slowly.

'A contest perhaps?' mocked Delpierre, taking a step towards Lausard who stood his ground, swaying slightly back and forth, his eyes never leaving his foe.

Delpierre swung his sword in a downward arc, the blade slicing air as it sped towards Lausard's left shoulder.

Nimbly Lausard ducked the stroke and thrust forward with his own sword, the point aimed at Delpierre's chest.

Delpierre recovered and knocked the blade away with a backhand stroke. The sound of metal on metal rang around the training ground.

Legier walked slowly around the two men, pushing the others back a few paces, watching as Lausard parried one of Delpierre's thrusts.

'Give them room,' Legier said, as fascinated by the contest as the other watchers.

Delpierre struck again, aiming for Lausard's head.

Lausard jerked back then jabbed his sword forward, catching Delpierre in the upper left shoulder. Not hard enough to puncture flesh but strongly enough to rip the material of his jacket.

Delpierre glared at him and swung his sword with even greater ferocity.

Lausard blocked the slash, ducked and drove a fist into Delpierre's stomach, then he jumped to one side and, with the point of the sword, slit open the lobe of the sergeant's right ear.

Delpierre roared in pain and rage and began hacking frenziedly at his opponent.

Lausard parried or dodged each murderous swipe of the sword, the clash of steel now filling the air.

Delpierre struck at Lausard's head, both hands gripping the sword.

Lausard felt the blade part air inches from his cheek but he edged sideways and struck Delpierre across the side with the sharpened edge of the sword, tearing his jacket again. Then he struck for the left shoulder, feinted to the right then carved a button from Delpierre's tunic.

The sergeant was raging now, hurling himself at Lausard, swinging his sword with the ferocity of a man possessed.

Lausard blocked the savage lunge and swung his foot across in front of his attacker.

Delpierre went sprawling, landing heavily on the ground and, as he rolled over, Lausard advanced towards him and thrust the point of the blade to within an inch of his throat.

Lausard was breathing heavily, perspiration running from his forehead, trickling down his cheek.

Delpierre tried to sit up but the point of the blade prevented him from raising his head more than an inch. 'I'll kill you,' he hissed, his eyes bulging madly.

'You just tried,' Lausard said quietly. '*Sergeant.*'

He increased the pressure on the sword, the tip breaking the skin, opening a tiny cut beneath Delpierre's chin. Stepping back, he glanced across at Legier then threw the sword, hilt first, back at him. The sergeant caught it, watching as Lausard turned his back on his defeated opponent.

Delpierre suddenly leaped to his feet, snatched up his sword and aimed for Lausard's unprotected back.

All Lausard heard was the arc of the steel as it moved in the air with incredible power towards him. He never had a chance to move.

There was a loud clang of steel on steel and he spun round to see that Legier had blocked the murderous downward cut.

'It's over,' Legier said to his companion.

Lausard looked at the two NCOs, watching as Delpierre sheathed his sword.

'This isn't over,' Delpierre snarled, pointing at Lausard. 'This is the beginning.'

'You should have killed him,' Rocheteau said, watching as Delpierre stalked away towards another group of men.

Lausard and Legier looked at each other for a moment but no flicker of emotion passed between them. Then Lausard nodded almost imperceptibly.

'Get back in line,' Legier ordered.

From the other side of the training ground, puffing contentedly on his pipe, Captain Deschamps watched.

CHAPTER 9

As the days stretched one into another, each becoming indistinguishable from the next, Lausard became aware that his life was beginning to take on something approaching order. There was a monotonous regularity to his existence in the army but it was preferable to the crushing feeling of worthlessness he'd been so accustomed to during his years in Paris. The nightmares still came, perhaps with slightly less regularity, but the pain was still there. Only now its severity was lessened somewhat as he channelled his feelings of uselessness into his training, concentrating every fibre on the task at hand. Only in the stillness of the night, when sleep still eluded him, did he find all the old familiar pain returning. In the darkness, alone in the barracks, his mind flooded with images of the slaughter of his family and, try as he might, he couldn't shake their possession of his waking thoughts.

No one mentioned the fight with Delpierre. No one asked him how he had learned to handle a sword so adeptly. No one seemed puzzled by his proficiency with the weapon and yet his comrades knew that to fight the way he had would have required training of the highest order. Instead they contented themselves with knowing that, among them, was a man they could trust and admire; a man who seemed as skilled as those who taught them. But Lausard wondered what their reactions would be if they knew he had learned his skills at a place many of them would see as a bastion of the class they had despised and helped to destroy. Only those with money, or their families at least, had been able to attend the Carabinier School at Chinon as he had. If his companions knew, would their admiration and respect turn to mistrust and hatred? Would they call for *his* head as they had called for the heads of so many like him?

As he stood on the parade ground glancing at his comrades, it didn't seem to matter either to him or to them. In their ignorance was his safety.

Most had adapted well to their present surroundings and to the new demands being made on them daily. They had been given wooden swords with which to practise the moves taught to them by Legier and the other NCOs. These they carried sloped, over their shoulders as they drilled, learning to march. As dragoons they would be expected to fight both on foot and on horseback.

Lausard found the entire concept a little absurd as, so far, none of them had seen so much as a musket ball, let alone the pistols, carbines and sabres they must learn to fight with. Every day they were told that the weapons would be arriving soon but from where no one seemed quite sure. It was getting to the stage where Lausard was beginning to think that he and his comrades would walk into their first battle wielding wooden swords and carbines, forced to stroll across the killing fields because they also had no horses.

Every piece of equipment, every mount, every uniform seemed to be second-hand and the greater proportion had been acquired from enemy forces currently engaged in Italy, Belgium and Prussia. Lausard could only guess at the state of the French forces fighting those enemies, but if they were suffering shortages as acutely as he and his companions then it seemed only a matter of time before the army and then the whole of revolutionary France collapsed.

Food was another commodity in short supply. Even the regular troops at the training depot sent out foragers on a daily basis to scour the land for provisions. Lausard and his men had been reduced to a diet consisting of biscuits and potatoes, the latter boiled in huge vats until they dissolved into a thick soup which the men were often forced to eat cold the following day. Drinking water too was at a premium and Lausard couldn't remember the last time he had bathed. The parade ground was full of reeking, hungry men all arranged in lines straighter than any sergeant had a right to expect. The smell of unwashed bodies was strong in the air.

Lausard could feel a flea crawling across his neck but he resisted the temptation to squash it. His eyes were fixed ahead of him, towards two dozen or more wooden objects which resembled barrels but were smoother, longer and narrower.

'These are your horses,' Sergeant Legier called, chuckling, gesturing towards the wooden objects. 'You will learn to mount and dismount on these.'

'Wooden swords, wooden guns, wooden horses,'

muttered Rocheteau. 'Our enemies will only need tinder boxes to defeat us.'

'We should be carpenters,' Giresse added. 'Not soldiers. I was a horse thief but I never stole anything like *that*.' He nodded towards the fake mounts.

'I hear the government pays four hundred francs for every horse captured,' Rocheteau whispered. 'Perhaps we should all become horse thieves. We'd be rich men.'

'You will all take your turns here,' shouted Legier, pointing at the wooden objects.

The unit was broken up into smaller groups, most of them taken away by other NCOs to drill while they awaited their turn at the wooden horses. Lausard could hear orders being shouted from all over the parade ground. He and Rocheteau were among the first called forward to the fake mounts.

'Stand beside the horse,' said Legier. 'Grip his bridle with your right hand, place your right foot in the stirrup and swing your left leg over the saddle.'

'There is no saddle, Sergeant,' Tabor said.

'There's no horse either, is there, boy?' snapped the sergeant. 'Use your imagination.'

'Just like climbing on top of a woman,' Delacor mused.

'You don't *climb* on women, you animal,' Giresse said reproachfully. 'You *ease* yourself on to them.'

'Mount up,' roared Legier, stepping back to watch his wards as they struggled to throw themselves on the wooden horses.

Lausard managed it effortlessly.

Bonet, too, accomplished the task with relative ease. As did Roussard, Carbonne and Rostov.

Joubert hoisted himself up, toppled over and

promptly fell to the ground on the other side of the object.

Charvet tried to grip the fake mount but could find no hand-hold and began swaying uncertainly.

'Use your knees,' Legier roared.

Charvet tried but failed. He fell forward.

Rocheteau swung his leg over but couldn't straighten up. With a grunt he finally fell to the ground.

'Grip with your knees,' shouted Legier again. 'Grip tightly.'

He watched those who had failed to mount struggling then shouted at those already sitting upright to dismount.

They did so with relative ease.

'Mount,' he shouted.

Again they tried. More succeeding this time.

'Dismount.'

The manoeuvre was repeated.

'Mount.'

Joubert hauled his mountainous frame upright for all of two seconds this time.

'Dismount.'

The order was becoming a litany.

Nearly every man was in position after fifteen minutes. After thirty, the orders were still being shouted with monotonous regularity.

Sonnier felt pain around his groin, his buttocks and the insides of his thighs. Some of the other men were also feeling the strain of constant friction against their inner thighs and knees.

The orders continued.

They clambered up with more precision but less speed.

Moreau saw blood soaking through his trousers at the knees, the flesh rubbed raw by the wood. Sonnier too was bleeding, crimson fluid trickling down his calves.

'Mount.'

It was all he could do to swing his bloodied leg over the fake mount.

Lausard felt the pain too and saw the flesh had been stripped from his thighs.

'Dismount.'

Rocheteau almost collapsed.

And it continued.

The men were drenched with perspiration, their tunics soaked through, hair matted to their faces. The unbearable friction was now causing intense pain with each movement, and the blood from many of them was now soaking into the wood itself.

Joubert could barely suck in the breath needed for the effort.

'Come on!' roared Legier. 'What will you be like on *real* horses? They kick, they bite, they panic. You must keep a firm grip on them. You must master them, you must pamper them, you must love them. They will carry you through battle. They could save your lives.'

Roussard toppled from the fake mount and hit the ground hard.

'Get up!' bellowed Legier, crossing towards him, glaring down at him.

Roussard struggled to his knees then dropped forward on to all fours, panting like a dog. Finally, with almost superhuman effort, he stood upright.

'Now mount up,' Legier ordered.

Roussard managed it at the second attempt and sat

astride the wooden object, eyes screwed up tight against the pain.

Lausard readjusted his position slightly, wincing at the discomfort, glancing down at the fresh spot of blood now smearing the thin material of his trousers. He wondered how much longer this was going to continue.

Thirty minutes later he was still wondering.

'They're trying to kill us,' groaned Sonnier, looking down at his bloodied legs.

'If any infection sets in you're done for,' Bonet added. 'That lot will turn gangrenous in days.' He nodded towards Sonnier's legs.

'Thanks for the information, schoolmaster,' Rocheteau grumbled, rolling on to his stomach on the straw mattress. 'I really needed to know that.'

'I just want to know what these bastards are playing at,' Delacor said. 'They want us for their army and yet, like Sonnier says, it's like they're trying to kill us before we even reach a battlefield.'

'If they didn't train us we'd be dead within seconds of reaching that battlefield,' Lausard told him.

'You call this training? This isn't training, this is torture.'

'It'll get better,' Lausard said, pulling free a piece of material that was stuck to some dried blood on his knee. He winced, noticing that the abrasions were still weeping.

'How can you be so sure?' Delacor demanded.

'Because it can't get any worse,' Lausard said flatly. 'They want us to get to the stage where we *want* to fight. Where being under fire is *better* than drilling and marching and climbing wooden horses. That's how this army works.'

'You seemed pretty sure of yourself today, school-master,' said Charvet. 'Where did you learn to ride?'

'My father had a farm. I grew up with horses.'

'What happened to your family?'

'Both my parents died of smallpox. I haven't seen my brother since 'eighty-six. He's probably dead too for all I know.' Bonet spoke quietly.

'He might be in the army like you,' Rocheteau chuckled.

Some of the other men laughed too.

'My brother joined the army,' Tabor said, inspecting his bloodied legs.

'You mean there's another one like you?' Delacor said disdainfully. 'A whole family of half-wits.'

'He was killed at Fleurus,' Tabor said. 'My mother told me. They sent his shoes back to her. Why would they do that?'

'So she could remember him,' Bonet said softly, tapping the big man on the shoulder.

'What about your parents, Alain?' Rocheteau said, looking at Lausard. 'Are they still alive?'

Lausard shook his head. He had no lie ready. He didn't speak. He didn't tell the truth. That his father had been a wealthy man branded as an enemy of the State by Robespierre and his bloodthirsty allies. He didn't speak of the executions. Of the murder of his family by men like those who now regarded him as a comrade. It was simpler to remain silent.

The candles in the barrack room were burning low and, outside, night was tightening its grip. Lausard knew that with the blackness would come the dreams.

The same dream he knew so well. And dreaded.

The conversation inside the barrack room gradually dwindled to a few whispers. Moreau said a prayer before lying down on his filthy mattress. Very soon the first snores began to fill the room. Those who could sleep through the pain and discomfort did so. Others, like Lausard, lay awake in the blackness, some craving sleep, others denied it by pain. Lausard fought it until, finally, he succumbed.

CHAPTER 10

Napoleon Bonaparte ran a hand through his hair and eyed the men who sat opposite him, aware of their appraising glances. He knew one or two of them well, Paul Barras in particular, but he felt neither confidence nor trust in these men. They were not soldiers, and Bonaparte found it hard to trust those who had not worn the uniform of his country.

'I thought you would have been more impressed with your appointment, *General* Bonaparte,' said Barras, smiling. 'For a man of your age, it is a huge responsibility. I do not know any other twenty-six-year-old General of Brigade.'

'You hide your gratitude very well,' Tallien echoed.

Bonaparte shifted in his seat and gazed at each man in turn. 'Is gratitude what you expected from me?' he asked. 'I was doing my job as a soldier, nothing more. A job, gentlemen, I might add, that ensures *you* sit where you sit now.' He took a sip of his wine.

'We appreciate that,' Barras said.

'Then perhaps it is you who should be grateful,' Bonaparte said. 'Not I.'

'Are you not happy with your position then?' Gohier asked.

'Of course,' the Corsican replied. 'I seek advancement just as any soldier should, just as any *man* should. A man should never be satisfied with his lot in life. There should always be more goals to strive for.'

'And what do you imply *we* should strive for?' It was Gohier who had spoken.

'I imply nothing,' Bonaparte said flatly.

'The Paris mob is defeated,' Barras said. 'You saw to that. They are no longer the force they were. Every citizen has been ordered to surrender his weapons to the government, to us. The city is in our power once more, as is the rest of the country.'

'Then it is time you looked beyond France,' Bonaparte told them.

'And where did you have in mind?' Tallien enquired.

'Italy. The Italian campaign is faltering. The army of Italy is a shambles. Every day the Austrians and Piedmontese take advantage of our position there. We will soon be driven out completely.'

'The men in command of the armies there are very able men,' Gohier protested.

'They are too old, too slow in their thinking,' Bonaparte countered. 'Massena is a good general. He won at Loano but the victory was not followed up. Schérer did not exploit it.'

'It is easy to conduct a war from the safety of the War Office, General Bonaparte,' Tallien said. 'We appointed men we felt were equal to the task.'

'Then why has there been no progress in Italy?' the Corsican demanded. 'The campaign being fought is one of defence, not attack. No war was ever won by defending. Battles are won by attacking, campaigns are fought on the offensive. Your men in Italy don't seem to realise this.'

'We are under-strength,' Gohier protested. 'The army is without food, clothes, weapons. We force our men to ravage the land because we cannot provide them with adequate supplies. The army in Italy is an army of scarecrows, General Bonaparte.'

'Commanded by farmers,' grunted the younger man with scorn.

'Your ignorance is matched by your arrogance,' snapped Tallien.

'It is neither,' Bonaparte said challengingly.

'You show no respect for your elders,' Tallien said. 'For officers who were in uniform while you were at your mother's breast. Some of these men have been in the service of France for over thirty years.'

'It shows,' snapped Bonaparte. 'They're still using methods from thirty years ago. They belong to a different time. There is a place for them, but not at the head of an army.'

'And where would you have them placed, *General* Bonaparte?' Gohier said irritably.

'As you say, they are able soldiers,' Bonaparte offered. 'What they need is an able leader. Someone who is not afraid to take risks. The men who command the army in Italy are too cautious.'

'They don't have the luxury of recklessness,' Tallien snapped. 'We cannot afford to lose men in wild undertakings. The army doesn't have the men to lose.'

'I said nothing of recklessness. There is a difference between boldness and stupidity. I don't ask for recklessness. I don't want stupidity. I want what you all want, what the entire country wants. I want victory for France.'

'Surely we would all agree with General Bonaparte on that,' Barras interjected.

'So you prescribe the same cures as he does?' snapped Letourneur.

'I agree with him that a certain boldness is called for,' Barras countered. 'Perhaps a boldness which comes with youth.'

There was a momentary silence in the room broken by Tallien. 'So, how do you see the situation, General?'

'We have thirty-eight thousand men hemmed in along the Ligurian plain. Held there by the Austrians and the Piedmontese. The Bay of Genoa is controlled by the British Navy. Our men need to break out. Turn defence into attack, push the Austrians back. If the army is forced to remain where it is for many more months it will starve to death. Hunger will do the Austrians' job for them.'

'Still easy to say sitting here,' Tallien said.

'Easy because it is true. If the men commanding the army of Italy do not act soon then everything will be lost and, if the Austrians defeat us, who is to stop them invading France itself? Remove the men who command. You need a new sword.' Bonaparte's eyes were blazing.

Again silence descended, this time broken by Barras. 'Would you be that sword?'

'The troops need someone they can believe in.'

'And you know of such a man?' Tallien said slowly, the words emerging more as a statement than a question.

Bonaparte nodded.

CHAPTER 11

'Horses,' murmured Tabor, almost mesmerised by the sight before him.

'Well spotted,' Delacor added, his eyes narrowing as he allowed his gaze to drift along the lines of mounts facing him and his companions on the parade ground.

Lausard too watched as more than one hundred horses were driven into untidy lines by more than a dozen dragoons, some wearing stable dress, the others resplendent in their full dress uniforms. Major Deschamps rode back and forth across the parade ground, his own bay neighing excitedly, its head tossing up and down.

There were animals of every size and colour. Small ponies, larger horses, even what looked like farm horses. Bays, piebalds, blacks, greys. Lausard even spotted a white animal among them. All were unsaddled but each one had been fitted with a bridle and reins. He saw a number rear up in confusion and hoped that he didn't get one of the friskier animals for his own mount. Not all of them were shod and a number were from the Camargue – fast, compact ponies shod only on the front hooves. The air was filled with the smell of horses and droppings.

Green saddle blankets had been set up in lines and each man was directed to take up position behind one. On top of each one was a saddle, some worn, some holed. There were stirrups missing from some, the irons bent and twisted in places.

'I wonder which enemy these came from,' said Bonet, inspecting his saddle. There was a dark stain just below the pommel which he was sure was blood. He shuddered involuntarily.

'Listen to me!' a familiar voice bellowed across the training ground and Lausard looked up to see Delpierre trotting back and forth on his horse. 'Today you become cavalry. You learn how to saddle horses, how to ride horses, how to manoeuvre horses. You obey orders, you make your horse obey *you*.'

Rocheteau glanced at Lausard but said nothing. His expression spoke volumes. Lausard managed to suppress a grin.

'Your training is nearly over,' Delpierre continued. 'You came here worthless, you will leave as soldiers, but you will only leave if you learn. In three days you must be able to fight on horseback, fight the way you've been taught. You will be given weapons, uniforms, but not until *we* think you are ready and you must be ready in three days.'

He wheeled his horse and rode back down the line of waiting men, past the horses that looked as nervous as their would-be riders. Delpierre slowed down as he reached Lausard, peering at the younger man from under his brass helmet.

'You will all be given help,' he said. 'But you are

responsible for your horse, for yourselves. I will be watching for any mistakes and I will punish them.' He glared at Lausard. 'It is also your duty to take care of your kit. Each man must carry with him one pair of trousers, two shirts, gaiters, stockings, boot cuffs, forage cap, stable jacket, needles, thread, scissors, awl, brush, wax, blanco, shoe buckles, curry-comb, powder bag, sponge, razor, two handkerchiefs and a nightcap.'

'Where the hell are we supposed to put all those?' Rocheteau murmured.

'It took them over a week to find us horses,' Lausard whispered, 'I doubt if they'll find us that lot too. I'm surprised they've even got weapons for us.'

'I won't believe it until I see it,' Rocheteau replied, nudging his saddle with the toe of his shoe.

'You'll never find a horse big enough to carry you, fat man,' Delacor said, elbowing Joubert.

'There's some good animals there,' Giresse said, running his gaze over the horses.

'How do *you* know?' Roussard said.

'I did used to steal them,' Giresse reminded him.

'What if I fall off?' Tabor murmured.

'You'll be fine,' Bonet reassured him.

'Pick up your saddles!' roared Delpierre.

The men on the parade ground did so with varying degrees of enthusiasm.

'Christ,' grunted Charvet. 'That's heavy.' He almost stumbled as he struggled to lift the saddle, cloth and portmanteau.

'Don't take the Lord's name in vain,' Moreau said reproachfully.

'I wish the Lord would give me a hand with this blasted saddle,' Charvet continued.

The men stood waiting, saddles held firmly.

'Select a mount and saddle up,' Delpierre shouted.

Most of the dragoons had formed a line close to the horses and were watching with amusement as the men struggled forward clutching their saddles. They pointed at those men who seemed to be having the most difficulty.

Delpierre walked his horse back and forth, eyeing the strugglers with something less than understanding.

One man threw his saddle on to the back of a grey horse which promptly reared up, threw the saddle clear and bolted.

The man grabbed for the bridle, missed and crashed to the ground.

Sonnier lifted the saddle carefully and slid it on to his animal's back, patting the hindquarters as he did so. Then without thinking, in his haste to mount, he placed one foot in the stirrup and prepared to swing himself over. Without the girth strap being fastened, the saddle, and Sonnier with it, crashed to the ground. His horse tossed its head, as if it too was mocking him.

Lausard fastened the necessary buckles on the saddle straps and tugged at the saddle to ensure it was secure, then he placed his left foot in the stirrup and lifted himself into the saddle. The horse bucked but he tugged hard on the reins, bringing the great black animal under control immediately, using one hand to pat its neck.

Giresse was also safely mounted, as were Bonet and several of the others. All across the parade ground men were beginning to haul themselves into their saddles. A number were still struggling, half-a-dozen were scurrying around trying to catch their mounts while NCOs bellowed at them.

Lausard sat straight in the saddle, his gaze meeting Delpierre's. The sergeant rode past him then turned his horse and headed back towards Lausard. He was less than ten yards away when a horse nearby suddenly reared up on its hind legs, hurling its rider to the ground. The man landed with a sickening thud, looking up in horror as the horse lost its footing and fell on top of him. The sound of breaking bone was audible even above the combined noise of neighing animals and yelling NCOs. The horse scrambled to its feet leaving the man clutching at one leg and shouting in pain.

Two dragoons dragged him away, one of them catching the bridle of the horse as it attempted to bolt.

Moreau felt his own mount bucking under him and he gripped the reins tightly and pressed his knees into the creature, feeling the power beneath him. But the animal would not be calmed and grew more agitated.

Lausard saw that the horse was about to unseat its rider and urged his own mount across. He grabbed at the muzzle of Moreau's horse but the grey snapped at him with yellowed teeth. Lausard took the bit and pulled hard, relieved to see the horse was steadying.

Moreau loosened his grip on the reins and the animal began to calm down. It kicked out with one hind leg then stood still. Moreau looked at Lausard and nodded almost imperceptibly.

'Quite the expert, aren't you?'

Lausard turned in the saddle as he heard the voice of Delpierre behind him.

'You can use a sword, you know how to ride . . . I wonder if you can shoot a carbine from the saddle too? I bet you can.' His smile was crooked. 'You will be a useful member of this regiment, if you live. A man like you should take his place in the front line for any battle. I will see that you do.' The two men locked stares for a moment then Delpierre rode off to shout instructions at two men who had managed to fasten their saddles on but could not manage to mount.

Rocheteau flicked his reins and was almost surprised when his mount walked slowly across to Lausard. He patted the chestnut thankfully.

'What was that bastard on about?' he asked.

'Nothing important.'

'He's a dangerous man, Alain. The sooner I kill him the better.'

'Once we get into battle the Austrians will do it for you.'

'I want to do it.'

Lausard smiled. 'You and most of the regiment.'

Joubert rode up to join them, his horse already lathered. The big man himself was sweating profusely, gripping the reins so tightly that his knuckles were white.

'I don't know who's more worried,' Lausard said, grinning. 'You or the horse.'

'It's taking the weight well,' Rocheteau added, nodding towards the huge black mare which Joubert was seated on.

'This isn't natural,' Joubert protested, grunting as the horse reared slightly beneath him. 'I should have joined the infantry.' Again it seemed as if the horse would throw him but his sheer bulk appeared to keep him there.

Rocheteau's horse also bucked and he was forced to dig in his knees to prevent himself falling.

'I think I know what you mean, fat man,' he said, clinging on.

Lausard saw that nearly all of the men were mounted now, some assuredly, others decidedly not. There were one or two stray horses galloping around the parade ground; a dragoon sped after one, clutching at the bridle to slow down the frightened animal.

Deschamps and two other officers had ridden on to the parade ground, the captain still puffing at his pipe. He looked over the ragged array of men and shook his head, more in amusement than disdain, and rode towards the gates of the compound with his adjutants in close attendance. Lausard watched him go.

'Wheel, right,' roared Sergeant Legier to the struggling horsemen and as many as possible tried to complete the manoeuvre. It met with mixed success. A number of men fell from their horses, several were thrown. Lausard saw one man trying to avoid the thrashing hooves of his mount, his scream echoing through the morning air when the horse stepped on his left hand, shattering it.

Delacor felt himself slipping to one side and gripped his horse's mane to prevent himself falling, but the pain this caused the animal made it buck more wildly. Delacor's right foot came clear of the stirrup and he was sent hurtling from the saddle. He landed with a thump, rolling over, trying to suck in air, clutching at his side in pain.

He struggled to his feet, grabbed his bridle and remounted, slapping the horse hard across the neck. It promptly threw him again.

'They respond better to kindness,' Lausard advised, watching as Delacor struggled painfully to his feet.

'I don't need your advice,' he grunted, snatching at the reins once more.

The horse reared up and he toppled backwards to avoid its flashing hooves.

'Sure?' Lausard sneered and turned his horse.

'Leave him,' said Rostov, joining Lausard. 'He'll learn.'

'He'll have to,' Lausard added.

The entire untidy column was moving away from the parade ground, stragglers bringing up the rear, men cursing their horses, their saddles, their NCOs and anything else that came to mind. As the pace of the unit picked up from a walk to a trot Lausard couldn't suppress a smile. It felt good to be riding again. He felt strong and in control, almost at one with his horse, and the great black beast cavorted beneath him as if it too felt the rider's elation. He could smell the animal's sweat and his own too as he urged it on to a canter, his companions forced to do likewise. The column picked up speed.

Some more men toppled from their saddles and landed heavily on the ground as Legier and Delpierre took the column on a circuit of the parade ground, looking behind them to see the progress of their wards. Some of the dragoons joined in on either side of the column, offering either encouragement or sarcasm depending on their mood.

Lausard saw that Rocheteau had settled more comfortably into the saddle. Bonet was also moving effortlessly with his horse, and Rostov too. Even Joubert was managing to keep up although the effort seemed to be wringing yet more perspiration from his huge body.

Giresse brought his horse up alongside Lausard, smiling broadly as he rode.

'Four hundred francs for each of these mounts,' he said. 'I could retire on what's on this parade ground.'

'Remember, you control the horse, he doesn't control *you*!' Delpierre's voice boomed out over the parade ground, audible even above the sound of so many hooves and the endless chorus of shouts, grunts and curses.

'All changes of movement and formation are carried out at the trot or the gallop,' Delpierre continued, riding around as if oblivious to whatever mishaps may be befalling the men following him. 'The walk is one hundred and twenty paces a minute. The trot is two hundred and forty paces a minute. The gallop is four hundred and eighty and the charge is six hundred. Remember that and when the orders are given, obey and make your horse obey.'

'What the hell does he think we're trying to do?' said Rocheteau, gripping his reins tightly.

The ragged column continued to move falteringly around the parade ground.

CHAPTER 12

The candle was burning low, casting long shadows over the desk. Bonaparte looked up briefly and gazed around the darkened room, peering into the blackness as if seeking something, or somewhere, beyond that gloom. Perhaps Italy? He smiled, amused at his own ponderings, then he dipped the quill back into the pot of ink and continued writing.

He'd been working for more than four hours now, stopping only for some wine and cold chicken and most of that still lay untouched on one corner of the desk. He looked up again, watching the flickering yellow flame as it danced in the breeze, smoke drifting from its tip. The desk was strewn with papers and maps, an organised chaos which he knew no one but he would be able to decipher. Every letter, map and piece of paper was clear to him. He began writing again, the scratching of quill on paper the only sound in the stillness.

His new position had brought not just advancement, an increase in pay, power and responsibility; it had also brought with it a plethora of administrative work.

Something Bonaparte had mixed feelings about. He was, after all, a soldier and a soldier's place was in the field, not in an office. He was a general now and his place was to lead men. To command men. To plan and scheme and use the army in a more constructive way than it had been used so far. He sat back in his chair and exhaled wearily. The men in command didn't have his ideas, his daring or his youth. The army needed that. France needed that, but he found himself in an office still distant from the theatres of war he longed to be a part of. He rolled the quill gently between his thumb and forefinger and continued to gaze into the thick shadows.

A knock on the door startled him from his musings.

'Come in,' he called, the quill still poised between his fingers.

The soldier who stepped inside the room saluted smartly and stood to attention.

'What is it, Sergeant?'

'There is someone to see you, sir,' the sergeant informed him.

'Is it important?'

The sergeant looked bemused for a second.

'Bring them in,' Bonaparte ordered and glanced down at the piece of paper before him, waiting as he heard the sound of hushed voices and footsteps in the corridor outside. Only when he heard the sergeant's voice again did he look up.

'Your visitor, sir.'

Bonaparte looked at the newcomer, a flicker of surprise crossing his face.

The boy facing him was in his early teens. A tall youth dressed in a dark blue jacket and white breeches.

He removed the bicorn hat he'd been wearing as Bonaparte ran appraising eyes over him. Then, as Bonaparte watched, the boy saluted. Sharply, smartly and correctly.

Bonaparte nodded towards the sergeant who took a step back, closed the door and left the boy alone with the general.

'I'm sorry to disturb you, General Bonaparte.'

'You know me?'

'All of Paris knows you, sir,' the boy said.

'But I do not know *you*.'

'My name is Eugène de Beauharnais, sir. You knew my father.'

Bonaparte nodded slowly. 'I knew *of* him,' he said. 'He was President of the Constituent Assembly at one time, wasn't he?'

'And Commander of the Army of the Rhine, sir. His name was—'

'Alexandre de Beauharnais. He was executed last year.'

'He was murdered by Robespierre, sir,' the boy announced defiantly.

'Executed by the State.'

'We quibble over terms, sir. It was political murder.'

'There have been lots of deaths in France in the last few years, whether they were murders or executions depends upon your political viewpoint.'

'Robespierre ordered the execution of my father, supposedly because of his military failings. He ordered my mother imprisoned too. She would have been executed if Robespierre hadn't been overthrown.'

'What happened to her dossier? All political prisoners have dossiers on them drawn up.'

'It was stolen, sir. Stolen and disposed of.'

'By whom?'

'I don't know who stole it but it was disposed of by Delperch de la Bussière, the actor. He ate it.'

'Ate it?' Bonaparte said incredulously, a slight grin flickering on his lips.

'He performed the feat for many people, he saved many lives that way,' Eugène continued. 'It was the only way to save my mother, sir.'

Bonaparte put down the quill, reached for his wine glass and sipped at the claret.

'So what has the death of your father to do with me?' he asked. 'I had no part in it.'

'I know that, sir, I didn't mean to imply that you did, but you have my father's sword.'

'*I* have his sword?' Bonaparte said in bewilderment.

'The Directory decreed that the citizens of Paris were to give up all weapons. My father's sword was taken. I'm sure you'll agree, sir, that a sword is no use to a dead man.'

'Quite so. How may I help you?'

'I wish my father's sword returned, sir. For myself and for my mother. We wish to honour his memory.'

'An admirable sentiment. Was it your mother who sent you here to beg for your father's sword?'

'I haven't come to beg, sir,' Eugène said defiantly. 'I came to *ask you* as a soldier. I thought you would understand, a general faced by the *son* of a general. I realise that you know the meaning of honour. My father too was an honourable man. Neither I nor my mother wants his memory trodden into the dirt, even if some do.'

'And what is your mother's name?'

'Joséphine de Beauharnais.'

'How old are you, boy?'

'Fourteen, sir. I hope you will forgive the intrusion of a child.'

Bonaparte got to his feet, walked around the desk and stood close to the boy. He extended one hand and placed it on the boy's shoulder.

'Your father was a soldier and, very obviously, his blood runs through your veins,' he said. 'You will have his sword.'

The boy dropped to one knee, took Bonaparte's hand and kissed it. The general felt tears against his flesh and heard the boy's muted whimperings.

'Stand up,' he said softly, helping the boy to his feet.

He tilted the boy's chin upward and wiped the tears away with his fingers. 'Your mother should be proud of you,' he said, smiling.

'Thank you, sir.' Eugène drew himself up to attention again.

'Have you other family?'

'A sister, Hortense.'

Bonaparte nodded. 'Go back to your family now,' he said. 'Come to me again and I will present you with your father's sword.'

Eugène saluted then bowed before leaving, closing the door quietly behind him. As Bonaparte sat back down behind his desk he heard the boy's footsteps echoing away down the corridor.

The candle had all but burned out. Bonaparte picked up the quill and again turned it slowly between thumb and forefinger. The word was that Joséphine de Beauharnais was the mistress of Paul Barras. Supposedly she had been the mistress of at least two other members of the Directory. What charms this woman must have.

He smiled and consulted his pocket watch, then dipped the quill in the ink and resumed writing.

CHAPTER 13

Lausard awoke with a start when he felt the hand on his shoulder. He sat up, blinking myopically in the gloom of the barrack room. He saw Rocheteau crouching beside him and realised that his had been the hand that had disturbed him.

Alongside the thief was Giresse. As far as Lausard could see, the other men were asleep, a chorus of grunts and snores filling the room.

'What's wrong?' Lausard asked.

'We've had an idea,' Rocheteau told him, hooking a thumb in the direction of Giresse. 'Joubert's right. The food they've been giving us isn't fit for pigs. I say we go and get some that's more suited to our tastes. There's a farm about a mile from here. Where there's a farm there's food.'

Lausard nodded and scrambled nimbly but quietly to his feet.

The three men made their way quickly through the barrack room, passing others who slept as soundly as they could on straw pallets. A huge man with a thick moustache lay nearest the door, his snores rattling throughout the building. As the three men passed him he grunted, rubbed his nose then rolled on to his side. The man beside him also stirred and Lausard paused for a moment, looking down at him, waiting for him to open his eyes. He didn't.

There were no sentries at the doors of the barrack room. Peering out, the three men could see across the parade ground towards the main gates. Either side of the gates two dismounted dragoons stood at attention. Two more walked their horses across the parade ground and disappeared around a corner towards the stables.

'We can get out the back way,' Rocheteau said with assurance and slipped out first.

Thick banks of cloud covered the moon and provided the three men with enough shadows to cover them. They moved swiftly through the gloom, ducking low, running between two barracks towards the rear wall of the compound.

When they reached it, Rocheteau stopped, clasped his fingers together and offered a leg-up to his companions. Lausard accepted the offer first, hauling himself up and on to the top of the wall. He looked out as far as he could into the countryside but saw nothing. There was a dirt track running around the perimeter of the compound and he could smell fresh horse droppings in the air. Dragoons obviously patrolled this outer area too; when they might return the three men could only guess.

'Hurry,' Lausard urged, dropping down on the other side of the wall, watching as his two companions scrambled over after him.

As Rocheteau hit the ground he hissed in pain.

'My ankle,' he grunted, shaking his foot, checking that he'd done no damage. 'I landed heavily.'

'Shut up,' Lausard snapped, holding up a hand for silence.

All three of them heard it in the stillness of the night. The unmistakable jingle of bridles. There were horses close by.

They bolted for a small copse of trees on the other side of the dirt track, ducking down amongst the thick underbrush.

A moment later two dragoons trotted past, the men chatting and laughing.

They disappeared into the night, the sounds of their harnesses dying away.

'All right,' Lausard said, and the three men turned and sprinted away from the compound, only slowing down when they found themselves in even deeper woodland. Satisfied that they were well clear of detection, they slowed down to a walk, Rocheteau sucking in deep breaths and banging his chest.

'I hope you're right about this farm,' Lausard said. 'Don't you think the others might have found it by now? Delpierre's probably had it scraped clean weeks ago.'

'I bet that bastard's not starving like we are,' said Rocheteau, pushing some low branches aside.

'If they catch us,' Giresse offered, 'they'll think we're deserting.'

'Deserting to what?' Lausard grunted, 'a life back on the streets of Paris, thieving for a living, scraping around for scraps that even a dog wouldn't touch.'

'There's nothing wrong with thieving,' Rocheteau said reproachfully.

The other two men laughed.

'Anyway, what's foraging if it's not thieving?' Rocheteau asked. 'Soldiers take from the land and it's called foraging. I take from other people and it's called thieving.'

'How long did it take you to work that one out?' Lausard smiled.

'He's got a point,' added Giresse, chuckling.

'The whole army's full of thieves,' Rocheteau continued. 'And I'm not just talking about stealing food.'

The other two looked puzzled.

'Officers steal,' Rocheteau clarified. 'Have you ever seen a poor one? They steal land, they steal gold.'

'It comes with the position,' Lausard explained. 'They call it the spoils of war.'

'I'm not interested in gold or land,' Giresse said.

'We *know* what *you're* interested in,' Rocheteau said and grinned, gesturing with his hands to illustrate the shape of a woman's body.

All three of them laughed, the sound abruptly shut off as they drew closer to the edge of the wood. The first of the outer buildings of the farm was less than fifty yards away and they could hear movement. Lausard was the first to spot something moving in the gloom and he jabbed a finger in that direction.

'Pigs,' he whispered.

'Pork,' Rocheteau echoed.

They advanced stealthily across the open space between the woods and a low fence which formed the perimeter of the farm. But as they drew nearer several of the pigs began snorting and squealing and, before any of the men could react, they had bolted, scurrying off around a corner.

Lausard led the chase, vaulting the fence and pursuing the fleeing pigs, his companions close behind him. The pigs ran into the yard and Lausard glanced around quickly, seeing a number of other outbuildings and a farmhouse. No lights burned in the windows.

Hearing a squeal behind him he saw that Giresse had caught one of the pigs and was trying to hold it by the head while it attempted to struggle free. Rocheteau ran across to help him, holding a rock the size of his fist. He brought it down with stunning force on the pig's skull and the animal dropped immediately.

Lausard left his companions to their triumph and headed towards the farmhouse, noticing that the windows were open, one hanging uselessly from its hinges. The place looked deserted and gave off an air of neglect. A dead dog lay close to the front door. Several lumps of wood were strewn across the path leading to the front door, obviously cut as fuel days or even weeks earlier. Lausard, suddenly feeling exposed without any weapons, knelt and picked up one of the heavy pieces, hefting it before him like a club. He pushed against the front door and found that it resisted.

'Alain, come on, we've got what we need,' called Rocheteau, holding up the dead pig as if it were some kind of trophy. But Lausard ignored him, pushing harder against the front door which finally swung open. He stepped inside, struck by the smell of damp.

The room was small, devoid of everything except one battered wooden chair. Beyond was what had clearly been the kitchen, pots and pans strewn over the stone floor. A rat scurried across the floor, its claws clicking on the slabs. Lausard watched as it ran over a metal ring in the floor, rusted and neglected like the rest of the house, and Lausard wondered if it might lead down to a cellar. He knelt down to open it.

'What are you doing?'

Lausard didn't turn when he heard Rocheteau's voice, instead he concentrated on pulling at the rusty metal ring.

'I doubt if there's a wine cellar down there,' Giresse said, ambling into the house, peering round to see if there was anything worth taking.

Lausard pulled the cellar hatch open. An overwhelming odour of decay rose up from the hole.

'There's nothing down there you'd want.'

All three men spun round as they heard the voice behind them.

Standing in the doorway was a small figure, no more than five feet tall, holding a gun which was aimed at the men. Lausard could see from the massive, yawning mouth and short barrel that the weapon was a blunderbuss; the figure brandishing it was a boy in his early teens.

'Why can't you leave us alone?' he said.

'Be careful with that, boy,' said Rocheteau, taking a step forward, a finger pointed towards the blunderbuss.

'What's in the cellar?' Lausard asked.

The boy swallowed hard. 'My family,' he said, his voice cracking. 'My father, mother and two sisters. My mother and sisters were raped and then killed. My father was shot trying to save them.'

'Who did it?' Lausard prompted.

'Soldiers,' the boy said. 'Soldiers like you.'

'Were they wearing these uniforms?' Lausard pulled at his white jacket with one hand.

'Some were. Others wore red, some had no uniforms at all. They came here a week ago. They robbed us. I hid in one of the barns. I've been there ever since. I came back in only to hide my family's bodies. I didn't know where to go or what to do. That's why I stayed here.'

'White uniforms, red uniforms,' Giresse mused. 'Deserters?'

Lausard nodded. 'We're not here to hurt you,' he reassured the boy. 'And the men who killed your family weren't soldiers. We *are*. Let us help you.'

'How?' the boy said.

'Come with us.'

Rocheteau shot his companion a wary glance. 'Are you insane? What the hell are we going to do with him? Eat him too?'

'We can't leave him here,' Lausard said, his eyes still on the boy. 'How old are you, son?'

'Thirteen.'

'Alain, we came here looking for food, not for orphans,' Rocheteau said.

'There's nothing here for you, boy,' Lausard said, one eye still on the barrel of the blunderbuss. 'Come with us. We'll help you.'

'The same way you were helping yourselves to whatever you could find here?' the boy said defiantly. 'The men who killed my family stole too. I saw you kill the pig. What else are you going to take?' Tears began to form in his eyes. 'You won't be able to have my mother's wedding ring because the others took that. They cut off her finger when they couldn't get the ring off by pulling.'

'We just wanted food,' Rocheteau said.

'We're hungry,' Giresse echoed.

'Come with us,' Lausard persisted. 'Join us.'

'We're supposed to be cavalry,' Rocheteau reminded his colleague. 'We don't have drummer-boys.'

'We have trumpeters though, don't we?' Lausard said. 'He can learn. We've learned to ride and to handle weapons. Why can't *he* learn too?'

'And what's Delpierre going to say?' Giresse enquired.

'Who cares?' Lausard said. Then, to the young lad: 'What's your name, boy?'

'Gaston.'

'I lost my family too,' Lausard told him. 'I know how you feel. I had no one to turn to, but we will help you. I swear it.' He took a couple of paces forward, hand outstretched.

The boy lifted the blunderbuss.

'Give it to me, Gaston.'

The boy's finger touched the trigger.

'Let us help you,' Lausard persisted.

He was close enough now to see tears coursing down the boy's cheeks.

Rocheteau and Giresse also took a step forward, their eyes fixed on the wavering barrel of the weapon.

'Gaston,' Lausard whispered.

The boy sniffed and allowed Lausard to pull the blunderbuss from his grasp. As he let go he felt a strong arm envelope him and he pressed his face against Lausard's chest, sobbing quietly.

'One pig, one boy,' said Giresse, smiling wanly.

'A trumpeter,' Rocheteau added.

'Another mouth to feed,' Giresse said and sighed.

Lausard ruffled the boy's hair and smiled down at him.

'Another soldier,' he whispered.

The boy stood beside the entrance to the cellar, head bowed and, watched by the three men, he whispered a prayer before shutting the trapdoor. It was like closing a tomb.

Lausard watched him, finally sliding his arm around the boy's shoulders and guiding him out of the farmhouse.

Rocheteau and Giresse followed, the former carrying the dead pig.

'And how do you propose to cook that when we get back?' asked Giresse glancing at the limp carcass.

'You let me worry about that,' Rocheteau told him. 'We'll be dining on pork for the next couple of days and no one will be complaining then, will they?'

'The men who killed your family,' Giresse said to the boy, 'what else did they take?'

'They took most of the animals, even the horses,' Gaston told him. 'They killed the chickens first and ate them.'

'How many of these men were there?' Lausard asked.

'Six,' the boy said. 'They smelled bad.'

Lausard smiled. 'A bit like us, eh?'

The boy wrinkled his nose and nodded.

'They could have been regulars,' Rocheteau suggested. 'I hear that men are deserting by the *regiment* in some places.'

'I thought the Army of the Interior was meant to deal with them,' Giresse said.

'They are,' Lausard said. 'We're fighting on three fronts and yet twenty thousand men are tied up within the borders of France chasing deserters, shooting Royalists and trying to find new recruits. It's a waste of troops.'

The trio of men and the boy made their way back through the woods, picking their way over fallen branches. Rocheteau stumbled once and went sprawling, dropping the dead pig.

Giresse looked on, laughing.

'Shut up and help me up,' Rocheteau snapped, accepting the helping hand which his colleague extended. The thief snatched up the dead pig once again and threw it across his shoulder as if he was carrying a piece of baggage.

The copse ahead of them masked the road so the men slowed down, knowing they were close to the compound once more. The moon was still hidden behind thick, scudding banks of cloud so they were well covered by the gloom but, nevertheless, they approached with caution.

Lausard was the first to set foot on the dirt track which ran around the perimeter wall. He looked to his left and right then waved the others forward.

'Stop!'

The shout echoed through the stillness of the night and, suddenly, the air seemed to fill with the sound of pounding hooves.

Six dragoons galloped into sight, three from each side. It was as if the horsemen had emerged from the very darkness itself. As they reined in their mounts, Lausard saw that two of them had their carbines pressed to their shoulders, aimed at him and his companions. One of the others had his sword drawn.

Something familiar struck him about one of the men. He was sucking on a pipe.

Captain Deschamps walked his horse towards them. 'What are you doing out of the compound?'

'Foraging, sir,' Lausard said, pointing towards the pig which Rocheteau held up proudly.

'And the boy?' Deschamps continued.

'We found him in a farmhouse back there,' Lausard replied. 'He wants to join us.'

Deschamps puffed on his pipe for a moment, eyeing the three men and the boy. Then spat out a piece of tobacco.

'Lausard, I want to see you in my quarters in ten minutes,' the captain said finally. He pulled on his reins and began to wheel his horse.

'What about the pig, sir?' Rocheteau volunteered.

'Give half to these men,' Deschamps said, nodding towards the dragoons. 'You are all in the same regiment. You share your provisions.'

Rocheteau opened his mouth to protest but Lausard shot him a warning glance.

'Ten minutes, Lausard,' said Deschamps. 'The boy can stay.'

'I thought as a trumpeter, sir,' Lausard offered.

'Can you ride, boy?'

Gaston nodded.

Deschamps looked carefully at the teenager.

Gaston met the officer's gaze, noticing the slightest flicker of a smile on his lips.

Deschamps rode off accompanied by two of the dragoons.

Of the three that remained, one, a large man with a thick moustache, slid off his horse and advanced towards the waiting men.

'Half, the Captain said,' the dragoon reminded

Rocheteau, pointing at the pig. 'Come on, put it down.'

Rocheteau reluctantly dropped the dead pig in front of him then looked up as he heard the hiss of steel. The dragoon had drawn his sword. He prodded the carcass with the point.

'It's dead,' Rocheteau grunted. 'You're safe.'

'Funny man,' said the dragoon with irritation.

'Ten francs says you can't split it with one stroke,' Lausard challenged.

'You haven't got the ten francs to bet with,' the dragoon said mockingly.

'All right,' Lausard continued, 'if you split the pig with one stroke you keep it all. If *I* split it with one stroke, *we* keep it all.'

'Go on, Charnier,' one of the other horsemen coaxed. 'Do it.'

'You're on.' The dragoon stepped forward, aiming the blade and raising the sharpened steel.

He brought the sword down with incredible power but the blade smashed into the pig's spine, sheared off and merely sliced a large chunk from the hide.

Lausard held out his hand for the sword which Charnier passed to him, watching as the young man raised the blade, paused a second then brought it down with stunning ferocity.

The blade struck across the spine splitting the pig cleanly in two.

'No one said which *direction* it had to be cut,' Lausard said smugly, tossing the sabre back to Charnier.

The dragoon looked at him angrily for a moment then his face creased into a smile. Behind him, his companions were laughing too. Charnier slapped him on the shoulder.

'Come on,' he said. 'We'll take you to Deschamps's quarters.'

The room was humble. As he looked around Deschamps's quarters, Lausard took in its contents: a desk, two chairs, a wooden bed with a mattress very similar to the one he and his colleagues slept on and, in one corner, a tin bath. Perhaps the only concession to luxury. The small dwelling place was lit by the dull orange glow of four candles.

'Sit down, Lausard,' Deschamps said, nodding towards the other chair, watching as Lausard did so.

'I trust you solved the problem with the pig?' the captain said and smiled.

'I can explain that, sir . . .' Lausard began.

'I didn't ask you to explain it, Lausard. The entire French army has survived over the years by its foraging skills. Now we move too quickly to be fed by a supply train. Our men carry three days' rations at most. Did you know that Austrian troops carry nine days' rations?' He smiled again. 'The French army is not dependent on the commissary but on the land. You showed initiative. You have since you got here. You've adapted well but I thought you would.'

'Meaning what, sir?'

'Come, come, Lausard. I *know* who you are, *what* you are. You told me back in the Conciergerie. Surely your memory isn't that short.'

'You know *about* me, sir, but you don't know me.'

'I know what I've seen. You ride better than most of my men, you use a sword as well as any man I've ever seen, you handle a carbine and a pistol with ease. If I had a regiment of men like you, men with your abilities, then I would be very happy. If I had a *division* of men like you then this war would be over very soon.'

'Thank you, sir.'

'I'm merely telling you the truth, Lausard. The others have seen it too. The men alongside you respect your abilities, they look up to you.' He smiled. 'These men you despise.'

'I never said that,' Lausard corrected him. 'I don't despise them.'

'Lausard. The blood of a different class runs through your veins. Not the same blood as the men you share your life with now, not the same class. You said yourself that if they knew your background they'd probably carry you to the guillotine themselves. Your family were aristocrats. Enemies to all the men in this training depot, enemies to all the men in this army. You are their enemy, they just don't know it.'

'And do you intend to tell them, sir?'

'I told you before, I don't care about your past, I don't care what you were. All I know is that you are a fine soldier and France needs men like you. I just find it ironic that you are so highly thought of by the very men who would have called for your blood two years ago. It seems too that you have an actor's skill for hiding your true feelings. Don't try to tell me you don't find these men abhorrent. They are beneath you, Lausard, and yet, around them, you act like the gutter rats that they are.'

'Perhaps I am more comfortable in the gutter, sir,' Lausard said.

'Perhaps,' mused Deschamps, pouring himself a glass of wine from the bottle on the table. He filled another glass and pushed it towards Lausard who accepted hesitantly.

'The other day,' Deschamps said, 'why didn't you kill Sergeant Delpierre? I saw the fight. You could have killed him. Why didn't you?'

'Are you sorry I didn't, sir?'

'A question countered with a question – don't you ever give a straight answer?' He sipped his wine.

'Which answer did you want to hear, sir?'

'You could have killed him but you didn't. You showed strength of mind as well as fighting ability. You have many qualities to be admired, Lausard. Be careful they do not trip you up.'

Lausard sipped at the wine, his gaze drawn to one of the candle flames. He watched it flicker in the slight breeze.

'Did you expect me to hate these men, sir?' he asked finally.

'I could have understood your dislike of them,' Deschamps told him. 'After all, you have more in common with our enemies than you do with our own soldiers. Britain, Austria and Prussia all retain monarchies. *Their* aristocracies have not been wiped out by those they formerly ruled. The Directory would have us believe that part of our mission in this war is to bring fraternity to countries ruled by monarchies.' He raised his glass in mock salute. 'We are on a mission of mercy and liberation, Lausard.'

'Excuse me if I do not join you in the toast, sir,' said the younger man.

A heavy silence descended.

Then Deschamps spoke. 'Each dragoon regiment is made up of three squadrons. Those squadrons need

NCOs. I am making you a sergeant in your squadron, Lausard. Pick two corporals to serve with you.'

Lausard looked momentarily stunned by the officer's declaration.

'This regiment leaves for Italy in two days,' Deschamps continued. 'The training is nearly over. All we can teach you we have. The next time you draw swords or fire carbines it will be at men, not straw dummies. And those men will fight back. Some of us will die, perhaps *all* of us. Who knows?'

'Who cares?' Lausard said flatly.

'Quite so, *Sergeant* Lausard.' Deschamps saluted.

Lausard rose and returned the gesture.

'You may go,' Deschamps told him, turning his back.

He heard Lausard's footsteps then the door closing behind him.

CHAPTER 14

'I should hate you,' murmured Joséphine de Beauharnais, tracing patterns across the sheets with slender fingers.

Napoleon Bonaparte handed her another glass of wine and slipped back beneath the covers with her, feeling the warmth of her nakedness beside him. He remained propped up on one elbow, staring down at her, intoxicated by her beauty, marvelling at the perfection of her features and the dusky hue of her skin, so rich against the perfectly white sheets. Her shiny black hair was spread across the pillow and he continued to gaze at her as she turned the glass between her fingers, eyes closed momentarily.

Gently, Bonaparte drew back the sheet, pulling it down to reveal the smooth swell of her breasts and the flatness of her stomach with the tiny triangle of dark hair at its base. Eyes still closed, she smiled, aware of his appraising look. She drew one long, slender leg up and nudged him with her knee.

As if he were wrapping some priceless artifact, after

first pulling down the sheets he then replaced them, hiding her exquisite body from view for the time being.

'Why should you hate me?' he said.

'You had my husband executed,' she said, touching his cheek with her hand, brushing his skin lightly.

'I had nothing to do with your husband's death.'

'The men you represent did.'

'They were politicians. I am a soldier.'

'So was my husband.'

He traced the outline of her lower lip with his finger.

'You fight for the politicians who had him executed,' Joséphine whispered, flicking her tongue out to lick the roving digit.

'I fight for France,' he said softly.

'You're a soldier in their pay.'

'Then feel free to hate me, but if you do then you have a strange way of showing it.'

Joséphine smiled. 'My son called you an honourable man.'

'He's a fine boy. A credit to you and your husband.'

'But was he right? Are you an honourable man? I know you are many things. Powerful, ambitious and influential.'

'Is that why you are here? Paul Barras had those qualities – is that why you were his too?'

'I was never his,' she snapped.

'You were his mistress. What would he say if he could see you now?'

'I don't care what he would say. What could he do to me? Or to you? You are the one with the power now.' She leaned forward and kissed him. Bonaparte felt her slide closer to him, her lean body pressing against him.

He enveloped her in his arms, gripping her to him. His hand looked almost iridescent against the tan of her skin. She was like some glorious living carving, hewn from the most supple bough. A monument to the genius of a master. And she was his.

'Why did you come to me in the beginning?' he asked when they finally broke their embrace.

'I wanted to thank you for returning my husband's sword. It meant so much, especially to my son. He wept when he held it. Perhaps he wept for the memory of his father and so many others like him.'

'He told me how you escaped the guillotine.'

'My family had been rich. To Robespierre I was an enemy, just like my husband. I was lucky to escape with my life.'

'And now you have that life, what do you intend to do with it? Would you share it? With me?'

She laughed and the sound was almost musical to Bonaparte's ears. He gazed at her with ill-disguised awe.

'I leave for Italy . . .'

She put a finger to his lips to silence him.

'Don't talk to me of war,' she said softly. 'I do not wish to know of it.'

'Of what shall I speak then?'

'Of love.'

Again that musical laugh. Again she kissed him.

'I know more of war than love,' he said, with a hint of sadness in his voice.

'Soldiers need to love,' Joséphine said.

'Love is a dangerous thing.' He gazed into her eyes and felt as if he were drowning there; but, mesmerised, he didn't attempt to fight the feeling. If this was love then he surrendered to it, allowed himself to be enveloped by it.

Joséphine saw that look in his eyes and she smiled. It was a smile of triumph.

CHAPTER 15

There were two bodies in the road. One was naked, the other retained some semblance of dignity, its trousers still intact.

Captain Deschamps held up a hand to halt the column and turned to Lausard who was in the front line of the cavalry detachment. He nodded towards the corpses and Lausard rode ahead, joined by Rostov who was having trouble controlling his horse; the animal, like most of the men in the unit, was troubled by the intense heat. A lesser horseman than the Russian might well have been forced to abandon the creature but Rostov was as good a rider as anyone in the regiment and, as he and Lausard trotted their horses along the dusty road, the chestnut pony he rode gradually calmed down.

The heat was almost intolerable. In a cloudless sky the sun had risen to its zenith and burned there like a massive blazing cannon ball. Despite the fact that they were on the coast road from Nice to Savona, currently eight miles south of Albenga, no sea breeze had blessed their passage. Nothing had eased the tortuous journey

and the murderous heat. Italy in April was as hot and
dry as any desert, the men had discovered. Their uniforms did little to help their situation. Their thick, green
woollen jackets were buttoned to the neck and the
brass helmets grew hot under the burning sun. Most
men had removed their usual thick leather gauntlets
but most officers retained them.

Inside his own bleached leather breeches, Lausard
could feel the sweat running down his legs and he was
sure it was puddling in his boots. He glanced across at
his companion and noticed how red Rostov's skin was;
he'd caught the sun, his fair skin exposed for too long
to the searing rays. Flesh was already peeling from his
nose and chin. But the Russian ignored the heat as best
he could, despite the rivulets of sweat pouring down the
side of his face. Every now and then he would wipe the
stinging, salty droplets from his eyes with his fingers.

Dust rose in small clouds every time the horses put a
hoof on the road, something else which exacerbated
the raging thirst suffered by men and horses alike.
Lausard had about half a canteen of water left but he
was saving it for as long as he could. Rostov had drunk
the last of his earlier that morning, allowing his horse
to lick some of the precious liquid from his cupped
hand. As they rode, the animal's tongue lolled thickly
from one corner of its foaming mouth.

Lausard's mount, a powerful black animal, was
sweating profusely. Forced to contend with not only the
heat but also the weight of its rider and his equipment, it
was lathered across much of its front and hindquarters.
The horse bucked once, as if anxious to be rid of both
but Lausard tugged on the reins to subdue it, bringing it
to a halt as he and Rostov reached the bodies.

The Russian dismounted and prodded the naked body with the toe of one boot, flipping the man over on to his back.

'Jesus,' he grunted, looking down at the corpse, waving a hand in front of him as the nauseating stench of decay attacked his nostrils.

There was a wound in the left side of the man's stomach and it was still choked with congealed blood, but what caused the Russian to recoil was the cut that had clearly killed the man. His throat had been slit from ear to ear, the wound gaping open like the gills of a fish.

He checked the other body and saw that it too had had its throat cut.

'They've been dead a couple of days,' Lausard said, gazing down at the corpses. The heat had accelerated their putrefaction.

Rostov swung himself back on to his horse while Lausard signalled Deschamps to bring the column on. The unit moved forward at a walk.

'Do you think they're our men?' asked Joubert, looking towards the tableau ahead.

'This far south, they must be,' Giresse said.

'Deserters probably,' Charvet added. 'Probably died of thirst.'

'Like hell,' Delacor said scornfully. 'The "Barbets" got them I'll bet.'

'What are "Barbets"?' Joubert asked.

'Local guerrilla fighters,' Delacor explained. 'You never hear or see them until they slit your throat.' He looked at Joubert and drew a hand swiftly across his own neck. 'Keep your eyes peeled, fat man.'

The head of the column drew level with the dead

bodies and many men glanced at the corpses with a combination of revulsion and morbid curiosity. Some looked on with relief. At least it wasn't *them* lying there.

Deschamps detailed two men to bury the bodies, telling them to rejoin the column as quickly as they could.

'Rather them than me,' Delacor offered, watching as the dragoons pulled the bodies to one side of the road. 'If those murdering bastards come back there'll be four graves there, not two.'

'Why don't they come out in the open and fight like men?' Tabor said.

'They're too clever for that, you half-wit,' snapped Delacor. 'They operate in small groups, keep to the hills and the woods, and pick their moment.' He looked around. 'They could be watching us right now.'

The ground to their left sloped upwards sharply about two hundred yards beyond, the hillside rising steeply. Outcrops of trees clung to the inclines as if gripping on with their roots. Elsewhere rocks stuck out from the slopes, baked hot by the scorching sun.

Gaston looked around and felt a shiver run up the back of his neck despite the heat. He was wearing the scarlet jacket of a trumpeter which was a couple of sizes too big for him, as was his helmet which he had to push back constantly because it kept slipping down over his eyes. His breeches were also too big and he'd been forced to pad them out around the backside with balled-up pieces of material ripped from an old shirt Lausard had given him. But this did have its advantages. He didn't feel as saddle-sore as some of the men who rode with him. Many a trooper shifted uncomfortably in his saddle, aware all too readily of the blisters that had formed on the insides of his thighs and on his buttocks.

Up ahead, the road turned sharply to the right and the column reduced speed as the hills rose to obscure their view of what lay around the bend.

Roussard was conscious of the sword bumping against his boot as he rode. He wondered how long it would be before he had to use it. As the column slowed down he glanced across at Moreau who was aware of his gaze. He tried to smile reassuringly but the gesture failed, coming across more as a crooked smirk. Moreau crossed himself.

'Take two men and ride ahead,' Deschamps said to Lausard. 'See if you can link up with the scouts you sent out earlier. We'll continue along this road.'

Lausard saluted, motioned to Rostov and Giresse and the three of them rode off down the road, great clouds of choking dust rising into the baking air behind them. Deschamps watched them go, disappearing around the bend in the road which wound through the hills and rocks like a parched tongue. Within minutes they were out of sight.

The column kept moving.

'Can't we find some water somewhere?' asked Giresse. 'I don't know who's going to drop first, me or my horse.' He patted the animal's lathered neck.

'Hopefully Rocheteau and the others will have found food *and* water,' Rostov said.

'There won't be much food around here,' Lausard responded, with an air of certainty. 'A combination of the locals and our men foraging . . .' He allowed the sentence to trail off, shrugging his shoulders.

'Where's the nearest village?' Rostov asked, wiping sweat from his face.

'A mile up ahead,' Lausard said, pointing to a range of low hills. 'My guess is that's where Rocheteau and the others are.'

'Talk of the Devil,' murmured Giresse and nodded in the direction of a lone figure on the crest of the ridge.

From the uniform and the horsehair mane which flew out behind the speeding rider the men could tell that the newcomer was a dragoon. He was riding hard, hunched low over his saddle.

'It's Bonet,' Lausard said under his breath, squinting to make out the features of the speeding horseman.

The ex-schoolmaster reined in his horse, pulling so hard on the leather that the animal reared up for a second.

'What's the hurry, schoolmaster?' Giresse said, smiling, but the smile faded as he saw the look of concern on his companion's face.

'The village is occupied,' Bonet said breathlessly.

'Austrians or Piedmontese?' Lausard asked.

'Frenchmen. Deserters,' Bonet said. 'They've got Rocheteau and Carbonne.'

'What do you mean *got them*?' Lausard prompted. 'Are they dead?'

Bonet could hardly suck in the breath to speak. He swallowed as best he could with a parched throat.

'We found the village,' he said. 'It looked deserted. There was food there, water too. Rice, some bread. We were loading up for ourselves when they appeared from some of the houses. We didn't have time to get back to our horses.'

'How did *you* get out?' Lausard queried.

'I ran for it while Rocheteau and Carbonne held them off,' the ex-schoolmaster said, still gasping for air. His face was sheathed in sweat, the skin crimson.

'How long ago did this happen?' Lausard pressed, watching as his colleague removed his brass helmet and ran a hand through his sopping hair. 'We didn't hear any shots.'

'There was none,' Bonet explained. 'They have muskets but no powder. They attacked us with bayonets.'

'How many are there?'

'A dozen, maybe more.'

Lausard leaned forward in his saddle and gripped Bonet by the arm.

'I don't want to know how many there *might* be,' he said. 'Think. How many? Exactly.'

Bonet nodded. 'Fourteen that I saw, that I counted,' he said finally.

'All carrying muskets?' Lausard persisted.

'Six have muskets,' Bonet told him. 'One, I think he's the leader, has a sword. The others are using bayonets.'

Lausard sat back in his saddle and looked towards the top of the ridge.

'Do we go back for the rest of the column?' Giresse asked.

Lausard shook his head. 'Is there any cover on the reverse slope?' he asked Bonet. 'Could we reach the village without them seeing us?'

'On foot, yes,' Bonet proclaimed. 'But if you go in, they'll kill us. They'll certainly kill Rocheteau and Carbonne. We couldn't reach them in time.'

'How many are guarding them?' Lausard demanded.

'Just two.'

'Four against fourteen, Alain,' said Giresse, falteringly.

'Are you a gambling man, Rostov?' Lausard asked.

'Those odds sound fine to me,' the Russian said and grinned.

'If there were fourteen *women* in that village you'd be in there quickly enough,' Lausard said to Giresse.

'That's true,' he said, chuckling nervously.

'Come on,' said Lausard and urged his horse on to a walk.

'Alain, they're Frenchmen,' said Bonet. 'You're going to kill Frenchmen?'

'Do you think they'd have had second thoughts about killing you?' Lausard pulled one of the pistols from its holster on his saddle and loaded it, replacing it carefully as the others looked on.

'They're soldiers like us,' Bonet protested.

'They're not like *us*,' Lausard snapped. 'And if you were down there, Bonet, would you expect Rocheteau or Carbonne to come back for *you*?'

There was a heavy silence, broken only by the low panting and occasional whinnying of the horses.

Bonet finally nodded.

'Come on,' said Lausard.

The tiny collection of dwellings which Lausard surveyed from the cover of thick bushes barely merited the description of village but, nevertheless, the huddle of buildings was called Villa Borghese. Or so a sign proudly displayed in what passed for the village square proclaimed. The square also had a well, but from where he was Lausard could see that the bucket was gone and the cranking handle rusty from lack of use. The well, like the village itself, had dried up long ago. Those who once called it home had left, either having fled or been driven out by any one of three armies currently in the area.

However, it was not empty now and Lausard carefully scrutinised those who inhabited its tiny square. He could see ten men, all dressed in blue jackets. Infantry. Another had removed his thick tunic. They were, without exception, shoeless and filthy. Their knapsacks bulged with whatever food they'd been able to collect and also with bounty they'd secured on their trek through Italy. Though most of it, he guessed, had been acquired since they fled from their regiment.

One of the men was busily wrapping pieces of cloth around his feet and Lausard could see that there was blood soaking through the makeshift bandages. Another had his arm in a sling. A third sported a bandage which covered most of the left side of his face and head.

Three, Lausard mused, who shouldn't offer too much resistance. But where were the rest? Bonet had said there were fourteen of them. Lausard counted again. He saw only ten.

Another, a tall man with a huge thick moustache, emerged from one of the tiny houses, a sword gripped in his fist.

The leader, according to Bonet. He looked fitter and sturdier than his colleagues and, despite the ragged uniform which he wore, the man seemed to exude an air of authority. As well as the bulging knapsack slung around his back he also carried several small leather pouches which hung from his belt. Lausard guessed that these contained more plunder.

Only one of the men was actually carrying his musket. The other Charlevilles were propped up against the side of the wall, bayonets glistening in the sunlight.

'Where are Rocheteau and Carbonne?' Lausard whispered.

Bonet pointed towards the house from which the tall man had emerged.

'So, there are three more of them in there,' Lausard mused.

He and Bonet were no more than twenty yards from the house, well hidden by thickly planted trees and tall hedges. Giresse and Rostov should now be around the other side of the house. The horses had been tethered about a hundred yards back in the trees, out of earshot. Each of the men carried his carbine, one of his pistols and his sword. The two horses which belonged to Rocheteau and Carbonne were tethered outside one of Villa Borghese's tiny dwellings with a young lad no older than fourteen watching them. Lausard looked at his companion and Bonet met his gaze and nodded.

They sprang to their feet as one.

Both ran towards the square, bursting from the cover of the trees.

The blue-clad infantry seemed stunned by the sudden intrusion. Two of them raised their hands in surrender immediately.

Bonet paused, swung the carbine up to his shoulder and fired.

The .70 lead ball struck one of the men in the shoulder, shattered his collar-bone and ploughed on deep into his back. Blood spurted from the wound and the man screamed, dropping to his knees, clutching at the wound.

Lausard came upon his first two opponents and used his pistol against the first, sticking the barrel against the man's face and firing. The man fell backwards as Lausard pulled his sword free of its scabbard and aimed a mighty backhand slash at the other deserter, who instinctively raised his hand to protect his face. The razor-sharp steel sliced effortlessly through the hand, between thumb and forefinger, sending blood spraying into the air. The man shrieked and turned to run but Lausard drove the sword into his stomach, feeling the muscles tighten around the blade as he first punched it in then ripped it free. The man fell at his feet.

Of the remaining deserters, six immediately ran for the trees, anxious to escape these maniacs who were attacking them. One ran straight into Rostov who was scurrying into the square from the opposite direction.

The Russian cut his foe across the face with his sword, slicing away one eyebrow and most of the forehead around it, but the man kept running.

Three men emerged from the house and hurtled after their fleeing colleagues.

Giresse aimed his carbine at one but, seeing the man was already more interested in escaping than fighting, he lowered the weapon and advanced towards the tethered horses. The young lad holding them was weeping uncontrollably, transfixed by what had happened.

'Run,' snarled Giresse and the boy did, a dark stain spreading across his groin.

The man with the moustache stood his ground, lifting his sword to confront Lausard, who met his furious gaze.

'Go while you can,' Lausard said forcefully.

The man looked at him then at the other dragoons who were closing in around him. He lowered the sword slightly and reached for one of the pouches fastened to his belt.

'Just go,' Lausard told him. 'I don't want your money.'

'I do,' Giresse interjected, holding out his hand for the pouch.

The man tossed it to him, dropped the sword and ran, disappearing into the woods.

Rostov walked into the house where Bonet had said that Rocheteau and Carbonne were being held. He emerged a moment later with his two colleagues, both of whom had been stripped of their boots and buttons.

Lausard laughed as he saw them.

Bonet meanwhile was staring down at the man he'd shot, inspecting the wound, noticing, with revulsion, that part of the collar-bone was sticking through the flesh. The injured man's face was the colour of rancid butter and he looked imploringly at Bonet for help.

The ex-schoolmaster felt his stomach contract as he continued to gape at the wound in the deserter's shoulder. 'What can we do for him?' Bonet asked, his own face now pale.

'Do for him?' Rocheteau shouted angrily, and he snatched the carbine from Bonet and slammed it into the face of the wounded man with incredible force, smashing his nose, splitting his lips and forehead.

'Stop it!' shrieked Bonet, trying to step between Rocheteau and the injured man but Carbonne pulled him aside, watching as Rocheteau struck again, the next blow cracking the man's skull. The third finished him off.

Rocheteau spat on the body and handed the carbine back to Bonet, who was staring in horror at the body. He turned away and vomited until there was nothing left in his stomach.

'They would have killed us,' Carbonne said, crossing to his horse. He found his own boots stuffed untidily inside his portmanteau. 'They're lucky *I* didn't get my hands on them.'

'We just killed three of our own countrymen,' blurted Bonet. 'Don't you understand that? They weren't Austrians or Russians or Prussians. They were French. Like us.'

'If you feel so strongly about it,' Rocheteau snapped, 'you stay behind and bury them.' He knelt beside one of the bodies and went swiftly through the pockets, pulling out the contents of the knapsack. The search didn't yield much apart from a small bottle of wine and some stale biscuits but it was better than nothing.

'There's rice and bread in one of the houses,' Carbonne said.

'Enough for all of us?' Lausard asked.

'*Some* of us,' Carbonne said.

'How can you talk about food after what we've done?' Bonet said.

'We'll do much worse before this war is over,' Lausard warned him.

'Will it make you feel better if they're buried?' Rocheteau snapped, grabbing the heels of the nearest corpse. 'Right, schoolmaster, I'll lay them to rest.'

He dragged the body to the edge of the well, sat it on the side for a second then pushed it in. There was a second's silence then a loud thump. 'Happier now?'

The other men laughed.

Bonet shook his head in despair.

'Load up and let's get out of here,' Lausard said.

'Have we turned into savages?' Bonet asked imploringly.

'Do you think you weren't before,' snapped Lausard.

Flies were already beginning to buzz around the puddles of blood in the square.

CHAPTER 16

The two men who waited inside General Bonaparte's tent could not have been more different. Diametrically opposed in every aspect ranging from age to social background, they were drawn together by the fact that both were divisional commanders in the Army of Italy. They had nothing more in common. Their only bond was the army.

Jean Mathieu Philibert Serurier was in his fifty-third year. He was a tall gloomy man with a scar on his lip acquired during his thirty-four years service with the old Royal Army before the overthrow of the Bourbons. He had an aristocratic air about him which seemed totally out of place within the new citizen army. He walked agitatedly back and forth before the desk inside the tent, which was strewn with maps and documents. Serurier seemed less interested in those than in the time, as he continually consulted a pocket watch retrieved from his uniform.

His companion inside the tent noticed this constant clock watching and felt compelled to check his own time-piece, wondering what his colleague found so fascinating about the slow advance of the hands around the ornate face of the watch.

Pierre François Charles Augereau was thirty-eight years old, a product of the Paris gutters, like many of the men who served beneath him. He rejoiced in his nickname 'child of the people'; clung to it as if it were some medal of great importance to him, bestowed with affection by his troops. He was even taller than Serurier and, combined with a huge hooked nose, this made him difficult to ignore.

'Staring at that watch isn't going to make the time go any quicker,' he told his companion. 'Leave the bastard thing alone.'

Serurier glanced at him with ill-disguised contempt.

'It's a good job that your abilities as a soldier outweigh your shortcomings as a gentleman,' said the older officer, making no attempt to conceal the distaste in his tone.

Augereau hawked loudly and spat on the floor.

'That's what I think of gentlemen,' he said. 'Gentlemen have no place in this army. This war is fought by ordinary men.'

'But we are not ordinary men who command them,' Serurier said. 'At least some of us aren't.'

'We are all the same under these uniforms,' the younger man said. 'We all bleed when we're cut. We all go hungry when we don't eat. We all ride the same way. Horses *and* women.'

'You really are quite appalling,' Serurier snapped, glancing again at his watch.

'Why are you so interested in the time?' Augereau asked.

'I wondered where our new commander was.' Again

there was disdain in his voice. 'My God, he looks more like a mathematician than a general and I suspect he is only a general because of Barras.'

'A political soldier, you think? Well, he's riding Barras's old mistress too. Seems Bonaparte got more than his rank from the Directory.' Augereau cracked out laughing but was not joined by his companion.

He was still laughing when the flap of the tent opened and a third man joined them.

'Massena,' Augereau said, still chuckling. 'You're late. If you don't believe me, consult Serurier's watch. It's all he's been doing for the past ten minutes.'

André Massena was a thin, dark man with pinched features. He was the same age as Augereau but looked younger. His dark blue jacket with its gold epaulettes and embroidery was immaculately pressed and clean. He looked as if he'd just left a tailor's shop, not ridden miles across parched, dry countryside. There was barely a trace of perspiration on him. He had served at Toulon with Bonaparte three years earlier and knew the abilities of his new commander.

'So, Massena,' Augereau continued, 'what do you think of General Bonaparte? Serurier here thinks he comes to us only because of Paul Barras and the Directory.'

'I didn't say that,' Serurier protested.

'And he has Barras's mistress too,' Augereau continued.

'Then he is a lucky man,' Massena said. 'She is a rare beauty.'

Augereau laughed again. 'You would ride her yourself, given the chance,' he joked.

Again Serurier looked on with contempt.

When the flap of the tent opened a second time all three men drew themselves to attention to greet the newcomer.

Bonaparte nodded a greeting to them and took up a position behind his desk. He ran his hands over the largest of the maps there, sweeping others to the ground.

'Italy,' he said, pointing at the map. 'It should be our triumph, it is becoming our graveyard. The Army of Italy was raised four years ago and it numbered one hundred and six thousand men. Now, it is disintegrating. Casualties, sickness and desertion have reduced it to sixty-three thousand. Of that number, less than thirty-eight thousand are effective. Of those, many have no shoes, no muskets, no bayonets, no powder. There isn't enough food to go around. The infantry fights in rags, the cavalry rides horses that have been on half rations for a year and, as I speak, we have less than sixty field guns working.' He sucked in a deep breath. 'Royalist agents are at work within the ranks, poisoning the minds of those who will listen to them. The Third Battalion of the Two Hundred and Ninth mutinied at Nice. Even your division, Serurier, defied orders. There is talk of mutiny every day and every soldier in the army is starving. And yet, with these men – men who cannot remember the last time they ate a good meal, had efficient equipment or received any pay – with men such as these we are expected to win this war.' A slight smile flickered on his lips. 'And I tell you, gentlemen, we will.'

'How, General, do you propose to win this victory?' Serurier asked. 'Or perhaps miracle would be a more apt word.'

'The army needs money,' Bonaparte said. 'The men need food but, above all, they need a victory.'

'I agree, sir,' said Serurier condescendingly. 'But that victory will be harder to gain with troops in the condition you described. It is a vicious circle. They need a victory and yet they will not fight well because they haven't the equipment or the supplies needed to gain one.'

'Massena here won at Loano with just such men,' Bonaparte corrected him. 'They will fight, trust me, I know these men. They are men like us.'

'Not like Serurier,' Augereau said scornfully. 'His men obey him because he is a tyrant.'

'I don't care what methods my generals use to command their men,' Bonaparte said. 'All that matters is that they obey.'

'You expect them to fight for no food *and* no pay?' Augereau challenged.

'The Directory entrusted me with some money,' Bonaparte said. 'I have already instructed my chief commissary to organise a small issue of pay. Loans have been secured from some of the merchants in Genoa and a captured privateer has been sold for fifty thousand francs.'

'You should get them to investigate those damned contractors too,' said Augereau. 'They've made fortunes for themselves by giving our men short rations.'

'It is all in hand,' Bonaparte reassured him. 'The rest of it is up to us. To *lead* these men to victory.'

'And what is your plan, sir?' Serurier asked.

'The mountains between Nice and Genoa can be crossed by six different passes and valleys,' Bonaparte said, indicating the area on the map. 'The fighting in this campaign will centre on control of those because, once through them, we are in Piedmont. Once their forces are destroyed we can concentrate on defeating the Austrians.' The other men drew closer to the map, listening to Bonaparte's excited voice, riveted by his passion. 'The Col di Tende, here, leads into the very heart of Piedmont. It is guarded by the fortress of Cuneo. Also leading into Piedmont is the second crossing point. Here, the valley of the River Tanaro. The Col di Cadibona offers us a way into Piedmont through Ceva or into Lombardy by the branches of the River Bormida. The Col di Giovo is more difficult to move through but we must still find a way. Finally, here, the Turchino pass and here, the Bochetta pass.' He stepped back slightly. 'Once these mountains are conquered, Lombardy is ours. No more barren hillsides and scorched plains, gentlemen, just the richness of Lombardy and Piedmont. Our men can live off the land without difficulty. We can replenish, recuperate and regain our strength before we push the Austrians out of Italy.'

'Do we know the opposition's strength?' Massena asked, his eyes still focused on the map.

'Somewhere around fifty-two thousand Austrians and Piedmontese.'

'And we are thirty-seven thousand,' Massena murmured.

'But our forces are concentrated. The Austrians and Piedmontese are thinly spread and, what is more, they do not trust each other. We will be up against armies who are not united and the weak point is here.' Bonaparte pointed to a place on the map. 'Carcare. Once we take that town we turn and defeat Colli and his Piedmontese. He will be cut off from his allies.'

'Where is the best place to cross?' The question came from Augereau.

'The Col di Cadibona,' Bonaparte told him. 'It is closer to Carcare and it also offers good ground for moving artillery. It means we can move quickly, before the enemy can concentrate its forces. Massena, your division will move to join Augereau's troops. You will attack through San Giacomo, joining to assault Carcare. In two days we should be able to concentrate twenty-four thousand men there.'

No one spoke.

The silence was finally broken by Serurier. 'A bold plan,' he said without enthusiasm.

'A *good* plan,' Augereau said and smiled.

'If it works,' Massena added.

'It *will* work,' Bonaparte assured them, total conviction in his voice.

CHAPTER 17

'Here,' called Rocheteau, emerging from the trees. 'Skin those.' He hurled two rabbits towards the camp fire, grinning as they landed with a thud at the feet of Joubert. The big man looked at them hungrily, as if prepared to devour them as they were. He rubbed his voluminous belly with one pudgy hand, listening to it rumble.

The other men also looked on longingly, watching as Bonet reached for one of the rabbits and slit the skin with the tip of his bayonet.

Lausard was surprised to see Gaston snatch up the other dead animal and proceed to do the same.

'Farm boy,' Giresse said smiling.

'Where did you find them?' Lausard enquired, watching as Rocheteau knelt beside the fire, warming his hands.

'The woods are swarming with them,' the corporal said. 'You just have to be quick enough.' He nudged Joubert in the side. 'You wouldn't have been much help to us, fat man.'

'He could have rolled on them,' Roussard offered.

The other men laughed.

A large tin pot was suspended over the fire, half filled with water. Rostov had taken it from one of the houses in Villa Borghese. The implement had been dangling from his saddle, attached by a piece of leather. The water had come from a small stream at the bottom of the ridge the men were now camped on. Fires had been lit all over the ridge, smoke rising into a sky the colour of burnished gold. However, despite the passing of the sun, the night was still humid. Mosquitoes hovered around, seeking any uncovered flesh. Delacor swatted one of the insects as it bit into his neck. He wiped the squashed remains on the grass.

The horses had been watered at the stream before any of the men had been allowed to set up camp. They were now tethered in long rows, watched by sentries. Dragoons ambled up and down with carbines sloped, some looking longingly up the ridge towards their companions, eagerly awaiting the time when they would be relieved, when they could eat and rest.

Sonnier was one of those who gazed at the array of comforting fires and trudged obediently back and forth, turning to look every so often when he heard a horse whinny or scuff the ground.

Sentries guarded the approaches to the wood as well. Like the men near the stream, they also carried their carbines sloped, the fifteen-inch bayonets fixed and twinkling in the light of so many fires. Like many men in their position in the French army, they had their weapons loaded with 'running ball', where the only charge of gunpowder was in the priming pan. It saved on powder which was, like most things on the campaign, at a premium.

Bonet and Gaston finished skinning and gutting the rabbits and set about cutting them into pieces which they then dropped into the boiling water suspended over the fire. Carbonne had found a few wild potatoes in the woods and he dropped those in alongside the rabbit pieces, not bothering to remove the dirt first. The entire potful of food began to turn a shade of brown but the men didn't care what it looked like, only that they were going to eat. Rice was also added and they gathered around eagerly awaiting their feast. None of them knew how long it would be before they ate again.

Most of the other units in the regiment weren't so lucky. They were forced to make do with biscuits. A fight had almost broken out between Charnier and a rival dragoon over who had claim on a dead dog they'd found at the roadside earlier that evening, but Charnier had taken it and the creature was now being turned on a makeshift spit over the fire, which he and his men had made.

Lausard sat gazing down the slope at the tents which had been erected for Deschamps and the other officers. He could see the captain strolling in and out of his tent, dressed only in a shirt and breeches. Lausard wondered if the officer was as anxious to see action as *he* was. Time seemed to have lost its meaning. The days had become a blur of marches beneath the blistering sun over roads sometimes barely wide enough to accommodate three horses moving abreast, most of them rutted, parched causeways. Hills crowded in on the roads in most places as if threatening to crush them out of existence and the thick growths of trees made the men nervous, wondering if their movements were being watched by the local guerrillas. Lausard didn't doubt for one second that they were.

They'd already lost over a dozen horses, made lame by the terrain. The only consolation was that the animals, once shot, had been cut up for food. That feeling of consolation wasn't shared by their riders, however, who trudged along on foot, finding it difficult to keep up and generally slowing the column as it advanced further towards the fighting which everyone knew would come soon.

They had passed regiments of infantry without shoes. Some without muskets, and stories had filtered through to them about battles already fought, of how the Austrians and Piedmontese were better equipped and fed, of how the hostility of the locals that remained made passing through every village that bit harder. In places, food had been burned to prevent the advancing French from making use of it and, in one village, two dozen oxen had been poisoned rather than let them fall into the hands of the invaders. A number of men in the regiment were sick too. Lausard thought it was mainly lack of food and bad water but rumours were circulating of a typhus epidemic. Everyone was on edge. Lausard thought that the chance of combat might be a good thing if only to relieve the worries of day-to-day campaigning. When faced with some of the problems they encountered, the prospect of battle didn't seem so terrifying after all. Combat, he mused, should go a long way to making the men forget the saddle-sores and the constant gnawing in their bellies.

But when would that battle come? He ran a hand through his hair and exhaled deeply.

'Alain.'

He turned at the sound of his name to see Rocheteau holding a metal plate towards him. A couple of pieces of rabbit meat were floating in brown gravy with some potatoes and rice. Lausard pulled a spoon from one of his pockets, blew the dust from it and began eating.

'We'd better save some for Sonnier,' said Giresse, 'for when he comes back from sentry duty.'

'To hell with him,' Delacor snapped. 'All the more for us.'

Lausard glared at the man then nodded to Giresse. 'Save him some,' he said quietly.

'This might be the last meal we eat for a while,' Charvet observed.

'It might be the last meal we *ever* eat,' Joubert added, gravy dripping from his chin as he stuffed the food into his mouth.

'With God's help we'll all get through it,' Moreau added.

'Do you honestly think God gives a damn about us or anyone else in this stinking army?' Delacor sneered.

'God cares about everyone,' Moreau continued. 'Even *you*.'

The other men laughed.

Delacor didn't see the joke.

'Well, I don't need *His* help,' he said irritably.

'When you run up against the Austrians you might change your mind,' Tabor added.

'Shut up, you half-wit, I don't need *your* opinion.'

'Stop squabbling amongst yourselves,' Bonet said. 'We're not here to fight each other.'

As he spoke he looked across at Lausard.

'If you're referring to those deserters, Bonet,' said

Lausard without looking up from his food, 'you know my opinion. They would have killed *us*.'

'Yes, they would,' Rocheteau added.

'What happened?' Roussard pressed.

'It isn't important,' Lausard replied. 'Forget about it. It's in the past and the past doesn't matter.'

Lausard tried to convince himself that was true. He'd been trying to, ever since the death of his family, but he knew that the past *did* matter. It did to him. It ate away at him like some canker and he knew it would continue to do so as long as he lived. As long as he walked, his guilt would walk with him like an extra shadow.

The sky was darkening rapidly now, bringing with it a chill but welcome westerly breeze, which ruffled the men's hair and caused them to draw nearer the fire. Some were already lying down on their blankets, saddles used as makeshift pillows. Rocheteau was busy sewing a button back on his tunic. Rostov took the now empty tin pot from the bayonet which held it above the fire and made his way down to the stream to wash it out in the cool water. All the men would fill their canteens from the stream in the morning before leaving. Most had drained the contents already as soon as the order had been given to make camp, urged on by their uncontrollable thirsts. The dust had stuck in their throats and noses until it seemed that it would suffocate them.

As Rostov washed the pot he heard the dull clank of a hammer and looked across to see that the regimental farrier and two of his assistants were shoeing a large bay. They wore the appropriate insignia on their sleeves; suitably enough, a silver horseshoe. The animal seemed unconcerned by the running repairs being performed on it and stood obediently as the farrier first removed the old shoe then replaced it with another, which he'd taken from a dead horse earlier in the day, pounding it into shape as best he could on a flat rock by the edge of the stream.

As Rostov made his way back up the slope he saw Charnier and his companions finishing off what was left of the dog they had cooked. One of the men was sucking contentedly on a pipe despite the fact that it had no tobacco in it.

Heading down the slope towards him was Lausard.

'Charvet and Roussard are taking first watch,' Lausard informed him. 'You try to get some sleep, you and Moreau can take the next one.'

'What about you?' Rostov asked. 'When will you sleep?'

Lausard smiled.

'I don't sleep too well,' he said. 'I haven't for a while now.'

'Nervous?'

'Bad dreams.'

Lausard patted his colleague on the shoulder then continued on down the slope alone, his cape now slung around his shoulders to protect him from the increasingly chilly wind. The material flapped in the breeze like the wings of a gigantic bat and, as he walked, his sword bumped against his boot.

Reaching the bottom of the ridge he found Sonnier still walking obediently up and down in front of the horses.

'There's food back there for you,' Lausard told him. 'Tabor's on his way down to relieve you.'

'Good, I'm starving.'

'You and half the army.'

Sonnier watched as Lausard walked off along the floor of the valley, following the gently flowing stream, walking as close to its edge as he could without losing his footing on the powdery dirt. Every now and then he kicked loose stones into the stream, watching the small geysers of water rise and the ripples spread.

The smell of horse droppings was strong in the air, carried on the breeze, but far from recoiling, Lausard inhaled deeply, savouring the odour which was mixed with the smell of grass and earth. It was the smell of freedom. A glorious aroma compared to the fetid stench he'd had to live with in his prison cell or the rank mephitis of the Paris gutters which had clogged his nostrils for so long before that.

He made his way back up the slope, skirting dying camp fires, drawing one or two glances from men who could not sleep. He wondered what *their* reasons for wakefulness were. Fear? Excitement? Foreboding?

He walked along the very outskirts of the camp, passing sentries every twenty yards, exchanging nods with them. Drawing nearer to the top of the ridge the trees grew so thickly and the darkness seemed so dense as to be palpable. He could barely see the dragoons who stood sentinel close to the trees. In fact, he was barely three feet away when he realised that the man ahead of him was busy urinating into a bush, his carbine propped against the tree beside him.

Moving quickly but stealthily, Lausard went over to the man who was sighing contentedly as he emptied his bladder. Then, with one swift movement, Lausard drew his pistol and pressed it to the back of the sentry's head.

He clicked back the hammer and the man raised both hands, his breeches still gaping.

It was all Lausard could do to suppress a grin. 'You're supposed to be keeping watch, not watering the land.' He removed the pistol and pushed the hammer back down.

'Sorry, Sergeant,' said the man who still had his breeches open.

'Delpierre would have had you shot if *he'd* caught you.'

The man saluted. 'I know, Sergeant,' he jabbered. 'It won't happen again, Sergeant.'

Lausard nodded. 'Trooper,' he said, again trying to keep a straight face, 'you should fasten your breeches now.'

The man did so hurriedly as Lausard walked on, heading for the next outpost.

Two sentries up ahead stood motionless, both seeming as if they were a part of the night; dark shapes which had detached themselves from the blackness and become tangible. Neither turned as he approached, despite the fact that his sword clanked against his boot as he drew nearer.

'Asleep on duty?' Lausard murmured to himself.

He reached out and grabbed the first man's shoulder. The dragoon toppled backwards, falling flat on his back at Lausard's feet. His throat had been cut from ear to ear. Blood was still draining from the riven veins and arteries.

Lausard looked across at the other soldier, realising now that his body leaned against the tree close by.

A knife had been used on him too. Driven skilfully, with great power and precision, into the base of his skull. His eyes were open and staring wide, bulging like a fish on a hot skillet. Thin trickles of crimson ran from his nose and ears.

Lausard spun round, pulling his sword free with one hand, his pistol with the other, while preparing to shout a warning to the other sentries, to rouse the regiment from its slumber.

It was then that he heard the first gunshot.

CHAPTER 18

The bang sounded like a thundercrack in the stillness of the night. The crack reverberated around the valley, followed all too soon by another. Then another.

Lausard turned in the direction of the sounds and realised they were coming from the bottom of the slope. He heard shouts now, not just from the base of the ridge but also closer by. Men, roused from their slumbers by the noise, were staggering to their feet, some reaching for weapons, others trying to regain their wits, to shake the sleep from their minds.

There were more gunshots. Then the whinnying and screams of horses. A carbine was fired, the muzzle and pan flash briefly illuminating the firer.

The light from the camp fires was dim, barely strong enough for Lausard to see the base of the slope but he hurtled towards it nonetheless.

The horses were restless now, many hooves pounding the ground. Their cries grew louder, their anxiety increased. Dark shapes moved amongst them and Lausard knew they were not dragoons.

One of the shapes raised a pistol and placed it

against the head of a grey horse. There was a loud bang and then the animal crashed to the ground taking two other horses with it as it fell. Now the animals became almost frantic. Steel glinted brightly in the gloom.

More dragoons were charging down the slope now and he saw Sergeant Legier, sword drawn, running past him. Other men ran to the aid of the horses, some stumbling in the darkness. Lausard saw one man go sprawling headlong as he tripped over a rock, his carbine falling from his grasp.

Then he saw the dark shapes among the horses again.

He rushed towards one, forcing his way through the lines of terrified animals. Clouds of dust were being raised by the churning hooves, further limiting his vision.

When no more than three feet away, the man turned to see Lausard; in the gloom the dragoon could just make out the face of his opponent – bearded, his hair long and dirty, his eyes wide and almost frenzied. He cursed at Lausard in Italian and aimed a pistol but he was too slow. Lausard drove the point of his sword forward, hurling all his weight behind the thrust. The blade punctured the man's chest just below the sternum and erupted from his back. Lausard pulled him on to the steel, twisted it once then pulled it free, striking at his dying enemy with a powerful backhand slash that almost severed the man's right arm at the shoulder. He dropped to his knees and Lausard drove the blade through his throat, ignoring the blood that jetted on to his breeches.

'Sergeant.'

The shout made him turn and he spun round in time

to see another of the guerrillas racing towards him.

Lausard ducked down, drove his shoulder into the man's chest and knocked him on to his back, stepping forward and driving his sword into the guerrilla's belly and chest.

'They're after the horses!' Lausard shouted as another shot exploded close by him and he saw Sonnier with a carbine and a cloud of smoke surrounding him.

The panic spreading through the horses was so great by now that Lausard feared a stampede. Many of the horses were rearing up, anxious to escape their attackers. One struck out with its hind legs, catching a dragoon in the face, the impact shattering a cheekbone and his nose. He dropped to his knees, his face a bloody ruin.

Elsewhere, men were grabbing animals, trying to calm them, but the guerrillas continued to run among them, firing into the air, sometimes into the mass of horses. Those without guns slashed with knives at the helpless animals.

Lausard could not tell how many guerrillas there were; the darkness hid them too effectively. But whatever their number they seemed to be succeeding in their mission. He saw another horse go down, hamstrung with two slashes of a knife. Two of the dark figures ran from the camp, scampering over the rocky terrain towards some trees on the other side of the stream.

'Sonnier!' Lausard shouted. 'Come on.' And he was scrambling for a horse, gripping its mane to haul himself on to the animal's bare back, hurtling after the fleeing guerrillas. Sonnier pulled another cartridge from his cartouche, bit off the ball, held it in his mouth while pouring powder down the barrel, then spat the ball after it, rammed wadding down and replaced the rod, all with a speed which surprised him. Then, gripping the carbine in one hand, he too hauled himself on to a horse and rode after Lausard and the fleeing 'Barbets'.

Lausard knew he had to catch the running men before they reached the relative safety of the woods and he could see that his horse was gaining on the fugitives. The animal splashed through the stream, almost stumbled, but then went on, closing the gap on the fleeing men. Lausard raised his sword and drew alongside the closer of the two men, swinging his sabre down with great power, catching the man across the shoulders, a blow which sent him flying. He hit the ground and rolled over moaning in agony, his cries rising to screams of terror as Sonnier rode over him, the horse trampling the body beneath its hooves.

The second Barbet had almost reached the woods. He turned and fired his pistol at Lausard, who actually heard the ball whistle past his ear. Then the horse slammed into the guerrilla, knocking him to the ground. He hit the ground hard but, despite being dazed, tried to clamber to his feet. Lausard leaped from the animal's back and hurled himself at the disorientated man, driving the pommel of his sword into his face. The man dropped to his knees and Lausard kicked him hard in the stomach. He went down, curled into a foetal position.

Sonnier approached seconds later.

'Watch him,' ordered Lausard.

Sonnier raised his carbine to his shoulder and aimed it at the fallen fugitive.

Lausard went back to the first man, prodding the body with the toe of his boot. He was still alive but for how much longer Lausard could only guess. What his sabre cut had started, the hooves of Sonnier's horse had all but finished. Blood was running freely from his mouth and nose, and he was clutching his stomach. Lausard guessed that the hooves must have caused some internal damage. The man would be no use to them.

Lausard ran his sword through the guerrilla's throat.

He went back towards the other guerrilla, who was still lying on the ground with Sonnier's carbine pointed at him. Lausard hauled him to his feet, aware now that the gunshots and sounds of panic from the camp had died away. Even the horses had quietened down, their exhortations now limited to the odd whinny. He could hear many voices.

The Barbets had obviously fled, disappearing back into the night like spectres. All except the one he now had a firm grip on. Lausard heard more horses coming towards him and he saw Deschamps, an officer he recognised as Lieutenant Royere and two troopers riding closer. Deschamps and Royere dismounted and approached Lausard and his captive.

'They killed six horses,' Deschamps told him. 'Four more will have to be destroyed.'

He regarded the captured guerrilla angrily.

'Ask him where he's from,' he instructed Royere, who did so in faultless Italian. 'Which village?'

The man muttered something under his breath then spat on the ground in front of Royere.

The lieutenant didn't react but simply repeated the question.

The guerrilla rasped a few words at him, leering into the Frenchman's face. Lausard took a step forward as if to restrain him but the officer merely held up a hand as if to dismiss the gesture.

'He said he hopes we all rot in hell,' Royere said, not taking his eyes from the prisoner.

'Ask him if he's seen any Austrians,' Deschamps instructed.

Royere repeated the question in Italian.

The man merely smiled.

He said something and, again, Royere's expression did not change.

'He won't cooperate, sir,' the lieutenant said.

Deschamps nodded and, with one fluid movement, Royere pulled his pistol free, pressed it to the man's temple and fired. From such close range, the guerrilla's entire face was blackened by the pistol's discharge, one portion of his skull staved in by the ball as surely as if he'd been hit with a red-hot hammer. The body rolled over and ended up face down in the stream.

'Post extra sentries,' said Deschamps. 'We move out at dawn.'

CHAPTER 19

Bonaparte saw the cloud of dust before he saw the horseman.

He rose slowly from his seat and placed one hand over his eyes to shield them from the sun, squinting into the distance to try to pick out the image hidden beneath the dense clouds of dust.

Beside him, Colonel Joachim Murat reached for his telescope, extended it and watched through the eye-piece.

The rider was dressed in a dark blue dolman jacket and matching breeches. A red cloth 'wing' flapped behind him as he rode, wrapped around his conical mirliton cap.

'Hussar,' said Murat quietly, handing the glass to Bonaparte, who fixed the rider in the single eye of the telescope.

As the hussar drew nearer, those infantry who were resting close by the road lifted their headgear into the air and cheered the speeding horseman as he swept past them. His horse was badly lathered, its tongue lolling from one side of its mouth.

The rider rode on through other troops, past a unit of horse artillery who were trying to manoeuvre a four-pounder into position on its limber, struggling to secure the cannon. The men were sweating profusely beneath the burning sun.

Bonaparte handed the telescope back to Murat as he saw the hussar heading up the hill towards his position. He could now see the man clearly. He was young, barely out of his teens, his hair long and plaited as was the manner of the hussars. He had the beginnings of a moustache but certainly nothing to compete with some of the massive growths sported by these most flamboyant of cavalrymen. Some of the younger troopers, unable to grow a sufficiently impressive moustache, had been known to blacken their top lips with burned cork until the sought-after facial hair appeared. As he rode, his black leather sabretache flapped behind him and Bonaparte could hear the harness jingling madly as he closed to within a few yards, tugging hard on the reins to halt his mount.

The hussar leaped from the saddle and almost over-balanced, such was his eagerness to reach Bonaparte. His jacket was soaked with sweat, great dark rings of it fanning out from beneath both arms and soaking through the back of his dolman. He wiped sweat from his eyes and saluted.

Bonaparte returned the gesture.

'I have news from General Massena, sir,' said the trooper breathlessly and he fumbled inside his jacket for a piece of paper, which he presented to Bonaparte.

Bonaparte read it swiftly, the expression on his face darkening.

'The Austrians have attacked at Voltri,' he said, not

taking his eyes from the paper. 'Two columns attacked Cervoni's brigade.'

'What damage?' Murat asked.

'It doesn't say what casualties he sustained, only that he managed to organise a retreat,' Bonaparte said, handing the piece of paper to his companion.

The hussar was still standing to attention before the general, still sucking in great lungfuls of air, sweat pouring from his face.

'Did you come from Voltri?' Bonaparte asked him.

'Yes, sir,' the exhausted horseman answered and, for the first time, Bonaparte noticed that there was blood on the man's uniform, some splashed on his left arm and breeches.

'Are you wounded?' the general enquired, pointing at the blood.

'That's not my blood, sir,' he answered, again sucking in a deep breath. 'Sir, General Massena requests orders immediately. He thinks he should move his troops to block the attack on Voltri.'

'No!' snapped Bonaparte. He looked towards Murat. 'The Austrians have shown their hand too soon. They have revealed their position.' He looked at the hussar. 'I need you to ride back to General Massena now. Can you do that?'

'If you will oblige me with a fresh horse, sir, I will go immediately.'

Bonaparte smiled, watching as the hussar pulled his saddle, complete with its sheepskin shabrack, from his exhausted animal and hurriedly flung it over the back of a small chestnut horse which had been brought over by Murat.

In a matter of moments the hussar was ready. He

swung himself into the saddle, took the order from Bonaparte and rode off.

'The Austrians thought they would take me by surprise,' Bonaparte said, watching the hussar galloping back down the slope and on to the road. 'They will see what a surprise I have for them.'

The road on which Lausard and his companions travelled seemed to be the only one in Italy capable of accepting the passage of troops and equipment. At least that was the way it felt to Lausard when he saw the number of men clogging it. During their march they had passed all kinds of infantry, most of them in the same ragged state they always appeared to be in. Some at least had shoes, a few even wore gaiters too, but the majority were barefoot as usual. One man, in a pair of cavalry boots which were clearly too small for him, walked as though each step were painful but, Lausard guessed, his feet were probably so swollen by now, it was impossible to remove the boots anyway. Other men had simply wrapped pieces of cloth around their feet. Some carried their jackets over their shoulders or slung atop their packs but this did little to alleviate their suffering beneath the sun which was still burning ferociously in a clear azure sky. Others merely trudged on, sweat pouring from them, some with muskets sloped, others dragging them by their straps. Those who *had* weapons were among the lucky ones. Whether those weapons had powder, ball or flint, Lausard didn't know. They had heard a rumour earlier in the day that the thousand men of Augereau's division had no firearms at all. Lausard himself, like most of the men in his regiment, carried twenty-five rounds, although Rostov and Joubert had traded some cartridges for biscuits with an infantry unit they'd passed not too far back.

However, for the most part, the woefully equipped foot soldiers moved with a speed and purpose that their commanders had little right to expect. They had suffered badly during the last year or so, desperately short of food and supplies, driven more by their hunger and desire to plunder than any revolutionary ideals. They didn't care for the politics of the war. Ethics and morality were for those 'pekinese' back in Paris; these men wanted nothing more than a good meal and the chance to gather some riches for themselves. If they had to fight battles to get those things, then so be it.

Lausard guided his horse carefully past three foot soldiers who were marching close to the roadside, aware of their glances up at him.

'New boys,' said one of the infantry, chuckling. 'Look at their uniforms. Not even a dust mark.'

'You'll have more than dust marks when we run into the Austrians,' quipped another.

'They're pretty, but not as pretty as the hussars,' said another infantryman, a large man with a thick growth of beard.

'The hussars,' snorted another. 'Those peacock bastards.'

A chorus of laughter rippled through those troops within earshot.

'Have you any spare powder?' one of the infantrymen asked Delacor, pulling at the cavalryman's stirrup.

'What are you offering in exchange?' Delacor asked.

'I haven't got much but—'

'Then I've got no powder,' Delacor snapped, pulling his foot away.

The infantryman overbalanced and almost fell as he stepped back, avoiding Delacor's horse which bumped him.

One of the other foot soldiers slapped the beast's flank and it reared up suddenly. Delacor was fortunate to remain in the saddle as the bay rose on to its hind legs. He gripped the bridle and managed to bring the animal under control but its sudden movement startled a handful of other horses close by.

'You bloody fool!' snapped Carbonne at the infantryman, who merely spat in his direction.

'He started it,' snarled one of the other foot soldiers, pointing at Delacor. 'You bastards are all the same. You think you're better than us. Well, you'll find out when you get into battle, it's not so easy to hide when you're on a horse.'

'Is that what you do during a battle then?' asked Lausard. 'Hide?'

The cavalrymen nearby laughed.

'You think you're a funny man,' the infantryman said. 'See if you're still laughing when you've got an Austrian bayonet up your arse.'

It was the foot soldiers turn to laugh.

'You let us do the dirty work then you ride in and take the glory,' the infantryman said scornfully. 'All of you bastards are the same.'

'Not all of us,' Lausard told him and guided his horse back towards the head of the column.

Ahead, blocking the road was an artillery train made up of four eight-pounder guns, their limbers and two caissons. A wheel had come off one of the ammunition carts and five blue-coated gunners were trying desperately to fix it while a sergeant bellowed at them. The barrels of the cannon sparkled in the sunlight.

Lausard watched as Deschamps and Royere took their horses past the stranded caisson, finding enough room to bypass it on the narrow road. Lausard waited a moment then spurred his own mount on, followed by Rocheteau and Giresse. The remainder of the men did likewise and soon the entire regiment was slipping past the cursing gunners who were still struggling manfully with the wheel. Lausard guessed that it would be another hour or more of struggling along this cramped, overcrowded road before the order to halt would finally be given.

They set up camp on a gentle slope overlooking a valley dense with trees. Several small streams snaked along the valley floor. The slope opposite was also thickly wooded. Beyond it, they all knew, the Austrians waited.

Lausard stood gazing at the far slope, squinting in the dying rays of the sun, one hand cupped over his eyes as he peered towards the opposite ridge. He could see figures moving there.

'Are they getting ready for us?'

The voice startled him and he looked around to see that Rocheteau had joined him and was also gazing in the direction of the figures on the distant ridge. He drew a telescope from his tunic pocket, pulled it to its furthest extension and began looking through it.

'Where did you get that?' Lausard asked.

'I took it off one of those deserters back at Villa Borghese.' Rocheteau said, passing him the instrument.

The troops moving about on the opposite ridge were, without any doubt, Austrians; their white jackets and breeches marked them out as such. But those in white jackets seemed to be outnumbered by those in brown.

'Artillery,' murmured Lausard, his observation confirmed when he saw six limbers being dragged into place by teams of horses, these guns in turn being manhandled into position by the brown-coated troops, the barrels facing the French position. Half-a-dozen six-pounders were arrayed along the ridge.

'They're not going to make it easy for us, are they?' Rocheteau mused, watching the guns.

'We're all going to be killed.' Joubert had joined them.

'Thank you for that cheerful thought, fat man,' Rocheteau said.

Lausard handed the telescope back to his companion, his attention caught by something much closer than the Austrians. Along the floor of the valley, two French demi-brigades were setting up camp and Lausard could hear their officers and NCOs shouting orders.

'There will be a battle tomorrow, won't there?' Joubert asked warily.

Lausard nodded.

'Our first battle,' Rocheteau echoed, his voice a little more solemn than usual. 'It makes you wish we were back in Paris, doesn't it, Alain?'

'No,' said Lausard, 'at least here we're free.'

'I didn't mean in prison, I meant—'

'I know what you meant. And I'd still rather be here than living like a rat in a sewer. We weren't free when we lived on the streets, we were just a different kind of prisoner.'

Rocheteau looked at him in bewilderment for a second then patted his shoulder. 'Perhaps you're right.'

'Charvet and Tabor are collecting wood for a fire,' said Rostov, coming up alongside. Then his attention was also drawn to the activity on the opposite ridge. More guns had been dragged into place, all barrels pointing towards the French. A number of camp fires had sprung up on the slope too as the Austrians tried to make themselves more comfortable.

'Do you think they're as scared as we are?' Joubert asked.

'Everyone's scared,' said Rostov. 'If they've got any sense. No man wants to die.'

Lausard didn't answer, he merely continued gazing at the Austrians. Below him, more infantry had arrived and were setting up camp. He estimated that there were close to fifteen hundred of them, perhaps more.

'I hope Bonaparte knows what he's doing,' Rocheteau said under his breath.

'Do you doubt our General?' Lausard asked and smiled.

'Ask me this time tomorrow.'

The sun sank a little lower in the sky, the heavens began to turn the colour of blood.

'"Soldiers. You are hungry and naked; the government owes you much but can give you nothing. The patience and courage which you have displayed among these rocks are admirable; but they bring you no glory. Not a glimmer falls upon you. I will lead you into the most fertile plains on earth. Rich provinces, opulent towns, all shall be at your disposal; there you will find honour, glory and riches. Soldiers of Italy, will you be lacking in courage or endurance?"'

Lausard watched and listened as the proclamation was read out by the aide-de-camp. The man was dressed in a dark blue hussar uniform with a red pelisse slung around his shoulders. The golden braid both on his dolman and pelisse seemed to gleam in the light of the setting sun, as though strips of precious metal had been stitched to the material. His uniform was undirtied by the dust of the roads, his boots sparkling; even his spurs glinted.

Lausard looked down at his own boots. They were two-toned where the dust and grime clung so thickly to them. Even his jacket carried a thin sheen of dust, making it look grey instead of green. He patted the sleeves to remove the choking particles.

All around stood the men of his regiment; they had been joined by infantrymen, sappers, artillerymen, even the farriers were present. These men cheered every so often and the aide paused, smiling sometimes at the raucous reaction garnered by the proclamation, but he continued reading, perched high on an artillery caisson.

'"You will fight a battle tomorrow which will open up the gates of Piedmont,"' the aide continued. '"I will lead you through those gates and on to glory and riches. I will be with you tomorrow, every one of you, at your side as you fight and together we will win a glorious victory. Your General, Napoleon Bonaparte."'

A huge cheer greeted the end of the reading and the aide looked around at the sea of faces as if he personally was enjoying the adulation, then he stepped down from the ammunition wagon and climbed on to his horse.

'Vive Bonaparte!' someone shouted and the cry was taken up by others.

Lausard looked on in silence, watching as some of his companions joined in the cheering.

Charvet even lifted his brass helmet up on the end of his sword and raised it into the air.

Gaston looked on with bewilderment, pushing his helmet back on his head.

'He's going to get us all killed,' grunted Delacor. 'Why cheer him?'

'It's thanks to Bonaparte that you've still got your head,' Bonet told him. 'If the army hadn't needed men, we'd still be in prison now.'

'*He'd* have had your head,' said Rocheteau, pointing at Carbonne and grinning.

The bald man didn't seem to be listening. Like Charvet he had lifted his helmet high into the air on the tip of his sword and was cheering wildly. The former executioner was shouting Bonaparte's name at the top of his voice.

Tabor began clapping but he wasn't really sure why. He was grinning maniacally, his huge hands slapping together excitedly.

Through a crowd of troopers, Lausard saw Sergeant Delpierre heading down the slope. He was chewing on a piece of tobacco.

Lausard took a step across towards him, forcing the older man almost to collide with him.

'Not joining in the celebrations?' Lausard said, staring at the other sergeant.

'I don't need to jump about like some girl,' Delpierre hissed. 'I *know* we'll win. You just make sure you do as you're told.'

'You have no authority over me,' Lausard snapped. 'We're of equal rank now, remember?'

'There'll be nowhere to hide tomorrow. Not for you or any of your scum.'

'I won't be hiding and neither will they. Where will you be, Delpierre?'

As Delpierre leaned close to him Lausard could smell the tobacco on his breath.

'I'll be right beside *you*, Lausard. If you feel steel in your back,' he snapped, 'you'd better check if it's Austrian or not.'

Lausard's eyes narrowed, but he held his tongue.

The two men glared at each other for a moment longer then Delpierre disappeared into the still cheering crowd.

'What did that bastard want?' asked Rocheteau.

'Nothing important.'

The cheering of Bonaparte's name was still going on. It had grown to almost deafening proportions by now but Lausard seemed unmoved by the show of adulation. He made his way slowly back up the slope.

Despite the fact that the slopes and the valley floor were seething with men, Lausard might as well have been alone. He glanced at faces as he passed, looking indifferently at them, sometimes even at men from his own regiment.

The sky had darkened and the glow of camp fires lit the ridges on both sides of the valley. In the middle, where the stream criss-crossed, the tree-filled floor was a black void. Lausard thought that it resembled an enormous open grave. He suspected that, the following day, that was precisely what it would become.

CHAPTER 20

Lausard couldn't remember the last time he'd watched the sun rise. He began to wonder if he would ever again see it perform its unstoppable climb into the heavens, spreading light, banishing the night and ushering in a day of warmth and beauty. A sunrise, he mused, like a sunset, should be watched with a lover. He should be lying with a beautiful woman now, her head on his chest, his hand stroking her hair. Together they should be watching the beginning of a new day and savouring the joys it might bring.

He blinked hard, trying to shake himself from his musings. Rather than watching this sunrise with a lover he was watching it from the saddle of his horse, the smell of sweat and horses strong in his nostrils, and the day that was breaking held the promise not of joy and beauty but of pain and suffering.

He looked along the line of dragoons. He and his men had been mounted for over twenty minutes and the entire routine had been conducted in an eerie silence, broken only by the jingling of harnesses and the occasional whinny of a horse. The animals were also nervous and troopers tried to reassure them; troopers who themselves were feeling anything ranging from apprehension to pure terror, men who had never fought a battle in their lives and many shuddered to think this could be their first and last experience of one.

The regiment was drawn up in lines because of the slope. Once the order to advance was given, that linear formation would be transformed into a column, Lausard thought, although, looking at the terrain they would be forced to cross, an open-order advance might be more advisable.

Below them, already on the valley floor, the infantry waited in line, standards still lowered, drums still silent. Those in possession of bayonets already had them fitted. As with the cavalry, a curious, almost reverential silence lay over them like a blanket.

On the lower reaches of the slopes there was a little more activity. Six eight-pounder guns had been placed in position the previous evening and now Lausard watched as their corporals made last-minute adjustments to the screw-elevators at the sealed ends of the barrels. The effective range of an eight-pounder firing roundshot was about fifteen hundred yards. As the battle wore on, Lausard had no doubt that these guns would be moved closer to the Austrian positions.

Captain Deschamps was walking his horse back and forth before the waiting dragoons, Lieutenant Royere close behind him, the younger officer glancing across the valley every few seconds.

The sky was a beautiful shade of orange now, white clouds scudding across it, pushed by the light breeze which had risen with the sun.

'What the hell are they waiting for?' whispered Roussard from the rank behind.

Lausard glanced around at him and shrugged.

'What is this place called?' Tabor asked.

'Why?' snapped Delacor. 'Do you want to know where you're going to die?'

'It's beautiful,' Tabor continued, 'very beautiful. It reminds me of my home.'

'Shut up, you half-wit!' Delacor berated. 'We've got other things to think about now.'

Tabor seemed mesmerised by the sky and the slowly rising sun. 'So beautiful,' he repeated quietly.

Moreau calmed his horse as it pawed the ground with one hoof. He patted its neck then crossed himself.

Giresse scratched thoughtfully at his unshaven chin and gazed out over the valley. 'Tabor's right,' he said, 'it *is* beautiful.'

'There's a town over that opposite ridge called Montenotte,' Bonet informed them.

'Keep the noise down,' shouted an all-too-familiar voice from further along the line and Lausard glanced along to see Delpierre pointing at a couple of troopers close by him. Further along Sergeant Legier was gently patting his mount's neck.

'How much longer do we have to wait?' Roussard whispered, perspiration beading his forehead.

Lausard saw Deschamps and Royere train their telescopes on the far ridge but it was somewhere off to the west that his attention was drawn towards. A sound like distant thunder suddenly rolled across the landscape. It was followed by another rumble, then another.

A number of horses whinnied excitedly, their riders gripping the bridles tightly.

Moreau crossed himself again.

Rocheteau slipped his telescope from his jacket and peered through it at the opposite ridge.

'Nothing moving,' he said quietly then handed the glass to Lausard, who could see the Austrian gunners standing statue-like beside their cannons.

More rumbling came from the west. Lausard turned in his saddle and tried to see something in the direction of the sound but it was useless. Hills rose all around them.

He handed the telescope back to Rocheteau.

Down below there were shouts from the infantry officers and movement beneath the tricolours waving in the gentle breeze.

'I think the wait is over,' he murmured.

The roar as the French eight-pounders opened up was deafening. All six pieces opened up simultaneously, a great spout of fire erupting from each barrel as it hurled its projectile towards the enemy. Huge clouds of thick black and grey smoke suddenly spread across the ridge. The sound reverberated around the valley, ringing in the ears of man and horse alike.

A number of the animals reacted violently, rearing up and bucking wildly and at least eight men were thrown from their saddles. Lausard saw two more horses bolt from the line, their riders desperately trying to rein them in. NCOs roared orders and rebukes, trying to make themselves heard as the second salvo of cannon fire was unleashed.

Lausard himself gripped the reins as tightly as he could, his own horse unnerved by the thunderous explosions. The smoke covering the ridge was now thick and noxious like black man-made fog. The stench of sulphur was strong in the air.

The eight-man crews struggled to push the guns back into position after each round had been fired. The eight-pounder, weighing over a thousand pounds, was capable of moving backwards anything up to twelve feet after each discharge. The blue-coated crews manoeuvred the pieces back into their original positions and waited for the corporal to sight it, while the spongeman furiously cleaned the inside of the barrel with a damp swab. Lausard saw pieces of burning ember falling to the ground around the gun and he watched as another artilleryman hurriedly stamped on the dry grass which threatened to ignite like a tinder box.

Rocheteau's horse reared wildly in the noise and he was lucky to remain in the saddle as it kicked out its forelegs, but he held on and managed to calm the beast.

Gaston was gripping his reins tightly, pulling on them, trying to whisper encouragement to his mount, aware of how hard his own heart was thudding against his ribs.

A number of dismounted dragoons were chasing after their fleeing mounts. One soldier grabbed at the reins and managed to regain control of his animal but another trooper wasn't so lucky and was forced to chase his mount towards the valley floor. Both man and horse disappeared from sight in the thick smoke.

All down the line the process of reloading continued, and fresh balls were shoved into the barrels of the guns. Expert gunners could expect to fire two rounds a minute, sometimes three, depending on the size of the piece and the ammunition they were firing. But, because of the immense recoil and the need to re-sight the gun after each shot, the process was slower than anyone would have liked. It was strength-sapping, back-breaking work, all performed inside a shroud of reeking smoke which stung the eyes and parched the throat.

From the valley floor there was a new sound – the staccato rattle of drums. Through the drifting smoke Lausard saw that the infantry were beginning to advance. The tricolours were raised high and, even from such a distance, he heard shouts of '*Vive la République*'. This was met by a loud cheer. The cheering, the drumming and the shouts of officers all rose into one mighty crescendo of sound. It was eclipsed seconds later as the cannon opened fire once more.

Again horses panicked and their riders tried to calm them. More smoke rolled across the ridge, joining the fog which already hovered there, pushed like low-lying cloud by the breeze sweeping across the valley.

Throughout each eruption, Bonet's horse stood motionless, only tossing its head once or twice. He looked on in amazement as the animal calmly bent its head and began nibbling at the dry grass on the slope.

'I wish *I* felt that calm,' said Giresse, indicating the animal. He swallowed hard and managed a small smile.

Bonet nodded in agreement but couldn't return the smile.

Sonnier screwed up his eyes as a bank of smoke drifted over him, millions of tiny cinders floating in it, some sticking to his face. His horse was pawing the ground impatiently and then it emptied its bowels noisily. A number of animals had done the same and the stench of gunpowder now mingled with the stench of excrement and urine.

Lausard could smell his own sweat, some of which

he tried to reassure himself was from the heat of the day. The sun had now risen to a much higher point in the clear sky. Its light twinkled on the bayonets of the advancing infantry, at least those that Lausard could see through the stinking fog produced by the guns. So dense was the black and grey haze that it was impossible to see the far end of the line. Visibility was down to about one hundred yards unless the smoke was dispersed momentarily by a breeze and, always, there was that choking stench.

Rocheteau hawked and spat in an attempt to clear the smell and the cinders from his nose and mouth.

Roussard was coughing uncontrollably, waving one hand in front of his face as the black smog closed around him.

'What the hell is going on?' he said.

'A battle, you bloody idiot,' said Rocheteau. 'What do you think?'

Most of the horses were calming down now, growing a little more accustomed to the massive blasts which came from the cannons in front of them. Lausard reasoned that those animals which remained most unaffected were remounts that had taken part in battles prior to their capture by the French. His own horse seemed to have overcome its initial shock and was now grazing. Like its rider it waited.

The opposite ridge was hidden from view for the most part by the smoke from the French guns but Lausard and the others began to wonder how long it would be before the Austrians started firing back. Lausard felt a shiver run up the back of his neck. He saw, through a break in the smoke screen, Deschamps and Royere walking their horses across the ridge past the front of the regiment. Deschamps was pointing at something in the distance that Lausard couldn't see. The two officers both looked through their telescopes then were hidden as more smoke enveloped them.

In the valley the infantry were approaching the first of the small streams which criss-crossed the valley floor, wading through the knee-high water with ease, splashing almost gleefully in the cool liquid before moving up a gentle slope towards some trees. Officers ran before them, urging them on, and the drums continued to rattle.

Ahead of the main body of men the voltigeurs raced, a body of sharpshooters who would try to pick off enemy gunners and officers once they were close enough.

The infantry had already manoeuvred into columns and they continued their steady advance, urged on by officers and NCOs and the constant shouts of encouragement which they themselves bellowed as if to reassure themselves and their comrades.

'Advance.'

Lausard heard the order, saw Deschamps standing in his stirrups to signal the movement and, as one, the dragoons began to move forward down the slope. Like everyone else, Lausard felt his heart begin to beat that little bit faster.

Bonet's heart was thudding so hard against his ribs he feared it would burst.

Moreau crossed himself.

'So this is it,' Rocheteau said, swallowing hard.

Lausard didn't answer, his eyes were fixed ahead. He and his comrades rode past the sweating artillerymen who were busily reloading their pieces.

'Good luck!' called a corporal, his face drenched, his skin blackened by powder. 'Give them hell.'

'We're going to die, aren't we?' Roussard said, his voice shaky, his breath coming in gasps.

Lausard didn't look at him, he simply shook his head almost imperceptibly and murmured, 'Some of us.'

He saw Deschamps and Royere ahead of him, their horses walking, apparently unconcerned.

Beside him Rocheteau was clutching his horse's reins tightly and gazing ahead.

Gaston looked around him at the pale faces of his companions, some of their expressions showing naked fear.

Rostov's features looked as if they were set in stone. The Russian sat upright in his saddle, sword bumping against his boot.

Lausard guessed that there was something like a thousand yards between the two ridges and he looked up towards the waiting enemy gunners, who were now swarming around their guns like flies round rotten fruit.

Up ahead, the infantry were quickening their pace, the drums beating with an ever-increasing tempo. It seemed to match the beating of Lausard's heart.

High above, the sky was clear, the last of the cloud having been burned away by the sun. It was going to be a beautiful day.

The Austrian guns opened up.

CHAPTER 21

A series of dull thuds followed by distant puffs of smoke was how the opening Austrian volley looked to Lausard as he guided his somewhat skittish horse across the stream. The enemy guns were still out of range as far as he could tell. Nevertheless, the very sight of them finally being brought into action was enough to send shivers up and down many spines, not least that of Roussard who watched the Austrian gun crews realigning their cannon. To him they seemed to be moving twice as quickly as the French gunners and, indeed, a moment later, another volley of roundshot came into the valley.

A few hundred yards ahead the infantry continued to advance, covered by the hordes of voltigeurs who as yet had not fired a shot. They darted back and forth, seeking cover behind rocks and trees, even ditches in the ground.

Lausard could still hear the beating of the drums and the shouts of the officers, even above the jingling of so many harnesses. To his left and right he saw that the line was breaking up in places as dragoons forced their mounts over the increasingly uneven terrain.

They were roughly halfway across the valley by now and – in addition to the cannon ahead of them – they could still hear the occasional rumbles off to the west as General La Harpe's men attacked the Austrians from the other side, their advance having started a little earlier.

Up ahead the infantry were coming into range.

Three roundshot struck the ground ahead of the leading line of foot soldiers. The first buried itself in the hard earth, the second hit a rock, shattered it, then rolled harmlessly into a ditch, but the third ploughed into the men with terrible results.

The men hit seemed to disintegrate, their bodies squashed; blood sprayed in all directions, spattering those nearby and slowing many men in their tracks, but the drums seemed to beat only louder, the officers to exhort more vociferously. The advance continued as more of the deadly balls began to find their mark.

Another struck the ground and ricocheted up again taking out three men.

A spent ball rolled towards the advancing cavalry, the iron covered in blood.

Lausard looked down at it, knowing that they themselves were in range now.

Fifty feet ahead there was an explosion and several men were catapulted into the air by the impact, their screams of agony audible above all other sound. Lausard realised that the Austrian gunners were firing shells as well as roundshot. The fuse on them was usually timed to burn for five seconds but sometimes they would explode in mid air, sometimes they would roll around on the ground for a while before detonating. However they worked, they were lethal.

Lausard looked again to his right and left. He saw Moreau cross himself and glance briefly towards the sky which was as clear as he'd ever seen it. A deep azure blue.

A roundshot struck a small tree less than twenty feet to the right, the metal ball smashing the trunk and bringing the tree down. It crashed to earth and a number of horses nearby reared up in fear.

'They're getting closer,' hissed Giresse, gripping his reins ever more tightly. A cloud of thick smoke from the explosion enveloped them and Lausard found that he had to guide his horse slightly to the left to prevent it stepping on the torn and bloodied corpse of an infantryman.

'Jesus Christ!' murmured Sonnier, gaping at what little was left of the soldier. He felt his stomach contract and looked away, the smell of gunpowder now strong in his nostrils as the smoke continued to drift across the valley floor.

'Where is your God now?' Delacor shouted at Moreau, pointing at the dead infantryman.

Moreau was about to answer when a roundshot struck the ground ahead of the advancing dragoons. It spun up and slammed into his horse. The animal let out a squeal of pain and fell in an untidy heap, both its front legs shattered by the impact. Moreau was thrown from the saddle as the animal went down and as he rolled over he felt its warm blood splash his face and neck.

The dying animal crashed into Delacor's mount, bringing it down too. Delacor hit the ground hard and rolled over groaning, clutching at his side, trying to scramble to his feet to avoid the oncoming hooves of his companions' horses. His own horse was up in seconds, leaping to its feet, bucking wildly and Delacor shot out a hand to grab its bridle.

To the right a shell landed and exploded with a deafening bang. Three dragoons were blasted from their saddles by the detonation, two horses went down, one dead before it hit the ground, its head almost severed by a lump of iron. Thick blood, of both animal and man, sprayed into the air and Lausard saw one of the dragoons lying on his back, stomach ripped open, screaming, but any sound was lost in the noise all around.

More thick black smoke drifted across the valley floor.

Moreau grabbed at the reins of a riderless horse as it passed and he managed, more by luck than judgement, to halt the frightened animal. He quickly swung himself into the saddle and looked across to see that Delacor had already remounted. The two of them rejoined the advancing regiment, aware now of the popping and cracking of musket fire both from their own voltigeurs up ahead and also from some Austrian infantry on the ridge.

Lausard guessed there were about seven or eight hundred yards between them and the enemy now.

The infantry drummers quickened the pace of their tattoo, shouts became more frenzied and the cry suddenly went up 'En avant'.

The infantry charged.

'Hold!' roared Deschamps, galloping across the front of his anxious horsemen. His sword was already unsheathed. Lieutenant Royere galloped after him, his attention fixed on the ridge and on the attacking infantry.

The Austrian gunners redoubled their efforts as the French swept closer and began to load their cannon with case shot. The canisters full of metal balls waited like gigantic shotguns as the infantry charged closer, still protected by the constant harassing fire of their own sharpshooters.

The dragoons came to a halt in two ragged lines.

'What the hell are we waiting for?' Rocheteau called, watching as the infantry began to charge up the slope, the incline slowing their hectic advance slightly. Tricolours waved proudly in the breeze. A number of the infantry had raised their bicorn hats up on the tips of their bayonets.

'Let the Austrians use up their ammunition on those fools,' said Delacor, nodding towards the infantry who were now less than one hundred yards from the waiting cannon.

Lausard watched intently as the waves of blue-clad troops rushed towards the Austrians. The beating of the drums had ceased, lost now beneath the cacophony of shouts and cries, some of fear because the infantry were less than fifty yards from the mouths of the cannon and they knew what the gunners were waiting for.

The six-pounders opened up with a deafening roar, spewing their lethal loads of case shot at the infantry who were struck at point-blank range. Dozens went down in the hail of metal, and those who didn't fall were splattered with the blood of fallen comrades. A tricolour fell from the hands of its bearer, the man having lost most of his face and the left side of his head. More willing hands snatched it up and carried it forward over ground now stained with the life fluid of dead and dying.

As if angered by the loss of so many of their companions, the blue-clad infantry threw themselves on the Austrian guns, using their bayonets on those gunners who had not turned and fled.

The first Austrian infantry column moved up to the crest of the ridge to meet the frenzied attack of the French, and Lausard watched as it moved ponderously into line in an attempt to fire. But the men in white tunics were shaken by the ferocity of the French attack; with musket fire peppering their own lines from the dozens of sharpshooters still swarming over the ridge, they couldn't unleash a complete volley. There was a series of loud bangs as several units managed to discharge their muskets into the French but it seemed to have little effect and now the French themselves were forming lines and firing back volleys.

The dragoons, from their position at the base of the ridge, sat in virtual silence watching as the foot soldiers battled. Moreau wiped blood from the pommel of the horse he'd acquired.

Gaston thought how alike were the colour of the blood and the hue of his own jacket. He shuddered involuntarily.

Other officers had joined Deschamps and Royere to look at the unfolding action through telescopes. Deschamps was motioning towards a depression in the ridge off to the right, beyond the extent of the Austrian line.

Rocheteau also saw the gaggle of officers and said: 'Do you think they'll send us?' He struggled to keep his frightened horse calm.

Before Lausard could answer there was a rumbling from behind them and the men turned to see three of the eight-pounders being hauled towards the Austrian ridge on their limbers, the horses straining under the effort of pulling. Artillerymen ran alongside, urging the animals on, occasionally helping to manoeuvre the cannon over particularly awkward stretches of ground.

The guns passed and continued up the slope to where the Austrian and French infantry were still facing each other, still firing into each other's massed ranks but Lausard could see that the white-coated Austrians were giving ground, falling back towards another steeper ridge about five hundred yards behind their first position. Smoke was lying thickly over the battlefield now, twisting and swirling around the fighting men.

'This waiting is driving me insane,' said Delacor.

'You're already insane,' Bonet retorted.

'Shut up, schoolmaster.'

'I'd rather be sitting here than stuck in the middle of that lot,' said Roussard, nodding towards the battle on the ridge.

'Why don't they get it over with?' Rocheteau wanted to know. 'Let's go now.'

Lausard shook his head. 'Soon,' he whispered under his breath, eyes still riveted to the infantry duel.

The eight-pounders had unlimbered by now and as he watched they fired a withering salvo into the tightly packed Austrian ranks, turning many of the white tunics red.

The column wavered then began to split.

It was becoming difficult to see what was going on, so great was the thickness of smoke. The dragoons were aware only of reeking black and grey clouds, the rattle of musket fire and the occasional roar of a cannon.

Deschamps emerged from a bank of smoke no more than ten feet from Lausard and he heard him roar the order for the dragoons to advance but, once more, it was a leisurely walk not a charge. Lausard felt cheated as he led his horse forward towards the fighting. He wanted Deschamps to give the order; he wanted to be sent at the Austrians riding at full tilt. It seemed it was not to be.

They advanced up the slope, many of them unable to prevent their horses stepping on the bodies of the dead and wounded.

An infantryman with one arm blown off below the elbow covered his head with his remaining hand as the horses passed. Another was sitting gazing down at a hole in his stomach. One of his hands was clutched to the wound while the other hand held that of a man who seemed to be little more than a mass of crimson from head to foot. As the soldier lay on the grass, his life blood seeping from him, he nodded at Lausard as he passed and the sergeant respectfully returned the gesture.

Parts of the parched hillside had been burned black, the dry grass which grew there so sparsely having been incinerated by fallen used cartridges. The smell of burned wood mingled with the coppery odour of blood, the stench of both human and animal excrement and the ever-present choking stink of gunpowder.

As the dragoons moved further up the ridge the smoke became thicker and the noise almost intolerable. Horses became more nervous. One reared, threw its rider and fell backwards, crashing into three more troopers behind.

Lausard heard horses' hooves away to his left but he could barely see where Royere was taking two squadrons of dragoons, leading them away at a canter. He and his companions continued to advance at a walk, through another curtain of fumes which nearly blinded them.

They passed an Austrian six-pounder which had been overturned by the French infantry.

To his right, one of the eight-pounder crews was limbering up again, attaching the cannon to the wooden wagon which transported it. Lausard thought that the horses which pulled it barely looked up to the task, the drivers perched precariously on their skinny backs. Most of the crew drivers were civilian contractors, even more reluctant to be on a battlefield than many of the troops who now surrounded him.

More bodies littered the top of the ridge and in many places the ground was slicked with blood. Screams of the wounded were inaudible over the crash of battle and those not shrieking in pain were crawling from body to body, desperately trying to find water in an unused canteen.

A breeze suddenly swept a particularly thick bank of smoke away and Lausard saw Austrian troops no more than five hundred yards away. And they had broken. The centre and left of the line still seemed to be holding firm but many of the white-coated troops were fleeing.

He felt a sudden surge of adrenaline pump through his body. The hair at the nape of his neck stiffened and he drew in a deep breath.

'Draw swords!' roared Deschamps, rising in his saddle.

The sound of hundreds of sabres being pulled from

their scabbards reminded Lausard of the hissing of a thousand snakes.

'At last,' he murmured, glancing at Rocheteau who looked back at him blankly, his own face already stained with powder and greasy with sweat.

'Advance by squadron,' shouted Deschamps. 'Trumpeters, sound the charge.'

Gaston, like the other seven trumpeters, did as he was ordered and the ring of the notes began to fill the air, rising above the shouts, screams, gunshots and jingling harnesses.

The dragoons moved off at a trot, their speed building gradually to a canter. This was what Lausard had dreamed of, what he had sought.

The canter increased to a gallop over the last two hundred yards, the sound of thundering hooves the only sound anyone seemed to be aware of. Swords glinted in the sunlight which also struck their brass helmets. As if caught up in the excitement of the charge the horses whinnied, eyes rolling in their sockets.

The Austrians had neither time nor opportunity to form squares to protect themselves from the sudden attack.

The front line of dragoons crashed into them and rode them down.

Lausard struck to his left and shaved off the ear of an infantryman.

He struck again, using all his strength to cut down through the shako of an Austrian, a blow which cut the headgear cleanly in two before ploughing into the top of the man's skull.

Other fleeing troops were trampled to death by the churning hooves of the French horses.

Rostov drove his sword down, skewering an officer through the cheek.

Delacor slashed at a running man's back and caught him across the nape of the neck, the blow causing him to stagger in front of his attacker. What the sword cut had begun, the hooves finished.

One or two Austrians turned and tried to protect themselves but it was futile. The sheer bulk of the horses was too much for them and those not cut down by swords were buffeted and crushed.

A corporal drove his bayonet at Charvet in a desperate attempt to defend himself but Charvet knocked the weapon to one side and slashed the man across the face.

Even Lausard's horse was snapping and biting at the Austrians as they ran, and Lausard cut down two more of the white-coated troops.

They rode over a small ridge, urged on by Deschamps but barely needing any encouragement. It was as if Lausard's frenzy had infected all the men around him.

A ripple of bangs sounded as a line of Austrian troops opened fire.

A number of horses were hit.

One close to Lausard went down, somersaulted and threw its rider from the saddle. Another fell sideways, crashing into those following, causing more to stumble and fall, many unseating their riders.

Roussard guided his horse over a tangle of struggling men and horses, urging the animal to leap the mêlée, which it did, landing surefootedly and charging on.

Rocheteau heard a loud clang and realised that one

of the musket balls had struck his helmet just above the crown. Allowing himself a brief sigh of relief, he rode on towards the line of Austrians, who were trying to reload. Only a handful managed it before the dragoons crashed into them. The volley they unleashed did little damage but Lausard saw more horses fall and, to his right, a dragoon was struck in the eye by one of the balls. He toppled backwards out of the saddle. Another clutched at his chest, his horse careering across the front of the charging dragoons, its dying rider still upright in the saddle.

The last few Austrians were ridden down, their screams lost beneath the thundering of hooves, a sound which was now mingling with the roar of cannon and the shouts of charging infantry.

'They're running!' bellowed Lausard, striking at another opponent.

The Austrians had broken.

All over the ridge and beyond, white-uniformed troops were fleeing for their lives, most of them throwing away their muskets. Some tried to surrender but many were just ridden down or sabred. An officer tried one final futile stand and swung his sword at Lausard who slashed at the man, severing his hand at the wrist. The officer screamed as his hand went spinning into the air, still gripping his sword. Blood spouted from the stump as he turned to meet a thrust from Joubert, who was almost pulled from his saddle as his sword remained firmly embedded in his foe. The officer dropped to his knees, hunched over as if in prayer, the sword still stuck through him.

Deschamps, his face and jacket spattered with blood, shouted for the trumpeters to sound the recall, and

Gaston and the others began to blow furiously.

The charge began to falter as horses slowed down, reined in by their riders who felt an exhilaration unlike anything they'd ever felt before. Lausard was breathing heavily, from the exertion but also from excitement. His face was sheathed in sweat and blood, his breeches and saddle also spattered with gore. His horse had been cut across the hindquarters by a bayonet but the wound wasn't deep and the animal seemed untroubled by the gash.

Carbonne wiped blood from his eyes and realised that a musket ball had grazed his forehead.

Bonet was nursing a bruised knuckle where a spent ball had struck him on the hand but otherwise he was uninjured.

Royere galloped out of a smoke-bank looking at the dragoons, trying to appraise the damage. He saw Lausard and nodded, a thin smile hovering on his lips. Lausard returned the gesture and noticed that the officer was bleeding from a wound in his shoulder.

'Are you all right, sir?'

'It went straight through.' Royere touched the wound tentatively with a gloved hand. When he brought the hand away his fingers were slick with blood.

'Get that wound seen to,' Deschamps instructed him.

Royere nodded. 'The Austrians are falling back, sir,' he said, smiling.

Deschamps didn't answer. He nodded curtly, then turned to Sergeant Legier who had also ridden up, his own sword bloody, his horse limping slightly from a cut on its left forelock.

'Take number two squadron and follow them,'

Deschamps told Legier. 'I want them watched, not engaged. Send back reports every hour.'

Legier saluted and wheeled his horse away.

Only now did Royere finally slip forward slightly in his saddle and Lausard shot out a hand to support him.

'See that the Lieutenant gets that wound attended to, Sergeant Lausard,' Deschamps told him. 'I want every trooper ready to move out in six hours.'

'Those thieving bastards,' said Rocheteau, glaring at the infantry who were busily robbing the dead Austrians. 'Look at them.'

'Yes,' snapped Giresse. 'They will take everything.'

'There'll be nothing left for us,' Rocheteau said smiling. Both men dismounted, the corporal running towards a dead officer who was lying close by. He flipped the body over and began pulling the buttons free.

Giresse was going through the pack of a dead private, delighted when he found half a bottle of wine inside.

Other troopers were dismounting now, eager not to miss out on the bounty.

Lausard looked around him at the scavenging dragoons, leading Royere's horse with his free hand.

'Once a thief always a thief, eh, Lausard?' said the officer, smiling weakly. 'I think they've earned it, don't you?'

Lausard didn't answer.

The dead Austrian was in his early forties. A distinguished-looking man with a thick moustache and sideboards flecked with grey. His face was relatively unmarked, the wound which had killed him having been received to the back of his skull. In fact, both his eyes were still open and Delacor paused to peer into those lifeless pools as if fearing that the man was still watching him. He waited a moment as if mesmerised by the staring eyes then, gently, he reached forward and closed the lids. He moved away from the body, scuttling across to another Austrian who'd been killed by a musket ball which had struck him in the chest. Delacor swiftly and expertly went through his pockets and pack, coming up with some tobacco, a pair of socks and a piece of cheese wrapped in muslin. He took a bite before stuffing it into his own pack.

Several dragoons were shepherding some Austrian prisoners towards the French ridge, which was all but deserted now. The prisoners had been stripped of everything except their breeches and shirts and they trudged along, some with their hands behind their heads, some walking sullenly, others supporting injured comrades.

Lausard watched the dismal little procession from his saddle then allowed his gaze to drift once again over the ridge and the valley. The dead of both sides were being collected together by some infantrymen, who were dragging the corpses towards a series of large holes that had been dug in the rock-hard earth. Lausard guessed that none of the mass graves was deeper than about two or three feet, barely sufficient to cover the corpses and sure to attract scavengers. Every corpse was naked, clothes, equipment and personal effects having been taken by the burial parties. The clothes and weapons had been piled high into two wagons drawn by some scrawny-looking mules. General Augereau's division of a thousand men, who had no firearms, had been forced to advance anyway and the captured enemy muskets were to be distributed amongst them.

A French artillery crew was busily limbering up an Austrian six-pounder in preparation for it to be hauled away. A shortage of horses for the campaign had ensured that not only were the bulk of the cavalry understrength but also the artillery lacked horses. Lausard was beginning to wonder if there was anything which the Army of Italy was *not* lacking. And yet, despite these shortcomings, they had won their first victory under Bonaparte and, again, Lausard found a certain irony in his situation. He, the son of an aristocratic family forced to hide in the gutters of Paris, driven to fight and live alongside men he would normally have shunned, was fighting in an army commanded by a Corsican peasant who was forced to prove himself to older and so-to-say socially superior officers, many of whom resented both his youth and his lack of social skills.

He walked his horse slowly across the ridge, guiding it past one of the mass graves, through dry, burned grass, avoiding bodies where he could. The ground was spattered with blood, which had dried so quickly beneath the scorching sun that even the flies had enjoyed only a brief feast. They swarmed over the bodies of the dead, of course, but those too were hauled away as swiftly as possible.

The smoke had cleared but the air still smelled of spent cartridges. The slope was littered with musket balls and roundshot, pieces of blackened wadding and burned paper from so many cartridges. In the clear sky overhead a number of crows circled, waiting to descend on the dead when the opportunity presented itself.

The sun glinted off something golden in the dry grass ahead and Lausard dismounted to see what it was, surprised that anything of value had been left behind by his scavenging comrades. What he found fitted into the palm of his hand. At first he thought it was a watch but as he flipped it open he realised that it was a locket. An inscription in the lid read:

To My Dearest Karl With Love From Madelaine.

He inspected the tiny painting of a young woman, her features as delicate as porcelain, then he snapped the locket shut and slipped it into his pocket, wondering where the owner was now. Had he fled with the other Austrian troops? Was he lying wounded somewhere or had his body already been pushed into one of the mass graves? Lausard swung himself back into the saddle, his gaze scanning the ridge and beyond.

In the distance he could hear the occasional popping of musket fire but, other than that, the battlefield and its surrounding area was relatively quiet.

He saw Gaston and Rostov approaching, also walking their horses slowly across the scorched ridge. The young boy was wiping his head with the sleeve of his tunic, his brass helmet held beneath the other arm. He was gazing around at the activity, occasionally looking intently at one of the dead. Rostov seemed unmoved by it all, hardly blinking as two drummer boys helped a French infantryman, his right foot shattered, down the slope towards the temporary field hospital. There, a group of surgeons and their assistants did their best for the injured of both sides, although the remedies were at best rudimentary and at worst as lethal as the wounds themselves.

'Not joining the scavengers?' Lausard asked, pointing at the French troops still busily searching the pockets and packs of the dead.

'I took some bread from one of them,' the Russian told him. 'We shared it.' He nodded towards Gaston.

Lausard reached into his pocket and pulled out the locket, allowing the Russian to inspect it.

'She's a good-looking woman,' he said admiringly. 'I wonder who'll be keeping her company from now on?' He tossed the locket back to Lausard.

'How many do you think died here today?' Gaston asked.

Lausard could only shrug. 'Does it matter?'

'I was curious,' Gaston told him.

'Death makes men curious,' Lausard said. 'It makes us realise our own mortality.'

'Our first battle, our first victory,' Rostov said, a note of pride in his voice.

Lausard nodded. 'It certainly won't be our last,' he said quietly.

'You don't sound too disappointed, Alain,' Rostov observed.

Lausard shook his head almost imperceptibly.

CHAPTER 22

General Bonaparte raised his wine glass, a smile on his thin features.

'Hannibal crossed the Alps,' he said, looking around at his officers. 'We have outflanked them.' A chorus of approving murmurs and laughs greeted the remark and the other men drank their wine, enjoying the occasion, celebrating the toast with their commander.

'In fifteen days we have brought Piedmont to its knees,' the general continued. 'We have won battles at Montenotte, Millesimo, Dego and Mondovi. We have taken twenty-one colours, fifty-five pieces of artillery, captured fifteen thousand and killed or wounded ten thousand. All for the cost of six thousand of our own casualties. I tell you, gentlemen, we are only at the beginning.' He took another sip of wine. 'I have already written to the Directory asking for another ten thousand reinforcements. We will need them to complete our task.'

'You expect help from those bastards?' Augereau snapped at his commander.

'*They* are our government,' Bonaparte reminded him.

'They care nothing for us. They are as corrupt as the Bourbons were. They know nothing of what happens here.'

'They know what I tell them,' Bonaparte said. 'They know what I allow them to know.'

A ripple of laughter travelled around the men.

'Do they know that La Harpe's men mutinied?' Serurier asked, not looking at his commander.

'That was an unfortunate incident but one which could not have been avoided,' Bonaparte said dismissively. 'The problem has been rectified now.'

'They mutinied because they were not allowed to share in the looting of Mondovi,' the older man sneered. 'They behaved like common thieves, not soldiers.'

'Most of the army consists of thieves,' Massena offered. 'That includes officers too.'

There was more laughter.

Serurier did not join in. He shook his head wearily.

'The French army exists by foraging, you know that,' Bonaparte reminded him.

'And by stealing?'

'They haven't been paid for so long they've forgotten what sous look like,' Massena interjected.

'They're entitled to share in our victory by whatever means,' Bonaparte continued. 'They obey orders, they carry out my wishes. That is all I ask of *any* man.' He fixed Serurier in an unblinking stare. 'Loyalty.'

'So we buy their loyalty by letting them ravage the countryside?' Serurier snapped.

'We already have their loyalty, we don't *buy* that with bounty, we *instil* it with victory.'

'And where will our next victory come?' Augereau

wanted to know. 'We've beaten the Piedmontese, we've even beaten the Alps. How do we beat the river? That bastard could destroy us, even if the Austrians can't.'

'The Po is a fast-flowing river,' Massena added. 'It would be difficult enough to cross even without Beaulieu and his Austrians so close. We have no bridging train. We will have to cross at one of the established points and they are all guarded and fortified.'

'So, how the hell do we get over this river?' Augereau persisted, filling his glass again and looking down at the map spread out on the table before them.

'Not only must we cross it,' Bonaparte said, 'we must force Beaulieu to fight, to commit his forces, but he seems more intent on running.'

'The north bank is a stronger position,' Massena observed. 'He wants to meet us there.'

'So, where do we cross?' Augereau asked.

'There are three places,' Bonaparte informed him, turning his attention to the map. 'Here, at Valenza, is the closest. But it is also the most dangerous because it is nearest to the main Austrian force. We could move quickly but we run the risk of being attacked while we're crossing.'

'If the Austrians catch us strung out, crossing those bridges, they'll destroy us,' said Augereau.

Bonaparte ignored the other man's comment and pointed at another spot on the map. 'Or we could cross here, south of Pavia,' he said. 'If we do that, it puts us *behind* Beaulieu. We will disrupt his lines of communication but, again, the problem is that the main Austrian force is very close. I suggest we cross here, at Piacenza.'

'But that's fifty miles away,' Serurier said incredulously.

'And the Po is at its deepest and widest there,' added Augereau.

'It looks the most hazardous of all crossing points,' Massena offered.

Bonaparte smiled. 'If we cross there,' he said, 'we cross as close as possible to Milan itself and we also turn the three lines of defence which Beaulieu has prepared along the Agogna, the Terdoppio and the Ticino. Pavia will be turned and if Beaulieu chooses to defend it we will be between him and his supply depots.' He stood back smugly, eyes flicking across the faces of his companions.

'It's dangerous,' Augereau countered.

'Wherever we cross is dangerous.'

'But it's fifty miles away,' Serurier said.

'Speed and surprise will be our allies. The risks are worthwhile,' Bonaparte proclaimed. 'At worst we might force Beaulieu to retreat piecemeal which will make him easier to destroy. At best, we will catch his entire force and *make* him stand and fight.'

'I still think it's risky,' Serurier reiterated wearily.

'It is, but you and Massena will help deflect interest from our main force by distracting the Austrians into thinking you and your men are crossing at Valenza,' Bonaparte told him. 'We need that diversion.' He looked around at his officers. 'Have faith, gentlemen. Victory awaits us.'

CHAPTER 23

The explosion brought down three horses and sent several more dashing madly to one side where they collided with other riders.

Lausard felt himself thrown through the air. He hit the ground with a thud and rolled over, desperate to avoid his falling horse which whinnied in fear then scrambled back to its feet. It reared but did not run.

Lausard hauled himself to his feet, caught the reins of the terrified animal and steadied it, glancing around him briefly at the damage the Austrian shell had caused.

One of the trio of horses brought down was lying motionless and even a quick inspection revealed that it was dead, blood spouting from a wound in its neck. The other two were back on their feet, one bleeding from a gash on its flank, the other limping slightly, a piece of flying steel having cracked its left front hoof. The riders were relatively unscathed: one was clutching his forearm, cursing the pain and the blood which stained his green tunic; the second had lost his brass helmet and was staggering around looking for it; while the third had sustained nothing more than a split lip when he'd hit the ground.

Lausard remounted, watched by Rocheteau, who seemed reassured by the nod the sergeant gave him.

Another blast erupted about twenty yards to their left and the dragoons saw several infantrymen drop.

The Austrian cannon on the north bank of the Adda River were keeping up a steady fire with both shell and roundshot, their fire concentrated on the bridge across the river which linked the two parts of the town of Lodi. It was the only crossing point and would have to be stormed if the French were to progress. Through a rolling fog of smoke, Lausard counted six guns at the far end of the bridge itself and another three on either side, designed to catch any charging French troops in a withering enfilade fire when they chose to attack.

The French artillery fired back and Tabor watched as a four-pounder was loaded, fired and then thrown backwards with the recoil, its shell hurled towards the Austrians on the far bank. He saw the speeding black object strike its target and there was a massive explosion as an enemy artillery caisson blew up, a mushroom cloud of black and red smoke rising into the air.

A great cheer accompanied the blast and many of the infantry shouted words of encouragement as they waited their turn to assault the bridge. Flags, some shredded by fire, were held proudly aloft in the smoke-darkened air.

'It looks like Bonaparte did a good job,' said Rocheteau as another salvo of roundshot exploded from the French guns, all of the shots striking targets on the far bank. Austrian troops went down and the cheering of the French grew in volume.

'I wouldn't want to be the first one on to that bridge,' said Joubert, eyeing the formidable array of firepower which the Austrians had amassed.

'I'd rather swim the river,' Roussard added.

'At this rate we might have to,' Lausard said, his voice drowned out by another explosion nearby.

Lumps of earth and a cloud of dust came out of the sky to envelope the dragoons.

Gaston was almost knocked from his horse by a large piece of rock which banged against his helmet with an audible clang.

Rocheteau shot out a hand to support the boy who swayed uncertainly in his saddle for a moment before steadying himself.

Lieutenant Royere, his wounded shoulder bandaged, rode past. His voice was barely audible above the roar of cannon but he was signalling for the dragoons to follow him and the men at the front of the column duly did so, galloping across the path of the waiting infantry. Others looked with trepidation towards the bridge, knowing that they would soon be ordered to charge its bristling defences. They had driven the Austrians out of Lodi with relative ease earlier in the morning but the bridge presented a different obstacle altogether. Many felt a twinge of fear at the thought of charging across it into such furious fire.

'They'll be slaughtered,' Roussard remarked as the dragoons rode by.

'God help them,' echoed Bonet.

'If God's got any sense, He'll be far away from here,' Rostov said.

'He is here with us,' Moreau rebuked, 'He is always with us.'

'Then I wish He'd tell us what's going on,' Giresse said. 'Where are we going? If the bridge is the only way across that river why the hell are we riding away from it?'

'There must be fords up and down it somewhere,' Lausard called, glancing across the fast-flowing water. He caught sight of more Austrian troops arrayed on the opposite bank but then they began to disappear from view among the trees along the riverside. The steeples of two or three churches strained above the tree-tops but the houses of Lodi were effectively hidden behind the green. Smoke rose into the air though, drifting up into the blue sky from buildings which had been set ablaze by the continuing bombardment. Pulling clear of the main hub of the battle, the dragoons found themselves surrounded on both sides by heavily leafed trees. Occasionally there would be a break in the screen and the river would come into view once more but, otherwise, the sounds of fighting began to recede.

Lausard saw men moving in the trees up ahead. Blue- or red-jacketed troops. There was a number of horses too, some tethered, others standing obediently, chewing at the short grass on the bank.

'Hussars,' said Rocheteau, catching a better view. One of their officers was sitting by the roadside chewing contentedly on a piece of stale bread. He nodded perfunctorily towards Royere who reined in his horse, waving a hand to slow the following dragoons.

'We're looking for a ford,' Royere announced.

'What do you think we're doing?' the hussar officer asked, grinning. 'Picking daisies? There's no way across this damned river other than the bridge.'

'There has to be a shallower crossing point somewhere,' Royere insisted.

'Bonaparte's sent men in both directions to find one but it's a waste of time,' the hussar continued, chewing the last of his bread. 'Still, it keeps us out of the Austrian fire, doesn't it?'

Royere shook his head irritably and prepared to lead the waiting dragoons on.

'You'll find nothing further up the bank,' the hussar insisted.

'How far up have you checked?' Royere demanded.

The hussar shrugged. 'Far enough. Why not wait? Let the infantry take the bridge, we can cross in peace.' He laughed.

Royere didn't share the joke; he waved his hand for the dragoons to follow him and they galloped off along the riverside road, leaving the hussars behind.

'Perhaps he was right,' offered Rocheteau, glancing back at the hussar officer. 'Perhaps there is no ford.'

Lausard looked at his companion briefly. 'Then we might have to charge the bridge.'

Rocheteau held his sergeant's gaze for a second and found the steely look in his eyes almost unnerving.

They were approaching a bend in the road where the trees were not so dense, giving a clearer view of the river. Behind them, the sound of musket fire seemed to have intensified and Lausard guessed that the French infantry had begun its assault on the bridge. Smoke was still rising in clouds above the town, part of which had caught fire under the shelling.

Royere suddenly reined in his horse and waved a hand to halt the column.

Lausard watched as the officer pulled out a telescope and scanned the far bank.

The trees on the other side were also more sparse and, clearly visible amongst them, even without the benefit of a telescope, was a number of cavalrymen, some of whom were formed up into lines facing the river.

Royere surveyed the Austrian troops, trying to pick out exactly which type of men he was facing. Most carried carbines and their grey uniforms marked them out as mounted hussars.

'That must be the ford,' said Lausard, pointing towards the enemy cavalry.

'How do you know?' Delacor asked him.

'Why else would the Austrians be guarding that part of the bank?'

Royere walked his horse towards the edge of the river and rose in his saddle. There was a crack from the far bank and a musket ball dropped harmlessly into the water about ten feet to his right.

'We're going across,' he shouted to the waiting dragoons. 'Draw swords.'

The air was filled with the familiar metallic hiss of fifty swords being drawn and the dragoons formed up into two lines behind the lieutenant.

'Charnier,' he snapped at one of the men closest to him. 'Ride back to Lodi and bring the rest of the regiment. Tell Captain Deschamps we need reinforcements now.'

The trooper nodded and galloped off.

'Why the hell don't we just wait for the others?' Roussard queried, peering across the river at the hussars, a number of whom had now dismounted and were taking up firing positions behind trees and bushes on the far bank. The rest were forming up into lines.

'Because the Austrians will be calling for reinforcements too,' Bonet told him. 'By the time the others reach us we could be facing twice that number.'

'We don't know how many there are now,' Sonnier protested.

'Forward!' ordered Royere and the dragoons advanced down the river bank at a walk, the officer's horse leading the way into the shallows, water splashing up around its hooves.

Lausard gripped his reins tightly as their horses entered deeper water which rose past the animals' forelocks to their hindquarters. Some whinnied fearfully as the water lapped around them and many of the men felt the river pouring into their boots. Water was splashing up all around them and now small geysers began to shoot up as more musket fire was directed at them by the Austrians. A ball whizzed past Rocheteau's ear and struck the helmet of the man behind him, spinning away harmlessly.

The depth of the water was slowing the advance of the dragoons and Lausard urged his mount on, realising that they were now halfway across; the water level would begin to drop again at any moment but the journey seemed to be taking an eternity. To his left a dragoon was struck in the face by a musket ball. He screamed and toppled from the saddle, his horse trying to rear up as the body fell with a loud splash, blood staining the water nearby.

A horse was struck in the neck and fell forward, pitching its rider into the water. He surfaced spluttering for air.

The water smelled rank, its odour mingling with a stench of sweat and a gradually more pervasive odour of gunpowder.

Downriver Lausard noticed that the bridge was being attacked, blue-clad French infantry swarming across it into ferocious fire. To him that did not seem as important as the realisation that the water was becoming more shallow again. The dragoons and their horses were beginning to rise up out of the water, the animals gaining a firmer footing.

A salvo of musket fire swept them and two more men were unhorsed.

'Jesus!' hissed Rocheteau, his gaze fixed on the far bank. 'They'll pick us all off before we reach them.'

Royere was urging his mount on, up into the shallows.

He waved his sword high above his head.

'Charge!' he bellowed.

The dragoons did as they were ordered, battling against the flowing water and also against the incline of the bank and driving their horses on towards the Austrians. The hussars moved forward at a canter, swords drawn, intent on meeting the French before they could clear the river.

The enemy cavalry came down the opposite slope led by a huge officer on a black horse, who headed straight for Royere.

Gaston pressed the bugle to his lips and blasted out the notes which signalled the charge and the dragoons flung themselves forward as best they could.

Royere met the Austrian officer, blocking his downward stroke and slashing at his face, carving a huge gash in his opponent's cheek, but the huge man scarcely seemed to notice and struck at the lieutenant once again, this time with such power that he almost knocked Royere from his horse. The animal reared and a thrust aimed at Royere caught it in the shoulder. Blood jetted from the wound and the horse whinnied in pain, toppling to one side, flinging the lieutenant from the saddle. He dragged himself to his feet, confused, turning in time to see the Austrian's sabre flash above his head. He had no chance to raise his own weapon in defence. He waited for the cut that would kill him.

There was a loud bang and the officer toppled from his horse trailing blood in the air behind him.

Royere, waist-deep in water, spun round and saw that Lausard had shot the man from point-blank range with one of his pistols, the weapon still smoking in his fist. He re-holstered it and extended the same hand to Royere who nodded and allowed himself to be pulled upright.

Rocheteau grabbed the reins of the dead Austrian's horse and Royere swung himself into the saddle. He looked both at Lausard then at Rocheteau but no words were exchanged. There was no time.

A second line of mounted hussars crashed into the dragoons now fighting their way through shallower water. The horses dug their rear hooves into the mud and headed for the bank.

Carbonne drove his sword deep into the chest of an attacker, hearing a crack as the steel smashed bone and grated against a rib before he tugged it free.

Delacor, meanwhile, ducked beneath a sword swipe and used his elbow to fend off the Austrian, slamming the point of it into the man's face. As his injured foe wavered in the saddle, Delacor stabbed him in the stomach and shoulder, smiling as the body toppled into the water.

The horses too seemed gripped by the savagery of the moment and they snapped and bit at each other and more often than not, at other riders as the two sets of cavalrymen clashed in the shallows where the water was already turning red beneath the churning hooves. The air was filled with the clanging of steel on steel and, to Bonet, it sounded as if dozens of blacksmiths were at work.

Charvet hissed in pain as a sword cut opened his arm from elbow to wrist, blood spurting from the wound. As the Austrian struck at him again he seized the man's arm with his free hand and yanked so hard that he pulled the man from his saddle. The hussar fell into the water, rising quickly to avoid the hooves of the horses. Charvet kicked out at him, his boot catching the man in the face. As he reeled from the impact, the Frenchman caught him across the shoulder with a devastating backhand slash.

Despite their own comrades now being in the line of fire, the dismounted hussars on the bank kept up their fusillade and several more dragoons went down, killed or wounded. But now, by sheer savage determination, the dragoons were beginning to force their opponents back, to reach the dry ground of the bank where their horses could get a firm foothold. The desperation in their fighting seemed to take the hussars by surprise and a number wheeled their mounts and galloped away.

Lausard and Rocheteau, alongside Royere, led the green-coated dragoons up the bank. Lausard, his face spattered with blood, struck down two Austrians, riding over one with his horse, his eyes scanning the bank for more enemies.

Sonnier pulled his carbine free and shot down one of the hussars, smiling as he saw the man clutching at his chest. Before he could reload, Sonnier was faced with another man and he swung the carbine like a club, smashing the butt into the Austrian's face.

Those hussars on foot suddenly ran for their tethered mounts and Lausard wondered why. Although the dragoons had reached the bank, they were still out-numbered, their horses exhausted.

'Look!' shouted Giresse and Lausard turned to see the remainder of the regiment, led by Deschamps, pour-ing into the river, churning across it. On either flank, hussars supported the attack.

Seeing the oncoming green mass Lausard managed a smile.

A number of the hussars were throwing away their weapons and raising their hands in surrender. Those who could were fleeing, some leaving their horses behind as they ran for sanctuary in the trees.

A cheer went up from the dragoons, but Lausard's attention was now concentrated on the fleeing hussars who were heading back in the direction of Lodi. He glanced downriver towards the town, which was shrouded in smoke now, the bridge a mass of blue-jacketed troops. He could see tricolours waving on the bridge, he could even see one or two on the northern bank.

'Victory?' said Giresse breathlessly, also seeing the French infantry swarming across the bridge.

Lausard looked back at the fleeing hussars then at the blazing inferno that was Lodi, flames licking towards the sky. He could feel the blood drying on his face but he made no attempt to wipe it away. It was dripping from his sabre too and he held the weapon aloft in triumph, his gesture suddenly copied by a dozen of his comrades. The sound of cheering began to grow louder.

CHAPTER 24

'They call him "The Little Corporal",' said Paul Barras, his voice heavy with scorn. 'The whole army loves him. *He* controls them, not us.'

'Did we ever?' Tallien asked. 'What's the harm in an army cherishing its commander? They will fight more vigorously for one they respect than one they despise.'

'And if that commander's aspirations are not just military but political, then he becomes twice as deadly,' Barras retorted. 'Bonaparte is as interested in the politics of this war as he is in the soldiery.'

'You sound as if you fear him, Barras,' Gohier said, polishing his spectacles with a small handkerchief.

'Perhaps we should *all* fear him a little. It may well prolong our careers, perhaps even our lives.'

'You overreact,' Letourneur said.

'Do I? Perhaps I know him better than you.'

'You were the one who was singing his praises until he stole your mistress,' Letourneur chided. 'Perhaps your dislike of Bonaparte stems from his personal achievements rather than any danger he may present as a political adversary.'

A heavy silence fell over the room, broken by Barras who glared at his companion. 'Bonaparte didn't steal my mistress,' he hissed. 'Our affair was over anyway. I had no further use for her.'

'As you say,' Letourneur murmured. 'The fact remains that, six months ago, when you recommended we give Bonaparte command of the Army of Italy, *you* were one of his leading supporters. Now you would see him deprived of that command because of a personal matter between the two of you.'

'I care nothing for Bonaparte in this matter,' Barras lied. 'My concern is for France and I fear for her with this Corsican in charge of our army. We tried to limit his power, we tried to split his command with Kellermann but he protested so we backed down. He has resisted *all* attempts to limit his control over the Army of Italy and we have *allowed* him to resist.'

'What choice do we have?' Tallien said. 'Before he took over the army was a shambles, the war was being lost. He has transformed those men with nothing but his personality and his skill as a leader, and you seek to restrain him.'

'For the good of France,' Barras said.

Tallien waved the suggestion away. 'The economy of France was collapsing,' he continued, 'the amount of plunder arriving daily from Italy, from Bonaparte, is what keeps this country on its feet. We need his victories for the financial gain they bring us and they give the people something to celebrate too. Conquests *outside* France make her people forget some of the hardships they endure. I say good luck to our "little corporal".'

'Why is he called by that name?' Gohier enquired.

'At Lodi he personally sighted some of the cannon during the battle,' Barras said haughtily. 'A task usually reserved for an artillery corporal.' Again there was scorn in his voice.

'His list of victories is impressive,' Tallien said.

'He has still failed to take Mantua,' said Barras. 'That fortress is the key to this campaign. Until it falls Bonaparte has achieved nothing.'

'So now you are a tactician as well?' Tallien challenged. 'How can you be so dismissive of what he has done? The summer is almost over and he has been triumphant in his battles; he has taken Milan, he has bled Italy to finance France and he has ensured that Spain has become our ally against the British. What more can he do?'

Barras had no answer. He sat back in his seat, clasping his hands before him as if in prayer.

'So, what arguments can you offer now?' Tallien continued. 'Do you still want to see Bonaparte replaced as head of the Army of Italy? Do you think Kellermann could do a better job?' He glanced around at his colleagues. 'Do any of you?'

The question was met by a chorus of grunts and headshaking.

'I still say that the Austrians were not *driven* out of Lombardy, they were *frightened* out,' Barras urged.

'They are out, that is all that matters,' Gohier said.

'In time we will all grow rich with Bonaparte's help,' Letourneur said, smiling. 'Why distrust him so?'

'At the moment he is harmless because he is five hundred miles away,' Barras argued, 'but mark my words, when he returns, *if* he does, then we may all do well to reserve a little mistrust for him and for his army because that is what it is. *His* army. We may have more to fear from Bonaparte, in the long run, than the Austrians.'

CHAPTER 25

Delacor reached out a hand, grabbed a fistful of grapes from the vine and squeezed them above his mouth, savouring the sweet juice that flowed from them. All around him other men were doing the same, slaking their thirsts with the liquid from the overripe grapes. Some had already begun to wither on the vines, unharvested and untended. Other bunches were fat and swollen with sweet fluid and the dragoons accepted the prize eagerly.

For the last twenty minutes they had been riding through countryside rich in provisions. Through rice fields, olive groves and vineyards, all but a few abandoned by their former owners whose tiled farmhouses stood empty. Many had been looted but the haul of valuables from these humble dwellings was nothing compared to the hoard of food which could be gathered, and the troops had collected as much as they could carry. What could not be stuffed into packs and portmanteaus had been eaten during the journey. They swept through the farms like locusts, stripping everything from the trees and vines.

Lausard chewed on a handful of grapes and looked up the road ahead to where Colonel Lannes and his aides were riding. Lannes was a tall, powerfully built man, a great friend of Bonaparte's and also the same age. Lausard could pick him out easily with his blue uniform and its sparkling gold epaulettes. Most of the army admired Lannes for his bravery. He had been the first man across the Po River and he'd sustained numerous wounds during the campaign so far. The troops respected and liked him. He also had a streak of ruthlessness about him which made him perfect for their present task.

'It's about time someone taught these Italian bastards a lesson,' Delacor opined, wiping juice from his mouth with the back of his hand. 'None of them are to be trusted. I mean to say, we liberate them and what do they do? Stab us in the back.'

'This isn't the first time they've revolted either,' Charvet offered. 'I heard that the garrison at Pavia actually surrendered.'

'Gutless bastards,' snapped Delacor.

'Bonaparte had the officer in charge shot,' Charvet continued.

'So what the hell are we supposed to do here?' Rocheteau said.

'Teach these Italians a lesson,' Delacor rasped.

'We're making war on women and children,' Bonet protested. 'They're innocent.'

'There are no innocents in war,' Lausard said, still chewing on some grapes. He spat out a couple of pips and pulled another handful from the vine closest to him.

'Our fight is with the Austrians,' Bonet persisted.

'These Italians have brought this upon themselves,' Rocheteau sneered.

'Yes, they should have kept out of our affairs,' Delacor echoed.

'We are not liberators to *them*, we are invaders, as unwelcome as the Austrians,' Bonet protested. 'What do you expect them to do?'

'It isn't just a matter of killing innocents,' said Giresse. 'How can we subdue the Austrians when we can't even control those people we've conquered.'

'Conquered?' Bonet said incredulously. 'In one breath we call ourselves liberators, in the next conquerors. What *are* we?'

'Soldiers,' Lausard said. 'Which is why we do our duty. Why we do as we are ordered and if that order is to burn a village then we do it. If that order is to charge an enemy position then we do it, and if that order is to kill women and children we do that too.'

'It isn't right,' Bonet said.

'Since when has war been right?' Lausard replied. 'But we are a part of it, schoolmaster, and we are here to obey orders, no matter what we think of them.'

'Maybe you should have stayed in Paris and kept your date with the guillotine,' said Rocheteau. 'At least you couldn't have moaned then.'

'*He* would,' Carbonne offered and the men around him chuckled. 'That's what you're best at, isn't it, schoolmaster? Complaining.'

'I was making an observation,' Bonet hissed. 'Just because we have to carry out orders doesn't mean we have to *like* them. My God, some of you actually sound as if you're looking forward to this.'

'And why shouldn't we?' said Delacor. 'Have you

forgotten what the "Barbets" did to us when we first came here?'

'These people we come to slaughter aren't guerrillas,' Bonet countered. 'They're innocent—'

'Oh, shut up!' Rocheteau advised, 'or you might find that the Italians aren't the only ones getting shot.'

There was more laughter among the men.

'You're worse than His Holiness there.' Rocheteau indicated Moreau with his finger. 'I suppose you disagree with all this too, do you, Moreau?'

'If it is God's will then I go along with it,' Moreau answered, crossing himself.

'You see, even the Almighty is against you,' Rocheteau said, turning his gaze back on Bonet.

Lausard said, 'God has nothing to do with this. He stopped caring about this army a long time ago.'

'God *is* with us,' Moreau objected. 'He *has* been from the beginning and He is now.'

'Well,' Rocheteau mused, 'I'd like a word with Him. I think my horse is going lame, I want to know if He can fix it.'

This was met with more howls of laughter.

'I hope He has patience with your blasphemy,' Moreau rebuked him.

'How can you still believe in a God after some of the things you've seen during this campaign?' Lausard asked.

'God is not to blame for this war or for the men who've died in it,' Moreau explained.

'Tell that to their families,' Bonet sneered.

'Most of them probably haven't even got families,' Lausard said. 'They're like us. They've got no one. Nobody's going to miss us if we die. Whether we'd have died back in Paris or here on some Italian hillside, we won't be missed.'

Giresse said, 'You speak for yourself. I can think of a couple of dozen women who'd be heartbroken if anything happened to me.'

Again there was laughter and even Lausard managed a smile.

'I'm surprised we haven't all died of hunger by now,' said Joubert.

'You know, you and Bonet make a good pair, fat man,' Rocheteau told the big man. 'Neither of you ever stops complaining. You about your belly and him about the rights and wrongs of this stinking war.'

'Why don't you *all* shut up,' Rostov interjected. 'You French, you're like a bunch of chickens, squawk, squawk, squawk.'

'And I suppose Russians never complain?' Joubert countered.

'No, we don't. We face each task as it comes and we get on with it. That is the nature of my people.'

'If you loved your people so much what were you doing in France?' Carbonne pointed out. 'That was why you were arrested, wasn't it, for being a foreigner?'

'My country is harsh,' the Russian told him. 'The climate, the land, the rich. Those who have plenty care nothing for the rest.'

'That was like those Bourbons,' Rocheteau said. 'And all the other rich bastards back in France. They weren't so powerful when they were walking to meet the guillotine though, were they?'

There was more laughter but Lausard didn't join in.

'I say all the rich in every country should be hung from the lamp-posts,' was Delacor's offering.

There were some cheers of agreement.

Lausard gazed blankly at Delacor, who was slightly puzzled by the darkness in the sergeant's expression.

'Then you'll have to hang most of the officers in the army,' Bonet interjected. 'They're all becoming rich from plundering Italian cities.'

'That's different,' Delacor said.

'How?' Lausard asked. 'Isn't one rich man the same as the next? Shouldn't they all be judged as harshly? There are no good rich men, are there, Delacor? Just as there are no innocents in this war. Everyone gets the same treatment.'

It was Rocheteau's turn to eye Lausard with something akin to bewilderment but, before he could question his friend's vehemence, the column was called to a halt and told to form up in lines at the base of a gentle slope. On the crest of the ridge, Lannes and his aides were sheltered by a clump of poplars, their attention drawn to whatever lay in the shallow valley beyond. After a moment or two of wild gesticulation from a number of the blue-clad officers, Lausard saw them, led by Lannes himself, riding back towards the waiting dragoons. The small group came to a halt ten yards from the leading cavalrymen and Lannes rose in his stirrups, waving his bicorn in his hand to attract their attention.

'Soldiers of France,' he began. 'Over that crest lies the village of St Vicini. It has risen against us, against General Bonaparte, against France. Its people have ignored our kindness, they have shown the kind of treachery which cannot be tolerated. They have murdered our soldiers, just as the people of Tortona, Pozzolo and Arquarta have risen and murdered our

men. This cannot be allowed.' Lannes looked from face
to face as if scrutinising each of the waiting dragoons.
'Where these towns and villages rise, others will follow.
If they see that we do not react to this treachery they
will think us weak. They will side with our enemies to
try to defeat us but we have fought too hard for that,
you have fought too bravely to be betrayed by such as
these.' He waved a hand towards the crest of the ridge.
'The village is yours. Everything it contains is yours.
Destroy it and those who dwell within it. Destroy the
traitors who would stab you in the back. Take from
them what you will. They must become an example.
The rest of this country must learn the folly of resisting
the French Republic.' He drew his sword and waved it
above his head, his features set in stern lines. '*Vive
Bonaparte! Vive la République!*'

The dragoons moved forward.

The dead woman was in her early twenties.

Lausard wondered if she might even be a little
younger but it was difficult to tell. The sabre cut that
had killed her had laid open one cheek to the bone,
shattered her jawbone and spilled several of her teeth
on to the cobbled street.

He rode slowly past the corpse, shielding his eyes
momentarily from a fierce eruption of flames spewing
from one of the many burning houses. The heat from
the fire combined with the scorching sun and the exertions of the past thirty minutes had caused Lausard to
sweat heavily and he felt droplets of the salty fluid
trickling down his cheeks and neck.

The entire village of St Vicini was ablaze, even the
tiny church which dominated the central square was

burning from door to spire. Two dozen bodies were piled unceremoniously in front of it. All of them men, all of them shot on the orders of Lannes. Blood had spread out around them in a wide pool, now slowly congealing. Elsewhere, bodies had fallen where they'd been hit; men, women and children shot, sabred or simply ridden down by the dragoons who had swept through their village like vengeful demons.

Two of the green-clad troops galloped past, blood still smeared on their swords, one of them carrying a small sack of rice he'd taken from one of the houses before incinerating it. It was a meagre bounty and the entire village had yielded little in the way of spoils. Some food, the odd piece of jewellery and that was all. But the object of St Vicini's destruction hadn't been gain. The village had been a sacrifice, an example.

Lausard wondered if the gesture would have the desired effect. He guided his horse down the street, the animal lifting its hooves to avoid stepping on the body of an old man who'd been stabbed in the chest and back. Slumped in the doorway of the house behind him was a younger man, his body half-devoured by the flames consuming the building.

Lausard took off his helmet and ran a hand through his hair.

'Another glorious victory for the Republic.'

He heard the weary voice and turned to see Bonet had joined him. The ex-schoolmaster was perspiring profusely too, his horse heavily lathered.

'It had to be done,' Lausard told him.

'Do you honestly believe that, Alain?'

'I believe that these towns and villages that have

risen against us are of strategic importance and that
they must not be allowed to stop us winning this war. Is
that enough for you?'

'Is that your justification for this butchery?'

'I don't *need* to justify it,' Lausard responded angrily.
'We did as we were ordered. It's as simple as that and
we'll do it again and again and again if we have to.
Because we have no choice.'

'Because we're soldiers?' Bonet chided.

'Yes, and if that is the only way this war can be won
then so be it.'

'Slaughtering women and children isn't going to
bring us victory. Where's the glory in that?'

Lausard laughed scornfully. 'In case you'd forgotten, none of us is a part of this army because we wanted
glory. We're here because there's nowhere else for us to
go. We're here because we chose to take our chances
here rather than die like sewer rats in some filthy
prison. Or perhaps you'd prefer to be back there.'

'Don't tell me you agree with this slaughter because
I won't believe you.'

Lausard didn't speak. He fixed the schoolmaster in
an unblinking stare and carefully replaced his brass
helmet.

'Don't expect me to pity them, Bonet,' he said finally,
glancing towards the burning church and the pile of
corpses which lay before it. 'There's no room for pity in
war.'

'Nor compassion?' Bonet said softly.

Lausard shook his head.

Rocheteau and Delacor brought their horses trotting up the street, a barking dog following them. It
seemed to be the only inhabitant of St Vicini left alive

and it darted back and forth behind and between the horses' legs as the dragoons guided their mounts towards their companions. Delacor shouted at the dog but it refused to leave them.

'Easy pickings,' said Delacor smiling, looking around at the blazing village.

Bonet threw him a disgusted glance.

'What's wrong with you, schoolmaster?' Delacor teased. 'Not got the stomach for it?'

'Not for *this*,' Bonet grunted.

'What about *this*?' said Delacor, reaching round to his portmanteau. He pulled a golden candlestick from it and held it before him like a trophy. 'I took it from the church.'

'And I got the other one,' Rocheteau echoed, holding up another candlestick.

Bonet was unimpressed.

'This'll be worth five loaves of bread,' Delacor chided. 'Don't expect me to share any of it with you, schoolmaster.'

'I wouldn't want it,' said Bonet and wheeled his horse, guiding it up the street to where a number of the dragoons had already formed a ragged column.

'What's the matter with him?' said Rocheteau. 'He's more pious than Moreau and that's saying something.'

'He's had an attack of conscience,' Lausard said dismissively. 'He doesn't think we should be killing women and children.'

'Do you?' Rocheteau asked.

'I don't know what to think,' Lausard said. 'Perhaps it's best not to. I don't know if what we're doing is right or wrong; I don't even *care*. Besides, since when have right and wrong mattered?'

Rocheteau pushed the candlestick back into his portmanteau. 'Did you get anything for yourself?'

'Nothing worth taking from here,' Lausard said, surveying the carnage. Large cinders were floating up into the bright sky, carried on the updraught created by so many fires. The roof of one of the small houses collapsed, sending up a shower of sparks. Lausard's horse reared at the sight but he steadied it. The dog continued to dash around the horses, barking wildly until it finally dashed off up the street towards the other dragoons. Delacor raced after it, yelling angrily at the animal.

'He raped one of the women before he killed her,' Rocheteau told Lausard. 'Giresse saw him, he told me.'

'That's what he was in prison for, wasn't it?' Lausard said, unmoved. 'Men like him don't change.'

'What about us, Alain? Have *we* changed?'

'We know how to kill now. That's all that's different about us. Men don't change and we're the same as any man.'

'We're better than Delacor. We're not rapists.'

'Thieves, murderers, rapists. What's the difference?'

Lausard rode slowly up the street, the heat from the burning buildings searing him from both sides. Moreau rode past him, also sweating from the effect of the roaring flames.

'They're like the fires of hell,' he said. 'And they're waiting for us all.'

'Let them wait,' Lausard whispered under his breath.

The stench was appalling but Bonaparte barely seemed to notice it. The air reeked with a foul combination of blood, sweat, urine, infection and vomit. He didn't recoil but the smell inside the field hospital at Albaredo caused his companion, Captain Jean Baptiste Bessieres, to wrinkle his nose visibly. Bonaparte suppressed a grin and leaned closer to his companion.

'For the son of a surgeon, my friend, you have a strong dislike of hospitals,' he said and chuckled.

Bessieres ignored the comment and scanned the rows of wounded who filled the building.

'As a soldier I have a strong dislike of death,' he said finally. 'This is a place of death, not healing.'

'These men were wounded fighting for France, do you expect me to abandon them? Those who recover will fight on once again. God knows, we can afford to lose no more men.'

'I don't expect you to abandon them, sir,' Bessieres said indignantly. 'I wish there was more that could be *done* for the poor wretches. Perhaps if the government hadn't abolished medical schools then there'd be more doctors to cope.'

'Larrey and Desgenettes do their best,' Bonaparte said, waving away one of his aides who attempted to accompany him to the nearest patient. 'They are even more acutely aware of the problem than we are.'

The man lying closest was opening and closing his mouth slowly and soundlessly like a stranded fish. His head was heavily bandaged from the scalp to the nose. Blood had soaked through the filthy bandages in several places. Bonaparte reached out and took the man's hand, squeezing it.

'Can you hear me?' he said quietly.

'Doctor?' the man croaked, his throat dry and parched from lack of water.

'No, it is not the doctor. It is your general. I am Bonaparte. At which battle were you wounded?'

'Lonato, sir,' the man told him. 'I would have given my life for you, my General; instead I gave my eyes.'

Bonaparte patted the man's hand and moved to the next patient, who was lying motionless on his straw pallet. His face was the colour of rotten cheese and thick saliva was dribbling from his lips. He didn't respond when Bonaparte spoke to him. Bessieres reached out a hand and pressed it to the man's throat, feeling for a pulse. He detected one but it was incredibly weak.

'He needs a priest, not a doctor,' said the captain softly.

Orderlies in ragged blue uniforms were tending to the men in the hospital as best they could and Bonaparte saw a tall man with black hair and a thick moustache moving swiftly from patient to patient but he could do little more than inspect their wounds. Finally he noticed Bonaparte and scuttled across to him, two orderlies in pursuit.

'I don't want to interrupt your work, Doctor,' Bonaparte said. 'Please continue.'

'I was not told of your visit, sir,' the doctor said apologetically.

'Just go about your business, please,' Bonaparte urged. 'We will follow.'

The doctor moved to the next man and began unbandaging his upper arm, finally revealing a mottled greyish-pink area of flesh surrounding a deep wound. Pus had formed yellowish nodules in many places around the wound and the smell was foul.

'Gangrene is beginning to set in,' said the doctor. 'We probed for the ball but it was too deep. I left it in, I thought it might work itself free but . . .' He shook his head in despair.

The injured man saluted with his good arm and Bonaparte returned the gesture with a smile.

'Where did this happen?' he asked.

'On the bridge at Lodi, sir,' the man informed him. 'I was in the charge that kicked the Austrians off.' He smiled, revealing a set of discoloured teeth.

'I'll have to amputate the arm,' the doctor said. 'Before the poison spreads.'

The patient ignored the comment, his face still beaming as he looked at Bonaparte, who was already moving to the next wounded soldier.

The next man was wearing a shirt and cavalry breeches. His right leg had been amputated below the knee, both his hands were heavily bandaged and there was a nasty cut across his forehead.

'A roundshot killed his horse at Borghetto,' said the doctor. 'The same one that took off his leg. He was ridden over by several other men. He'll probably lose his hands too.'

The cavalryman tried to salute but the movement was impossible. Bonaparte patted his shoulder then followed the doctor to the next bed.

'Fever,' the doctor said. 'More than half the men in here are suffering with it. Field hospitals up and down the country have more men out of action through sickness than with wounds. And there isn't a thing we can do to help them,' the doctor added. 'Those who are strong enough usually survive but the weaker ones have no chance. Without fresh water and enough food these men have less chance of survival.'

'Another victory will be all the nourishment they need,' Bonaparte said.

'I hope you're right, sir,' the doctor said quietly.

The next man had sustained several wounds but he looked strong enough and tried to rise to salute as Bonaparte drew nearer. The general shook his head and helped lay the man down again, looking over the mass of bandages covering him.

'You look like a brave man,' Bonaparte said, smiling.

'Those Austrian bastards won't kill me easily, sir,' the soldier replied. 'They sabred me at Mondovi.' He pointed to his bandaged head. 'Shot me at Lodi.' He indicated his shoulder. 'And two of them stabbed me with bayonets at Lonato.' He gently touched his thigh and calf. 'But they couldn't kill me.'

'Good man,' Bonaparte encouraged.

'I want to get back into action again,' the soldier informed him proudly. 'I want to fight for *you*.'

'Which unit are you with?' Bonaparte enquired.

'The Eighty-first Demi-Brigade, sir.'

'Will he survive?' Bessieres said to the doctor, his voice a whisper.

The medical man nodded.

'Do you have a family back in France?' Bonaparte asked the man.

'I have a wife and two sons, sir. When they are old enough they will fight for you too. We would all fight and die for you, General.'

Bonaparte smiled and moved on.

He passed two men being tended by orderlies. One was vomiting dark fluid into a metal bowl, some of it spilling on to the stone floor. The other was being held down while a wound in his upper thigh was re-bandaged. His eyes were rolling wildly in their sockets, his lips fluttering.

'He has fever as well as the wound,' the doctor muttered.

'Haven't you seen enough, sir?' Bessieres asked.

Bonaparte fixed him in a stare for a moment then followed the doctor towards the next man. An infantry-man with a stomach wound. Then the next. An artillery sergeant paralysed by a piece of metal that had shattered part of his lower spine.

Men with fever. Men with dysentery. Men slowly bleeding to death internally. Men without limbs. Men with no eyes. The parade of misery continued.

'We will win,' Bonaparte said, finally turning back towards the main doors of the hospital. 'We will beat the Austrians *and* whatever nature sends against us. Malaria, smallpox or your Walcheren fever will not stop us. Caesar and Alexander faced the same problems but they conquered despite them. So will we.'

'Alexander died of fever, sir,' Bessieres reminded him.

'In Babylon,' Bonaparte mused. 'Not in Northern Italy. Do you not feel it, Bessieres? Destiny. I *know* we will win as surely as if God Himself had told me.' He turned and headed out of the hospital.

The cries of the sick and wounded echoed behind him.

CHAPTER 26

The breath of both men and horses clouded in the chilly early-morning air. The sun was a watery circlet in a washed-out sky and the feeble rays it emitted twinkled dully on the blanket of light frost covering the ground. A narrow stream ran parallel to the cavalry's route and Lausard noticed that parts of it were frozen. Elsewhere the clear water bubbled up through rents in the ice and the men had already stopped to fill their canteens.

Lausard shivered slightly as he rode. The weather had turned decidedly colder during the last two days and he thought back to the beginning of the campaign when they had all ridden across Italy in scorching heat, complaining about the stifling temperatures. Now, halfway through November, there wasn't a man amongst them who wouldn't have traded these chill mornings and cloudy days for just one of the searing April afternoons. Like the other ten men with him, Captain Deschamps included, Lausard wore his cloak and he was glad of it. The garment, like the rest of his equipment, was showing signs of the rigours of eight months' campaigning. His boots had a hole in one sole. His breeches were worn at the knees and his tunic had been repaired more times than he cared to remember. He'd lost a gauntlet at Arcola a week earlier, the glove mislaid in one of the dykes which surrounded the town. The horse he'd been riding had been hit by an Austrian bullet and as it went down, it had catapulted him into the stagnant water of a swampy tributary of the River Alpone. Many others had followed him but not all had been as fortunate. The three-day battle had cost the lives of at least fifty of the dragoon regiment and many more had been wounded. He had heard that the army itself had sustained over four thousand casualties and Bonaparte himself had only been saved from death by the intervention of two mounted guides who had swept him from the bridge into a quagmire below.

Since then the fighting had petered out into a series of clashes between foragers or scouts, never more than a hundred men at a time. Indeed, since the battle, the whole of the cavalry had been used mainly for reconnaissance as Bonaparte sought to find his foe and bring him to one final, conclusive battle. The days had passed but the French cavalry patrols had made no contact.

Food was still scarce and patrols usually combined their searches for the Austrians with hunts for sustenance. The patrol on this chilly morning was doing the same.

'What time is it?' Lausard asked Rocheteau who rode alongside him.

The corporal pulled a gold pocket watch from his tunic and flipped it open. He'd taken it from an Austrian officer at Arcola, along with a ring from the man's little finger. Unable to loosen the gold band,

Rocheteau had simply cut the digit free with a knife then pocketed it.

'It's just after seven,' he told his colleague, slipping the watch back inside his tunic. Like Lausard, Rocheteau had lost a horse at Arcola. The unfortunate beast had slipped on one of the muddy banks of the River Adige and broken a foreleg. Rocheteau had had to shoot it. The animal had then been cut up and the meat eaten by the men. Waste was something the Army of Italy could not afford.

'I should be in bed with my woman at this time of the morning,' Giresse complained.

'Which woman?' asked Lausard.

'*Any* woman,' Giresse said and chuckled.

'Do you ever think about anything other than women?' Rocheteau asked him.

'Yes, I think about food and wine and a warm fire and a soft bed and I think about women again. Didn't you have a woman, Rocheteau?'

'I was married for a time,' the corporal announced.

Both Lausard and Giresse looked at him incredulously.

'She was a fine-looking woman too,' Rocheteau continued, 'but she caught a fever back in 'eighty-five and died. I missed her. I didn't get much for her clothes when I sold them either,' he added with disgust. 'Barely enough to pay for her burial. She was a good woman though and a damned fine pickpocket.'

The other men laughed.

'It sounds like a match made in heaven,' Lausard said, grinning.

'I taught her everything I knew, all the tricks of my trade,' Rocheteau proclaimed proudly.

'Your trade was thieving,' Giresse reminded him.

'At least I only stole watches and money and food, not horses like you,' Rocheteau said indignantly.

'What about you, Alain?' Giresse asked. 'Tell us about the women in your life, the ones you left behind.'

'There was no one special,' he said flatly. 'There *were* women but none that I loved, none I would have married like Rocheteau here.'

How could he tell them about the women he'd known? How could he tell them of the grand parties and balls his parents organised, of the cultured, sophisticated and beautiful women who had attended – women he had seduced so easily. Most of them had probably met their deaths beneath the blade of the guillotine by now. Just like his family. They were either dead or they had fled the country along with the rest of the rich and the privileged. How could he tell these two men about a world they could never hope to understand, a world they had helped destroy?

'I wanted my freedom,' he said, forcing a smile. 'I didn't want to be tied to one woman all my life.'

'Quite right,' Giresse said with a chuckle. 'Why pick one apple when you have an entire basket before you?'

'I knew a woman once,' Tabor interjected, his words slow, almost slurred.

'And who was she, my friend?' Lausard asked, looking at the big man.

'She was a friend of my sister,' he said, smiling at the recollection. 'I can't remember her name,' he added.

'And did you become close?' Giresse wanted to know, grinning.

'She taught me how to dance,' said Tabor. 'My mother would sing and I would dance.'

'You don't look very graceful,' Rocheteau offered.

'My mother said I was a good dancer,' Tabor said, his voice now lower, his tone softening. 'I miss her but I suppose we all have people we miss, don't we?'

Lausard didn't answer, he merely directed his gaze ahead, as if that simple action would wipe away his own memories. Images of his family hovered inside his head but he struggled to push them away.

A shout from one of the leading dragoons helped him complete the task. He looked across to where the trooper was waiting on his horse, gesturing through a copse of trees towards a small group of buildings – a barn, a house and a pigsty. The other dragoons reined in, two of them dismounting and pulling carbines from their saddles.

'We can ride through those trees,' Rocheteau said. 'There's enough room for the horses.'

To prove his point he guided his mount into the small wood, the animal nuzzling at a frost-covered branch as it passed.

'Watch the road,' Deschamps told the two dismounted troopers, then the captain followed Rocheteau and the others into the wood, discovering, like his troopers, that the trees had not been very densely planted. The mounted men moved through them with ease, the hooves disturbing piles of fallen leaves.

A bird rose suddenly into the air, disturbed by the intruders. It went up into the morning sky, squawking loudly, and Lausard gripped his horse's bridle tightly to prevent it rearing at the sudden outburst.

Up ahead, something moved.

The men clearly saw the first of two figures wander

into view. Both hussars. Both dismounted. They were dressed in dark blue pelisses and grey overalls and were chatting happily, apparently unaware that the dragoons were less than one hundred yards from them.

'Austrians,' said Deschamps. 'I wonder how many there are?'

Another trooper came into view, mounted on a small bay and he paused to speak to his two dismounted companions.

'I think it's just a patrol,' said Lausard, noticing two more of the enemy cavalrymen.

'They're probably looking for food, like us,' Giresse added quietly, his gaze never leaving the Austrians.

'If this is an advance patrol then the main body must be close,' Deschamps mused. 'We'd better report this.'

He wheeled his horse slowly and silently and began heading back through the wood.

The gunshots sounded like thundercracks in the stillness of the morning.

The sudden noise caused the horse to Lausard's right to rear up, snorting loudly. The dragoon riding it was unable to control it and, spinning round, the horse clattered into a tree, knocking several of the lower branches down and churning up the ground with its hooves.

The Austrian hussars turned towards the sound of the commotion and Lausard saw one of them point, then heard him shouting something.

Then there were more shots and the dragoons realised that they were coming from behind them, in the direction of the road.

Rocheteau pulled his carbine free as he saw three hussars galloping towards the wood. He took aim and

shot one of them in the chest, the heavy lead ball toppling the man from the saddle.

The other two kept coming, although Lausard did
notice that one had slowed his pace, wondering exactly
how many adversaries were hidden by the wood. But
the dragoons had already turned and were heading
back through the trees towards the road where the
sound of firing had ceased.

Lausard and Rocheteau burst from the copse to be
confronted by a dozen hussars. Glancing quickly to his
right Lausard saw that one of the dragoons was lying
face down on the road, his horse having bolted, the
second man was on his knees, clutching at a wound in
his chest. A sabre cut had opened his throat and blood
was spilling down the front of his tunic. But this
tableau had barely registered with Lausard before the
hussar closest to him attacked, aiming his sabre at the
Frenchman's head. Lausard ducked sideways, feeling
the air part close to his left ear. Pulling one of his pistols
free, he jammed it against the stomach of his attacker
and fired. The retort was muffled by such close contact
and both men were enveloped by a small cloud of black
smoke as the hussar toppled from his saddle and fell
heavily.

Rocheteau dragged his sword free and drove it at his
nearest opponent, spearing the man through the top of
the right arm then again in the face. The hussar's horse
reared wildly, dumping its rider from the saddle.

More of the dragoons were emerging from the wood
but Lausard realised that the road seemed to be a mass
of men on sleek ponies in dark-blue uniforms. There
were at least thirty Austrian cavalry, all eager to attack
the emerging French.

Deschamps saw their numbers and had no doubt of what to do.

'Retreat!' he roared and the men wheeled their horses and put spurs to them, hurtling back down the road with a number of hussars in pursuit. The thunder of churning hooves filled the early-morning air and Lausard heard the crack of a carbine from behind him, ducking involuntarily as the ball whizzed past him.

He risked a glance over his shoulder to see how close the pursuing Austrians were, and saw several of the blue-clad horsemen no more than ten yards behind, sabres waving wildly in the air. Their horses looked fresher but, he thought, not as powerful as those of the dragoons. If the chase went on much longer then the dragoons should be able to outdistance them. However, none of the Austrians was showing any sign of giving up the chase.

There was another shot and Lausard heard the sound of a horse neighing in pain; he looked across to see that Deschamps's mount had been struck in the hindquarters by a bullet. The animal was faltering, blood pumping from the wound. Deschamps urged it on but the injury was beginning to slow it down.

Lausard leaned across and caught the bridle, nodding towards a sharp incline which led down to a stream. Deschamps understood and guided his mount in that direction, Lausard and Rocheteau riding with him.

Several hussars also darted off the road to pursue this quarry. Lausard counted six of them. The remainder continued to chase the other fleeing dragoons.

There was a hedge at the top of the incline formed by some small bushes. Lausard rode his horse straight through the barrier but Deschamps's wounded mount tried to jump it. The animal cleared the obstacle but lost its footing on the other side and pitched forward, spilling Deschamps from the saddle and rolling over him.

The full weight of the fallen beast crushed the captain's left leg and he screamed as he felt several bones snap. The horse tried to scramble to its feet and almost trampled him in the process, but he covered his head with both hands and waited for the stricken animal to move clear. When he tried to rise it felt as if someone had set fire to his leg. Searing pain spread from his calf to his thigh and he fell down again, aware of the ground vibrating as the Austrian hussars drew nearer.

Lausard and Rocheteau had both turned their mounts to meet the onrushing light cavalry. Lausard drew his other pistol and shot the leading horse in the head. It dropped like a stone, its rider flung from the saddle; two animals immediately behind it crashed into the carcass and also fell.

With three of the hussars unhorsed, Lausard and Rocheteau drove their own mounts forward.

Rocheteau stabbed the first man in the chest then swung his sword in a devastating backhand swipe which sent the hussar crashing to the ground.

Lausard parried a sabre cut and drove his fist into the face of his attacker. As the dazed hussar reeled in the saddle, Lausard's sword was driven into his stomach and chest. The horse bolted, the dying rider still hunched over his saddle.

The hussar still mounted wheeled his horse and rode off. The remaining three were trying to swing themselves back on to horses but Lausard cut one down as he tried to grab the horse's bridle.

Rocheteau simply rode his horse into another, knocking him to the ground, allowing the animal to trample on the fallen Austrian who lay still on the frozen earth. The riderless horses bolted and the one hussar who was still alive raised his arms in surrender.

Lausard looked at the man and for a second thought about cutting him down, but then he lowered his sword, his breath coming in gasps from the exertion of the fight.

'Watch him,' he said to Rocheteau then dismounted himself and scuttled back over the incline to Deschamps, who was lying on his back, his face crumpled in pain, his left leg bloodied. He could see something white and gleaming poking through the material of his breeches and realised that it was a portion of splintered bone.

'You should have left me,' the officer croaked. 'When the surgeon sees this, he'll have my leg.'

'Can you stand if I help you?' Lausard asked, offering himself as support for the injured officer, virtually carrying him back towards the crest where Rocheteau was holding the remaining hussar at pistol point. The Austrian was in his early twenties and his face was ashen. There was a small cut on his forehead from his fall and his uniform was stained with mud. Rocheteau had already taken his weapons.

'I ought to shoot you here and now, you bastard,' Rocheteau snapped.

'No, please,' said the hussar, looking to Lausard as if expecting help.

'Give me one reason why I shouldn't?' Rocheteau said.

'Gold,' the cavalryman said. 'Lots of it.'

Rocheteau looked at Lausard.

'I can tell you where it is,' the hussar blurted out.

'That's not important now,' Lausard said, helping Deschamps towards his horse. The captain's own mount could barely walk now, weak from loss of blood and its crashing fall.

'I can't ride like this,' Deschamps said, nodding to his shattered leg. He stood on one leg leaning on Lausard's shoulder.

Lausard left him hanging on to his wounded horse while he mounted his own. Then he reached down, offering the captain his arm.

'Pull yourself up, sir,' he said, steadying the horse while Deschamps hauled himself up by the strength of his arms alone.

'Jesus!' gasped Deschamps, the effort bringing fresh pain, but he fastened his arms around Lausard's waist and clung on.

'What about him?' Rocheteau said, indicating the hussar.

'He's ridden long enough,' said Lausard. 'Let's see how well he runs.'

'You try to escape and I'll put a ball through your skull,' Rocheteau said. 'What about the others, Alain?'

'We'll worry about them when we get back to camp,' said Lausard. 'Come on.'

They set off at a trot, the hussar running alongside Rocheteau's horse. 'I could ride with you,' he suggested.

'Shut up and save your breath,' Rocheteau hissed. 'You're going to need it. And if you're lying about this gold I'll personally cut your throat. Now keep running.'

CHAPTER 27

'I swear to God it's getting colder,' said Rocheteau, pulling his cloak more tightly around him and staring into the flames of the camp fire. 'Mind you, I don't suppose that bothers you, does it, Rostov? I mean, you Russians, you're used to the cold, aren't you?'

'It isn't cold all year round in Russia, you idiot,' Rostov said, grinning. 'We do have summers too you know.'

'How do you know when it's summer? Do you get only one inch of snow instead of six?'

The men around the fire laughed.

'We're cold because we haven't had enough to eat,' said Joubert forlornly, cupping his much-reduced waist. 'I haven't eaten for four days.'

'You liar, fat man,' said Delacor. 'We all ate yesterday.'

'I wouldn't call a piece of rabbit a *meal*,' Joubert complained.

'We should be thankful for whatever we get,' Moreau said. 'We should thank God for it.'

'Do we thank Him for frostbite too?' Delacor
rubbed his hands and held them closer to the fire. 'I bet
the Austrians aren't suffering like this.'

'Everybody's suffering,' Bonet said. 'Us *and* them.'

'Well, I care about myself, not the stinking Austrians
and I'*m* cold,' Delacor hissed.

'No sign of them for four days,' Rocheteau mused.
'Not so much as a horse apple.' He chuckled. 'Perhaps
they've all gone home.'

'Good,' Roussard said. 'Then we can go home too.'

'To what?' Rocheteau asked.

'If the Austrians go home then this war will be over,'
Roussard continued. 'Isn't that what we all want?'

'I think they've got something in store for us,'
Giresse mused. 'There's a battle coming, you mark my
words.'

'Did anyone get anything out of the prisoners you
took?' Giresse said. 'They must know where the main
Austrian force is.'

'The one I took was too frightened to say much,'
Rocheteau said. 'I don't know about the others.' He
had wondered whether to mention the gold that the
Austrian had spoken of but thought better of it. If it did
exist and they found it, Rocheteau didn't plan on sharing too much of it with his companions. Not if he could
help it.

'I wonder how Captain Deschamps is?' Tabor said.

'They'll have had his leg off by now,' Delacor stated
flatly. He held up a piece of wood, ready to toss it on
the fire. 'Perhaps we ought to save this for him. He
might need it.'

Some of the men laughed.

'What for?' Tabor said blankly.

'For a wooden leg, you half-wit,' Delacor sighed, then threw the stick on the fire.

Around them, a dozen other fires burned in the darkness.

The hills which rose on three sides of the encamped dragoons did little to lessen the effect of the freezing wind sweeping across the night-shrouded land. As Lausard walked through the camp he passed many men trying to sleep, huddled around fires, wrapped in their cloaks and saddle blankets, some with their heads resting on their saddles.

Sentries, shivering in the chill of the night, walked ceaselessly back and forth, patrolling the perimeter of the camp, while others guarded the horses. Two farriers were busy shoeing some captured Austrian ponies. A number of dragoons were cleaning their weapons. Some were smoking. Others, like himself, were strolling around the camp, unable to sleep, either because of the cold or through restlessness. This was the case with Lausard. He walked past a corporal who was snoring loudly, oblivious to the cold and the chatter of his companions. How Lausard envied him. What he wouldn't give for one peaceful, uninterrupted night of slumber, untainted by dreams.

'So, I'm not the only one who can't sleep.'

The voice startled him and he spun round to see Lieutenant Royere striding towards him, his cloak flapping.

'I hate the cold weather,' Royere said. 'I always have. I suppose that's what comes of being brought up in Navarre. I don't ever remember seeing snow when I was a child.'

'Whereabouts in Navarre?' Lausard asked him.

'A village about ten miles from Biarritz. My father was a miller.'

'Why did you join the army?'

'Patriotic zeal,' said Royere, laughing. 'That's the answer most officers in this army would give you, isn't it?'

Lausard regarded him quizzically.

'There isn't a man in this army who could tell you what he's fighting for now, Lausard,' the lieutenant said wearily. 'It isn't patriotism and it's certainly nothing to do with politics. Perhaps at the beginning there was a handful of men who actually believed that the object of this war was to spread the Republican doctrine but no one can even remember what *that* is any more.'

The two men began walking slowly, Royere glancing up at the velvet sky and watery moon.

'This war was supposed to be one of liberation,' Royere said. 'Our armies were going to march across Europe freeing the masses from the yoke of Royalist tyranny.' He laughed again but it had a bitter, hollow sound. 'It's a war of conquest, like all wars. There's no gallant motive behind our struggle.'

'You sound disappointed, Lieutenant.'

'Perhaps I am. There's a little bit of the idealist still left in me but I'm sure the years and the battles will grind it away.' He exhaled deeply. 'But what about you, Lausard? What do you think of this war?'

'I'm a soldier, Lieutenant. I'm not supposed to think, just obey orders.'

Royere smiled. 'Come on then,' he said. 'I've bared my soul to you. Tell me something about yourself. Where are you from?'

'Is it important?'

'I'm curious. I think I have the right to know something about the man who saved my life.'

Lausard shrugged.

'You seem to be making a habit of saving men's lives, Lausard,' Royere observed. 'You saved mine at Lodi and then you saved the life of Captain Deschamps.'

'I did what anyone in that position would have done,' Lausard said.

'Not every man would have displayed such courage. You underestimate yourself.'

'Men with little to live for usually possess more courage. If a man sees no worth in life, then death holds no fear. It is easy to be brave when dying is easier then living.'

'And you have nothing worth living for?'

'I have no family, no friends. All I own is this uniform and that was given to me by the State.'

'But you must have had someone before you joined the army? A family, a wife perhaps?'

'There is no one. If I die there will be no one to mourn for me and that is how I want it. I live day to day, hour to hour, like the other men in the army. If I hadn't joined I'd be dead by now. Executed. You seem to forget, Lieutenant, I was a thief.'

'Well, what you *were* is not important any longer,' Royere told him. 'It is what you *are* that matters.' He extended his right hand. 'For my life.'

Lausard shook the offered hand.

'I thank you,' said Royere with genuine warmth.

The two men continued walking slowly.

'You still haven't told me where you're from,' Royere reminded him.

'South of Paris, my family had a house and . . .' he allowed the sentence to trail off.

'I thought you had no family.'

'I haven't any longer, they're dead.'

'I'm sorry.'

'So am I.'

'What was it? An illness? An accident?'

'A mistake,' Lausard said, and smiled at the puzzled look on the officer's face.

Before either of them could say any more a shout filled the night and both of them spun round towards its source.

'Horsemen approaching,' a sentry called.

Royere and Lausard scurried across towards the man who had called out and, quite clearly, they could see two mounted men making their way to the camp.

'If they were Austrians I think there'd be more of them,' Lausard said quietly, squinting through the gloom to make out the men's uniforms.

'They're wearing dragoon uniforms,' Royere said, noticing the swirling horsehair manes on their helmets.

The horsemen were no more than twenty yards away and Royere, Lausard and the sentry moved towards them, the sentry raising his carbine. Lausard touched the hilt of his sword.

'Identify yourself,' Royere called.

The horsemen slowed virtually to a halt, while the sentry kept his carbine aimed at the first of them.

'Who are you?'

The leading man removed his helmet to reveal a youthful face, short-cropped hair and cheeks which had not long felt the caress of a razor. His companion was a little older.

'Who's in charge here?' the younger man asked, eyeing Royere, Lausard and the sentry almost with contempt.

Lausard noticed how clean his uniform and horse furniture were compared to the men of the squadron. Gold epaulettes on his shoulders marked him out as an officer.

'I am in charge,' Royere said.

'You owe me a salute, Lieutenant,' said the younger man. 'I am Captain Joseph Cezar. I am your new squadron commander.'

Both Lausard and Royere looked puzzled for a moment, taken aback by the appearance of this new officer, then they both saluted stiffly.

'This is my adjutant, Lieutenant Marquet,' Cezar told them, motioning towards the man at his side who looked a little older. He had a thick moustache which had not been trimmed in months, swarthy skin and dark, hooded eyes.

'Have you any news of Captain Deschamps, sir?' asked Royere.

'I am an officer of dragoons, not a surgeon,' snapped Cezar. 'But if you men are an example of the rest of this squadron then Deschamps couldn't have been much of an officer.' Cezar swung himself out of the saddle and stood close to Royere and Lausard. 'Your uniforms are filthy, they are a disgrace.' He wrinkled his nose. 'And when was the last time you bathed?'

'We don't have much opportunity for bathing, sir,' Lausard said. 'We've been too busy fighting. That is why our uniforms are so dirty. However, may I compliment you on how clean yours is?'

'What is your name?' Cezar said, stepping closer to Lausard.

'Sergeant Lausard, sir.'

'The army must be very short of good men if someone as insolent as you can make the rank of sergeant.'

'I agree, sir, but then again, it is usually officers who make such appointments, isn't it?'

'Sergeant Lausard saved Captain Deschamps's life,' Royere interjected. 'And mine too.'

'Am I supposed to be impressed by that?' Cezar snapped. 'He was only doing his duty.'

'Not *all* officers are worth saving, sir,' said Lausard, looking past the captain.

Cezar glared at him momentarily then turned his attention back to Royere.

'I want a full inspection of this squadron at five tomorrow morning. Do you understand?' he hissed.

'Yes, sir,' Royere answered.

'Every man is to be present.'

'We have some sick—'

Cezar cut him short. '*Every* man,' he shouted. 'I want no excuses. Any man not present will be punished. Understood?'

Royere nodded.

'You're dismissed. You too, Lausard. I'll be keeping a special eye out for you tomorrow.'

'Thank you, sir,' said Lausard. 'I hope you won't be disappointed.'

'I'd better not be, for your sake.'

The men saluted and turned to walk away.

'Wait,' Cezar said. 'There are two more things. I understand that you took some prisoners recently.'

'Only three, sir,' Royere informed him.

'I want to speak to them,' Cezar said.

'We've already interrogated them, sir, they know

nothing of any importance. Nothing our own reconnaissance hasn't already told us.'

'I will speak to them in the morning after the inspection,' said Cezar dismissively. 'Lausard, you can show Lieutenant Marquet and myself to our quarters.'

'Your quarters, sir?' Lausard queried quietly.

'Yes, you idiot. Where are they?'

Lausard motioned around him.

'You're looking at them, sir,' he said softly. 'I hope you will be comfortable on whichever piece of open ground you choose.' He saluted and walked off, Cezar glaring at his broad back as he disappeared into the gloom.

Royere caught him up. 'It seems he's taken a strong dislike to you, Lausard.'

'I'll survive,' Lausard grunted.

'Be careful with him. He doesn't live in the same world we live in.'

'I know. He's living in *my* world now.'

The fire had burned down to little more than embers by the time Lausard returned, warming his hands over the glowing fragments, pulling at his cloak as the wind whipped by ferociously.

Most of the men of his unit were sleeping fitfully, cocooned beneath cloaks and saddle blankets. Lausard settled himself beside the fire, glancing across at Charvet who was snoring loudly enough to wake the dead. Beside him Gaston lay with his head against the man's chest, seeking the extra warmth of human contact. On the other side, the mountainous frame of Joubert at least kept some of the wind from blowing in Roussard's face. He stirred in his sleep, murmured something incomprehensible, then rolled over.

'Where the hell have you been?'

Lausard looked around to see a bleary-eyed Rocheteau looking up at him.

'Walking,' said Lausard quietly. 'Thinking.'

'About what?' Rocheteau asked. 'The only thing I can think about is trying to sleep in this bloody wind.'

'Deschamps's replacement has just arrived,' Lausard said. 'Captain Joseph Cezar.' He spoke the words with disdain. 'Our new squadron commander.'

'What's he like?'

'You'll see for yourself tomorrow morning when he reviews the unit.'

Rocheteau sat up. 'A review? Where does he think he is? In some training school?' he snorted. 'What kind of officer is he?'

'A clean one. I doubt if he's been in the field for more than a week. He knows about our prisoners. Don't ask me how. He says he wants to talk to them.'

'What if he finds out about the gold,' Rocheteau said.

'There is no gold. That Austrian told you that to save his skin.'

'You know your trouble, Alain, you've got no faith.'

'Even if the gold does exist, *we'll* never get our hands on it. The Austrians have probably got it locked up inside Mantua and God knows how long it will be before we get inside *that* place.'

'It could be part of their baggage train,' Rocheteau said hopefully.

Lausard smiled and said, 'Go back to sleep. Dream about your gold.'

'This Cezar,' Rocheteau persisted, 'what's he really

like? He doesn't sound much like old Deschamps. Not one of us, eh?'

Lausard shook his head.

'No,' he mused. 'Not one of us.'

But what, he wondered, was he now? He was an important part of this unit but he wasn't like these men he fought with, or shared his meagre rations with. They coexisted in blissful ignorance. They had welcomed him as one of their own and Lausard had embraced that. Perhaps, he reasoned, as time went on the façade would become reality. He would become like the thieves, rapists, forgers and pickpockets he shared his new life with. After all, there was nothing of his old life left.

He watched the embers dying, one last tiny yellow flame rearing up defiantly before the breeze killed it.

Lausard settled down to try to sleep but it was many hours before that merciful oblivion claimed him.

CHAPTER 28

Dawn rose grey and dirty, spreading over the land like the smoke from a thousand guns. The heavens were crowded with grey cloud which scudded and shifted uneasily, swollen and dark as bruises. Rain was in the air although the icy wind threatened to turn it to sleet. Horses and men shuddered in the early morning, many of the animals skittish and unsettled. Like the men they carried, the animals ate sparingly and rarely enjoyed enough to fill their bellies. Troopers in threadbare, torn and holed uniforms sat in lines, some calming their mounts with reassuring pats, others rubbing their own eyes to force the weariness from them. They felt stinging spots of icy rain and shivered in their cloaks. Brass helmets were covered by oilskins, designed to protect the metal against the elements. Saddle cloths, some singed by fire in battle, others torn or ripped by bullets or bayonets, flapped forlornly in the breeze. Some horses pawed the ground impatiently, others merely stood shivering, heads lowered.

Lausard patted the neck of his own horse as it

chewed at the grass. On one side of him Rocheteau sat upright, watching to the left and right, his face set in firm lines. To his left Delacor gazed ahead blankly, his cheeks flushed, his eyes heavy from lack of sleep. None of the men had enjoyed much rest the previous night. The wind which had whipped across the land all through the hours of darkness had gradually increased in severity until even the thickest garments could not keep out its stinging chill. Even Rostov, seated in line behind Lausard, was shivering. The Russian glanced to his right and saw that Sonnier was slumped forward slightly in his saddle, his eyes half-closed. The Russian dug him in the ribs and Sonnier sat bolt upright as if pricked with a sword.

'Who is this bastard anyway?' said Delacor. 'A field inspection. Who does he think he is?'

He cast a quick glance towards one end of the line where Captain Cezar, Lieutenant Marquet and Royère were moving slowly along the ranks of dragoons, the captain pausing every so often to take a closer look at one of the men or his horse.

'He's our new commander,' Lausard said quietly. 'That's who he is.'

'Where is old Deschamps?' Rocheteau asked.

'Your guess is as good as mine,' Lausard murmured, aware that the officers were drawing closer. 'But even if he's still alive, it looks as if we're stuck with this fool for the time being.'

'God help us,' Moreau added, crossing himself.

'What do you know about him, Alain?' Rocheteau whispered.

'Only what I saw last night. He's ambitious and he's keen.'

'What about the other one? His adjutant,' Rocheteau persisted.

Lausard could only shake his head. 'I don't know,' he murmured. 'Not yet.'

Cezar was less than ten feet away now, leaning forward to inspect Charvet's tunic which still bore a hole in one shoulder.

'Your tunic is damaged,' the officer snapped. 'Repair it.'

He looked at Tabor. 'That shabrack is filthy. If you keep the rest of your equipment in such a disgusting state then you can expect regular visits from me. Clean yourself up.'

Tabor saluted.

'All of you,' Cezar bellowed. 'You are a disgrace. You are dirty, your horses are badly cared for, your uniforms are fit for rags. *You* are not fit to wear them as soldiers of France.' He turned his attention to Lausard. 'Let me see your sword.'

Lausard pulled it free in one fluid movement and held the point inches from the officer's face.

Cezar looked at Lausard then at the gleaming blade, the wicked point poised close to his nose.

'*Keep* it clean,' he hissed.

Lausard slid the weapon back into its scabbard.

'All of you, remember that,' the officer called. 'Never sheath a damp or dirty sword. It will rust, the metal will rot.' He shot Lausard a final, withering glance then moved on, immediately spotting a hole in Delacor's breeches.

'How do you explain that?' he said jabbing at the rip.

'It was a bayonet cut at Arcola, sir,' Delacor announced.

'And why has it not been repaired?' Cezar demanded. 'This is a sign of ill-discipline.' He wheeled his horse and rode to within a few yards of the leading rank of dragoons. 'The officer before me was weak. He allowed lapses of discipline which I will *not* allow. I am not here to be your friend, I am here to lead you. You are here to obey *my* orders. I know about this squadron, I know about this regiment. I know some of you were criminals, taken from prisons to fight for France. Well, if your discipline doesn't improve you will be treated like criminals again.' He rode his horse slowly back and forth, his eyes never leaving the lines of green-clad troops. 'There will be inspections every morning. I will drive you hard, sometimes to breaking point, sometimes beyond. Any man who cannot adapt will be punished. I have no need of fools in this squadron. I will not tolerate indiscipline. You are scum and, until you prove otherwise, that is how you will be treated. All of you.'

Lausard caught Royere's eye and something passed, unspoken, between the two men. The lieutenant shook his head almost imperceptibly then fixed his piercing stare on the captain.

'For those of you who do not know my name, it is Captain Cezar,' the officer proclaimed. 'I attended the same military school at Brienne as General Bonaparte. I learned what he learned. I know what *he* knows. Remember that.' He turned to Royere. 'I want patrols sent out. They will ride for fifty miles north and west and report back to me every hour. The rest of the squadron will move north. Understood?'

'Yes, sir,' said Royere, preparing to leave.

'When that's done, I want to speak to the prisoners.'

*

Lausard guessed that not one of the captive Austrians was any older than twenty-five. One of them sat on a fallen tree rubbing his hands together, the other two stood, aware of the watchful eyes of their captors and the carbines which were trained on them. They looked weary more than apprehensive, cold rather than terrified. The gold braid had been stripped from their dolman jackets which hung open. Most of their equipment had also been taken. One still had his sabretache but it had been emptied of personal effects.

'Which regiment are you with?' Cezar asked one of the prisoners standing up.

He was about to answer when one of the other men stepped close to him and put a hand across his mouth.

'It would be easier for all of us if you cooperated,' the captain said, drawing his sword. 'Which regiment?' he repeated, pressing the point of the blade against the cheek of the second hussar.

The man eyed the officer warily for a moment but still didn't answer.

Cezar cut him. Blood ran from the gash on his cheek and the man yelped.

'The Eleventh,' said the third man, jumping to his feet, holding up his hands in supplication.

'Ah, some cooperation,' Cezar said and smiled.

Two Austrians stepped back slightly, the one with the cut cheek pressing his hand to the gash in an effort to stem the flow of blood.

'Where is the main Austrian army?' Cezar addressed the hussar who had spoken.

The hussar shook his head.

'Come, come, you're not in a position to lie,' Cezar insisted. 'Where is your main force? Ten miles, twenty? Thirty? Which direction? North? West?'

'I cannot tell you,' the hussar said.

'Very well,' Cezar said.

The sword flashed forward with such dizzying speed and accuracy that everyone was taken by surprise.

The blade pierced the hussar's throat just below his larynx. The body remained upright for a few seconds then fell forward.

'I will ask again,' Cezar said, stepping towards the trooper who was already cut on the cheek. 'Where is the main force of your army?'

'Sir, you can't do this,' said Royere, stepping forward. 'The rules of war state that prisoners must be cared for until their exchange can be arranged.'

'Don't tell me what I can and can't do,' snarled Cezar. 'Besides, we scarcely have enough food for our own men – do you think I'm going to waste any more supplies keeping these enemies of France alive?'

Royere stepped back and shot a helpless glance at Lausard who was gazing not at the Austrians but at Cezar.

'Is the baggage train with the main force?' the captain demanded.

Lausard looked puzzled.

Even the Austrians looked bewildered by the question.

'Where is the baggage train?' Cezar raised the sword so that it was pressed against the tip of the injured man's nose.

'What's so important about the baggage train?' Royere said.

His question was met by a withering stare from Cezar.

The Austrian swallowed hard.

'It's true, isn't it?' Cezar asked quietly. 'It's true about what's being carried?'

The wounded man didn't answer.

Cezar whipped the point of the sword across his face, splitting open a nostril. Blood burst from him and sprayed the hussar's companion, who looked frantically around at the other Frenchmen, but none of them moved. No one tried to prevent this madman from pressing the end of his sword against the Austrian's ear.

'How much gold is there?' Cezar demanded.

Lausard looked at the hussar. So, what he'd said to Rocheteau had been true?

'How much?' the captain snarled.

Still no answer.

He sliced off the Austrian's left ear.

The man shrieked and clapped a hand to the bleeding hole.

'How much gold?' Cezar persisted.

'I don't know,' the hussar said, his face now a mask of blood.

Cezar stabbed him in the stomach, pushing the blade until it exited through the hussar's back, blood dripping from the tip. He tugged it free, the dying man falling at his feet.

The third hussar took a step back, his face the colour of rancid butter.

'How much gold is being carried on the baggage train?' Cezar said evenly.

'One hundred thousand marks,' the young hussar blurted out. 'Coin.'

Lausard stroked his chin thoughtfully then glanced

at Royere who was still looking on with bewildered anger.

'And the gold is with the main baggage train?' Cezar persisted.

The hussar nodded.

'And that baggage train is with the main force?'

Again the hussar nodded.

'Which is where?'

The hussar shook his head.

Cezar raised his sword.

'Where?'

'I can't tell you,' the trooper said, his face pale.

'Very well,' said Cezar almost resignedly, then drove the sword twice into the hussar's chest, ignoring the blood which just missed his tunic. He stood over the dead hussar for a moment then wiped his blade on the dead man's dolman and slid it back into the scabbard.

Lausard watched him.

'Sir,' said Royere, stepping forward. 'I must protest strongly about your treatment of these prisoners.'

'These spies,' said Cezar.

'They were not spies, sir. They were captured several days ago in combat. They were ordinary soldiers who should have been afforded the dignity—'

Cezar stepped closer to him snarling, 'Don't preach to me about dignity, Royere. This is a war. They were enemy soldiers and I killed them. They would have done the same to me given the chance.'

'They were unarmed,' Royere snapped defiantly.

'What did you see, Lieutenant Marquet?' Cezar asked his own adjutant.

'I saw you attacked and forced to defend yourself, sir,' Marquet said, a slight grin hovering on his lips.

'And you, Lausard?' the officer asked. 'What did *you* see?'

'Nothing very impressive, sir,' Lausard said, his gaze never leaving the officer.

Cezar and Marquet turned to walk away but the captain paused a moment, turning to Royere.

'I want full reports as soon as the patrols return,' he said. 'Understood? And get these' – he nodded to the three dead Austrians – 'out of the way. Bury them, throw them over the nearest gorge. Just get rid of them.' He and his adjutant walked away.

'Murdering bastard,' hissed Royere, glancing down at the nearest of the dead Austrians.

'I wonder why he's so interested in that gold?' Lausard mused.

'If it's part of the Austrian baggage train I don't know how he thinks he's going to get hold of it anyway,' Royere said.

'I'm sure our new captain has already thought of that.'

'One hundred thousand in gold coins – how is he going to carry it, even if he manages to find it?' Royere said dismissively.

'I don't somehow think he'll be doing it alone,' Lausard murmured. 'My guess is he'll want some help.'

The two men looked silently at each other.

CHAPTER 29

Bonaparte pulled up the collar of his greatcoat and stuffed both hands into the deep pockets. As he walked he seemed to be gazing off into space, his eyes attracted by some far-off object which Bessieres himself could not see. He walked slightly behind his commander, matching the Corsican stride for stride as they moved briskly along the top of the ridge.

Below them on the road, moving slowly due to the narrowness of the thoroughfare, the massed ranks of infantry, artillery and a few cavalry flowed like a human river. Many of the men marched stiffly, their feet frozen and painful from so many days of similar marching. Others merely slouched along, muskets by their sides. The artillery drivers did their best to force some effort out of animals that were practically starving to death. But, despite their wretched condition, the French soldiers moved with purpose and an almost robotic determination.

Bonaparte paused and gazed down at them, his pinched features expressionless.

'They are starving, freezing and homesick,' he said,

'and yet, they have conquered most of Northern Italy.'

'Under your command, sir,' Bessieres added.

'And they never question it, Bessieres. They obey my every order willingly, almost blindly.'

'Because they trust you, sir. They love you. You have brought them victories they could never have dreamed of.'

'I wish Barras and those other ninnies in Paris could see them. They want peace, Bessieres. Those preening *pekinese* want an end to this war. Barras, Carnot, Tallien. All of the Directory want this conflict finished. They want peace.'

'There's nothing wrong with that, sir, is there?'

'I myself want peace. I want it for those soldiers,' he nodded towards the men below. 'I don't enjoy sending men to their deaths. I lose a son every time one of them dies.' He took off his bicorn and ran a hand through his long hair. 'But I will lose many more if it brings about a lasting peace and gain for France. The Directory see no further than the ends of their noses. They believe I triumph here for *them*. And now they want me to make peace, even if it is a peace of compromise.' He shook his head. 'If peace is to be made it is for me to make it and I will not consider that until the Austrians are beaten once and for all.'

'They will not give up while Mantua holds out,' Bessieres observed.

'I know, and I know that their only hope is to relieve it,' Bonaparte mused. 'It is the key to the door of Italy, Bessieres. Once that fortress falls, this country is ours, but it is a hindrance to me. I have ten thousand men besieging it, the same number protecting our lines of communication from it. Men I need here. As long as I am short of men I must defend, but this war, these gains, they have been made from attacking not sitting around waiting for the Austrians to attack.'

'We have nearly thirty-five thousand men on the move, sir,' Bessieres reminded him.

'And the Austrians have over forty-five thousand.'

'We've beaten them before with smaller numbers.'

'But that was while we were on the offensive. No. I must wait for the Austrians to attack. It's just a question of where that attack will come. There are three ways they can approach Mantua. They can use the Brenta valley to Vicenza, they can move down the Adige or they can move along our rear using the River Chiese. The problem is that we are thinly spread. If they attack we will need to concentrate all our forces at that one point, and quickly, otherwise all may be lost. Everything you and I and these men have fought for could be worthless. But I can do nothing until the Austrians show their hand.'

He stopped walking and stood, arms crossed, looking down into the valley where the steady stream of men, horses and equipment continued to flow past.

Bessieres looked up at the cloud-bruised sky and, as he did, he felt the first drops of rain against his skin.

Lausard didn't know the man's name. He'd seen his face on a number of occasions but he'd never bothered to ask his name. It hadn't seemed important. After all, like all the men in the squadron, he could be dead soon, why get close? But now, as he stood with the rest of the dragoons, he was curious as to the identity of this man. This man who stood naked on a small boulder, his carbine held in one hand, his sword in the other. His arms were extended on either side of him in cruciform shape and Lausard could see the muscles bulging as he struggled to hold the weapons aloft. In a soggy heap in front of him lay his uniform. His horse stood close by, Marquet holding the reins, his own gaze fixed on the rows of watching dragoons with that almost imperceptible smile playing across his thin lips.

The rain, which had begun over an hour ago as fine drizzle, was now hammering down, blasted by the chill breeze. The naked man holding the weapons was shivering almost uncontrollably. His knees buckled slightly and it looked as though he was going to fall but by a supreme effort of will he remained upright.

'If you release those weapons before I give you the order you will be flogged,' shouted Captain Cezar, who sat astride his horse gazing at the naked man. 'That goes for all of you. Commit a crime and you will be flogged. Step out of line and you will be flogged. Question my authority and you will be flogged.'

'He can't do that,' murmured Bonet. 'Punishment like that has been banned.'

'Try telling that to Cezar,' Lausard said.

'This man,' shouted the captain, pointing at the bedraggled figure before him, 'was told to keep his powder dry, to keep his sword clean. He did neither. He disobeyed. He is no use to me. He is no use to you. If the Austrians had attacked he would have been unable to fight. I do not want men like this in my squadron.'

Lausard fixed the captain in an unblinking stare.

'He's insane,' whispered Rocheteau.

Lausard didn't answer, his stare was still riveted on the officer.

With a grunt, the naked man finally lost his battle and fell forward, sprawling on the wet grass. Marquet kicked him in the ribs in an effort to revive him but the action drew only groans from the prone figure.

'Get up, you bastard!' the lieutenant shouted but the man wouldn't move.

Moreau crossed himself.

Marquet kicked the man again but he could only drag himself up on to all fours.

'You should stay in that position,' chided the lieutenant. 'You are nothing more than a dog.'

Both Marquet and Cezar laughed, watching as the man tried to drag himself upright.

He finally managed it but could stand there for only a second or two before he crashed backwards and lay still.

'Leave him there,' Cezar said. Then, turning to the watching men: 'The rest of you mount up and remember what you've seen here today. The next time it could be one of you. Or it could be worse for you. I'll see the skin taken off any of your backs if you disobey me or slip below the standards I demand.' He walked his horse slowly back and forth. 'There will be a new inspection at dawn tomorrow, before we rendezvous with the rest of the army.'

'If I had my way, Cezar would have a rendezvous with my sword,' hissed Rocheteau, hauling himself up into the saddle.

Lausard heard his companion but his attention was elsewhere. His interest was drawn towards the crest of the ridge ahead of them, his eyes fixed on the single horseman galloping towards them.

*

Bonaparte read the despatch once more then handed it to Bessieres.

'It is as you feared, sir,' said the captain, scanning the report.

'As I had *hoped*, you mean,' Bonaparte said, then turned to the horseman who had brought the news. He was a thick-set man in his early twenties, his long hair plaited at the temples and the back, a red pelisse fastened over his jacket. His horse was badly lathered but still fresh.

'Ride back immediately,' he told the hussar. 'Tell the General he must hold firm at all costs. Tell him that we will join him before nightfall.'

The rider saluted, wheeled his horse and raced off.

Bonaparte turned as he heard another horse approaching and saw Murat riding to join him.

'What news?' Murat asked.

'The enemy's plan is at last unmasked,' said Bonaparte gleefully. 'They have attacked La Corona, Joubert has been forced to withdraw to Rivoli. Another Austrian column has attacked Legnano and the main force is advancing through the Adige valley.'

'To Rivoli you say?' Murat asked.

Bonaparte nodded. 'It is there we will find our victory,' he said defiantly.

'And what if Joubert's men can't hold them until we arrive?

'They *will* hold,' Bonaparte asserted.

Murat was less impressed. 'I hope to God you're right.'

CHAPTER 30

Lausard heard the screams before he saw their source. The wagon carrying the wounded was packed to overflowing and bumped over the rough road which led towards the village of Rivoli; the constant jarring only intensified the suffering of the already agonised human cargo.

The column of dragoons parted to let the wagon through, which was followed by a second and then a third, each filled with wounded and dying men.

Beneath the light of the full moon, their faces looked like those of ghosts. Blood, which stained so many of them, appeared black in the silvery glow and Lausard could see that the dark liquid had splashed the drivers in places and, occasionally, even the horses that drew the wagons.

The procession of pain passed through the centre of the horsemen and out of sight, although the groans and shrieks seemed to hang in the air, ringing in the ears of the dragoons.

All around the men steep mountains rose up into the blackness, as if the outcrops of rock were reaching for the heavens themselves. To the east was a view across the plateau of Rivoli and also the Adige River. Above all was the huge edifice of Monte Pipolo. Lausard could see several units of infantry camped on the rocky ground close to the village of Rivoli itself and many fires burned in and around the hamlet as the foot soldiers tried vainly to arm themselves against the chilly night breezes.

The ground began to slope upwards sharply and Rocheteau had to grip his reins tightly to prevent his horse from stumbling on the rock-strewn slope. Elsewhere, other troopers were finding similar problems. Horses strained under the weight of their riders and their equipment, trying to find a foothold on the treacherous terrain.

As the cavalrymen climbed higher up, they moved past increasing numbers of infantry but these were not sitting around camp fires; many were receiving treatment from overworked doctors and their assistants who had set up a number of dressing stations on the reverse slope of the plateau. Lausard could only guess at how many had been wounded in the fighting earlier that day, but of that number it appeared that many were due to be sent back into conflict as soon as they had been patched up. The men waited obediently in lines, those who were having trouble standing supported by comrades. Their wounds were not treated, simply bandaged and then they made their way back across the plateau to rejoin their units.

The huge silver moon glinted on the surface of the Adige and beyond the river Lausard could see more camp fires. He could even see cannon. It took him only a moment to realise that they were Austrian.

Four horsemen galloped past and Rocheteau nudged Lausard as he saw the white plume on the bicorn of one of the men.

'That's Bonaparte, isn't it?' he said, pointing in the direction of the swiftly moving men.

But they had already been swallowed up by the gloom before Lausard could pick out the general. All he saw was the small geysers of dust thrown up by the horses' hooves.

A chorus of cheers from up ahead told him that Rocheteau had indeed been right. Great shouts of '*Vive Bonaparte*' echoed across the plateau and seemed to reverberate off the mountains and cliffs, which closed around the French position like granite fingers.

The ground was finally beginning to level out slightly as the dragoons reached the top of the plateau and Lausard heard the order to dismount and set up camp.

'Perhaps we'll get something to eat now,' said Joubert feeling hopeful.

'You'll be lucky,' Rocheteau snorted. 'The infantry will have scraped this place clean by now. We'll be fortunate if we can find enough wood to make a fire, let alone some food.'

'I don't know how you can think about eating when we're going to fight a battle tomorrow,' said Roussard.

'You might as well die on a full stomach,' said Rocheteau, chuckling.

'If that bastard Cezar has anything to do with it, we'll probably all be killed anyway,' Delacor sneered. 'Bloody glory boy.'

'May God have mercy on all of us,' Moreau prayed.

'Except Cezar and that lap-dog of his, Marquet,'

Delacor added. 'They'll kill more of us than the Austrians ever will.'

'You could just be right,' Lausard murmured and headed off into the darkness.

'Alain, where are you going?' Rocheteau called after him.

'For a walk in the moonlight,' Lausard said, smiling.

'That should be done with a woman,' Giresse told him.

'If I find one, I'll remember that,' Lausard called back.

The breeze whipped the horsehair mane of his helmet around his face as he walked, passing between more camp fires and more troops. Some horse artillery had set up a fire close to their four-pounder gun and they sat around smoking, casting cursory glances at the dragoon as he passed.

Two hussars were walking across the plateau too, inspecting the ground over which it was likely they would have to charge the following day. Both nodded as Lausard passed them and he returned the gesture.

Drummer boys were using their instruments as seats as they huddled around fires, warming their hands. Most of them were shoeless, as were the bulk of the infantry. Some had already settled down to sleep, heads resting on their bulging packs, some resting on their comrades. Other men lay talking quietly or smoking. Some were praying.

Some men were playing cards, using pebbles to bet with in the absence of money. Anything to pass the time, to take their minds off the coming battle, to banish, even momentarily, thoughts of their impending death.

As Lausard walked, the scabbard of his sword trailed on the rough ground and a number of heads turned to watch him pass by. An artilleryman, sitting on the trail of the gun smoking a pipe, waved to him.

'Lost your horse?' he called.

'Last time I saw him, he was with your mother,' Lausard told him and heard the other members of the crew laughing heartily.

Ahead of him, the plateau began to slope away once again and, across the valley, in the direction of the village of Caprino, he could see hundreds of flickering yellow spots. The camp fires of the Austrian army. There seemed to be five distinct camps, each belonging to a column. Spread from Lake Garda in the west, across to the Adige in the east, the enemy were encamped across a four-mile front. It reminded Lausard of thousands of candles burning in the gloom.

The terrain favoured the defenders and most of the French troops were drawn up along the horseshoe formation of the Trombalore heights. The only good roads available to the Austrians were either side of the Adige but only the western route offered the attackers a clear and direct approach to Rivoli itself by way of the gorge and village of Osteria. Another village, called San Marco, clung precipitously to the easternmost edge of the plateau, and Lausard, like his commanding general, realised that this position could be crucial to the outcome of the battle.

He stood with his arms folded, looking across the plateau at the masses of French troops and then, once more, looked out towards the myriad Austrian camp fires. Somewhere down there was the baggage train which Cezar wanted to find so badly. One hundred thousand in gold. Lausard stroked his chin thoughtfully. He knew that officers and private soldiers alike had spent time and effort pillaging Italy for riches. Stories of entire shipments of art treasures being escorted back to France had reached the men. Commanders, it seemed, were as eager to line their pockets as common soldiers. Lausard shook his head. Those same commanders who had helped to destroy the rich were now setting *themselves* up with fortunes. People said that war was insane; then so too were the men who waged it. Perhaps the whole world was insane, himself included. He gazed up at the sky, past the thrusting peaks of the mountains, at the stars shimmering against the black backdrop. They looked like distant camp fires, Lausard thought. The moon passed momentarily behind a bank of cloud and the plateau was plunged into darkness for precious seconds, but then the silver light slowly began to creep across the rocks once more, illuminating so many men waiting for the coming day. Waiting and wondering if they would see the next moon.

Lausard turned and headed back towards his unit.

'That is one of the keys to our position,' said Bonaparte, pointing towards San Marco. 'If we hold it we will divide the Austrian attack in two. The entire battle could hinge on that position. That and how quickly your men get here, Massena.'

The dark-haired general nodded.

'My men should be here in less than three hours,' he said, confidently.

'Good,' Bonaparte said. 'When they arrive you will hold the valley on the left flank. Use one brigade. The rest of your division I want as a reserve around Rivoli itself. Understood?' He turned to one of the other officers. 'Joubert, you will use one brigade to hold San Marco and the Osteria gorge. Use your other two brigades to meet the first Austrian advance against the heights.'

'How can you be sure that's where they'll attack first?' Joubert asked.

Bonaparte waved a hand towards the mass of camp fires before them.

'There must be ten or twelve thousand men there,' he said. 'They're not there for show. That is where the first attack will come. Trust me.' He pushed his telescope shut and slipped it into the pocket of his tunic. 'They are spread too thinly,' he said. 'Our opponent chooses to use a scythe, not a hammer.' He smiled to himself.

'What if they cross the river and outflank us?' Massena said.

'You and your men will make sure they do not.'

'My men are tired, General,' Joubert said. 'They have fought today and now you expect them to fight again in the morning.'

'And the morning after that and the morning after that if necessary, Joubert,' Bonaparte said. 'I want them to fight for as long as it takes to win this war and I know they will. I know *you* will.' He placed one hand on the officer's shoulder.

'My men will not fail you, General,' Joubert assured his commander.

'The total Austrian strength is around twenty-eight thousand,' Bessieres said. 'Our strength, at the moment, is ten thousand.'

'Two Frenchmen are worth four Austrians any day,' Bonaparte said, smiling. 'Our troops move quicker and that is what this battle will depend on. It will be a race against time, gentlemen. Let us hope that our watches are working.'

The men laughed.

'If we fail tomorrow then everything we have won so far in this campaign will be lost,' Bonaparte said, his voice now low, his gaze fixed on the Austrian camp fires. 'If the Austrians defeat us, drive us back, then they will be able to reinforce Mantua. If we beat them then the fortress cannot hold out. The war will be won.' He looked around at his companions. 'Now, gentlemen, I suggest you get some sleep while you can. We have pressing business in the morning.' He glanced at his pocket watch. 'And morning is not that far away.'

CHAPTER 31

The air was thick with the cloying smell of gun-powder. Great clouds of noxious smoke drifted across the plateau like choking banks of hissing fog, occasionally parted by a breeze to reveal the ebb and flow of battle below.

Messengers galloped frantically back and forth on lathered horses, clutching orders, bringing reports to Bonaparte from every part of the French position.

The sound of cannon fire was accompanied by a non-stop crackle of muskets as both sides poured fusil-lades relentlessly into each other. The sounds drifted up from below, carried to the top of the Rivoli plateau on the wind and the swirling banks of smoke.

Lausard's horse pawed the ground impatiently. He himself peered to right and left in an attempt to see something of the battle which he and all his comrades could hear raging. The din of fighting seemed to be coming from all around them, the most intense clashes coming from the eastern end of the French positions around San Marco and the Osteria gorge.

The Adige, which had looked like a strip of silver

the previous night beneath the moonlight, now resembled a dark-blue snake writhing amidst the rocks and mountains. From its eastern bank, Austrian artillery were shelling the French troops in and around San Marco and, every now and then, great plumes of fire would shoot skyward, sometimes blasting men in the air.

The initial Austrian advance against the Trombalore heights had been checked but bitter fighting was still going on all across the front of the French positions.

Lausard sucked in a gunpowder-tainted breath and nudged Rocheteau. 'What time is it?'

'Just after ten.'

'How much longer are they going to leave us sitting here?' Giresse asked in agitation. 'We've been in the saddle more than three hours already.'

'I don't care if they leave us here for the whole battle,' Roussard said.

'It sounds as if we're surrounded.' Carbonne looked around. 'There's gunfire coming from all directions.'

'And all we can do is sit and wait,' Giresse hissed.

Captain Cezar walked his horse past the front line of the dragoons, his interest drawn to a rider who was galloping hell for leather across the plateau towards the tent where Bonaparte had set up his headquarters.

'Something's going on,' said Giresse.

'A battle, I think,' said Lausard cryptically.

Moments later, Bonaparte, Bessieres and a dozen mounted guides followed the horseman back across the plateau, heading for the western end of the French line. The dragoons watched as they disappeared down the sharp slope, swallowed up by dense clouds of smoke.

'If only we knew what was happening,' Giresse said.

'It's probably best that we don't,' Roussard offered, trying to calm his own skittish horse.

The cannon and musket fire were growing in intensity. Again Lausard took a deep breath, again tasting gunpowder. He saw three four-pounders being limbered up, the crews sweating and straining under the effort, then the drivers leaped into position and the guns were hurried away in the direction of the gorge.

Even the mountains themselves appeared wreathed in smoke, the gunfire reverberating around them.

Lausard and the rest of the dragoons continued to wait.

'My God, they're running,' said Bessieres, seeing dozens of French infantry streaming towards them, many throwing their weapons away in panic.

'The Eighty-fifth has broken!' someone shouted and Bonaparte saw a big sergeant reeling towards him, blood pouring down his face. 'Save yourself,' the man said and dropped to his knees close to Bonaparte's horse. Fleeing men streamed past him, some of them bumping into the horses of the guides in an effort to escape the oncoming Austrians, some of whom were already forming a line preparatory to delivering a volley of fire into the backs of the running men.

The fusillade swept the French and more men crashed to the ground.

A guide close to Bonaparte fell from his horse, blood streaming from a chest wound. Another man pitched forward as his horse was hit in the neck and head by bullets.

A dozen infantrymen went down, shot in the back as they fled.

'They'll cut us off from our reinforcements,' said Bonaparte, watching the advancing Austrians with apparent calm. 'Outflank us. Massena, you must plug the gap now.'

More French infantry were sprinting over the rough ground, some even discarding their packs in an attempt to make themselves lighter as they ran. Others had paused and were trying to rally, officers bellowing at them.

Bessieres and half-a-dozen of the guides rode forward and joined fifteen infantrymen who had rallied close to an outcrop of rocks and were preparing to fire back at the Austrians. From the saddle, the mounted guides aimed their carbines and, when the order was given to fire, added their own to that of the infantry.

A number of Austrians went down but the sheer mass of men was unaffected by this minor annoyance and they now lowered their bayonets and continued to advance with well-ordered determination.

'Bring up the Eighteenth,' Bonaparte shouted, watching as Massena led three columns of men forward, drums beating and colours flying in the smoke-filled air. A battery of horse artillery galloped up alongside them. The columns of men began to spread out into lines, preparing to bring their full fire power to bear against the Austrians.

'Sir, you must take cover,' Bessieres called to Bonaparte who merely wheeled his horse and galloped back and forth across the front of the deploying Eighteenth Demi-Brigade, his bicorn held high above his head.

'Brave Eighteenth,' he shouted. 'I know you, the enemy will not stand before you.'

The men cheered.

Stragglers from the broken Eighty-fifth were still streaming past and some of the other troops spat at them as they ran but they ignored it, anxious only to be away from the battlefield.

'Cowards!' roared a corporal at the fleeing men.

Massena drew his sabre and walked his horse back and forth in front of the Demi-Brigade.

'Comrades,' he called. 'In front of you are four thousand young men belonging to the richest families in Vienna. They have come with post-horses as far as Bassano. I recommend them to you.' He smiled and pointed his sabre at the oncoming Austrians who were now less than two hundred yards away.

The men of the Eighteenth roared their approval and steadied themselves, squinting down the barrels of their muskets as the white-coated masses drew nearer, urged on by their own officers. But the ground between the two sets of troops was uneven and also littered with discarded weapons, equipment and bodies. The Austrians began to break formation slightly, unable to retain their rigid column on such terrain.

One hundred yards and they were able to see the faces of the French waiting for them, muskets primed and ready.

Fifty yards.

The crews at the trio of four-pounders awaited the order of fire.

Bonaparte, Bessieres and a number of the guides had taken shelter behind the front line of French troops. They watched intently as the Austrians came to within forty yards, their bayonets glinting.

Thirty yards.

'Fire!'

The shout seemed to fill the valley and a series of thunderous blasts followed as both the French infantry and the artillery opened up, sweeping the Austrian columns with fire and pouring canister shot from cannon into them from close range.

Huge blankets of smoke covered the field but the French fired again, unable to see their enemy but knowing where the Austrians were. They could hear screams of agony, shouts of officers. Through the fog, some of the men saw a colour fall and the sight drew another huge cheer from the infantry.

The gunners on the four-pounders worked quickly to reload, preparing to fire yet more shot into the shaken enemy.

When a gust of wind finally blew some of the choking smoke aside, Bonaparte saw that dozens of Austrians were lying dead or dying on the littered ground, their white uniforms spattered with crimson. The advance had halted, the remaining troops wavering, unsure whether to move forward or not.

A volley of fire from the four-pounders seemed to make up their minds for them. The barrels flamed and canister shot erupted from the barrels, scything down dozens more of the bewildered Austrians.

Smoke again obscured Bonaparte's view but he heard Massena roar out the order to fix bayonets and the French infantry did so with mechanical precision.

'They will not stand,' Bonaparte said, squinting to see through the rolling smoke. 'They *cannot*.'

Bessieres pointed to a break in the smoke and they both saw the Austrians retreating, trying to retain as much order as possible but many were stumbling over the bodies of their fallen comrades.

Bonaparte smiled, his white horse bucking excitedly beneath him.

'They are safe with Massena,' he said, seeing the general rise in his stirrups and urge the infantry forward. 'We must see what the situation is elsewhere.'

The French infantry swept forward with a huge cheer.

The village of San Marco was on fire.

Every dwelling in it seemed to be aflame and the smoke rose like a black shroud over the Osteria gorge.

French infantry occupying the houses fled. Those unable to were burned to death inside buildings that had been transformed into funeral pyres. The stink of gunpowder began to mingle with another, sickly sweet stench – that of burning human flesh.

In the narrow streets, Austrian and French troops fought hand-to-hand amidst the raging inferno, as cannon balls from the Austrian batteries across the Adige tore into the village, sometimes killing friend and foe alike.

French artillery fired back, although most of the time they were firing blind due to the choking smoke. Their faces blackened, their throats parched by the choking fumes, they sweated over their guns, keeping up a more or less constant fire in an effort to keep the Austrian infantry back, but it seemed to be a useless effort. The French were forced back up the slopes towards the plateau of Rivoli itself and the white-coated Austrians pressed on through the blazing inferno of San Marco.

'Pull back!' shouted an officer but his words were

silenced seconds later when a roundshot took off his head. The decapitated body remained upright for a second, spouting blood into the air, then fell forward.

The wounded were left where they fell, such was the French infantry's desire to escape the burning village. In places the smoke was so thick that men couldn't see more than a foot ahead. Some had abandoned their weapons and were attempting to climb the craggy outcrops of rock which led upwards to the top of the plateau.

Lausard saw the first of these bedraggled, smoke-stained and blood-splashed figures stumble out of a bank of smoke then fall to the ground less than a hundred yards away. He was followed by another, then another, the last of them carrying a faded tricolour which was singed and blackened.

Captain Cezar saw them too and walked his horse across towards the men. Lausard saw him leaning down speaking to the dazed infantrymen.

'How much longer are we to sit here?' Lausard asked, his words directed at no one in particular.

However, they were heard by Lieutenant Marquet.

'You will sit here for as long as you are ordered,' he hissed.

'Our men are being slaughtered down in that valley,' Lausard said. 'Are we to sit and watch it?'

'Just keep your mouth shut, Lausard,' snapped Marquet. 'The Captain cannot move without orders either.'

'But will he move *with* them?' Lausard challenged.

Marquet was about to answer when several loud shouts of '*Vive Bonaparte*' echoed across the plateau and the dragoons turned to see Bonaparte riding ahead of two columns of infantry, Bessieres and a dozen mounted guides with him. Rumbling up alongside came a battery of four-pounders.

Cezar saw him too and rode back to join his regiment.

The infantry passed by, drums beating, some of them looking disdainfully at the stationary cavalry before they disappeared down the steep eastern side of the plateau, picking their way over the difficult terrain leading down into the blazing hell of San Marco and the Osteria gorge.

The four-pounders were taken to the rim of the plateau and then unlimbered. They began firing immediately, blasting the oncoming Austrians with case shot.

Suddenly, there was a fearsome explosion less than twenty yards from Lausard. The blast caused several horses to rear, one throwing its rider.

'Where the hell did that come from?' said Rocheteau, looking around anxiously.

Lausard looked up and saw several puffs of smoke coming from the north-east, from the slopes of Mount Magnone which rose above the plateau.

Another blast erupted nearby and Lausard pointed to the Austrian guns that had begun to fire down on the French. Smoke, lumps of earth and metal flew into the air only to rain down again on the men below. A lump of metal the size of a man's little finger pierced the shoulder of a horse close by and passed straight through the animal, embedding itself in the rider's thigh. The dragoon shrieked and clapped both hands to the wound as blood stained his gauntlets. Next to him another man toppled from the saddle clutching his face. Three horses went down, only one of them getting to its feet again, blood pouring down its hind leg from a wound in its flank.

Another piece of flying steel cut cleanly through the ear of Rocheteau's mount and he had to use all his skill to prevent the animal throwing him.

Lausard saw Bonaparte's white horse rear then fall, hurling its rider to the ground.

'No,' he rasped, seeing Bonaparte hit the ground hard. But he rolled over and sprang to his feet, splashed with the blood of his wounded mount. One of the aides leaped from the saddle and held the bridle of his own horse, offering it to the young general, who nodded and prepared to swing himself astride the new mount.

Men all around looked on in horror as they saw their leader wiping blood and dust from his uniform, but he rose in his stirrups and waved his hat above his head to signal he was unhurt. Deafening cheers greeted his reappearance but those cheers themselves were eclipsed a moment later by two shattering explosions. They came from just below the rim of the valley but were so enormous that the shock waves could practically be felt across the entire plateau. Two massive plumes of black and red smoke mushroomed up into the already blackened heavens.

'We've hit two powder wagons,' an artilleryman bellowed triumphantly.

Pieces of wood were still spiralling upwards, propelled by the savagery of the blasts. Lausard even saw part of a wheel spinning into the air.

Bonaparte rode to the lip of the plateau then turned and looked towards the dragoons.

'Ride them down!' he roared. 'They are lost. Drive them from the gorge.'

'Draw swords,' bellowed Cezar and the dragoons did so as one man, the three-foot lengths of steel brandished above their heads.

'At last,' said Lausard.

'A charge down the side of a mountain,' Roussard murmured. 'We haven't got a chance.'

Moreau crossed himself as the lines began to move forward, Cezar at their head. Gaston spurred his mount up alongside the officer, ready to sound the notes which would signal the charge. He could see down into the gorge now, to the bewildered Austrians and the exploded powder wagons. All around the remains of both there were dozens of bodies. Two cannon had been overturned and Gaston could see a man trapped beneath the carriage of a six-pounder, his legs pulped by the weight of the artillery piece. All around him, the crew of the gun were dead and no one else was helping to free him.

Lausard saw more horsemen to the right, their blue uniforms and shabracks marking them out as chasseurs. Their officer was carrying the curved sabre of light cavalry and he was waving it frenziedly in the air above his head, screaming instructions to his men. Lausard watched as the chasseurs hurtled over the rim of the plateau and the charge began.

'Charge!' roared Cezar and the dragoons followed, swept along by a sudden insane exhilaration. The release of so much tension was mixed with a sheer exultation of moving at speed on horses that were every bit as anxious to flex their muscles. Over it all, the trumpets sounded the charge and the green- and blue-clad horsemen rushed down the slope towards the Austrians.

Those in the front ranks had little chance.

Lausard sabred one man across the face, then cut right and slashed downwards so violently that he split a man's cranium open.

Rocheteau rode his horse into two white-clad grenadiers, one of them crushed beneath the hooves, the other knocked to one side where Giresse drove his own sword through the man's neck.

Slashing to right and left, Delacor cut down more infantrymen.

Cezar struck a sergeant so hard across the back of the neck that he almost severed his head.

Blood from their helpless foes splashed the raging horsemen and this seemed to inflame them even more.

Moreau cut down three men, one of them a boy in his teens.

Some of the Austrians turned and ran, others tried to take shelter behind rocks or near to the burning houses of San Marco. They managed to get off a volley of musket fire in an attempt to halt the charge.

A dragoon close to Lausard was hit, his horse slipping on the slope, falling and catapulting its wounded rider from the saddle. He fell shrieking beneath the hooves of his comrades who were unable to avoid him.

Two more horses went down, taking their riders with them. Those dragoons behind tried to jump the fallen animals but the steep incline made it impossible and more fell.

Lausard could see the burning inferno that was San Marco now, he could smell the burning flesh.

A French artilleryman with one arm blown off knelt and cheered as the cavalry swept past, the hooves sending clouds of dust into the air to mix with the reeking smoke. The air was practically unbreathable. It clogged the nostrils of men and horses alike, millions of tiny cinders from the burning town also stinging their eyes, but most of the men barely noticed as they were swept along, swords raised high, dripping blood, ready to be brought down whenever more enemy troops came within striking distance.

The smoke enveloped them making it almost impossible to see. They could have been charging off the edge of the world for all they knew. Insistent blasts from the trumpets were all that guided them. The vast, swiftly moving mass thundered down the slope and through the scorched, burning remains of San Marco, many of the horses whinnying in fear as flames licked from the blazing buildings. The roof of one fell in, collapsing with a huge shower of sparks, smoke and flame and it was all Lausard could do to keep control of his horse.

Another dragoon was hit in the chest and face and toppled sideways, falling from his mount into what was left of a burning house. Lausard heard his screams as he galloped past, his own voice rising to a shout of furious exultation. Smoke filled his lungs and pieces of burning debris singed his skin and his uniform but he rode on, searching through the inferno for any Austrian troops who had escaped the first mad charge. Most of the enemy soldiers had either fled or simply thrown away their weapons. Lausard saw many with their arms raised and he could hear their shouts through the din of men and horses.

'Prisoners!' they called helplessly.

A number of the dragoons ignored their pleas to surrender and Lausard saw a group of Austrians ridden or sabred down despite their desire to be taken alive.

Anything to escape the ferocity of these charging cavalry.

French infantry were spilling down the slope too, bayonets fixed, and it was they who took most of the prisoners.

Some of the cavalry rode on almost as far as the banks of the Adige but a few shots from enemy batteries on the far bank soon halted them.

Despite the speed of the charge, few of the horses seemed to be blown; they were as enthusiastic as their riders and leaped around like spring lambs, seemingly oblivious to the burning buildings and wreckage all around. Bodies were everywhere. French and Austrian. Dead and dying horses, shattered cannon and caissons, overturned wagons. An Austrian standard bearer, his left leg holed by a bullet, his face gashed open by a sword cut had crawled up against one of these wagons, the colour still gripped in his bloodied hands. Lausard galloped over to him, grabbed the standard and yanked it from his grip, lifting it into the air.

Those who saw him do it shouted in triumph, their delighted cries heard even above the continued explosions and the fire from San Marco.

Lausard rode towards Captain Cezar and thrust the standard at him. 'A present for you,' he said, his face set in hard lines, his cheeks blackened, his uniform splashed with blood.

Cezar took it then handed it to a trooper and told him to take it to the rear.

Lieutenant Royere rode past and slapped Lausard on the back. The officer's horse was limping slightly where a musket ball had grazed its hindquarters but it seemed lively enough. One corner of the lieutenant's shabrack had been shot away and there was a dent in his scabbard where another musket ball had struck the metal but the officer seemed untouched. He wiped sweat from his face with his sleeve and looked around him to see how many of the dragoons had fallen. Then Lausard lost sight of him as he disappeared into a swirling bank of smoke.

Prisoners were being escorted away now, their faces pale, their heads downcast but they seemed relieved to be out of the fighting and although they outnumbered their captors, they strode along obediently. An entire battalion of the Deutschmeister regiment had surrendered *en masse* and now trudged towards the rear escorted by the jubilant French infantry.

Lausard looked around him and saw more blue-clad infantry taking up positions in the remains of San Marco and on the ground beyond.

The Osteria gorge was firmly in French hands once more.

Bonaparte raised the telescope to his eye and squinted through it, watching the troops moving before him. His uniform was stained with sweat and mud, splashed with blood and torn on one sleeve but he himself was uninjured and he rode his horse slowly along the body-strewn length of the Trombalore heights with half-a-dozen guides and messengers in attendance.

Bessieres, his face blackened by powder and smoke, rode with him. He wiped his face with the back of his hand and inhaled, sucking down the acrid air.

All around dead and wounded men lay. An eight-pounder stood close by, its crew scattered around it, every one of them dead or dying. Even the limber horses were dead, still strapped in their harnesses.

Bonaparte kept his telescope trained on the slopes of Mount Baldo, certain now that the Austrians were retreating in disorder.

'It is the victory you wanted, General,' said Bessieres, looking through his own telescope.

Bonaparte nodded slightly.

'Take some cavalry and pursue them,' he said. 'I don't want to give them the chance to regroup.'

He pulled a pocket watch from his tunic and flipped it open.

Six minutes past five.

He swept the battlefield with his telescope once more and saw that, along the length of their line, the Austrians were falling back.

CHAPTER 32

Lausard surprised even himself with the speed that he fell asleep, exhausted by the exertions of the day. He and the remainder of the squadron had withdrawn to the village of Rivoli and had found quarters in several of the houses, competing with some infantry for the right to occupy the dwellings. Lausard couldn't remember the last time he'd slept with a roof over his head and, what was more, he slept without the intrusion of dreams. Even Joubert's snoring didn't wake him.

What did rouse him from his slumber was a sharp kick.

He woke suddenly and spun round, immediately alert, one hand reaching for the pistol he kept close to him. He thrust the barrel in the direction of the intruder and saw Lieutenant Marquet standing over him. Lausard kept the pistol aimed at the officer for a few moments, his eyes narrowing and, briefly, he saw the uncertainty in Marquet's expression. As if he was unsure whether or not Lausard was going to pull the trigger. Lausard finally replaced the weapon.

'Captain Cezar wants to see you,' said Marquet. 'Now.'

Rocheteau had also woken and he turned over and looked contemptuously at the officer.

Lausard got to his feet and watched as Marquet left the room.

'Alain,' said Rocheteau. 'Be careful of that bloody butcher.'

Lausard nodded then followed the lieutenant out into the street.

'You fought well this afternoon,' Marquet said. 'You are a good horseman.'

Lausard didn't answer.

The men crossed the main square of the village and headed towards what had once been an inn. Several horses were tethered outside, one of them urinating gushingly as the two men passed. Lausard grinned as the steaming liquid splashed on to Marquet's boots.

The rooms downstairs were occupied by dragoons, also sleeping. But Marquet ushered Lausard upstairs where, as he climbed the stairs, he could see the dull yellow light of a candle burning in one of the upper-storey rooms. Marquet knocked on the door and walked in.

Inside the room there was a bed and a small fire had been lit in the grate. Elsewhere, only the candlelight illuminated the occupants of the room. Seated on a chair close to the window was Sergeant Delpierre. The bed was occupied by Captain Cezar who was wearing just his shirt and breeches. He was sipping from a glass of brandy.

'It's good brandy,' he said, raising the glass. 'I

liberated it from the cellar.' The officer grinned.

Lausard didn't even smile; rather he drew himself to attention and saluted.

'Is that why I was brought here in the middle of the night, sir, to discuss the merits of Italian brandy?'

'No, it wasn't, you insolent bastard,' Cezar snapped. 'Now sit down.' He motioned towards a chair close to Delpierre.

'I'd rather stand, sir,' Lausard insisted.

'Sit down!' Cezar barked and watched as the sergeant did as he was ordered, removing his helmet in the process.

'You know Sergeant Delpierre,' Cezar said.

The two NCOs merely glared at each other.

'You don't need *him*, sir,' Delpierre hissed. 'Or any of those scum like him. They're prisoners you know, convicts . . .'

'I know what they are. Shut up. I even know a little about Sergeant Lausard here.' The officer swung himself upright and padded across to the window, looking out over the square.

Lausard stiffened slightly wondering just how much the officer *did* know. He couldn't know of his background, he reasoned. But if he did and he spoke of it with Delpierre in the room then word would spread. He would become an outcast amongst men who called themselves his comrades. Nevertheless, his concern did not show in his expression.

'I know that he is a good fighter,' said Cezar. 'The kind of man I need for this mission.'

'What mission?' Lausard said.

The officer took another sip of brandy.

'You heard me speak of the Austrian gold,' he said.

'You were there when those Austrian prisoners told me about it.'

'I was there when you murdered three prisoners of war, sir.'

'You heard them speak of the gold?'

'They could have been lying. What makes you so sure it even exists?'

'I've been aware of its existence for over a month,' Cezar said. 'Those Austrians merely confirmed it. I spoke to some of the men captured today and they mentioned it too.'

'What has this got to do with me?' Lausard said.

'You are going to help me retrieve it,' Cezar told him.

'Why should I?'

'Because I'm giving you an order. Disobey and I'll have you shot.'

'Then do it, sir,' Lausard challenged.

'Don't you want to end this war a rich man, Lausard? I am giving you that opportunity,' Cezar said. 'Men have made fortunes already from this war. Every day thousands of francs' worth of art and gold head back to France. I don't intend to leave this country with less than I came in. Sergeant Delpierre is more than willing to help.'

'He would be, he'd sell his own mother for ten francs.'

'The money on that Austrian baggage train is to finance this war,' Cezar said. 'It is to finance troops and equipment to be used *against* France. If you refuse to help me capture it I will have you charged and tried for treason.'

Lausard's expression revealed nothing, his face cast

in deep shadow by the candlelight, but there was a fire burning in his eyes – a fire of anger.

Delpierre looked on with a twisted grin.

'The Austrians are beaten, they are running,' Lausard said. 'But they still outnumber us, unless you're planning to take the entire army with you to steal their gold.'

'Ten men,' Cezar told him. 'Myself, Delpierre, Lieutenant Marquet, you and six of your men. That is all it will take. A small unit will have more chance of success.'

'You're insane,' Lausard said. 'Ten men against an entire army? What chance will we have? You won't have any use for gold. All you'll need is a hole in the ground.'

'*Not* an army,' Cezar snapped. 'A disorganised rabble. Beaten men who want nothing more than to escape, to get back to their homes and families.'

'How do you know where the baggage train is?'

'Intelligence reports say that it is thirty miles north of here.'

'Thirty miles behind enemy lines and we're just going to ride in and take it?' He shook his head. 'How can you threaten me with a firing squad when all you're promising me is suicide?' He chuckled.

Cezar nodded towards Marquet who disappeared momentarily into the next room. He reappeared a second later and threw something in Lausard's direction. It landed with a thud at his feet and he looked down at it.

A white tunic, breeches, gaiters, shoes and a battered shako were held together in an untidy package by a piece of rope.

'An Austrian uniform,' said Lausard.

'And there are nine more like it in the next room,' Cezar informed him. 'Taken from prisoners tonight. We locate the baggage train, ride in dressed as Austrians and take it, then we ride out again.'

'Just like that?'

'Select six of your best men and report back here before dawn. Now get out. You too, Delpierre.'

Lausard replaced his helmet and saluted, pausing for a moment.

'There are over a hundred thousand marks in gold in that baggage train. Are you going to take all of it for yourself?'

'There will be one thousand marks for each man who returns,' Cezar told him.

Lausard nodded then saluted again and left, closely followed by Delpierre.

Cezar heard their footsteps echoing away down the stairs and looked at Marquet.

'One thousand marks for each man who returns,' he repeated.

Both men began to laugh.

CHAPTER 33

The sentries standing sentinel at the ford across the Adige near Ceradino watched in silence as a single line of dragoons crossed the freezing water. One of the men counted ten of them. He even nodded a greeting as they passed but none of the men acknowledged the gesture; they seemed too intent on controlling their horses who shook themselves free of water on emerging from the river. The sentries watched as the small column headed off up the valley at a canter, disappearing into the early-morning gloom. Dawn was still over an hour away and the horsemen were soon out of sight.

The valley floor was strewn with discarded weapons and spent musket balls. An artillery caisson lay on one side of the narrow road, two of its wheels blown off. Its contents had been spilled on to the rocky ground and Lausard noticed absently that a dead dog was lying among the spilled roundshot. In addition to weapons, there were also discarded packs and even a few items of clothing. Shakos, jackets and a few dozen overcoats were strewn across the valley floor – evidence of the speed of the Austrian retreat.

A dead horse lay near the road, stripped of its shabrack. When the light came, Rocheteau reasoned, crows would swoop down to feast.

Behind him Sonnier, Carbonne, Charvet, Giresse and Moreau rode, while up ahead, past Lausard, he could see Delpierre, Marquet and Cezar.

Rocheteau urged a little more speed from his mount and drew up alongside Lausard, who barely seemed to notice him.

'Did he really say a thousand for all of us?' Rocheteau asked.

Lausard nodded.

'That's ten thousand he'll have to give away then,' Rocheteau said and grinned.

'It still leaves the bastard ninety thousand to himself, doesn't it?' Lausard observed. 'He thinks he's being generous.'

'Do you trust him?'

'I don't trust *anyone*.'

'I wonder why he wanted that bastard Delpierre with him?' Rocheteau mused. 'What's that pig going to do with a thousand marks in gold?'

'We've got to get our hands on it first,' Lausard reminded him. 'The Austrians aren't just going to sit back and let us carry it away.' His horse snorted as if in agreement, its breath clouding in the freezing air.

Lausard glanced up at the sky and saw that dawn was trying to force its way across the heavens, straining over the peaks of the mountains surrounding the men ominously like the walls of a huge tomb. The sky remained the colour of wet granite and clouds bulged menacingly with the threat of rain or even snow. It was certainly cold enough, the ground bone hard with frost.

The route they were following sloped up sharply and one or two of the horses found it difficult to keep their footing on the slippery, unforgiving terrain, but their riders urged them on towards the crest of the next ridge. Leafless trees waved skeletal branches at them, coaxed by the breeze which seemed to dart down every rift in the land.

Every few hundred yards they passed discarded weapons, abandoned cannon, dead horses and sometimes men. Bodies were twisted into unearthly positions by a combination of rigor mortis and the biting cold, and Lausard guessed that the freezing temperatures had probably claimed many lives during the night. That combined with a lack of medical care had probably killed as many of the enemy troops as the French had the day before. One corpse was sitting upright, eyes still wide open, the skin already beginning to darken. The dead Austrian toppled over as the horses passed close by, his feet now pointing towards the sky. Near him two other bodies were also frozen solid, hands outstretched as if soliciting help.

Up ahead, Cezar turned his horse and set off up a particularly steep incline, followed by the other men. Lausard glanced up the slope to see a church perched about halfway up looking strangely incongruous with no other buildings anywhere near it and none, as far as he knew, within five miles in any direction. Whoever had built this place had enjoyed solitude, he decided. There was a barely discernible dirt track leading to the church and it was up this that the dragoons spurred their mounts, Cezar slowing his pace slightly as he drew nearer the building.

There was a wagon outside, one wheel missing

from the back, the horses gone. When closer, Lausard saw another wagon and, as he rode his horse around it, he saw that there were four dead Austrians in the back. All had been stripped of their uniforms and equipment, their naked bodies mottled with the cold, the blood from their death wounds now congealed black.

The silence was overpowering, broken only by the jingling of harnesses as the dragoons brought their horses to a halt outside the church.

Moreau looked up at the short steeple and muttered a prayer.

Cezar swung himself out of the saddle, followed by Marquet, and pulled his sabre free of the scabbard. He approached the church door, signalling for the other men to cover him.

Sonnier pulled his carbine from the boot on his saddle and swung it up to his shoulder, moving the barrel from steeple to door, alert for any movement.

Lausard, armed with both a pistol and a sword, drew up close to Cezar. Rocheteau eased back the hammer of his pistol, ears and eyes alert.

It was Carbonne who heard the sounds first.

The former executioner whistled gently through his teeth then tapped one ear, an indication for his colleagues to listen.

At first they heard nothing but the whining of the wind over the freezing hillside, then Lausard also heard something. A low, barely audible moan and it was coming from inside the church.

Cezar pushed the door and it swung open, the rusty hinges groaning.

The men looked inside.

'Jesus!' hissed Rocheteau, taking a step inside the church.

There must have been thirty or forty Austrians inside.

Lausard could see immediately that all but a handful were already dead.

'They must have left their wounded here,' he murmured, noticing that one man was lying on the altar at the far end of the church.

'Left them to die,' said Rocheteau, inspecting a man who had been shot in the stomach and arm. 'Their wounds haven't even been dressed.'

Moreau knelt beside a man who was clearly clinging to life by a monumental effort, and as the Austrian looked up at him, Moreau traced the sign of the cross on the dying man's forehead. The Austrian managed a weak smile, blood clogging his mouth, spilling over his lips. He had a bayonet wound just below the sternum.

Cezar walked without concern among the bodies, inspecting each one for any signs of life, ignoring the puddles of blood that had formed on the freezing stone floor of the church. In one corner a man was shuddering violently although he had a thick cloak wrapped around his shoulders. His eyes were bandaged, the dressing soaked with blood. He turned towards the sound of footsteps, his lips moving soundlessly. In his lap he cradled a head which had most of its left side missing and the blinded man was drenched in its blood.

He babbled something in German but Cezar turned away.

'What did he want?' Lausard enquired.

'Some water,' Cezar said. 'I don't know why, he'll be dead in an hour.'

'Charvet,' Lausard called. 'Fetch my canteen.'

'I said he'll be dead in an hour,' Cezar snapped, grabbing Lausard's arm.

'Why wait an hour?' Delpierre said and with one fluid movement drew his sword and ran it through the throat of the wounded Austrian.

Lausard glared at him.

'How dare you take a life in the house of God?' Moreau shrieked.

'It looks like God gave up caring about this lot a long time ago,' Delpierre insisted, wiping his sword on a dead Austrian's tunic.

'You would have wasted your own water on an enemy?' Cezar asked Lausard.

'There are enemies I would sooner share with than some of those I'm supposed to call comrades,' Lausard snarled, looking first at Cezar then at Delpierre.

'This isn't a mercy mission, Lausard,' Cezar reminded him. 'Why don't you stop behaving like some angel of mercy and start acting like a soldier?'

'Is it the act of a soldier to murder wounded men?' Lausard retorted angrily. 'Is it the act of a soldier to chase after personal gain when there is still a war to be fought?'

'I told you before, the gold which we are to seize would be used against France,' Cezar insisted. 'It is as much a part of our duty as fighting the enemy and you and your men will obey my orders. Fetch the uniforms from your horses.'

Lausard hesitated a moment then walked out to his horse followed by his men. From inside his portmanteau he took out a bundle which he carried back into the church.

The men changed quickly, prompted to speed by the chill as well as the desire to get away from this place of death.

'Not you,' said Cezar, pointing at Giresse. 'You stay here. Guard the horses and our equipment. You will ride with us until we reach the Austrians then return here with our horses. Once we have taken the gold we will rendezvous back here.'

'There isn't enough food for all the horses,' Giresse complained.

'Find some,' Cezar instructed.

'What about them?' Giresse wanted to know, gesturing around him at the dead Austrians.

'You want something to fill your time, don't you?' Cezar said with a chuckle. 'Bury them.'

Rocheteau smoothed his hands over the white Austrian tunic then propped the shako on his head. 'What if we're stopped?' he queried. 'They'll know we're French.'

'Just keep your mouths shut and stay close to me,' Cezar instructed, wiping a piece of fluff from the sleeve of his jacket.

Lausard fastened the gaiters around his calf then stamped his feet, pushing them more firmly into the boots.

'If he's staying here,' said Delpierre, pointing at Giresse, 'I don't think he should get a share of the gold. He's not risking his life the way we are.'

'Go to hell!' snarled Giresse. 'I have to sit here surrounded by all these bloody corpses. That makes my job worth payment.'

'He should get half of what we get then,' Delpierre persisted.

'He can have *your* share,' Rocheteau said. 'How do you know you'll be coming back alive?'

'Yes,' Carbonne echoed. 'Someone might put a bullet in you. Someone in an Austrian uniform.' He grinned and tugged at his sleeve.

'You try it and I'll kill you,' threatened Delpierre.

'If you kill him you'd better kill me too,' Moreau said menacingly.

'Shut up, all of you!' Cezar snapped.

'Captain.'

Marquet's shout made them all turn, and Lausard saw that the other officer was by the window of the church, looking down into the valley.

'Austrians,' he said.

The other men joined him at the window and squinted through the gloom.

A ragged column of white-uniformed men was making its way along the valley floor. A mixture of infantry and artillery accompanied by three blue-clad horsemen, two of whom were on one horse.

'What now?' Lausard asked.

Cezar smiled.

'We join them,' he said quietly.

Lausard counted twenty-seven Austrians in the ill-assorted group struggling along the valley floor. Two brown-uniformed artillerymen were stumbling behind the infantry, one of them still carrying the sponge used to swab out cannon barrels after every round. It seemed to be all he had in the way of a weapon. The three hussars looked similarly worse for wear, one of them seated on the back of his companion's horse, his head on the leading man's shoulder, one arm dangling uselessly at his side. Blood dripped from his frozen fingers and the sleeve of his blue jacket was heavily stained. The other man who rode a bay carried just a carbine; there was no sign of a sabre. The infantry were nearly all armed although few of them still retained their packs and most were without headgear. One had wrapped a scarf around his face to keep out the biting cold but his ears were scarlet, his eyes streaming. All the men were powder-blackened and moved with the gait of defeated, frightened individuals. A private with a huge moustache was dragging his musket along the ground, the butt scraping over the frozen terrain.

It was he who noticed Lausard and the others moving down the hill from the church and gestured to his comrades.

'Remember, just keep your mouths shut and stay close to me,' Cezar reminded them as they drew nearer.

The fugitives were without an officer so he approached the corporal who marched at the head of the lowly band.

'Have you come from Rivoli like us?' Cezar asked in perfect German.

'No,' said the man, breathlessly. 'From La Corona. The French attacked there this morning. It is over.' He carried on marching, his eyes as lifeless as those of a fish on a slab. 'This general of theirs, he is a young madman. He attacks from the right, the left and the rear. It's an intolerable way of making war.'

'We sheltered up there last night,' Cezar said, motioning towards the church but the corporal merely nodded without looking around.

'Where are you heading for?' the captain persisted.

'Home,' said the defeated corporal.

'I need to find my brother,' Cezar lied. 'He is with the baggage train.'

'It went west, to Allenta. Half a day's march from here. It is over.' He repeated the words like some kind of litany.

'West,' Cezar muttered under his breath. He raised an arm and motioned for Lausard and the others to follow.

'The French are still advancing,' said the corporal. 'It is over.'

Cezar ignored him and marched on, the other men close behind him.

Lausard cast a quick glance back at the shattered Austrians.

'And *we* did that to them?' said Rocheteau, affording himself a brief smile. 'We must be better soldiers than we thought.'

'Half a day's march,' said Cezar. 'And that gold will be ours. Come on.'

Lausard felt the first flecks of snow beginning to fall.

'To hell with this marching,' said Charvet, breathlessly. 'I wish I had my horse with me now.'

'We're supposed to be able to fight on foot as well as horseback,' said Lausard, striding along.

'Yes, get your feet up, you lazy bastard,' snapped Delpierre. 'Otherwise we'll leave you here.'

'The only one we're leaving behind is *you*,' Lausard said, pushing the other sergeant.

Delpierre shot him a warning glance but Lausard returned the stare with a look even more venomous.

Rocheteau moved closer to his colleague as if to reinforce the words.

'I said I'd kill you back at the training depot,' he told Delpierre. 'When you feel that steel in your back, Delpierre, you'll know it's mine.'

'Is that the only way you dare face me then, convict? The coward's way? From behind?' Delpierre spat on the ground close to Rocheteau who lunged forward.

Lausard shot out a hand to restrain his colleague.

'Go on,' Delpierre chided. 'Let your dog off his leash.'

'Bridge ahead!'

The shout came from Cezar and it distracted the feuding men, drawing their attention towards where the officer was pointing.

A wooden bridge spanned the Adige and offered the only crossing point for five miles in either direction. On the far bank, the men could see more Austrian troops, another motley collection of fugitives from various regiments. All with one thing on their minds. To escape the pursuing French. There were cavalry amongst them, grey-clad mounted jägers, and Lausard spotted half-a-dozen cuirassiers, their laquered black cuirasses gleaming even in the dullness of the morning. A number were walking, leading horses by the bridles and the animals looked as weary as their riders. Some had been wounded and were limping along, trying to keep up with the others. Many of the men had discarded their portmanteaus in order to lighten the load. Two jägers had even thrown away their carbines and were now equipped solely with swords. A leading cuirassier rode with his right thigh heavily bandaged, blood seeping through the dressing. An infantryman was stumbling along behind him, gripping his horse's tail. Behind them were two ammunition wagons and a pair of six-pounders was being dragged along by horses that looked ready to drop. The gunners rode on the caissons, heads down, uniforms stained and blackened.

Cezar led the French across the bridge, raising his hand to one of the cuirassiers in greeting but the man could only nod in return. None of the Austrians appeared to even notice the group of nine joining them.

'Have you any wounded?' the cuirassier with the leg wound asked, leaning over in his saddle slightly, his face pale.

'We left three men back there,' said Cezar, motioning behind him. 'We heard that some of the army were regrouping at Allenta.'

'No one is regrouping anywhere,' the cavalryman told him. 'We're not retreating, we're running.'

'Is it far to Allenta now?' Cezar persisted.

The cuirassier pointed towards an outcrop of low cliffs about a mile ahead.

'There's a pass that leads through those mountains,' he said. 'Allenta is just beyond it.'

Cezar nodded and he and the others joined the forlorn little column.

Lausard looked swiftly around at the dispirited Austrians and saw the same resigned look on all their faces. It was the face of defeat.

One of the infantry touched his arm and said something which he didn't understand.

Lausard could only shrug, wondering how many more eyes were focusing on him.

The Austrian repeated whatever he had said but Lausard merely tapped his ears and shook his head, feigning deafness.

The Austrian seemed to accept this and nodded but

then moved to Rocheteau instead and spoke the same words again.

Cezar turned and saw what was happening, aware that the continued silence of his men was beginning to arouse suspicion, even amongst troops whose spirits were so battered. Beaten they may be, stupid they were not.

Rocheteau pulled away from the insistent grip of the Austrian infantryman and eyed him menacingly, aware now that other eyes were turning towards him. The Austrian was now raising his voice, snapping angrily at Rocheteau in German.

Lausard stepped forward and pushed the man away but he was undeterred.

Cezar caught Lausard's eye, nodding slightly.

There were about fifteen Austrians. Seven of them mounted, three wounded, the others trudging along dejectedly, and a number had no weapons. The odds seemed fair.

One of the jägers spurred his horse forward to see what the fuss was between Rocheteau and the infantryman, then he too called something to Rocheteau in German which was also ignored.

He rode close to Carbonne and said the same thing to him, meeting with a similar blank response.

'Who the hell are you?' the jäger barked and Cezar saw his hand drop to his sword.

'Now!' bellowed the captain.

Carbonne grabbed the jäger's bridle and pulled with all his strength, tipping the horse and its rider over, the cavalryman spilling from the saddle. Carbonne kicked him hard in the face and snatched up his sword.

Rocheteau pulled the musket from the hands of his

startled opponent and fired it, point-blank, into his chest.

One of the cuirassiers swung his sword at Rocheteau but he managed to parry the blow with the butt of the musket, using the weapon like a club, knocking the horseman from his saddle and then driving the bayonet into his face, watching as the man rolled away screaming, clutching the gaping gashed wound. Rocheteau took no chances and ran the bayonet into his back.

Charvet grabbed an artilleryman close to him and drove one powerful fist into his face, lifting him bodily into the air before hurling him down on to the bone-hard ground with incredible force.

Lausard grabbed the stirrup of the cuirassier officer and pulled, jerking the man from the saddle. He landed on his bandaged thigh, shouting in pain. Lausard swung himself into the saddle, the Austrian horse rearing in panic. It brought its front hooves down on the wounded officer, one of them caving in part of his forehead.

Rocheteau ripped the sabre from the hand of his dead foe and flung it to Lausard who caught it by the hilt, hefting it before him.

Delpierre pulled a pistol from one of the cuirassiers and shot an infantryman as he raised his hands in surrender.

The remaining Austrians raced back down the road as fast as they could, anxious to be away from these madmen who butchered them despite wearing the same uniform. Delpierre snatched up a musket and swung it up to his shoulder, taking aim at the fleeing men but the shot missed and Cezar knocked the barrel down.

'Let them go,' he said, looking at the carnage around the Frenchmen.

Six more bodies lay on the ground around them. The terrified Austrians had also abandoned the ammunition wagons and the six-pounders.

Apart from the horse Lausard rode, the others had bolted in terror, one of them dashing off across the wooden bridge towards the other bank of the Adige. It galloped off into the distance, reins flapping around its head.

'They'll bring reinforcements,' said Delpierre. 'We should have killed them all.'

'Reinforcements from where?' snorted Cezar. 'By the time they reach the rest of their army we'll have got the gold and be on the way back.'

Rocheteau was busily rifling the pockets of the dead men. He found little: some coins, a piece of gold chain and a letter he couldn't read so he balled it up and tossed it away. Charvet found a fork on one of the infantrymen and slipped it into his pocket. Rocheteau's only other discovery was a knife. About four inches long, double-edged and wickedly sharp. He smiled and slid it into his belt.

'This is perfect,' Cezar said, 'we'll take the gold and come back this way, we'll use this bridge to cross back to the other bank but I want to make sure no one follows us over. You two' – he pointed a finger at Moreau and Sonnier – 'take some powder from those ammunition wagons and set charges on the bridge. Both banks.'

'But how do we do that?' Sonnier said. 'We're not engineers.'

'You're supposed to be soldiers,' Cezar snapped. 'Work it out and do it. Understood?'

The two men nodded and began unloading barrels of gunpowder from the first of the wagons.

'You're leaving two more men behind?' Lausard queried. 'That means there're only seven of us going in to Allenta to get the gold.'

'The fewer of us there are the more chance we've got of getting in and out quickly,' Cezar told him.

'And more chance of getting killed,' murmured Rocheteau.

'What if more Austrians come along this road?' Lausard offered. 'We'll be trapped between them.'

'Not if we move quickly,' Cezar said, looking up at Lausard who had managed to bring the Austrian horse under control. 'Now get off that horse, Lausard.'

The two men locked stares.

'Get down!' Cezar insisted. 'I need the horse. I will ride ahead into Allenta, locate the gold then we can strike tonight.'

'Why you?' Lausard said.

'Because I'm the only one who can speak German, you idiot.'

Lausard hesitated a moment then swung himself out of the saddle. He held the reins then, as Cezar moved to take them, he let them slip from his hand. The officer glared at him. 'You are all under the command of Lieutenant Marquet for the time being.' Cezar swung himself into the saddle. 'Through the pass to Allenta. You must be there before nightfall.'

He rode off, the other men standing watching as he guided the horse along the road towards the mountains.

'I don't trust that bastard,' Rocheteau said under his breath.

Lausard didn't speak.

'Get these bodies out of the way,' Marquet shouted.

'What shall we do with them?' Carbonne asked.

'Throw them in the river, you fool,' the lieutenant hissed, watching as Sonnier grabbed one of the dead Austrians by the ankles and hauled him to the bank, pushing to propel the body towards its watery grave.

'This one isn't dead,' Carbonne said, kneeling close to one of the fallen Austrians.

'Throw him in,' ordered Marquet.

Carbonne hesitated.

'Do it, damn you!' Marquet snarled, watching as the former executioner lifted the man bodily then rolled him down the bank.

'Who cares if they're alive or dead?' Delpierre sneered, pulling a cuirassier towards the bank. 'To hell with them.' He watched as the body rolled into the water. 'What's wrong? Haven't you got the stomach for it?' He looked at Lausard and grinned.

'It's *you* I can't stomach,' said Lausard.

His companions laughed.

'You think you're clever, don't you?' Delpierre said, taking a step towards the younger man.

'Compared to you, a mule is clever. *And* more useful.'

'Funny man,' hissed Delpierre. I'll wipe that smile off your smug face.'

'Shut up,' Marquet snapped. 'Enough of this petty stupidity.'

'When this is over, Lausard,' Delpierre continued, 'I'm going to kill you.'

'You can try,' Lausard told him. 'Any time you can try.'

Delpierre suddenly felt something cold against the back of his neck. He turned slightly to see that

Rocheteau had the tip of the knife pressed against his skin, only a fraction more pressure required to puncture it.

'But you'd better watch your back,' Rocheteau said softly. He pulled the knife away and slid it back into his belt.

'Come on!' Marquet shouted, striding off down the road. 'We're wasting time. Move.'

The mountains towered above them, their peaks thrusting up into the sky as if threatening to puncture the clouds.

Sonnier and Moreau waited a moment, watching their colleagues trudge off towards the pass, then they began rolling barrels of powder across the bridge to the far bank. Despite the deep cold, they were soon sweating from the exertion.

'I hope to God this works,' grunted Sonnier, lifting another of the barrels from the ammunition wagon.

Moreau nodded in agreement then looked towards the pass. 'I don't know how they're going to get out of there in one piece,' he said.

Sonnier patted his shoulder. 'Come on,' he said. 'Let's get the rest of this powder unloaded. Then we can try to work out what to do with it.'

They continued with their task.

Moreau glanced across the abandoned six-pounders, his eyes lighting up.

'I've got an idea,' he said, grinning.

CHAPTER 34

The village of Allenta sheltered within the towering peaks of the mountains like a moth in a cocoon. Houses had been built not only on the floor of the ravine but also on the lower slopes. Many buildings seemed barely to cling on to the rock which rose, in several places, as sheer walls with hardly a handhold. Higher up there were ledges, some so precarious they didn't look capable of supporting the weight of a man, but others had been cut into the rock either by nature herself or by the inhabitants of the region so that the mountains could be crossed through the ravine or by way of the precipitous paths.

A number of Austrian troops were in the village, seeking warmth in the abandoned houses where they could. The streets were filled with wagons of all description, jostling for a place with artillery and cannon. Infantry and cavalry added to the congestion, some stopping in the village, others only too anxious to continue through the pass.

The inn had been taken over by meagre Austrian medical services and was being used as a dressing station. Wounded troops, those at least who could stand, queued up outside waiting their turn, shivering in the freezing wind. Elsewhere, wagons full of injured men trundled with difficulty through the already clogged streets, their forlorn cargoes moaning and shouting with each bump of the wheels.

Exhausted horses stood motionless in their harnesses, waiting for equally tired drivers to guide them through the streets and away from the place. But the tide of humanity which flowed through Allenta was moving slowly, far too slowly for those who sought sanctuary beyond the mountains. Infantry and cavalry alike had chosen the more hazardous mountain routes to speed their escape. Word had reached the village less than an hour ago that the French were no more than fifteen miles away and this rumour served only to increase the panic and fear already rife among the survivors of the Austrian army.

Cezar had heard these rumours as he wandered through the town, dressed in the uniform of his enemy. He'd even paused to eat some scraps of food with a group of infantrymen who'd arrived from La Corona that day. They had told him of the fighting and he, in turn, had lied about his own unit's involvement at the battle of Rivoli. Not for one second did he feel that they suspected he was an impostor, such were his demeanour and the quality of his German. His command of the language was virtually flawless and the men he spoke to had no reason to doubt his sincerity. Talk had inevitably turned to the baggage train – although most of the men seemed more concerned with moving on – and Cezar had been forced to suppress a smile when some had discussed the amount of gold concerned.

Now he sat on the steps of what had once been the entrance to a blacksmith's shop gazing across at the wagon which held the gold. It was being pulled by four stout grey horses which looked fresher than most of the beasts passing through. They stood obediently, heads down, waiting for their driver to urge them forward when he was ready. But of the driver there was no sign. The wagon and three other wagons which made up the rest of the baggage train were surrounded by sentries. Cezar could see the driver of the second wagon perched on his seat puffing on a pipe. Tarpaulins had been secured over all four wagons, held in place by thick rope. There were a number of bullet holes in the side of one wagon but otherwise the train and those who guarded it looked in very good condition. The men, particularly, looked more confident than their beaten comrades who passed through the village. Cezar told himself that those who guarded the gold probably hadn't fought in either of the actions of the last two days.

He got to his feet and wandered across to where he had tethered his horse, the animal flicking its head back and forth agitatedly. Patting its neck to calm it, his eyes remained fixed on the baggage train. He was still gazing at the collection of wagons when he felt a hand on his shoulder.

He spun around.

Lausard was standing behind him, his cheeks scarlet from the cold.

'Where the hell have you been?' Cezar said angrily, his heart thudding against his ribs. 'Where are the others?'

'Around,' said Lausard.

'What's that supposed to mean?' Cezar hissed. 'I told you to be here before nightfall. To be ready.'

'We *are* here and we *are* ready, Captain,' Lausard said. 'There were more Austrian troops on the road into the village. We had to avoid them. It took time.'

'Where are the rest?'

'They are in the village.'

'What about Lieutenant Marquet?'

As if in answer to the officer's question, Marquet appeared through a group of infantrymen and strode towards his commander and Lausard.

'Carbonne is waiting outside the village with horses for us all,' Lausard said.

'Did you order this?' Cezar demanded, looking angrily at his subordinate.

'Sergeant Lausard's idea seemed like a good one, Captain. I saw no reason to disagree with him,' Marquet said.

'What idea?'

'The Austrians aren't going to just let us walk out of here with that gold, are they?' Lausard offered. 'We're going to have to take it and, once we've got it, we're going to have to move fast. Like it or not, Captain, you might be in charge but the success of this whole operation relies on *my* men.'

'You insolent bastard,' Cezar snarled through gritted teeth.

'That may be,' Lausard replied, 'but if you want that gold then *you'll* do as *I* say.'

'I'll have you shot when we get back,' Cezar threatened. 'I will not stand for this.'

Two hussars riding past glanced at the trio of squabbling men but said nothing. Lausard noticed their interest and glared at Cezar. The officer turned to the horsemen and spoke some words in German and Lausard was relieved when the hussars nodded and continued on their way.

High above them, the sky was beginning to darken, the onset of dusk that much quicker due to the thick banks of dark cloud.

'Another hour,' Lausard said quietly. 'We should get off the street.'

'If this plan of yours doesn't work, Lausard, I'll kill you myself,' Cezar told him.

Unconcerned by the officer's comments, Lausard said: 'If it doesn't work, Captain, you won't have to kill me, the Austrians will do it for you.'

He turned and walked away.

Rocheteau looked at his pocket watch, squinting in the gloom as the hands crawled round.

Beside him, Charvet and Delpierre sheltered in a stable next to the inn, watching through the slits in the door, their eyes on the baggage train.

Straw had been built up in a pile at the back of the building and, at a nod from Rocheteau, Charvet scuttled over to it and began striking a flint he'd taken from a musket against the stone floor. At the third attempt sparks flew upwards and Charvet grinned, pushing more straw into the flashes of fire. The straw caught light, crackled then died. Charvet tried again, cursing under his breath.

'Come on,' urged Rocheteau.

'It's damp,' Charvet said angrily. 'The damned straw is damp.'

He struck the flint again but this time the sparks

flared. Some pieces were beginning to smoulder but there seemed to be more smoke than fire – reeking black and grey smoke that stung his eyes and stuck in his throat. Gradually flames began to lick upwards, dancing in the gloom and Charvet pushed more straw on to the growing blaze.

He nodded towards Rocheteau and Delpierre. The other two men got to their feet, pushing open the door of the stable and slipping out into the street. Charvet followed seconds later, leaving the door open, allowing the chill night air to fan the flames which were growing by the second.

Lausard saw the smoke beginning to rise into the air and he smiled. A number of horses tethered near the stable were pawing the ground, able to smell the smoke. Sentries, disturbed by the nervous horses, began looking around to find the cause of their distress.

The wagon transporting the gold was thirty or forty yards from the stable and the sentries guarding it were still unaware of the commotion. Their horses had just been fed and they remained contentedly in harness.

Lausard got to his feet, looking up and down the street, seeing that it was clear apart from some hussars who were standing around smoking and talking almost directly opposite the stable. It was one of them who first noticed flames leaping from the building, his shouts echoing around the street.

'Come on,' said Lausard, drawing a knife from his tunic. He'd taken it from an Austrian corporal earlier in the day and now he held the blade before him, gripping it tightly in one fist.

Cezar and Marquet followed him, heading towards the gold wagon.

Men were spilling into the street now from many of the houses, alerted by the cries of fire and shocked to see that the stable was ablaze. The flames leaped high in the air, illuminating everything roundabout with a hellish red glow.

Lausard ran at one of the sentries and drove the knife into his back before he could turn, twisting it, feeling warm blood on his hand. He snatched the man's musket from his grasp then let the body fall.

Cezar took out another Austrian, grabbing him by the back of the head and ramming his face against one of the wheels. The man staggered, dropped his musket and fell to the ground. Cezar snatched up the weapon and threw it to Marquet, who caught it and swung it up to his shoulder.

From the other side of the wagon, Rocheteau slid his arm around an Austrian's neck, jerked him off his feet and drove the knife into his neck at the point of his jaw and his ear, feeling it scrape bone. He too took the dead man's musket, using the bayonet to despatch the other guard who came at him.

Fire was now rising high into the air, huge sheets of flame devouring the stable, black smoke belching from the inferno. But the blaze seemed secondary to some of the Austrians who had spilled into the street. They had noticed the scuffling around the baggage train and a number of them began to move towards it, bewildered by what was happening.

'Get in!' shouted Lausard to the others, clambering into the back of the wagon while Rocheteau and Delpierre took their position on the driver's seat,

Rocheteau snapping the reins to force the horses forward.

A musket cracked and Lausard heard a ball whizz past his ear. Another struck the side of the wagon blasting a piece of wood free.

'Go!' Lausard ordered as more Austrians ran into the street, their faces illuminated by the blazing stable.

The horses reared, whinnied, then set off, urged on by Rocheteau.

An officer tried to clamber into the wagon but Cezar struck him hard in the face and he fell to the ground, screaming as the wagon passed over him.

Charvet fired his musket at three men chasing the wagon and saw one of them fall, skidding on the cobbled street.

Lausard fired off a shot from one of the captured muskets, the bullet hitting one of their pursuers in the shoulder.

'Come on!' yelled Rocheteau, snapping the reins almost frenziedly, the horses using all their strength to haul the wagon along, the wheels rumbling over the ground, the precious cargo bumping about beneath the tarpaulin.

The wagon was moving quickly now, easily outstripping the chasing foot soldiers.

The explosion was deafening.

Even the men in the wagon ducked down at the ferocity of the detonation. The stable was ripped apart by the blast, lumps of wood spinning fully fifty feet into the air, a mushroom of flame leaping skyward.

Lausard smiled with relief as he saw the pursuing Austrians reeling. 'I was wondering when that powder keg was going to go off,' he said, slapping Rocheteau on the shoulder, but the corporal was more concerned with guiding the horses along. The wagon was now careering out of Allenta at speed, its occupants forced to cling to the sides to stop themselves being thrown out.

In the blinding light of the explosion Cezar saw horsemen in the street, sabres raised above their heads. Half-a-dozen hussars were charging down the street in pursuit.

'We'll never outrun them,' Cezar shouted as Rocheteau roared encouragement to the horses, their hooves thundering on the uneven road. The wagon bumped and swayed alarmingly but Rocheteau remained hunched in the driver's seat, his face sheathed in sweat.

The hussars drew nearer. One tried a shot with his carbine but the bullet sang harmlessly through the air and smacked off a tree.

'I hope Carbonne is ready with those horses,' said Charvet, reloading the musket, tasting powder in his mouth as he bit the end off the cartridge. Crouching in the back of the speeding wagon, he rammed both ball and wadding down the barrel then swung the weapon up to his shoulder, firing at the hussars.

More by luck than judgement he hit one of their horses, the bullet catching the animal in the eye. It reared, squealing in pain, then toppled forward, pitching its rider from the saddle and tripping two of the other horses. They went down in an untidy heap but the others rode on.

'Get rid of some of the gold,' shouted Lausard, undoing the ropes which held the tarpaulin firm. 'We've got to lighten the load or they'll catch us.'

'Leave it!' roared Cezar, grabbing Lausard's wrist. 'We're not leaving any of it behind.'

'It's slowing us down,' Lausard bellowed back.

Cezar kept a firm grip on the sergeant's wrist until Lausard shook loose.

The leading hussars were only about a hundred yards from the speeding wagon by now and one fired a pistol at the vehicle.

Marquet hissed in pain as the ball clipped his ear, ripping away part of the lobe and splashing his face with blood.

The valley was narrowing, the rocks climbing precipitously on either side of the road.

'There's more of them,' shouted Charvet, spotting that about a dozen more Austrian cavalry had joined the chase and were bearing down on the wagon. 'We'll never do it.'

Lausard took his knife and, with one swift movement, cut a rope, pushing one of the boxes from the back of the wagon.

'What are you doing?' shrieked Cezar, watching in horror as the chest cracked open, spilling its precious cargo all over the ground. Gold pieces were flung up into the air by the churning hooves of the pursuing hussars; some of them slowed their mounts, looking down at the gold.

'Leave it alone,' Cezar roared, trying to wrestle the knife from Lausard's grip.

'Up ahead,' Rocheteau bellowed, finding it difficult to make himself heard above the thundering hooves of the horses.

Horses were waiting by the roadside and Carbonne stood in his stirrups signalling. Lausard knew that they were not going to have time to transfer to the waiting mounts.

'Ride!' he shouted to Carbonne, who hesitated a moment then set off with the other horses. Tied together by their bridles, they galloped along behind him.

'How far to that bridge?' Rocheteau hissed, still urging more effort from the horses pulling the wagon. Moving at such speed and hauling such a heavy cargo was causing them to tire; despite his maniacal shouts and snapping of the reins, they were beginning to slow down. 'Come on, come on!' he yelled frantically.

Carbonne guided the spare horses closer to the speeding wagon, the leading mount no more than three feet from the side of the vehicle.

'Hold them there,' Lausard called, steadying himself.

'What are you doing?' Cezar demanded, watching as Lausard crouched, his eyes fixed on the lead horse.

Lausard knew that if he mistimed his jump he would either be crushed beneath the wheels of the wagon or trampled by the hooves of the horses, but he had no choice. There was no time to think of failure.

Or death.

The wagon hit a bump and he almost overbalanced.

It was now or never.

He jumped.

For what seemed like an eternity he appeared to hang in empty air then he landed on the back of a grey horse, grabbing at its mane to pull himself upright. He snatched at the reins and immediately dug his heels into the horse, driving it fiercely.

'Come back, you stinking coward!' Delpierre

shouted after him, shaking his fist at Lausard, who was disappearing rapidly into the darkness ahead.

The wagon thundered on.

The hussars drew nearer.

CHAPTER 35

They had heard the explosion. They had watched the sky above Allenta turn red. Now Sonnier and Moreau listened to the popping musketry echoing through the stillness of the night, drawing ever nearer.

Moreau paced back and forth, looking at the bridge across the river then towards the sound of the gunfire. Sonnier was squatting beside the river bank, absently throwing small stones into the dark water. Their horses were tethered on the far bank, both animals chewing at shrivelled grass growing sparsely on the stony ground.

A keg of gunpowder had been set at each corner of the bridge, slightly below the parapet. Long dark trails of powder up to fifty yards long led from each barrel. These would serve as fuses when the time came and, from the sounds of gunfire heading their way, that time was approaching fast.

'I wonder what's happening?' Moreau mused aloud.

'They've probably all been killed by now,' Sonnier suggested, throwing a last stone into the river and getting to his feet.

'Look,' said Moreau, pointing into the gloom.

Both men squinted through the darkness and saw a solitary figure galloping towards them.

'Austrian?' Sonnier murmured.

Moreau lifted his musket to his shoulder in readiness.

'No, wait,' Sonnier said, pushing the barrel aside. Even in the dull light he could make out Lausard's features.

'Get across the bridge now!' Lausard yelled. 'Light the powder.'

'What about the others?'

'They're coming and they've got company,' Lausard said, wheeling the horse.

All three men heard the sound of thundering hooves and the wagon lurched into view, Rocheteau almost standing in the driver's platform.

'Light it!' Lausard shouted again.

Sonnier and Moreau ran across the bridge to the far bank and, for the first time, Lausard noticed that Sonnier was carrying something in his hand. Something which glowed red at the tip. It was a portfire from one of the discarded cannons. But then his attention was wrenched back to the wagon which was turning quickly – too quickly. It was carrying too much weight. It was going to topple over.

'Swing the leaders wide!' Lausard roared at Rocheteau. 'It's tipping. Rocheteau felt the wagon begin to list to one side.

Carbonne raced across the bridge ahead of the wagon, after releasing the spare horses, allowing them to run back towards the pursuing Austrians, causing at least a temporary hindrance.

One of the wagon's rear wheels was actually leaving the ground.

Charvet gripped the edge of the vehicle, convinced he was about to be sent flying. Delpierre gripped the seat more tightly, his eyes bulging in their sockets. Rocheteau tugged on the reins, trying to slow the horses to make the turn easier. He dragged hard on the leather until the muscles in his forearms bulged.

The rear wheel rose higher off the ground.

Lausard could only look on helplessly as the wagon swayed, teetering precariously. It was inches away from going now.

'No!' roared Rocheteau and hauled the two lead horses back with all his strength.

For interminable seconds the wagon lurched sideways, then it slammed back down on all four wheels and the horses were thundering across the wooden bridge, the sound reverberating through the night.

Sonnier lit one of the gunpowder trails, ran across and lit the second. A hissing sound followed and the ball of fire began to devour the streams of black powder.

Rocheteau felt another enormous jolt, the impact strong enough to send Marquet falling from the back of the wagon.

'What the hell was that?' Rocheteau hissed, then cursed as the wagon rolled backwards.

One of the rear wheels had crashed through the flimsy wooden struts of the bridge and was firmly wedged.

Rocheteau whipped up the horses but they couldn't budge the stricken vehicle.

Lausard pulled a pistol free and fired it in the

direction of the oncoming hussars, a number of whom had now dismounted and were preparing to fire their carbines at the stricken wagon.

'Push!' bellowed Cezar and the men jumped down and ran to the rear of the wagon, throwing their collective weight and strength behind it while Rocheteau urged the horses on to greater effort.

'Hurry!' shouted Sonnier. 'The powder's lit.'

He saw the trail burning up with alarming speed, each trail heading for its allotted keg, sputtering and crackling as the fire danced along it.

'Get this wagon free,' snarled Cezar, watching the sweating, straining men who were all too aware that they were going to be shot by their pursuers or blown sky high.

The black powder trails were now less than fifty feet long, the flame speeding along them.

Moreau rushed back on to the bridge to add his weight to that of the men already pushing and the wagon began to lift slightly.

Lausard leaped from his horse and ran to one of the powder kegs on his side of the river. He lifted it and pushed it towards the Austrians, watching the powder spill out behind the rolling barrel. Holding the pistol close to the stream of coarse grains he fired, the spark from the pan igniting the powder, the fireball chasing the explosive stream to its source.

The Austrians who realised what was happening had scattered, trying to escape from the rolling barrel which was spewing out its own fuse behind it. A fuse which was being devoured rapidly by the flame.

And then it caught up.

The keg exploded, a shrieking ball of red and yellow

flame which seared the eyes of those watching. It was accompanied by a concussion blast which flattened anyone within a twenty-yard radius. Men and horses were sent tumbling by the blast and even the French troops pushing at the jammed wagon chanced a glance behind them at the pall of black smoke spreading upwards into the night sky.

'Keep pushing!' roared Cezar, now aware of Lausard's presence on the bridge, of his considerable strength shoving against the wagon.

'Come on,' bellowed Sonnier, watching the trails of powder burning down rapidly towards the kegs.

Twenty feet.

The wagon began to move.

Fifteen feet.

Rocheteau shouted encouragement to both horses and men alike as he felt the wagon lurch forward.

Ten feet.

The wagon pulled free and rolled several yards. He whipped up the horses who bolted forward, dragging the vehicle across the last few feet of bridge and on to the far bank.

Sonnier had one eye on the speeding flame, the other on his companions who were now running for their lives to reach safety, oblivious to the musket balls which whizzed through the air around them, aware only that the bridge was about to be obliterated and them along with it.

Lausard was at the back of the fleeing band and he actually saw the last length of black powder burning down.

Five feet.

He pushed Carbonne ahead of him, urging him on.

Two feet.

Two Austrians had spurred their horses on to the bridge in pursuit of the Frenchmen. They reached the middle of the bridge as the twin kegs exploded simultaneously.

One end of the bridge simply vanished, obliterated by the ferocity of the blast. Lumps of wood were sent spiralling up in the air, carried on a shrieking plume of fire and smoke. The parapet was ripped apart by the explosion, the sound deafening.

Lausard hugged the ground and shouted, his bellow drowned by the ear-splitting bang and then the shrieks of men and horses as they plummeted into the water below. Debris rained down on the ground or into the water.

On the other bank the Austrians could only look on with dazed awe as the end portion of the bridge rose into the air, splitting and disintegrating to matchwood.

When Lausard finally scrambled to his feet he looked across at the other bank and saw that the hussars were gone. The bridge had tipped into the river, portions of it now being carried away by the current. Smoke drifted across the ground in a poisonous fog.

Charvet struggled to his knees, his ears still ringing.

Rocheteau shook his head and grinned, gazing at the remains of the bridge.

'Jesus,' he whispered. 'That was some firework display.'

Moreau, looking heavenward, mumbled a few words of thanks.

Charvet and Carbonne walked over to the river bank, the ground there cratered deeply in two places. Smoke was rising from the holes.

They merely looked at each other.

'I think we did a good job there,' Sonnier said and grinned, regarding the devastation with something akin to pride.

Lausard wiped his forehead with the back of his hand, leaving a black streak across his skin where the powder had stained it.

'The gold is ours, Captain,' he said to Cezar. 'Time to take it home and share it out.'

Rocheteau laughed, a whooping sound of pure joy.

Cezar looked at Lausard then at the wagon full of gold.

He said nothing.

Lausard finished buttoning his green tunic then ran a hand along one sleeve, a faint smile on his face. It felt good to be wearing his own uniform once more. The Austrian one he'd taken off lay discarded in a pile with others that his colleagues had taken off. Rocheteau, Sonnier and Charvet, on the other hand, still wore the white uniform of their enemies.

'Why the hell do we have to keep these on?' Rocheteau wanted to know.

'You've been told once,' Cezar said, adjusting his girth strap and green saddle cloth. 'We're heading back towards Rivoli now, towards our own lines but we don't know if we might run into some more Austrians. If we do then those of you dressed as dragoons will pretend to be prisoners and pass through them. If we reach our own men first then the opposite will apply.'

'So why are you riding on ahead then, Captain?' Lausard asked.

'It will be easier for one man to get through unseen,'

Cezar said. 'I can warn our troops that you're coming.'

'And you trust us with all this gold?' said Lausard.

Cezar met his baleful gaze.

'What if we decide to just run for it?' Lausard said. 'Take the gold with us.'

'You wouldn't dare,' Cezar hissed.

Delpierre looked at both men then at the gold-laden wagon and licked his lips like a starving man before a banquet.

'Is that back wheel all right?' Carbonne said, watching as Giresse and Sonnier tugged and pulled at it.

'It'll hold long enough to get us back,' Giresse told him.

Cezar swung himself into the saddle and pulled out a pocket watch.

'It shouldn't take me long to reach our lines,' he said. 'You follow on in an hour.'

Rocheteau checked his own watch and showed it to Lausard who noted the time.

'Lieutenant Marquet is in command until you reach our lines again,' Cezar continued, then he dug his knees into his mount and set off down the steep slope which led away from the church and back to the narrow road snaking along the valley floor, parallel to the Adige.

The other men watched him go.

'And what if he doesn't make it back to our lines?' said Delpierre. 'What if the Austrians stop him first?'

'There are no Austrians between here and Rivoli,' Marquet said with an air of certainty. 'None that could be a threat to us.'

'How do you know that?' Delpierre insisted.

'They're still too busy running.'

'He's got more chance alone,' Rocheteau said. 'We're the ones who are more likely to run into trouble if there *are* any Austrians about.' He looked at Lausard. 'That's right, isn't it, Alain?'

Lausard ignored him. He was walking around the wagon peering at it suspiciously.

'What are you doing?' Marquet asked.

Lausard slid the knife from his belt and moved closer to the tarpaulin covering the contents of the wagon.

'I'm going to see what else is in this thing,' he said, cutting one of the ropes with the knife, pulling it away from the canvas covering.

'Get away from there, Lausard,' the lieutenant ordered angrily.

'Don't tell me you're not curious, Lieutenant,' Lausard said, cutting a second rope.

'That property belongs to France now,' Marquet said, sliding a pistol from his belt. 'Get away from it.'

'Am I not a soldier of France?' Lausard challenged. 'If it belongs to France then surely it belongs to me.'

Marquet raised the pistol.

'I'm warning you,' he said, the gun aimed at Lausard's head.

Only then did he feel the chill brush of steel against his neck.

Out of the corner of his eye he could see that Rocheteau had a sword pressed against his flesh.

'If I was you, Lieutenant,' Rocheteau warned, 'I'd put the pistol down.'

'You raise a weapon against one of your own officers?' Marquet said.

'Absolutely,' Rocheteau breathed, pressing a little harder with the sword point.

Sonnier lifted his carbine to his shoulder and aimed it at the officer.

'You forget, Lieutenant,' he said, thumbing back the hammer. 'We're criminals. We have no respect for anyone or anything. That is what we've always been told.'

'Delpierre,' Marquet said, swallowing hard. 'Place them under arrest.'

'You stay where you are,' Charvet said, lifting his musket and prodding the bayonet in Delpierre's direction.

'Look for all I care,' Delpierre said. 'See how much gold there is. See how much richer we'll be when we get back.'

Lausard pulled the canvas away to reveal what lay beneath.

There were several bundles of cloaks, tied together with thick rope. Blankets, greatcoats and a number of small, square chests. Lausard leaned close to one and inhaled.

'Coffee,' he said approvingly.

There were other chests which he prised open. Inside these were tin cups, plates, knives, forks and spoons.

It was only as Lausard clambered further on to the wagon that he realised the whole floor of the vehicle was covered by a thick coating of gunpowder. Two barrels of the stuff were secured to the side of the wagon but one had been holed by a bullet, causing the coarse black grains to spill out into the wagon itself.

He came to the first of many, identical, wooden chests and slid his knife beneath lid and frame, prising the top off. It came away with a groan of splitting wood.

He stuffed a hand in and lifted it above his head.

The other men saw the gold coins gripped in his fist. He let them fall and they heard them chinking against other coins inside the box.

'Let's take it,' Delpierre suggested.

'And go where?' said Lausard. 'What are we going to do, desert?'

'Let's share it out and go our own way,' Delpierre insisted. 'Every man for himself. Equal shares.'

'You can't do that,' Marquet snapped, taking a step forward.

'We can do what we like,' Delpierre hissed.

'No,' Lausard said, 'the gold goes back and so do we.'

'You're mad,' Delpierre snarled. 'We won't get another chance like this, you fool.'

'We go back,' Lausard repeated, pulling the canvas back into position over the gold and fastening it with one of the heavy lengths of hemp.

'I'm pleased you've seen sense, Lausard,' Marquet said, relieved also that Rocheteau had pulled the sword away from his neck.

The sergeant jumped down from the wagon, wiping his hands on the tarpaulin in an effort to remove some of the spilled gunpowder that blackened his hands. He looked indifferently at Marquet.

'You're in charge, Lieutenant,' he said. 'Take us back.'

CHAPTER 36

'Rider coming in!'

The shout from the sentry echoed around the low valley where the advanced unit of French infantry had halted.

The sentry, a private named Caron, watched as the horseman spurred his grey mount down the sharp incline leading from the top of the valley towards the road which bisected it. He could not see the identity of the rider as yet, the uniform colour being difficult to distinguish in the early-morning mist which hung over the valley. All Caron knew was that the rider looked to be in a hurry.

Caron called to one of the other sentries and asked him if he could see the colour of the tunic on the oncoming horseman, and together the two men peered more closely at the rapidly approaching figure.

'Green,' said the other, nodding.

'Green,' echoed Caron in agreement. 'It's a dragoon. One of ours.' The rider was close enough now for the men to see the horsehair mane of his helmet trailing out behind him as he rode.

Even so, both levelled their muskets as he drew nearer.

Caron held up a hand to halt him.

Cezar pulled on his reins and his horse reared up panting, its tongue lolling from one corner of its mouth, its hide lathered.

'Where have you come from?' Caron asked, his Charleville still levelled at the dragoon.

'Where is your commander?' Cezar demanded, ignoring the question.

'I asked where you had come from, I—'

Cezar slapped angrily at his epaulettes. 'Do you know what these are, you bloody fool? I am a captain of dragoons. Do not question me like some common foot soldier. Get your commander.'

Caron and his companion looked at each other for a moment then the other man scuttled off over the lip of a depression in the ground. He returned a moment later with a huge man dressed in a torn and powder-stained blue jacket. The man was chewing on a piece of bread.

'Are you in charge of this regiment?' Cezar snapped at the big man.

'No, sir,' said the big man. 'Colonel Declerc commands the Twenty-third Demi-Brigade. I am Sergeant Bertrand of the Twenty-third's light infantry.'

'How many men have you under your command?'

'Fifty, sir,' Bertrand told him. 'We were sent ahead to act as foragers and scouts.'

'How far away is the main army?'

'About three miles to the south. May I ask which unit you are from, sir?'

'Fifth Dragoons. We have been on a scouting mission.'

'I thought all the cavalry were either with General Bonaparte or General Massena,' Bertrand said. 'That is why *we* were scouting.'

'Well you were wrong, weren't you? I need your men, Sergeant, and I need them now. Myself and my men ran into some Austrians last night and I think they are following us. We captured one of their supply wagons.'

'We heard that the Austrians were running, sir,' Bertrand insisted.

'Are you calling me a liar, Sergeant? I'll have use of your men – now get them into line and get them ready now. Do you understand?'

Bertrand hesitated, taking a last bite of his bread.

'Do it, you imbecile,' snarled Cezar. 'The longer you hesitate, the more danger my men are in.'

Bertrand nodded then spun round and sprinted off.

Rocheteau turned in his seat and looked at the contents of the wagon, a grin on his grizzled features.

'Gold, food, wine,' he mused. 'Perhaps Delpierre is right. We ought to take it for ourselves. As a reward. After all, that bastard Cezar did nearly get us all killed.'

Riding alongside the wagon, Lausard shook his head. 'We go back,' he said flatly.

On the other side of the wagon Giresse also glanced at the tarpaulin covering the gold and clucked his tongue. 'One hundred thousand in gold,' he said, shaking his head. 'We wouldn't see that much if we lived to be a hundred. What do you think Cezar's going to do with it all?'

'Just what the other officers who've been picking this country clean over the last few months have been doing,' Lausard said. 'Buy himself a house and mistress back in France.'

'With money like that he could buy any woman he wanted,' Giresse said enviously. 'He could buy a princess.'

'Royalty is in short supply in France these days in case you hadn't noticed,' Carbonne threw in from his position in the back of the wagon.

The other men laughed.

Up ahead, Lieutenant Marquet glanced back to see what was going on but he said nothing and rode on, accompanied by Delpierre. They rode twenty yards ahead of the wagon, Lausard and Giresse on either side of it, with Charvet and Sonnier bringing up the rear. Rocheteau drove the wagon while Carbonne and Moreau were nestled in the back of it. Moreau was looking intently at a small box hidden amongst the gold crates and he reached for it, surprised at how light it was.

'What do you think is in here, Alain?' He flicked at the small padlock which sealed the box.

'Have a look,' Lausard told him, slowing his horse slightly, watching as Moreau used the butt of his musket to smash the lock. He lifted the lid.

'Hardly worth it,' said Carbonne, looking in at the collection of papers, maps and documents within.

'Let me see that,' Lausard said, holding out his hand, waiting until Moreau handed him the top sheet.

He scanned it quickly. 'My God,' he whispered under his breath.

'They're probably love letters,' said Giresse, grinning.

'They're a lot more than that,' Lausard said. 'Give

them to me,' he said to Moreau, who handed him the
remainder of the documents.

Lausard stuffed them into his portmanteau.

'What's so important about them, Alain?' asked
Rocheteau. 'They're only maps and numbers.'

'I'll tell you when we get back.'

The early-morning sun was fighting its way up into
the sky, but the mist was burning off slowly and the
wagon was forced to move with care over the treacherous, stony roads. One of the wheels bumped jarringly
over a rock, almost tipping Carbonne out of the wagon
but he held on to the side, muttering as he saw more
spilled gunpowder blacken his already filthy trousers.

Lausard looked back to where Sonnier and Charvet
were riding, also leading the spare horses.

Sonnier raised a hand to signal that they were all
right.

'We can't be far from our own lines now,' said
Rocheteau.

'That depends how far the army advanced,' Lausard
reminded him.

'Look,' Giresse said, pointing down into the valley
below.

Even through the mist, they could see blue-jacketed
French infantry.

Rocheteau smiled. 'Looks like we made it,' he said
and grinned.

Lausard watched the swiftly moving column of
troops marching along the valley floor, muskets sloped,
bayonets glinting in the watery sunlight.

Cezar lowered his telescope, able now to see the wagon
and riders more easily as they carefully negotiated the

steep incline leading down from the hills to the valley floor and the road.

'Deploy your men across the road, Sergeant,' Cezar instructed Bertrand and the large man barked out a series of orders, forcing his men into a double line across the narrow track.

Cezar watched the wagon, a slight smile on his face. The gold. At last.

He could see Marquet riding ahead of the wagon with Delpierre at his side, with Rocheteau, still wearing a white uniform, holding the reins which guided the tired horses.

'Make ready,' Cezar shouted and watched as the infantry loaded their muskets. 'On my order, Sergeant. We have to be sure they're not Austrians.' He peered through his telescope once more, picking out Lausard's features. Set hard, his cheeks powder-stained.

The two lines of French infantry had their muskets ready waiting for a command. Some could see the white uniforms now but Bertrand also spotted some green dragoon tunics.

'There are French soldiers in the wagon, sir,' he said.

'It could be a trap,' Cezar said. 'Can't you see the Austrian uniforms too?'

Bertrand nodded slowly but his eyes were riveted on the green uniforms.

The wagon was less than two hundred yards away now and drawing closer.

'On my order,' Cezar said quietly.

'Sir, I'm sure they are all French soldiers,' Bertrand insisted.

'Then explain the Austrian uniforms. I'm telling you, it's a trap.' He drew his sword. 'Prepare to fire.'

'Sir, I can't give that order until we're sure—'

'Damn you, Sergeant!' Cezar yelled. 'Then *I'll* give it.'

'It looks like a welcoming committee,' said Carbonne, smiling as he saw the lines of blue-clad troops.

Lausard said nothing. He guided his horse on at a walk, his eyes scanning the rows of infantry.

Then he saw Cezar.

For brief, interminable seconds, it felt to Lausard as if he and the officer were looking directly into each other's eyes, despite the distance between them.

Lausard saw the officer raise his sword.

He saw the two lines of troops raise their muskets to their shoulders.

'What the hell are they doing?' Rocheteau murmured, pulling slightly on the reins to slow the wagon a little.

Ahead, Marquet and Delpierre also saw the twin rows of Charlevilles now pointing at them.

From such close range, in the stillness of the morning, Cezar's shout was clearly audible.

With a great sweeping motion of his sword he roared: 'Fire!'

CHAPTER 37

The shout reverberated around the valley and the men in and around the wagon flinched involuntarily, expecting a hail of musket balls.

Nothing happened. Neither of the lines opened fire. The valley remained silent.

Suddenly Lausard understood why Cezar had insisted that not all of them revert to their dragoon uniforms. He realised that he was staring death in the face.

The muskets wavered, some men perhaps as uncertain of the identity of those ahead of them as Bertrand.

Cezar roared the order once again.

Marquet actually looked round at Lausard, a questioning, pitiful look on his face.

Then the front rank opened fire.

The valley was filled by a rolling wall of sound as the muskets crackled, spewing smoke, wadding and lead towards the men and the wagon.

Marquet was hit in the chest and face, his horse crumpling to the ground bleeding from a dozen wounds.

A musket ball hit Delpierre in the shoulder, the impact shattering his collar bone and lifting him from his saddle as his horse reared in pain and terror. The animal itself had been hit in the side and the neck.

Rocheteau heard bullets singing past his ears. One struck his right arm and tore a hole in the material without puncturing flesh. Another grazed his cheek.

Two of the horses pulling the wagon went down in an untidy heap. A third was hit in the muzzle and began bucking wildly despite the confines of the harness.

'No!' shrieked Carbonne, hissing in pain a moment later as a musket ball struck him in the fleshy part of the side and tore its way through.

'Stop it!' screamed Moreau, riding forward.

He, like the other men, heard the order Cezar bellowed.

'Second rank. Fire.'

There was another rolling volley, more choking smoke and death came flying towards them once again, propelled by the charges from each pan.

Moreau's horse was hit.

Sonnier felt a ball strike his helmet and clang off the brass. Another hit him in the leg just below the knee, passing through his calf. A third took off his left little finger.

Lausard drew his sword and rode forward waving it in the air.

'We're French soldiers!' he roared, his face blackened by powder, his features contorted with rage.

Cezar was ordering the infantry to reload.

However, Sergeant Bertrand was pushing many of his men's guns to one side, the look of horror on his face telling Lausard that he realised a dreadful mistake had been made.

Smoke seemed to fill the valley and the choking stench of gunpowder filled the air.

'It's a trap, keep firing!' roared Cezar but, by now, Lausard had reached the infantry and he stood in his saddle to allow the men a clear sight of him and his dragoon uniform.

'*Vive Bonaparte!*' he bellowed, his sword still gripped in his fist.

Cezar saw him and his right hand fell to his pistol, ready to pull it from its holster.

'I'm sorry,' Bertrand said, gazing first at Lausard and then at the other men and horses who had been fired upon.

They were walking or riding towards the French lines.

Marquet, however, lay motionless beside his horse.

Charvet was supporting Sonnier. Rocheteau used his knife to cut the wagon traces and release the one horse that hadn't been hit by the fusillades. Blood was running down his face.

Moreau crossed to Delpierre and helped him to his feet, noticing that a piece of jagged bone was protruding through his jacket from the wound he'd received.

'Help them!' Bertrand shouted and several of his men scurried forward to aid the stricken dragoons.

Lausard and Cezar remained within feet of each other, their stares locked.

'You wanted us all dead, didn't you?' snarled Lausard.

'You'll never prove it,' Cezar said under his breath. 'It was a mistake. An understandable mistake. I saw

Austrian uniforms, I suspected an attack, I ordered these men to fire on what I thought to be enemy troops.'

'You *knew* who we were,' Lausard rasped, shifting his sword to the other hand.

Cezar's hand closed over the butt of his pistol.

'Your gold is there, Captain,' Lausard said, motioning towards the wagon, now abandoned eighty yards away. 'Don't you want it? You wanted it badly enough to kill your own men for. Why not take it?'

Lausard suddenly wheeled his horse and rode back towards the wagon, sheathing his sabre as he did.

The other men turned to watch what was happening. They saw Lausard reach into the wagon and pull something free.

'You want your gold, Captain?' Lausard shouted. 'Come and get it.'

Rocheteau saw what his companion clutched in one fist. It was one of the portfires they'd taken from the Austrian cannon.

Lausard fired his pistol close to it, the flash from the pan igniting the portfire.

In a flash, Cezar realised Lausard's intentions.

He saw the lighted portfire hovering above the wagon.

Lausard dropped it, put spurs to his horse and ducked low over the saddle, hurtling back towards the French lines.

The gunpowder in the bottom of the wagon ignited immediately, the entire floor of the vehicle rapidly turning into a glowing red carpet of fire, with probing tongues of flame flickering and reaching for the barrels of gunpowder on either side of the wagon.

Cezar opened his mouth to shout something.

It was drowned by the deafening roar as the wagon exploded.

Lumps of wood, metal and flapping tails of tarpaulin were sent spiralling into the air but, propelled highest by the massive blast, was the gold. A great gleaming fountain of the precious coins rose into the air before raining down like gilt tears, spinning and bouncing all over the hard ground.

The men looked on in dumbstruck amazement at the explosion and its aftermath but then, as the first gleaming circlets began falling close to them, the infantry seemed to understand what was going on, what this precious rain really was.

The shout went up and spread along the lines until it seemed to fill the valley.

'Gold!'

The word was echoed again and again and then everything else was forgotten as the entire unit surged forward, scrabbling for handfuls of the scattered metal.

Lausard rode towards Cezar who was sitting motionless on his horse, his face drained of colour as he watched the infantry swarming over the ground, stuffing coins into their pockets and packs, some of them whooping with delight.

'Your gold, Captain,' Lausard said softly, motioning towards the scattered treasure.

The knot of muscles at the side of Cezar's jaw throbbed furiously.

'You ordered us to bring it back,' Lausard continued. 'There it is.'

Cezar was shaking with rage, the reins gripped tightly in his fists. He sat there a moment longer then wheeled his horse and rode away.

Away from the scenes of ecstatic scavenging and laughter, from the wreck of the wagon and the spilled gold.

Lausard dismounted, spotting one single gold coin close by. He looked at both sides carefully then slipped the coin into his pocket.

When he looked over at his men, Rocheteau was smiling.

'You're insane,' he told Lausard. 'We could all have been rich beyond our wildest dreams.'

'Or dead,' said Lausard, pulling the gold coin from his pocket. He flipped it towards Rocheteau who caught it in his palm and looked down at it.

'Now you're rich,' Lausard told him, grinning.

The other men began to laugh. And it was a sound so joyous they wondered how long it would be before they heard it again.

CHAPTER 38

'And you blew up a hundred thousand in gold? You must be mad,' said Delacor, shaking his head.

'You might just be right,' Lausard said, warming his hands and gazing into the leaping flames of the camp fire.

Nearby other fires burned and men huddled around them seeking what meagre warmth they could, and taking any protection from the biting wind which was whipping through the hills and valleys. A line of trees at the top of the ridge swayed and bowed dependent on the wind. Lausard looked over at them for a moment; around them sentries moved about, some occasionally stopping to chat as they patrolled. Two men were sharing a pipe, thinking they were hidden from prying eyes by some tall bushes.

'So, what now?' asked Giresse. 'The Austrians are beaten. When do we get to go home?'

'Home?' said Delacor scornfully. 'Home was a prison cell before we joined the army, wasn't it? I don't want to go back there.'

'Do you want to carry on fighting then?' Giresse persisted.

'What choice do we have?' Bonet said. 'We're soldiers now. It's our job to fight, isn't it?'

Lausard nodded. 'There's nothing back in France for any of us.'

'What about the women?' Giresse said and the other men laughed.

'There'll be plenty of women in Vienna when we reach it,' Rocheteau reassured him.

'*If* we reach it,' Roussard threw in.

'Roussard's right,' Bonet echoed. 'There aren't enough of us to advance on Vienna. The army isn't strong enough.'

'Since when did you become a military genius, schoolmaster?' Delacor snapped. 'How the hell do *you* know what's going on?'

'Just look around you,' he said, making an expansive gesture with his hand. 'This army is tired, ill-equipped and starving.'

'It's been like that ever since last summer,' Lausard reminded him.

'I agree with the part about starving,' Joubert interjected, rubbing his reduced but still prominent belly.

'Shut up, fat man,' Delacor said, slapping his colleague on the shoulder. 'I should think your horse must be grateful that you've lost some weight.'

The other men laughed.

'I heard that we're not advancing to Vienna,' Rostov offered. 'I heard a rumour that we're to pay the Pope a visit.'

'We're going to attack Rome?' Moreau said incredulously. 'That's blasphemy. God will strike us all down.'

'That old bastard has been against us ever since this war began,' Rostov said.

'He did try to raise an army against us last year,' Rocheteau reminded Moreau.

'He thinks we're all heathens,' Giresse said, smiling.

Lausard laughed and said, 'I think he might be right. Can you imagine what it would be like if the whole of Italy, including the Vatican, became a republic? A republic of thirty million with our morals and vices.' He shook his head.

'I haven't got any vices,' Charvet said innocently.

'What are vices?' Tabor wanted to know.

'Shut up, you half-wit,' Delacor snapped. 'It's not important.'

Bonet patted Tabor lightly on the shoulder. 'Whichever way we march there'll be bloodshed,' he said.

'What else do you expect in a war?' Lausard said dismissively.

Hunkered down on his haunches he continued to stare into the dancing flames of the fire.

It was Rocheteau who noticed the six men marching down the slope but he didn't know at first that they were heading for himself and his comrades. Only when he saw Lieutenant Royere leading them did he guess their target. He wondered why the five dragoons with the officer were all carrying their carbines over their shoulders.

'We've got company,' he said, nodding towards the men.

Lausard turned, saw Royere and got to his feet.

The officer extended a hand which Lausard shook warmly.

'It's good to have you back, Lausard,' the lieutenant said. 'I wish that my visit was for a different reason.'

'What's wrong, Lieutenant?' Lausard glanced at the other dragoons who flanked the officer.

'This isn't a social call, I'm afraid.'

'Is it me you want?' Lausard asked.

Royere nodded. 'I'm going to have to ask you to come with me, Sergeant,' he said almost apologetically. 'I'm placing you under arrest on the orders of Captain Cezar.'

'What's the charge?' enquired Lausard, straightening his cape.

'Deliberate destruction of Republican funds.' He shook his head. 'Believe me, my friend, I wanted no part of this.'

Lausard smiled and said, 'When is the hearing?'

'Now. Before General Bonaparte himself. I am to escort you to his tent.'

'I know the charge,' Lausard said. 'What is the penalty?'

'Death by firing squad,' Royere said. 'And I tell you now, that bastard Cezar means to see you dead.'

'Then we'd better go,' Lausard said.

'I said we should have killed the pig,' hissed Rocheteau.

Lausard stepped into line beside Royere, the other dragoons closing ranks around them. Rocheteau and the others watched as the sombre little band disappeared up the slope, moving swiftly through the maze of camp fires, past men who sometimes gave them cursory looks before returning their attention to the warmth of their own fires or to conversations with comrades. Others were trying to sleep. Those fortunate enough to have food ate it, savouring the tiniest morsel like gourmets at a banquet.

At the bottom of the slope Lausard saw a large tent, a tricolour flying high above it. Outside, a number of dismounted guides stood sentinel, others walked their horses back and forth. Three staff officers were standing close to the tent entrance smoking and talking but their conversation ended abruptly as they saw the procession of dragoons drawing closer.

Lausard recognised one of the officers as Colonel Lannes who had led them in the attack on St Vincini. Lannes watched indifferently as Lausard and his escort halted by the two guides closest to the entrance of the tent. One disappeared inside and, a second later, Lausard heard a voice call for them to enter.

He passed through the tent flap behind Royere.

Bonaparte was sitting in a chair sipping from a glass of wine, a cloak around his shoulders.

Bessieres stood close by him and, to their right, Lausard saw Captain Cezar standing at ease, one hand on the hilt of his sword.

'You are Sergeant Alain Lausard of the Fifth Dragoons?' said Bonaparte, suddenly rising to his feet as if galvanised by Lausard's appearance.

Lausard drew himself to attention and saluted.

'Yes, sir,' he said sharply.

'And you know why you're here?' Bonaparte continued.

Lausard didn't answer.

'Do you know how many muskets could have been bought with one hundred thousand in gold?' Bonaparte said, moving closer to Lausard, his eyes blazing angrily. 'Do you know how many men could have been provided with shoes? How many horses that money could have bought? How much food it would have provided? This army lacks everything except courage and belief. I have fought an entire campaign with just those qualities. Qualities which you yourself must have. Were you at Montenotte? At Arcola? At Rivoli?'

'Yes, sir,' Lausard replied flatly. 'And many more.'

'Then you have these qualities,' Bonaparte snapped. 'You know their value. You also know what it is like to fight on an empty stomach, to ride tired horses, to scavenge like a jackal in order to stay alive. If you know these things why did you not know the value of one hundred thousand in gold?'

A heavy silence descended, finally broken by Bonaparte himself.

'You disobeyed a direct order when you blew up that wagon and destroyed the gold.'

'I disobeyed no order, sir, because I had been *given* no order,' Lausard protested.

'Captain Cezar says that you were told to bring the wagon back to our lines,' said Bonaparte.

'And I did, sir. If I'd thought that money was to be used by the Republic I would not have destroyed it.'

Cezar's smug expression disappeared and he looked anxiously first at Bonaparte then at Lausard.

'That gold was for Captain Cezar's personal use,' Lausard continued. 'It was never intended for the Republic.'

'That's a lie,' hissed Cezar.

Bonaparte raised a hand to silence him. 'Can you prove this?' he asked Lausard.

'No, sir, just as Captain Cezar cannot prove that I

blew up that gold deliberately,' Lausard said with an air of finality.

'So it is Captain Cezar's word against yours, Sergeant,' Bonaparte reminded him. 'Who do you expect me to believe?'

'I trust you will believe your own judgement, sir.'

'And if that judgement is in favour of the Captain, then you will die.'

'Every man dies, sir, it's just a matter of when.'

Bonaparte smiled.

'You show no fear for a man who might shortly be facing twelve muskets, Sergeant,' Bonaparte observed. 'What can you offer in your defence?'

Lausard reached inside his cloak and pulled some papers from his tunic pocket. He handed them to Bonaparte who looked at the top sheet then motioned Bessieres to him.

Cezar looked on in bewilderment as they pored over the pieces of parchment.

'My God!' murmured Bessieres.

'I have more in my portmanteau, sir,' Lausard said.

'Where did you get them?' Bonaparte asked.

'From the wagon,' Lausard said. 'I thought that perhaps some things might be of even more value to the Republic than gold.'

Bonaparte held up one of the pieces of paper, a smile on his thin lips.

'Details of Austrian dispositions,' he said. 'Orders from and to the Aulic Council, requests for men and equipment.'

'There are unit strengths here too,' Bessieres added. 'These papers must contain the composition and position of every Austrian unit in Italy and the Tyrol.'

'We have their secrets in our hands.' Bonaparte laughed.

Bessieres joined him in the cheerful sound.

Royere grinned broadly.

Even Lausard managed a smile.

Cezar looked on furiously.

'Sergeant, bring the rest of your treasure to me as soon as possible,' Bonaparte said. Then he smiled and turned to face Cezar. 'I congratulate you too, Captain. You acted on your own initiative. It took great bravery to seize that baggage train. Your risks have paid dividends. The entire army, France herself, will benefit.' He raised one of the pieces of paper triumphantly.

Cezar forced a smile.

Lausard looked across at him.

'But such initiative must not go unrewarded,' Bonaparte continued. 'Good officers are always difficult to find. Your daring has been put to good effect here. I think the Army of the Rhine would benefit from your ideas and courage. They have more need of you now than I have. With these documents the Sergeant found we will force the Austrians to negotiate. They cannot run from us because we know where they will hide. They cannot escape us because we know where they will run. I need men like you elsewhere. You will leave for the Army of the Rhine tomorrow, Captain. Well done.'

'But, sir—' blabbered Cezar.

'I will hear no arguments,' Bonaparte said. 'No false modesty, Captain. Your skill will benefit France's other main army as it has done here.'

Lausard looked impassively at his commander, then

at Cezar. 'Congratulations, sir,' he said, unable to conceal his smile.

Cezar glared back at him.

'If you leave before dawn you should reach the Aviso in a matter of days,' Bonaparte said. 'I will send four of my guides with you.'

'You are very kind, sir,' said Cezar through clenched teeth. He was almost shaking with rage as he saluted.

Bonaparte turned to face Lausard, his expression darkening somewhat.

'Sergeant Lausard,' be began, 'while I applaud your courage, you must understand that the loss of so much gold cannot be allowed to pass without some gesture from me. There must be a punishment for destroying funds which would have been so useful to the Republic.'

It was Cezar's turn to smile.

Lausard stood at attention, his face impassive.

Bonaparte was only a foot or so from him, his eyes fixed on the dragoon.

'You will lose one month's pay for this action,' Bonaparte said quietly.

Cezar clenched his fists so tightly he felt as if his knuckles would crack. He wanted to scream that the punishment should be more severe. A flogging at least. The knot of muscles at the side of his jaw throbbed furiously.

Bonaparte eyed the sleeves of Lausard's tunic, his gaze drawn to the chevrons that signified his rank.

'You will lose your rank too, Sergeant. Although, I suspect, not for very long.'

Lausard thought he caught the hint of a smile on Bonaparte's lips, then he turned his back on the men.

'You may leave us, gentlemen,' he said.

Lausard, Royere and Cezar saluted then trooped out of the tent.

They were less than ten paces from the entrance when Cezar turned on Lausard.

'You think you've won, don't you?' he snarled furiously.

Lausard didn't answer. He simply held the officer's gaze.

'You haven't seen the last of me, Lausard, I promise you that,' Cezar insisted.

'We'll see, Captain. I hope the men under your command in the Army of the Rhine feel the same way about you as myself and my men have.'

'I should have killed you,' Cezar hissed. 'And one day I will.'

'I'll look forward to the day you *try*, Captain,' Lausard said, smiling.

He turned and walked away, accompanied by Royere.

'You lead a charmed life, my friend,' said Royere with a smile. 'One would think that God is personally protecting you.'

'God has nothing to do with it,' Lausard said. '*These* are my protection.' He tapped his forehead with one index finger then gently patted the hilt of his sword with his other hand. 'They are all I need.'

Royere looked up at the cloud-filled sky and muttered something under his breath. He felt the first drops of rain against his face.

'They say that when it rains the angels are weeping,' the officer observed.

Lausard nodded. 'Then there'll be lots more tears

shed before the end of *this* war,' he said. 'And not just by angels.'

Royere watched him as he set off down the hill back towards his unit, the darkness swallowing him up. The lieutenant looked up once again at the bloated clouds.

The rain continued to fall.

THE CONQUEST
Elizabeth Chadwick

When a comet appears in the sky over England in the spring of 1066, it heralds a time of momentous change for Ailith, a young Saxon wife. Newly pregnant, she has developed a friendship with her Norman neighbour, Felice, who is also with child. But when Felice's countrymen come not as friends but as conquerors, they take all that Ailith holds dear.

Rescued from suicidal grief by Rolf, a handsome Norman horse-breeder, Ailith is persuaded to become nurse to Felice's son, Benedict, but the situation soon becomes fraught with tension. Ailith leaves Felice's household for Rolf's English lands and, as his mistress, bears him a daughter, Julitta. But the Battle of Hastings has left a savage legacy which has bitter repercussions, not only for Rolf and Ailith but for the next generation, Benedict and Julitta.

From bustling London streets to the windswept Yorkshire Dales, from green Norman farmland to the rugged mountains of the Pyrenees and the Spain of El Cid, this is an epic saga of love and loss, compassion and brutality, filled with unforgettable characters.

DISORDERED LAND

Helen Cannam

Fresh from the ravaged battlefields of Flanders, the relative
tranquillity of England seems decidedly strange to Ludovick
Milburn on his homecoming in April 1640. And yet, despite
the lack of sacked villages and barabaric cruelty, there are
inescapable tensions, particularly for a Catholic nobleman
returning to claim his inheritance.

The uneasy truce between King and Parliament has spread its
aura of instability throughout the land, and further stirrings of
unrest in Scotland and Ireland serve only to heighten the sense
of impending disaster. As the situation steadily deteriorates,
Civil War becomes bloody reality, changing Ludovick's life
irrevocably and bringing him into contact with a disparate
handful of people who affect him as much as the war itself.

Sir Ralph Liddell, a landowner and Royalist, has ambitions to
make him his son-in-law. Walter Barras is an ardent
Parliamentarian, whose hatred of wealth and privilege makes
him a natural enemy of Ludovick's. And Richard Metcalfe, a
devout Puritan and Member of Parliament who is nominally a
rival for the attentions of the most significant of Ludovick's new
acquaintances: Susannah Fawcett, a doctor's daughter whose
forthrightness and independence are years ahead of their time,
but who cannot resist an affair of frightening intensity when
she and Ludovick are thrown together.

As the war plots its inevitable course, Susannah and Ludovick
undergo a profound reassessment of their lives and values as
the horror of war between countrymen teaches them to be
grateful for the power of love and friendship.

Other bestselling Warner titles available by mail:

☐ The Conquest	Elizabeth Chadwick	£5.99
☐ The Champion	Elizabeth Chadwick	£5.99
☐ Disordered Land	Helen Cannam	£6.99
☐ Kingdom of Shadows	Barbara Erskine	£6.99
☐ Waterfront	Richard Woodman	£5.99
☐ The Darkening Sea	Richard Woodman	£5.99

The prices shown above are correct at time of going to press, however the publishers reserve the right to increase prices on covers from those previously advertised, without further notice.

(W)

WARNER BOOKS

WARNER BOOKS
Cash Sales Department, P.O. Box 11, Falmouth, Cornwall, TR10 9EN
Tel: +44 (0) 1326 372400, Fax: +44 (0) 1326 374888
Email: books@barni.avel.co.uk.

POST AND PACKING:
Payments can be made as follows: cheque, postal order (payable to Warner Books) or by credit cards. Do not send cash or currency.

All U.K. Orders	**FREE OF CHARGE**
E.E.C. & Overseas	25% of order value

Name (Block Letters) _____

Address_____

_____

Post/zip code:_____

☐ Please keep me in touch with future Warner publications

☐ I enclose my remittance £_____

☐ I wish to pay by Visa/Access/Mastercard/Eurocard

Card Expiry Date

_____